"WHY DON'T YOU TRY ME?"

Gavin was standing in the living room when they entered. His eyes swept over Summer, then Nicholas.

"I want to talk to you," he said after a long silence.

"Good luck," Nicholas whispered in her ear, and he was gone from the room.

Summer squared her shoulders and prepared to do battle. "Look," she began, "nothing happened between Nicky and I . . . and nothing will ever happen. I'm not one of your brothers. You're not my parent. You're not my anything. So don't treat me like a half-witted child."

"You're my employee . . . or have you forgotten that?"

Summer forced herself to count very slowly to ten. For some reason, Gavin needed her to get upset. Well, not this time. "I'm going up to my room."

"We're not finished yet."

She gave him a cool stare. "Yes we are . . . and don't even think of kissing me," she said, as he made a move toward her.

He rocked back on his heels. "Kiss you? You are a conceited miss, aren't you?"

"You want me," she said, "why pretend you don't, when we both know you do."

A muscle in his jaw bulged and relaxed, but he made no denial of what she had just said. She continued, driven by some crazy need. "If I walked across to you now, and kissed you softly on the mouth . . . are you saying you would push me away?"

His voice was silky soft when he replied, "Why don't you try me?"

BOOK YOUR PLACE ON OUR WEBSITE AND MAKE THE ARABESQUE ROMANCE CONNECTION!

We've created a customized website just for our very special Arabesque readers, where you can get the inside scoop on everything that's going on with Arabesque romance novels.

When you come online, you'll have the exciting opportunity to:

- View covers of upcoming books
- Learn about our future publishing schedule (listed by publication month and author)
- Find out when your favorite authors will be visiting a city near you.
- Search for and order backlist books from our line catalog
- Check out author bios and background information
- Send e-mail to your favorite authors
- Join us in weekly chats with authors, readers and other guests
- Get writing guidelines
- AND MUCH MORE!

Visit our website at
http://www.arabesquebooks.com

MADE FOR EACH OTHER

NIQUI STANHOPE

BET Publications, LLC
www.msbet.com
www.arabesquebooks.com

ARABESQUE BOOKS are published by

BET Publications, LLC
c/o BET BOOKS
One BET Plaza
1900 W Place NE
Washington, D.C. 20018-1211

First Printing: May, 1999
10 9 8 7 6 5 4 3 2 1

Printed in the United States of America

DEDICATION

Thanks to:

God; my parents, Malcolm and Joyce; my brothers, Maurice, Michael, and Myles; the Prime Minister of Guyana and his wife (Uncle Sam and Aunty Yvonne); Publisher, Leticia Peoples of Odyssey Books; my best friends, Allison Joseph Carew, and Daniel K. Mackenzie.

Special Thanks to:

Mr. Charles Cook, publisher of the *LA Watts Times Newspaper*. A great soldier. Mentor. Friend. You touched my life in ways you will never know. Thank you for showing me how. I will never forget you. Rest in peace, my *Oba* (King).

CHAPTER ONE

Summer Stevens circled the parking lot again. The rows and rows of cars were beginning to make her dizzy. It was Murphy's law, pure and simple. There was not a free space in sight anywhere, and she was in serious danger of being late. Of course this would happen on the most important day of her life. It didn't matter that she had been stuck in traffic on the 405 freeway for more than an hour, or that she had subsequently driven at a hellish pace down Sherman Way, breaking several local speed limits. It didn't matter that she had even cut short the very extensive fittings that were needed on her wedding gown just so she wouldn't be late. The chairman of Aztec International, who by all reports was a stickler for perfection, would most likely give the project to another design firm if she, the head designer, rushed in sweating and out of breath, in the middle of the presentation.

She closed her eyes and said a quick prayer. She would not be late. There was still time. If only someone would come out of the building right now. She eased her foot down on the gas, and the little red Miata surged forward. She checked her watch again, and a bead of perspiration broke out on her nose. It was becoming increasingly clear that she was either going to have to park the car in the middle of the lot, and deal with the problems that would cause later. Or, park it in the forbidden loading zone at the back of the building.

She took a steadying breath. Her heart was beating like a trip-hammer. What could happen after all if she did park there? Maybe a couple trucking companies might be a bit late in making deliveries. That wasn't so very terrible, was it? She spun the wheel and decided. There was nothing else to do. It was just shameful that such a large office building should not have adequate parking to accommodate both staff and visitors. On the best of days, there were probably only one or two empty spaces in the entire lot. God forbid that there be a meeting of any sort. Clients were actually forced to use metered parking on the street. Those, of course, were all taken today because of the meeting.

Summer pulled around the corner in a screech of rubber. The nose of a large and very battered car, appeared around the opposite corner, at almost the exact moment, effectively blocking her way forward. Summer honked impatiently.

The large man in the driver's seat, turned his head to look in her direction. She pointed at the loading area that his car was now blocking. He seemed not to understand, for he proceeded toward her in the most unhurried fashion.

Summer rolled down her window, and prepared to lean out. The wind blew several long strands of hair across her face, and she pushed the tendrils back with an impatient hand.

"Sir . . . excuse me, sir. I'm . . ."

The man turned away from her, and with expert precision, swung the nose of his battered car into the very spot she had intended taking. Summer leaned heavily on the horn. She couldn't believe it. Some people were simply unbelievable. The only spot available in the entire lot, and he was going to take it.

She pulled her car to a halt, and slid out. She was tall and slender, and appeared even more so in her well-fitted navy pinstriped suit. The stylishly slung cream scarf about her neck, and thick gold hoops hanging from each ear, gave her a very high-fashion look, and her long legs looked very well indeed in the sheer silk stockings and shiny black pumps.

Adjusting her sunglasses, then taking very brisk steps, Summer walked toward the wreck and its rude owner. The man paid not the slightest bit of attention to her. In fact, it almost seemed as though he were going to great pains to ignore her completely. He had by now of course, snugly maneuvered himself into the spot, and was preparing to get out.

She knocked sharply on the driver's side window. Through the glass, she could see that there were papers strewn across the passenger seat. A trace of irritation rippled across her brow. The bum quite probably lived in his car. She knocked again, and waited with barely concealed impatience. Surely he was not deaf.

He continued to shuffle his papers for a few moments more, then, with what seemed like deliberate leisure, stacked them into a neat pile, and secured them with a thick paper clip. Only then did he turn to lower the window by just a fraction, to inquire in a cold and somewhat humorless manner: "yes?"

Summer took a long, slow breath. So, this was the reason for his abominable behavior. He was drop-dead gorgeous, and quite probably well used to thinking that the entire world revolved around him exclusively. Hordes of women probably threw themselves at his feet daily.

Well, he was in for a surprise. Her eyes flickered over him with analytical thoroughness. His deep black eyes did nothing at all for her. Granted, his cheekbones appeared to be exactly the right distance apart, and his nose was the very image of what every nose should resemble; not to mention the fact that his lips were just tailor-made for kissing . . . among other things.

None of this though, made one iota of difference to her. Men were men, and the handsome, conceited ones in particular were often in need of a good dose of shock therapy. From his general demeanor, it was very evident that this one just oozed with that certain quality of arrogance and conceit that just made her blood run completely cold. She would have to remember not to lose her temper though, no matter how generally unpleasant he was. The situation would not be helped at all, if she flew into a tearing rage and was forced to tell him a few home truths about his gender.

Maybe a softer approach might work. If she asked him nicely, perhaps explained how very important it was that she park exactly where he was now situated. Surely no red-blooded man would refuse such a very reasonable request.

She gave her watch a lightning glance. In exactly ten minutes, she would be officially late. She gritted her teeth, and plunged in. "Sir . . . I've got a really important meeting that I've just gotta be at. . . ." Her lips parted to reveal beautiful white teeth, and a soft pink tongue. "I've been driving around for fifteen minutes, searching for somewhere to park. I know this is a lot to ask, but . . . I really need this spot . . . it's very important. . . ." She let her words taper off with just the right hint of helplessness.

The face looking up at her was completely unresponsive. For a minute, Summer wondered if he had even heard her. His eyes flickered over her person with what she was certain was extreme distaste. Then, in a voice as deep and as cold as gravel, he said: "Step back, please."

For a second, she could only gape at him. "Wha . . . ?"

"Please step away from the door. I'd like to get out."

Summer's tight control slipped a fraction.

"Did you hear what I said?" she bellowed at him through the crack. The black eyes looking up at her were utterly calm, and completely devoid of any trace of concern.

"I would think," he said, once she was through hollering, "that if your meeting was as important as you say it is, you would have had the sense to get here in good time."

And, with that, he neatly closed the window and returned to his papers.

Summer stood where she was for a moment more, then, she spun on her heel and walked quickly back to her little convertible. She could feel the blood singing wildly in her ears. What a rude, condescending, utterly insufferable oaf. Well, two could play at that game. She threw her car into gear and roared forward, pulling to a screeching halt directly behind the battered blue thing. She cut the engine, collected the black leather portfolio lying beside her on the passenger seat, and stepped from the car, slamming the door behind her with excessive force.

The man was now standing at the driver's door of the blue monstrosity, and for the first time, she appeared to have his full attention. Summer tilted her head up, flung her scarf across her right shoulder, and walked past him in a cloud of expensive perfume. As she passed, she was certain that the corners of his lips curled upwards into a whisper of a smile.

In a few minutes, she was in her office in the *Design International* suite. She rang her secretary's extension, and hit the speakerphone button.

"Am I late?" she asked.

The crisp, efficient voice of Jessica Andrews came back. "No. There's been a delay. They haven't started yet. It'll probably be another half hour or so. I'll let you know when they're ready."

Summer looked at her watch again. Thank God. The swine downstairs hadn't really ruined a thing. There was still time to freshen up a bit too. She pressed the button on her phone again. "Jess, could you bring in the mail?"

Summer was in the little efficiency powder room attached to the office when the outer door opened. For a moment, she listened to the soft thud of sensible shoes. A fond smile flickered across her face. Jessica Andrews was a marvel. They had worked together for the last several years, and never once, even under the most trying conditions, had she ever lost her aplomb. She was never late to work, had never missed a day, and was always in the best of humor.

Summer smoothed a dab of powder onto a shiny spot on her nose and gave her reflection a considering glance. When the contract negotiations with Aztec were concluded, she would make a point of recommending her secretary for a raise. It was only right. She had helped so very much with the project.

''Anything really important Jess?'' she asked as the footsteps retreated.

''No. There're a few design magazines . . . some invoices. But nothing earth-shattering.''

''Uhmm . . . good,'' Summer said, and went back to her busy activities.

In five minutes, she had repaired the damage the wind had done to her sleek shag of black hair. Her makeup had been freshened, and a new coat of mascara added to the thick fringe of black lashes surrounding her fawn-colored eyes. Every immaculate inch of her looked the part of the beautiful sophisticate.

She gave her shiny burgundy nails a final critical look before returning to her desk. A neatly stacked pile of mail awaited her there. Before starting in on it, she made a short note in her daily planner. A visit to the manicurist was in order, and possibly a relaxing hour spent at the masseuse. Saturday would be ideal for both.

Summer found herself humming softly as she waded through the short stack of envelopes. For the first time in weeks, she could actually see the light at the end of the tunnel. The bidding war which had ensued over the Aztec contract, had required all of her creative skills and business savvy. Several dozen design firms had made bids and counterbids. Each one promising to create the most comfortable and efficient work environment for Aztec's fifty-odd offices. She had decided to take the most senior corporate manager at Aztec to dinner. She had wined and dined him on huge slabs of steak, pink lobster tails, honey-glazed potatoes, and ample quantities of robust cognac. During the course of the evening, while expertly fending off various sexual advances, she had managed to astutely determine the kind of office environment that Aztec required.

The following day, she shut herself away for eight hours, and step by very painstaking step, designed a scaled down, completely color-coordinated model of a typical office suite. By the next day, the model, along with a very attractive bid proposal, was sitting on the desk of the chief executive officer of Aztec. The call had come in almost immediately. They were interested, but not convinced. Another design firm had sent in a very enticing CD-ROM catalog with state-of-the-art point-and-click capabilities. And they were just as competitive cost-wise. So, a final decision between the two companies would be made, based on an oral presentation.

Summer had listened to all this, then together with her team of designers, set to work on the oral. They had worked twelve-hour days, and many weekends. She scoured the hardware stores and specialty shops, taking copious notes on shades of paint, fabric, venetian blinds, office furniture, and plants, carefully cataloging and pricing each item.

There were many nights when she had returned to her condo and just fallen into bed, too exhausted to eat. On these days, she had come to fully appreciate the wonderfully considerate man she was engaged to marry. Kevin supported her efforts fully, and would often call her during the long workday, just to give her a pep talk or a gentle mental nudge when her spirits were beginning to flag under the tremendous pressure. It wasn't unusual to walk into her office in the mornings to find a bouquet of mixed roses sitting on the polished lacquer surface of her desk, with a large I Love You balloon attached.

Kevin understood her. And she respected him. There would never be any grand passion between them. At least, not from her end of things. Romantic love was a silly creation dreamed up by Hollywood gurus. It had no place in her life or in her plans for the future. All that talk about hearing music and feeling chills racing up and down the spine actually made her angry. She had never heard even the faintest chime or experienced one solitary shiver when Kevin touched her. Their lips fit well enough together, and their bodies were of a similar type. They enjoyed opera on lazy Sunday mornings, fresh Italian pasta with thick tomato sauce on Friday nights, and the occasional smothered steak with generous helpings of macaroni and cheese and corn bread on special occasions. They both wanted the same things: a condo in the city; a house at the beach, maybe in Laguna Nigel; and eventually, when Kevin made partner, two children; a rabbit; and a cocker spaniel. Their lives were well on course, and there was absolutely no reason for juvenile suggestions about "true love" and "soul mates," to muck everything up.

The well-modulated ring of the phone interrupted Summer's train of thought. She had been right in the middle of opening the final piece of mail, when she had drifted off. She looked at the flashing red light, then lifted the telephone receiver. "Are they ready?"

Jessica Andrews' cheerful voice came back: "Yes. Everything's set. Mr. Cameron would like to see you first though. He wants you to meet the designers from our competitor before going in."

Summer suppressed a sigh. "Thanks. I'll be right there."

This was the part of the job she hated. It was such a very competitive, cutthroat industry. There were always lots of smiles and handshakes all around, but none of them were ever genuine. Her job could be made decidedly easier if her boss did not force her to resort to tactics bordering on industrial espionage. The only reason he wanted her to meet the designers before the presentation was so that she might pick their brains, maybe whittle out a trade secret or two. He knew very well that because of her face, her success rate with male executives was always high. It often took little more than a direct glance from her soft golden eyes, or a gentle touch on the arm from well manicured fingers, and a flash of good white teeth, to encourage a confidence. The general power she had over men was something that not even she fully understood. But she acknowledged it, and had come to rely on it during tricky business negotiations. And, now more than ever, she would need to bring all of her considerable skill to bear, if they were to bring home the ten-million-dollar Aztec account. Everything had to be just so. Including the way she looked.

With that in mind, she made a quick stop in the attached powder room. Her hair was immaculate, but she still gave it a final brush, and a quick blast of hair spray. The smallest hint of gloss was added to her lips, then expertly blotted away with a square of tissue. Her favorite fragrance was squirted into the air so that just a hint of it remained with her. Then, she hiked up her skirt and carefully perused the golden-brown length of each leg. Once she was satisfied there were no runs, she returned to her desk to gather her things.

Minutes later, she was nodding a polite good morning to her boss' executive secretary.

"Is everyone in the conference room?"

Francine Turner smiled at her. "They're all present and accounted for. There's coffee and Danish, too, if you'd like to have a bite to eat before the presentation begins."

Summer wrinkled her elegant nose. "Nothing for me thanks. My stomach is doing back flips right now."

Francine laughed. Of all the designers on their current roster, Summer Stevens was her favorite. Even though she was a trifle ritzy, and probably used a bit too much makeup, she was a pleasant, well-mannered young woman, who was, by all accounts extremely talented. She was too thin by half though, and maybe a little too aware of her looks.

The secretary picked up the phone. "I'll let them know you're here."

Summer thanked her with a smile, and perched daintily on the corner of a burnished leather chair. On most mornings, she could have walked right into Mr. Cameron's office. But, today, all the necessary office protocol would be strictly observed.

Francine Turner replaced the receiver in its cradle. Her softly wrinkled face creased into lines of encouragement. "You can go on in now."

Summer stood, took a deep breath and said, "This is it. Wish me luck."

Francine gave her hand a little pat. "There's no such thing as luck dear. You've done all the work. Just trust yourself and trust God."

Summer nodded. Francine was right. All the work had been done. Every angle had been thoroughly explored. Design International, with her at the project's helm, was the best company for the job. There wasn't any doubt in her mind now that they would get the contract.

She knocked on the polished-oak door, and entered when her boss' booming voice bade her: "Come in."

She scanned the huge office. The senior Aztec manager whom she had so thoroughly charmed during dinner was not there. A thoughtful frown puckered her brow for a moment. It was still a mystery which of the senior executives would make the final decision. She had tried in vain to find out, but that information had been closely guarded.

She clipped smartly across the room. It did not bother her a bit that she was the only woman present. Quite a few years spent in the corporate environment had shown her how to use this to her advantage. She gave the entire gathering a beautiful smile. Mr. Cameron was standing behind the elaborately curved wet bar, dropping thick chunks of ice into four neatly arranged glasses. He waved her toward a stool. "This is our resident genius, gentlemen. Summer Stevens."

The two men at the bar greeted her warmly. She recognized one of them. He was known as simply Adrian. He was small and frail, and gave the appearance of being in a state of perpetual nervousness. His designs were well-known in Los Angeles. And the rumor mill had it that he had been commissioned to redecorate several of the private rooms at the White House.

The other man, Summer did not know. He was about the same height as she, and looked more like a football player than an interior designer. His eyes were hard and calculating, and when he extended his hand to engulf hers, and said in smooth dulcet tones, "Brian Massey," she knew that he would be no pushover for her.

She selected one of the glasses of club soda, seated herself between the two men and commenced chatting about nothing of particular consequence. Cameron retired to his desk, and out of the corner of her eye, she watched him aimlessly shuffle papers. She knew that he was listening very carefully to every word that was being said. She very dutifully prodded the conversation into more interesting waters, making sure that she divided her attention equally between the two men. With deliberate intent, she occasionally crossed and recrossed her long, shapely legs, all the while taking mental note of the many times the eyes of the taller designer lingered on the soft curve of her calf. A little smile flickered around the corners of her lips. It was always the same with men. They were so very typical. With a little skillful prodding, she would undoubtedly be able to get Brian Massey to talk shop. For now though, she would content herself with idle chitchat.

CHAPTER TWO

After a period of maybe five minutes, the phone on her boss' huge desk rang. He barked an abrupt "right," hung up, then announced to the room at large.

"Okay, people. It's show time."

They walked the short distance to the conference room in companionable silence. At the mouth of the huge double doors, Cameron bent to whisper in her ear:

"The owner's here too. Be very careful with him. He's a bit of a queer fish I've heard. Sent me a personal fax this morning refusing to participate in any meetings prior to the actual presentation."

"What?" Summer whispered back. "Why? Does he think we might try to unfairly influence?"

Her boss nodded. "Yep. That's the long and short of it. We've had him and his CEO shut away in the small conference room. We're giving them the VIP treatment of course. Continental breakfast . . . the whole nine yards."

Summer grimaced. She didn't like the sound of that at all. How terrible it would be if the boss of the operation turned out to be one of those rare straight shooters.

''What is his name?'' she asked as Cameron stepped aside to let her enter ahead of him.

''Pagne. Gavin Pagne.''

She nodded. Already she had a mental image of the owner. Pagne was the perfect name for a boring, stodgy little man with thick black-rimmed Coke-bottle glasses, and a pronounced lisp. She would have to remember not to flirt with him though, since it would probably not work to their advantage.

Minutes later, she was seated up front beside her team of designers, waiting impatiently for the proceedings to begin. The room was crowded. Employees from both design firms had been invited to attend. Summer gave the small group of women seated on either side of her a confident smile.

''We're ready. Don't worry.'' She squeezed each of their hands. ''Besides,'' she whispered, ''we have a small advantage. Budget Designs gets to go first.''

The words were barely out of her mouth when the large double doors at the head of the room swung open, and two men walked in. Summer swallowed audibly. She recognized the taller of the two immediately. The broad shoulders, athletic build, cold black eyes. Her long fingers clutched unconsciously at the sides of her chair. It couldn't be true. Surely fate would not be that unkind. How did the insufferably rude man whose battered car she was now very deliberately blocking into an illegal parking zone, turn out to be one of the Aztec VIPs? Her brain churned as both men stopped to exchange a greeting with her boss.

Maybe he might not remember her, she thought wildly. After all, given his generally unpleasant demeanor, it was quite likely that he was accustomed to being accosted by all manner of people on a very regular basis.

Her heart gave a little flutter as he came closer. She gritted her teeth and mentally prepared herself for the worst. It was clear that he had not yet seen her. He was stopping to shake the hands of all the men first. Very typical, she fumed. It was the same thing, time after time. The old boys club, where women were definitely second-class citizens. Of course he would stop to talk to the men first. It would have been surprising had he done anything else.

"Our advantage is now back to zero," she muttered to herself. "In fact, I'd now put it in the minus region."

A smile was firmly planted on her face by the time her boss had managed to bustle both men up to the front of the room.

"And these . . ." Mr. Cameron panted, "these are my designers. I won't tell you that they're the best in the business," he guffawed and clapped his chubby hands together, "because, I don't want it said that I influenced you in any way."

Summer forced her teeth to unclench. Sometimes her boss was the most unsubtle human being on the face of the planet. Mr. Cameron stepped behind her to place a none-too-gentle hand, squarely in the middle of her back.

"Gavin, this is Summer, our head designer . . . Summer, Mr. Pagne is the guy who runs things," And, he gave her behind a sharp smack with the flat of his palm. Summer felt a wave of angry heat rush to her face. How dare he treat her like a cheap backroom girl, and in front of one of their most important clients. She made a firm resolution to have it out with him as soon as the presentation was over. She had tolerated his overfamiliar behavior for far too long. She had let him get away with a lot more than he should have just for the sake of her career. But, no more. This was the limit.

Her eyes sparkled with angry challenge as she firmly shook Gavin Pagne's hand. His cold midnight-black gaze swept over her, and for a second, Summer was shocked by the expression of acute distaste that ran like quicksilver through his eyes.

"A pleasure," he grated, and her hand was instantly dwarfed by his.

"Welcome to Designs International, Mr. Pagne," she said, and her voice was equally frosty. She let her hand remain in his only for as long as politeness would allow. The skin of his palm was hard and callused, and the simple feel of it gave her an uncomfortably hot sensation in the pit of her stomach.

Behind the serenely beautiful face, her mind churned. What a terrible way to begin the proceedings. First, she had hollered at him in the parking lot. Granted, she hadn't known who he was then, but that would hardly matter at all. And now, her asinine boss, had given the impression that she was some sort of tramp.

Uncertainty clamored at her for a moment. She had been counting on being in the good graces of the boss of Aztec just in case both design firms came out of the oral, neck and neck, and the decision came down to one of personal choice. If such an eventuality did occur, it would certainly help a good deal if Gavin Pagne thought favorably of her.

Her fine brow crinkled for a moment. In fact, it would help a great deal if he liked her. She observed him from out of the corner of her eye as she turned her attention to his CEO. There were two ways of approaching the current situation. If he was heterosexual, there would be many avenues of attack. If he was not, things would be more challenging, but not impossible. After all, there had never been a man whom she could not charm.

By the time everyone had taken their seats and the lights dimmed for the commencement of the slide show, Summer was feeling much more positive about things. She had decided that Gavin Pagne was exactly like any other man she had ever met. Even though he appeared unmoved by her appearance, she had caught him glancing her way on more than one occasion. This was a very good sign. It meant that she would not have to work nearly as hard on him as she had originally thought. It would probably take little more than a good dinner and a worthwhile play to cement herself within his good graces. She would invite him, and he would accept. She would drive him there and back in her sparkling new convertible that still had the smell of fresh leather. There would be light, entertaining conversation. She would almost flirt with him, but not quite. She would tell a joke or two, he would laugh. They would sit in companionable silence through the play. And, at the end of the evening, the desire to kiss her would be there in his eyes.

Gone, would be the fleeting dislike he had felt for her. She would let him kiss her on the cheek. Maybe allow him the barest glimpse of the softly rounded, dusky gold tops of her bosom. By the time she dropped him off at his hotel door, the contract would be theirs.

She smiled happily, and cheered along with everyone else, through the first segment of their competitor's oral. The slides had been good. The colors, fabric, furniture, and other fixtures, had been chosen well. The office environment that Budget Designs depicted on the pull-down screen, was ultramodern, yet warm and comfortable in appearance. There were neatly printed captions beneath each slide, and overlays that cleverly changed little details in each office.

At subtle intervals, Summer stole a glance at Gavin Pagne. He was hunkered down in his seat with fingers steepled beneath his chin. He did not seem terribly impressed by the efforts of the Budget Designers, even though anyone could see they had done a fantastic job. This made her happier still.

By the mid-morning break, she was almost pulsing with excitement. In her mind, she saw the ten-million-dollar contract being signed under her boss' spidery fist. It was almost theirs, she could feel it. All she had to do now, was give everything a soft push.

While everyone else mingled and grabbed a bite to eat, she excused herself and put in a quick phone call to the Los Angeles Music Center. She had heard of a wonderful new Broadway musical that she had promised herself she would just have to see, if it ever passed through Los Angeles. She couldn't remember the name, but did remember that, Savion Glover, was the main choreographer.

The clerk on the other end of the phone, was more than happy to jog her memory once she mentioned the name *Glover.*

"You mean, *Bring In Da Noise, Bring In Da Funk,*" he said with great enthusiasm. "Excellent choice. I've seen it more than once. It's a great production."

"Yes, that's the one," she told him. "I'd like two front-row orchestra seats for tonight."

She listened with great impatience to the seemingly endless clicking of computer keys. After an interminable pause, the clerk said, ''No front-row orchestra seats left. Actually, for tonight's performance, the only seats still available are one in the mezzanine, and two in the last row of the balcony. I can get you orchestra seats for the following night though, if you like.''

''No. No,'' Summer said with a tinge of ire in her voice. ''It has to be tonight. It's very important that it be tonight.''

''Balcony then?'' was the helpful response.

''Yes. Alright. Give me the two in the balcony.'' They weren't the best seats, but at such short notice, they would probably have to do.

She spared her watch a quick glance before hanging up and calling the Bonaventure Hotel. Dinner reservations were quickly made, along with a pleasant request that the maître d' have the finest bottle of champagne chilled and waiting for them at 6:00 P.M. sharp. With that little business nicely concluded, she then hurried back to the conference room to begin her part of the presentation.

CHAPTER THREE

Everything broke up at around 2:00 P.M. By then, Summer was not a little exhausted. She had carried the lead role on the entire thing. Carefully she explained how the tiny subtleties of light and color, when matched with the correct carpeting, furnishing, and fixtures, could create a bright and breezy office environment, which was highly conducive to productive work. She pulled out numerous transparencies, pointing to and circling key areas of interest. Pausing every so often to lighten things a bit with a little humor. The gathering broke into spontaneous applause when she finally revealed the finely crafted model, which said more about what Design International could do for Aztec, than she could herself.

She was very pleased with the way things had gone when she walked back to her seat, nodding and smiling, as everyone still continued to cheer. Mr. Cameron was wreathed in smiles, and Summer knew that he felt exactly as she did. They had won the contract.

It took several minutes for the heady sensation of success to diminish. As the lights went back up, and everyone began to mill around again, she stole a glance at Gavin Pagne. He was standing with his back to her, talking to her boss. And, she thought she knew exactly what was probably being discussed.

"I guess congratulations are in order?"

She turned to face Brian Massey, the taller of the two Budget designers. He stood with hands in pockets, an admiring smile beginning to twist the corners of his lips.

"I'd heard you were good. But, this . . . even I have to admit, was outstanding."

"Thank you." Summer gave him a smile and a saucy little wink. "I have my moments."

He leaned closer, his eyes shining seductively at her. "How about dinner one night this week?"

Summer's laughter tinkled sweetly. "I know you've also heard that I'm engaged to be married, in no less than six months."

Brian Massey was thoroughly charmed by the soft beauty of her. This was the kind of woman he wanted by his side. Smart, beautiful, and very sexy.

"Where's your ring?" he asked.

Summer gave her left hand a quick glance. For some inexplicable reason, she wasn't overly fond of wearing the tiny diamond solitaire. "I never wear it to work," she said.

Massey smiled at her in a knowing manner. "A lot can happen in six months."

"Not this time." She pressed soft fingers against his arm.

Massey felt an uncontrollable thrill work its way through him. Her lips were soft and unconsciously appealing. Her breath, sweet and warm against his face. In that moment, he decided. He had to have her. He was known about town as a voracious ladies' man, but there came a time in every man's life, when thoughts of settling down, seriously presented themselves. And, Summer Stevens was exactly what he needed right now. She would fit in nicely with the image he had built for himself. And, he would be willing to bet an entire year's salary, that she would be more than adequate in bed.

He gave her a sleek perusal, and stroked a long forefinger across the fine hairs of one arm.

"We'll see."

Summer favored him with another smile, then turned away. Her mind was already elsewhere. For the brief moment she had spent exchanging pleasantries with Brian Massey, her boss and Gavin Pagne had disappeared. Her eyes hunted the room frantically for them now. And, a multitude of questions popped into her head. Why had they left? What could it mean? Surely the contract would not be signed immediately. Or would it? She was still in the process of learning how the business side of the design industry worked. And, learn it she would. Every last detail. In five years, she intended to own her own design firm. But first, she needed to know the business, inside and out.

"Betty, did Mr. Cameron go back to his office?" she turned to ask one of the designers on her team.

"Let me check for you." The attractively dressed young woman picked up a wall phone and dialed. After a minute she hung up to say, "No, Francine hasn't seen him yet."

"Maybe he's just outside then."

Summer bent to retrieve her portfolio and other things. A tiny niggle of worry had crept into her. The events of earlier in the day flashed back into her mind. It was often hard to tell what people would hang on to and use against you later. Gavin Pagne had appeared to be a fairly well-balanced person. A trifle cold, but well-adjusted nevertheless. But, one could never be absolutely certain. He could turn out to be as petty and vindictive as the next person. Would he hold their little shouting match in the parking lot against the firm? Her brow puckered. She had been the one doing all the shouting, really. Would that make a difference? Her heart pounded for a minute. Because the presentation had gone so very well, she had been thinking of asking her fiancé to dinner and the play instead of having to endure an entire evening in the company of Gavin Pagne. But, maybe the deal was not yet sewn up. Maybe there still was a chance that Design International might not get the Aztec contract. She had to go find them, quickly, so that something could be done before it was too late.

She threaded her way through the thinning crowd, stopping once or twice to shake a hand, exchange a greeting. The left side of the room was lined by tables bearing crusty sweet pastries oozing ripe jellies, jams, and creams. Most of the people remaining were sipping contentedly on thick cups of hot coffee, and munching on the delicious assortment of sweet breads.

Summer hardly spared the delectable selection a glance. Her brain was quite firmly in overdrive. She pushed through the doors, then came to a dead stop. Gavin Pagne was standing by one of the water coolers, talking animatedly to a man she recognized. The chairman of Budget Designs. Her heart tilted a little. *God, let them not be personal friends*, she silently prayed. They both looked toward her as she approached. She was unsure of whether to nod and walk past, or stop and chat for a bit. It was imperative that she get Gavin Pagne alone, so that she might extend her dinner invitation.

Since they were looking her way, she decided to stop.

"Hello Mr. Rudolfo," she smiled widely, so that Gavin Pagne was included in the greeting. "It's such a pleasure to meet you . . . and to see you again, Mr. Pagne," she added, somewhat hastily.

Mike Rudolfo peered at her through very thick glasses. "So, you're the gal everyone's talking about. Summer . . . isn't it? What kind of a name is that? Summer?"

Before she could answer, he charged on, "We'll talk later Gavin. I've got a doctor's appointment in an hour. My prostate's giving me trouble again . . . isn't what it used to be you know. But, then, at my age, nothing's as it used to be."

And, with that, he beat a speedy retreat down the hall, leaving Summer standing there alone with Gavin Pagne.

In the wake of his abrupt departure, and somewhat startling personal disclosure, Summer was momentarily thrown off balance.

"Well . . ." she said, when the silence stretched on. "How did you like us in there?"

The black eyes met hers directly, and she tried in vain to read them. There were no two ways about it. He was a handsome man. The way his suit fell smoothly about his body, only hinting at the firmly packed muscle beneath. The long column of his throat. The strong fingers. Striking nose. Firm lips.

"Pardon me?" She raised her eyes to his in startled surprise. She had been so involved in her inspection of him that she hadn't realized that he'd spoken.

"I was saying that I'm a very hard man to influence. So, if you have that in mind, you're wasting your time, Ms. Stevens."

Summer blinked at him. He was rude. Completely and intolerably rude. Had she yet said or done anything out of the ordinary? How dare he think that she would stoop that low? She would, and had done so before, of course, but how dare he think her capable of it?

She widened her beautiful eyes and dug down deep for some suitable rebuke. But, before she could summon one to the surface, he said in a matter-of-fact manner: "Now, do you still want to invite me out to dinner? Or, should I make other arrangements for my evening meal?"

Summer's mouth opened and closed like a recently landed fish. How had he known? During the morning break, had he followed her out and overheard her conversation on the phone? She discarded that possibility almost as soon as it occurred. No. He must have found out that she had taken one of his executives to dinner before, and had drawn the conclusion that she would try to do the same with him. Oh, but he was a shrewd one. He could probably match her wit for wit too. She had not run into one like him before. It would be interesting though to bring him down a notch or two. The experience might even do him some good.

She forced her lips into a sweet smile. "Was I that transparent? I'm not as bad as you seem to think you know."

He looked down at her without considerable emotion. "Really? And how bad are you?"

Summer tilted her head sideways and flung a swatch of hair back over her shoulder before she could prevent herself. To flirt was as natural to her as breathing.

"I'm actually . . . very good."

His expression grew suddenly shuttered, and he appeared to lose all interest in the conversation. The distaste that she had seen earlier was suddenly back in his eyes, and she could have kicked herself for her lack of caution.

He looked very pointedly at his watch, "It's been interesting, Ms. Stevens, but . . ."

She stopped him with a hand on the arm. A familiar ploy that worked so well with other men, including her fiancé.

"Since you seem to have no firm plans for dinner. Why not let me show you around town tonight? How does dinner and a play sound?"

He stepped away from her so that she was forced to remove her hand from his sleeve. A flash of amusement came and went in his eyes.

"Show me around town? Believe me Ms. Stevens, there's very little that you could show me in Los Angeles, that I haven't already seen . . . or done," he added.

She blinked at him, quickly weighing exactly how to proceed. She had just naturally assumed that he was an out-of-towner. He didn't have the west coast demeanor at all.

"I'm sorry, I thought you were . . ."

"From somewhere else?" he asked. "No. Sorry to disappoint you. I was born and bred in L.A. . . ." He seemed about to say more, but then appeared to change his mind.

After a moment of silence, he said, "I'll pick you up."

Summer opened her mouth to object. Things were not going the way she had so carefully planned. "I made reservations for six . . . and I thought you might enjoy the change if I drove you. . . ."

He laughed down at her. It was a hearty sound that for some odd reason caused the hairs on her arm to stand at rigid attention. "You . . . drive me?" And the sound of his voice, ricocheted again down the hallway. Summer felt the blood rush to her cheeks. So, he was not only rude, he was also a chauvinist. Oh, what fun she was going to have bringing him down.

She took a breath and gave herself time to suitably collect her thoughts. "Let me give you my address and phone number then. I guess since you're so familiar with L.A., you won't be needing directions.''

She handed over one of her business cards. Her home address was printed neatly on the back.

He accepted the card, and pocketed it without even checking the address.

''Now, if you would kindly move your car. . . .'' he said, ''I've important things to take care of this afternoon.'' And, with that, he walked off down the hall, leaving her standing there looking after him.

Summer took a deep breath, and forced herself to count very slowly to ten. She had seen him interact with many others today. Why did he only take this attitude with her?

She thought on this for a bit as she followed him down to the parking lot. By the time she had made it to the lower level, she had seized on the answer. It wasn't her who he disliked. It was women in general. Gavin Pagne quite probably had a problem with her entire gender. After all, she had been perfectly charming. Had invited him out to dinner with her, no less. He had to be psychologically challenged. There could be no other explanation.

She threw the car into reverse, and watched the battered blue wreck pull slowly out of the parking space, and drive off with its various appendages shaking and rattling. A soft smile curved her lips. So, Gavin Pagne was a misogynist. What an interesting eventuality. Well, she was going to have some fun with him all right. After tonight, he would have a very valid reason to cling to his many misogynistic beliefs.

CHAPTER FOUR

''Have you gone completely crazy?'' Alyssa Davis asked. She stood directly behind Summer, watching her busy activities in the mirror, with increasing horror. ''You can't go out looking like that.''

''Why not?'' Summer paused to wipe a smear of dental adhesive away from her top lip, then tested her handiwork by opening and closing her jaws. The new set of teeth that she had so painstakingly glued in, made a solid clicking sound.

''Why not?'' her roommate almost shrieked. '' You look . . . you look completely ridiculous. I can understand you wanting to play a joke on Gavin Pagne. But, is this the way to do it? False teeth . . . orthopedic shoes . . . and . . . oh my God. . . .'' She paused to pull a few strands away, '' . . . the hair in this wig is beginning to shed.''

Summer grinned at her, and the false teeth bulged, white and shiny.

''I'm nowhere near as vain as everyone thinks, you know. I don't mind going out in public looking like a wreck.''

Alyssa gave her a dubious little look. ''Oh yes? Then why

are you always so . . . so well put together? . . . never a hair out of place . . . always glamorous?''

A sober expression came and went in Summer's eyes. ''Image my girl. I've worked long enough in the male-dominated corporate world to know how much that counts.'' She clacked the teeth again, ''So . . . tell me . . . do I look believable? I mean, the teeth and the hair . . . do they look like mine?''

Alyssa stood back again and gave the reflection in the mirror a critical once-over.

''The hair could pass as yours . . . I guess. As long as you manage to keep the shedding to a minimum. The shoes are okay too. But, you've got to do something about the teeth.'' She giggled suddenly. ''You look a bit like that horse in those old reruns . . . Mr. Ed. . . . Nothing but teeth.''

Summer exploded into deep chortles, and her eyes shone with amusement.

''Okay, okay, I'll do them again. He has to believe that they're mine, though. That I really wear dentures. . . . So you have to stay until I'm all done.'' She turned back toward the mirror. ''Oh, and find me something really ugly to wear. It has to be a blouse of some sort, and a pair of pants. . . . because of the shoes.''

''What color?'' Alyssa was already hunting through the stacks and stacks of dresses, suits, skirts, and pants that hung neatly bagged in the huge walk-in closet. She pulled out a gorgeous navy-blue oriental-print silk dress, and looked at herself in the mirror. If she lost a pound or two, it just might fit.

''When did you get this one? I've never seen you wear it.''

Summer turned. ''Oh that. I think Kevin gave it to me. A present for my last birthday.''

Alyssa put it back, and continued to search. Her voice was slightly muffled as she delved deeper still into the back of the closet.

''Well at least he's good for something.''

Summer squeezed a thick dollop of adhesive onto the wooden spatula. ''I still can't figure out why, after all this time, you two still don't like each other.''

Alyssa's head popped back out of the closet. Over her shoulder she carried several garment bags.

"I can't tell you why exactly. He's just too . . . too something, you know? Ultrasmooth and ultraslick. Besides, I hate lawyers anyway."

Summer turned back to the dentures. "Well, that's a good reason not to like him. What did you find in there?"

Alyssa held up a pair of checkered polyester pants. "How about this? It's got a fringe of threaded fabric around the waist and wide bell bottoms."

Summer wrinkled her nose. "God, those are terrible. When did I buy them?"

Alyssa grinned. "It was probably another gift from the jerk."

Summer made a noncommittal noise. "One of these days, I'm going to get you two to like each other. After all, you are my best friend, and he is going to be my husband."

"Don't remind me," Alyssa said. "So what do you think, is this ugly enough? Or, would you rather be ugly-chic tonight?" She held up a pair of bright-red satin balloon pants.

Summer shook her head. "No . . . no red. It has to be something really drab . . . .but at the same time, slightly attractive."

Alyssa's lips pursed. "Attractive . . . .and drab . . . hmmm. Let's see . . . let's see." She held up a hand. "Wait a minute. . . . I've got it." She darted into the closet, and returned to exclaim: "Ta-dahhh . . . " She held a mousy-brown crushed-velvet top and a matching pair of slacks.

"See . . . the legs are nice and wide . . . perfect for your shoes. And it is kinda attractive in a very watered-down way. The color is perfect too. Faded looking and for want of a better word, my girl . . . drab city."

Summer kept the fingers of one hand firmly pressed against the set of false teeth. She beckoned her roommate closer with the other. After a few minutes of hard pressure against the gum, she released.

"You're a peach Lyssa. These are exactly right." She bounded up from her padded stool, to press an enthusiastic kiss against her friend's cheek. They hugged each other for a bit.

Summer was the first one to break the embrace. ''Okay, back to business. How are the teeth now.''

Alyssa frowned. ''Let's see you smile again.''

Summer obliged, baring her new set of teeth, but somehow managing to keep the gum line completely hidden.

''Hmmm,'' Alyssa said after a moment. ''I have to give it to you. They don't look bad at all. Very realistic actually.''

''Could they pass for my real teeth though. It's really important that he doesn't guess what I'm up to. And, trust me, he's a shrewd one.''

''I still don't understand what this whole charade will accomplish other than maybe helping you lose the contract you worked so darn hard for.''

Summer shook her head, and succeeded in shedding a few more hairs onto the carpet. ''Oh, I'm not worried. The contract's in the bag. Besides, he told me today that nothing influenced him. He was very superior about it when he said it too. So, we shall see if he really is the upstanding citizen he claims to be. When the Ms. Stevens he met this afternoon turns out to be a down-home hag. . . .''

Alyssa giggled. ''You're just plain wicked you know that. . . . Just plain wicked.''

Summer grinned back at her. ''I'm willing to bet you that once he gets a good look at me this evening, he'll call the entire outing off.''

''And then you'll be able to spend the entire evening with darling Kevin. Where is he by the way. He hasn't called you all day. Unusual for him.''

Summer walked into her gold and cream bathroom and began to prepare her bath. ''He's tied up downtown with that double murder.''

''You mean the one where the son killed his parents?''

''Yeah that one. He's going to plead temporary insanity I think,'' Summer said above the noise of the running water.

''The usual scum-ball lawyer argument,'' Alyssa shouted back. ''That kid was just plain evil. I could see it in his eyes.

He should get the death penalty. He's eighteen years old. I don't believe in slapping the wrists of these juvenile offenders."

Summer poured a sizable quantity of shampoo into her hands and vigorously massaged it into her hair. "Well, we'll see what happens. I feel sorry for the kid. Maybe he was abused or something terrible like that. I mean, children just don't wake up one day and decide to kill the parents they love."

Alyssa made a sound of disgust. "Should I open up your mail for you? Looks like you got a variety. There's Publishers Clearinghouse . . . . a couple bills . . . and one that's addressed by hand. Looks personal."

"Open the personal one," Summer said, giving her long black hair another rinse under the shower.

"The personal one . . . are you sure? It might be private."

Summer laughed. "Come on. You know we don't have any secrets from each other. How long have I known you?"

"Okay . . . here goes." There was a sound of tearing paper, then Alyssa said in a disappointed voice: "It's only a chain letter."

"A chain letter? Throw it out." Summer stepped out of the shower, patted her long legs dry, then commenced the process of getting ready.

Alyssa walked across to the bathroom door. "No you shouldn't do that, it's bad luck not to pass them on."

Summer turned on the blow-dryer full blast. "I can't believe how superstitious you are, Lyssa. How could a simple letter, written by some crazy person, bring you good or bad luck? It doesn't make any sense."

"Okay Madame Pragmatic. Believe me, there are supernatural influences at work in this world."

Summer gave her an airy, "Whatever," and continued to dress.

With her hair nicely blown dry, she gathered the thick mass up, and twisted it into a tight bun atop her head. This was securely pinned, and a brown stocking cap added. She powdered her face lightly with a delicate shade of foundation, ran a ruby pencil around the circumference of her lips, then stroked in a deep burgundy. She tested the strength of the teeth with her tongue, and was satisfied that they were still as firm as when she had tested them earlier. She wouldn't wear any mascara tonight, maybe not even any eyeliner.

The humor of the whole thing appealed to her again, and, she chuckled heartily. She couldn't wait to see his face.

"Are you all right in there?" Alyssa called. She was now reclining on the soft pink and white bed, her feet propped on one of the large pillows. "Laughing to yourself is the first sign you know?"

Summer grinned. "Sign of what?"

"Nothing good, I can tell you. It's always the ones who stand and laugh to themselves in the corners of elevators, and other secluded places who end up stalking people and hacking them to pieces in dark alleys."

Summer chuckled. "You read too many of those mystery novels. I think they're beginning to affect your brain." She paused to skillfully apply a soft kohl pencil to her eyebrows. "When are you going to get yourself a good man, girl?"

Alyssa sighed. "You make it sound so easy. Let me tell you since you haven't been out there for a while. The pickings are slim."

Summer carefully positioned the wig atop her head, and pressed it firmly into place, pulling and patting the hair until it looked just right.

"I met a guy today. He'd be perfect for you. He's a designer from Budget."

"A designer?" Alyssa said, with a hint of derision in her voice. "Be serious. I don't want that kind of man. He's probably prettier than I am."

"He's not like that. He's about my height. Kinda buffed . . . you know, like a football player type. Name's Brian Massey."

"Is he cute?"

"As a button. I'd guess he's probably very popular with the women."

"Oh, I don't want a man who'll run around on me."

Summer stroked fragrant cream beneath her eyes, and across

her forehead. ''You have to train them not to girl. Let's face it. They're all dogs anyway. Look at Kevin, and what he used to be like. He'd go after anything in a skirt.'' She brushed a final hint of gloss across her lips. ''But, look at him now. Completely reformed.''

Summer emerged from the bathroom, clad only in a lacy white bra, and her stockinged feet. Alyssa let out a squeal of laughter.

''Oh my God. . . . you really do look like a hag. The effect is so realistic.''

Summer checked her reflection in the mirror. She had done a decent job. The wig had been a great help though. It added just the right touch to everything. She slid into the crushed velvet two piece and then stepped into the cloggy orthopedic brown shoes.

Alyssa propped a hand beneath her chin. ''Where'd you get all this stuff from anyway? The shoes . . . wig . . . teeth?''

''A little knickknack store in Van Nuys. There were some wonderful things in there. All very cheap too.''

''You sure the wig doesn't have cooties?''

''Nope. That was the first thing I checked for.''

Alyssa pushed herself into a sitting position. ''You're crazy. . . . you know that? I think your mind has come unhinged because of the pressure you've been under.''

Summer smiled. ''Some call it crazy . . . others call it genius.''

Alyssa shoved her away from the bed with a foot. ''Ohhh . . . shadup.''

The phone rang just then, and Summer hurried to answer it. In a sweet voice she said, ''hello Mr. Pagne. Yes, I'm almost ready. No, no, I won't keep you waiting. Okay. See you then.''

She crashed the phone into the cradle. If she'd been a bit sorry about what she was about to do, she certainly wasn't now. ''I have never . . . never in my life met a ruder person.''

Alyssa sighed. ''What now? Did he hang up on you?''

Summer attached a loopy gold earring to each ear. Sprayed

a hint of fragrance beneath her neck, and onto the pulse points of either wrist, before answering.

"He told me he'd be here in five minutes, and not to keep him waiting. Then, he practically hung up in my face . . . without even saying good-bye. Can you believe it? I mean he doesn't even know me . . . and yet he feels comfortable enough to tell me not to keep him waiting. I've a mind to make him wait, just for that."

Alyssa looked at her with a speculative gleam in her eyes. "Hmmm . . . I've never seen you this hot about a man before. Is there something more here?"

Summer snatched up her brown leather bag, and began to empty the contents of her purse into it. "I would never be interested in him. Trust me. He's not even my type. He's too tall . . . his . . . his fingers are too long, and . . . the skin of his palm feels as rough as sandpaper. He'd probably tear great gashes in my skin if he ever tried to be tender."

"Uhmm-hmmm," her roommate said, unconvinced. "And of course . . . there's Kevin to worry about too . . . not to mention, an upcoming marriage."

Summer swatted her with her bag. "I'm not Gavin Pagne's type either. So, we're perfectly mismatched. There's not a chance of anything happening between us. Besides, I'm the faithful kind. You know that. It's one man at a time for me."

"Right," Alyssa said. "Now, let me have a look at you." She walked around Summer, clucking her tongue in approval. "You look wonderfully mediocre. Even I might not have recognized you if I'd seen you on the street."

"Take a picture," Summer said, and she struck an elaborate pose. "I'll show it to Kevin later. He'll get a big kick out of this."

At about a quarter after five, Gavin Pagne pulled to a stop outside 123 Terrace Street in old Pasadena. The brownstone condominium complex had a very upscale, bourgeois look to it. With its neatly manicured green lawns, symmetrically shaped rose bushes, and assortment of water spouting stone sculptures. It was exactly the kind of place he would have expected someone like Summer Stevens to live. It so very completely reflected everything that she was: ritzy, superficial, and not a little predictable.

The evening ahead though, would be an interesting one. Summer Stevens was exactly the type of woman he could not stand. That she was promiscuous, was obvious. He had watched her flirt with various men earlier in the day. At a distance, her little shallow brained ploys had amused him. She was after all attempting to do her job to the best of her limited ability. But, when she had tried the same tactics on him, she had unwittingly disturbed a deep, brooding anger. He remembered another woman who had been very like her. All sugary tongued, and doe eyed. She, too, had set her sights firmly on the Champagne family money. But, when her harebrained schemes had failed to work on him, she had turned her attentions to one of his younger brothers. Now, a child was on the way, and they were constantly besieged by numerous demands for money. And, whenever these were not met with adequate speed, there would erupt a stream of petulant threats of impending legal action and public embarrassment.

Anger made his fingers tighten reflexively around the steering wheel. He sat there for a moment, until the feeling left him. Summer Stevens and all of her kind, were a blemish on the face of good and decent humanity. But, she would benefit greatly from their dinner tonight. The experience might even help make her a better person. So much so, that maybe at some nebulous point in the future, she might actually succeed in finding herself someone who was willing to marry her. A lesson in humility was what she greatly needed. And, he was just the one to give it to her. It was, in fact, the only reason he had agreed to have dinner with her at all.

He cut the engine, reached over to adjust the tattered leather on the passenger seat, then climbed from the ancient blue car. A minute was spent in the careful adjustment of his jacket and tie, then, he walked with determined purpose up the winding cobblestoned pathway.

Alyssa had just taken the first snapshot of Summer's ensemble, when the doorbell rang. The melodious three-toned chime echoed through the two-storied condominium. They both froze for a minute, and Summer felt her fingers go cold.

"He's right on time," Alyssa said.

Summer nodded. "I wouldn't have expected any different. You get it Lyssa . . . and tell him I'll be down in a few minutes. I want to make a grand entrance."

Alyssa smothered a giggle. "I can't wait to see his face." She tapped the Polaroid camera that was now slung about her neck. "I'll see if I can get a snapshot of his very first reaction when he sees you."

"Good," Summer said, "that's one I'll definitely keep for my scrapbook."

Alyssa gave her a final conspiratorial wink, then was gone, clattering down the stairs. There was the sound of the door opening and closing, Alyssa's cheerful voice, and a deep, surprisingly polite response.

Summer checked her appearance again, then went to sit on the bed. She would show him that he couldn't order her around. Be on time indeed. Who did he think he was? She was certainly not one of his employees, or a willing floozy who was after his money. If it were not for the contract that his company would quite probably give to Design International, in addition to all she would do tonight, she would also have given him a very well deserved tongue lashing.

After what seemed an eternity of waiting, there was the sound of footsteps on the stairs. Alyssa walked quietly into the room, closed the door, then turned to Summer with bright excitement in her eyes.

"Why didn't you tell me?" she whispered. "I thought he was old, fat, and ugly."

Summer adjusted the wig, which obligingly shed a few more hairs. "I don't care much for his looks . . . he would probably be much more agreeable if he had a face like a bulldog, and not a penny in his pocket. . . .''

Alyssa shook her head in amazement. ''He's gorgeous . . . or haven't you noticed? I'm talking . . . absolutely drop-dead, keel over in a faint, gorgeous. He makes your Kevin look like a bulldog . . . and we all know how cute Kev . . . well . . . how cute Kevin thinks he is.''

Summer slung the leather bag across her shoulder. ''I'm more concerned with non-superficial qualities like kindness, and . . .''

''Give me a break,'' Alyssa interrupted. ''This man has both money and looks . . . I wouldn't care if he was the worst creature on earth . . . I'd still take him.''

''Well . . . after tonight, you're welcome to him . . . though,'' and a little smile curled the corners of Summer's lips, ''he might not want to have anything to do with women in general for a good long while after I'm through with him.''

''Don't do it . . .'' Alyssa grabbed at her as she made to open the door.

Summer laughed and pinched her friend's cheek. ''Don't be influenced so easily by a pretty face my girl. Believe me, this will actually do him some good . . . the women of the world will thank me for this.'' And, with that, she was through the door, and as quickly as her orthopedic shoes would allow, went clumping smartly down the stairs.

At the foot of the staircase, she whispered to Alyssa, ''got the camera ready?''

A soft ''yes,'' was whispered in response.

Summer approached the living room door. Gavin was sitting on the large sofa, with his back to her. With all the clumping that the shoes were making, she was a little surprised that he did not turn in the direction of the sound. She took a deep calming breath, for her heart had begun to flutter a bit. Then, very sweetly, spoke: ''Hello again.''

He turned in the direction of her voice, and Summer felt a tiny blaze of happiness burst into glorious life in the pit of her stomach. The urge to laugh was so strong that she was forced to succumb to a sudden rash of coughing. Various expressions chased rapidly across his face. There was first shock, then what Summer liked to think was panic, then finally, bald incredulity.

He appeared to have lost his powers of speech, so, gladly, she helped him.

"I'm sorry to keep you waiting . . . but my arches were giving me some trouble tonight . . . they've fallen again, you see."

She watched with wicked delight, as his eyes darted to her feet, then rebounded almost immediately to her face.

"Are you ill . . . Ms. Stevens?" And, Summer thought she actually heard a note of solicitude in his voice.

She waved his suggestion away. "Ill? . . . no, Mr. Pagne . . . I'm in the peak of health . . . except for my arches . . . of course. Why do you ask?"

"You seem a bit . . . different."

Summer struggled to maintain her composure. "I usually get comfortable after work. You know how we women are?"

"Ah . . . yes." He bent to retrieve his jacket, and Summer knew beyond a shadow of a doubt, that he had no clue how women were at all.

She continued, undeterred. "After a long day of struggling with makeup, weaves, and very painful heels . . . which are largely responsible for my arches anyway . . . I like to let the real me shine through . . . I hope you're not too disappointed with me?"

He appeared to be in an awful hurry to leave, and Summer's heart pounded with vicious delight. She was certain that he was going to invent some excuse to call the whole thing off. But, he extended his arm, and she experienced a little plunge of disappointment. He was a bit stronger than she had originally assumed.

"Shall we go?" And, he very politely tried to avoid looking at her hair, which was, at that very moment, a little longer on the right side than on the left.

Summer clumped nearer, and shed a few more hairs as she did. She put her arm through the crook of his, then said with a plaintive note in her voice, "Do you mind if we take a picture together?"

CHAPTER FIVE

Once she was well situated in the front seat of the car, she said nicely, ''could you turn on the roof light for a minute, I'd like to fix my dentures. I just got a new pair today, and I haven't quite gotten the hang of them yet.''

Obligingly, he flipped on the roof light, and Summer went into another spasm of coughing. There was actually blank disbelief on his face now. And, the laughter came in such unrelenting waves, that she must have coughed for a lot longer than she had originally intended. For, not long into it, he reached across to thump her on the back.

''Should I go back in for some water?'' he asked.

Summer smiled, and her dentures were grotesquely displayed.

''Thanks, but I think I'm over it now.''

He gave her teeth another look, then started the engine. ''Where are we going?''

''The Bonaventure Hotel. Downtown.''

Within minutes, they were on the freeway. Summer observed him from out of the corner of her eye. She had to hand it to him, he had weathered the whole thing very well so far. But, the evening was young yet, and she had a lot more in store for him.

"I'm sorry?" He was actually speaking to her again. She had been certain that the entire journey would have been one filled with nothing but cold silence.

"Your dentist . . . have you been seeing him for a while?"

"Her," Summer corrected. "I have a female dentist."

"Well . . . it might not be a bad idea to look into obtaining a new female dentist," he said. "This one probably never graduated from dental school."

This time, the laughter escaped before she could control herself. Could it be that he was really concerned about the way her teeth appeared? Could he be that human after all?

He glanced at her, then returned his attention to the road. "Did I say something funny?"

A tear slid from the corner of her eye, and she wiped it away hastily.

"Are you saying that there's something wrong with my teeth, Mr. Pagne?"

A thoughtful frown rippled his brow. "I'd be hard-pressed to find anything right with the set of teeth you now have . . . and since we're going out to dinner, don't you think we can drop the formality for a while?"

Summer smiled again, and this time it was genuine. "It's all well and good for you to criticize when you've got the teeth you were born with."

There was a moment of silence, and Summer chuckled internally.

He appeared unsure of how to proceed. "You . . . have no teeth of your own then?"

Summer clacked the dentures with enthusiasm. "I've a couple in the back that are still mine. I lost the rest when I was in high school though. A combination of sports injuries and gum disease. But," and she turned to look directly at him. "I'm going to do all I can to hang on to the ones I have left."

"Yes . . . that would not be a bad idea." He flipped on the right signal and prepared to exit the freeway. Summer adjusted her position on the seat. The torn leather was beginning to gouge her in various places.

"Tell me," she began, "don't you think it might be a good idea to fix your car up a bit? After all, you do have a certain corporate image to maintain." His jaw clenched and relaxed, but she ignored his wordless signal of irritation. If he could get personal about her teeth, then she could certainly question his taste, or lack there of, in cars.

"This car is a classic," he said in a cold voice.

"A classic what?" Summer asked, enjoyment sparkling in her eyes.

"You obviously know nothing at all about cars, so it would be pointless having a discussion about them."

Summer took a deep breath. So, he had gotten over her appearance, and was back to his usual rude self. She would just have to remind him that he was dining with an extremely wretched individual. She would force him to be civil if it killed her.

"Is the torn leather part of the classic look too?" She asked, fingering the rips and tears, and poking her fingers into the protruding foam.

He glanced down at her busy hands. "Would you mind not doing that?"

Her plucking fingers stilled. "Sure." She leaned back against the headrest, and closed her eyes, a beatific smile curving the corners of her mouth. She couldn't remember ever having such an absolutely wonderful time. What could be better than spending an evening deliberately irritating a man, who, for perverse reasons of his own, had decided to not only dislike her, but her entire gender. She knew that out there somewhere, the feminists of the world were cheering her efforts heartily.

Gavin took his eyes off the road for a moment to glance at the woman beside him. With all the paint and polish of earlier in the day gone, her looks had dwindled away to absolutely nothing. It was clear that the lesson in humility that he had so carefully planned for her, would have to be saved for a more worthy adversary. This one, with her bulging teeth, and thinning hair, would be lucky if she managed to make it through dinner without keeling over from a heart attack or some other such malady.

Summer opened an eye to peer at him. His face was always so unreadable. She would be willing to pay good money to know exactly what he was thinking right then.

"You're so quiet Gavin . . . is something wrong?"

"I thought you had fallen asleep. Are you on any medication . . . that . . . ? I mean . . . are you suffering from any major ailments? It might be helpful to let the restaurant staff know . . . if you are. . . ."

Summer swallowed hard, and did her best to control the chuckle that was determined to bubble to the surface.

"Are fallen arches a major ailment?"

He turned a speculative glance in her direction, and a whisper of a smile twisted his lips.

"No. I don't think they are."

With expert skill, he swung the big car into the entrance of the hotel. Summer realized that somewhere, somehow within the last half an hour, she had gained a modicum of respect for him. He appeared to be completely unashamed to be seen with her. And, given the general state that she was now in, this was an accomplishment indeed.

For a moment, her thoughts wandered to her fiancé. Kevin would never be seen in public with someone who looked as she did. He demanded perfection in all areas of his life. It was only the best wines, designer clothing, upscale neighborhoods. In fact, the condominium complex where she now lived, had been his choice. She had gone along with it at the time, because there had seemed no reason not to. But, of late, she had been getting the urge to have something more substantial, more real. The condo was okay for city living, but, what she really wanted was a nice solid house. A white picket fence. A patch of green grass. A big backyard. A couple of fruit trees, ideal for tree houses or tire swings. A house not unlike the one her parents had up in Mammoth Lakes.

"Are you ready to go in?"

"Yes. I'm all set." Valets stood waiting at either door. Summer blinked a couple times. It was not like her to daydream. Maybe old age was beginning to set in early, or it could be that her biological time clock was starting its merry ticktock.

She gave the wig a quick pat, checked the teeth with her tongue, then stepped from the car. They rode up to the restaurant in the bullet-shaped elevator that ran up and down the side of the hotel. She watched the rapid retreat of the ground with quiet excitement. The sensation of climbing at top speed, never ceased to thrill her. And, of course there was the added enjoyment of seeing the lights of the city spread out below like a blanket of white diamonds.

"You enjoy elevators, do you?"

Summer experienced a moment of embarrassment. She'd been unaware that her very private emotions were written so clearly on her face.

"I like the external ones. It's like taking a balloon ride on a Sunday afternoon."

He laughed. "You're a romantic."

Summer objected immediately. A romantic, she was certainly not. And, no one had ever accused her of suffering from such a half-witted condition.

"In fact," she told him, "I don't even believe in the existence of romantic love."

A thoughtful glint came into his eyes. "Well, I won't argue with you on that score. It doesn't exist."

Summer nodded. For once, they were in absolute agreement. She took his arm again, and together, they left the elevator.

CHAPTER SIX

''No soup for me,'' Summer declined with a wave of her hand. She was on her second glass of champagne, and was beginning to feel very mellow. Her eyes swept the room in an expansive manner. She loved hotels, and was especially fond of eating out.

''Have you noticed the wonderful color scheme in here?'' She made another sweep with her hand, and almost dislodged her wig.

''You're not much of a drinker are you?'' Gavin waved a waiter over. ''Some coffee please. Black.''

She pouted. ''You're not supposed to drink coffee before the first course. Besides, I can't drink it . . . my teeth will come out.''

''Well, you can take them out and put them in a glass of water on the table for . . .''

''What?'' Summer exclaimed, a little too loudly. ''Are you saying I'm drunk?''

''Not yet. But, you're well on the way there.'' He removed the bottle of champagne from the table, and replaced it in the bucket of crushed ice. Why he didn't just call a halt to the entire evening, was beyond him. His only reason for wanting to have dinner with her in the first place, had been to show her that she couldn't have any man she wanted. But, now that she had turned out to be such a pitiful toothless creature, the reason no longer existed.

There was some strange intangible quality about this woman that pulled at him though. It was like being buffeted by the raw edge of a winter gale. Elemental. Powerful. Even though she was quite possibly bald beneath the hideous wig she was now wearing, there was a depth of spirit to her, one that he had completely failed to notice earlier.

"Tell me . . . how do you manage that whole glamorous getup you wear to work?"

Summer took a sip of black coffee, and waited for the bitter taste to settle warmly in her stomach. "You mean the hair, and everything else?"

He nodded. "I imagine it probably takes you a while to get yourself together in the mornings."

The coffee was beginning to clear away the warm, fuzzy feeling. Across the white linen tablecloth, with the candlelight flickering and the piano keys tinkling, she felt the first stab of guilt. Maybe he wasn't so bad after all. She ignored his question, and decided to ask one of her own.

"Is it women you don't like . . . or just me?"

He met her eyes directly. "I don't like beautiful women. They are invariably vain, selfish, superficial. . . ."

"Ah," Summer interrupted. "So, you can tolerate me now because I'm not attractive?" She still couldn't bring herself to utter the word *ugly* even though it would be a lie.

"In a nutshell, yes. I can see you more clearly without the eyelashes and the paint."

Summer sat back. It would seem as though she had chosen the wrong strategy entirely. He felt comfortable and at ease with her because he felt sorry for her. What a twisted psychological mess he was.

"You mean when I see you at work later on, and the attractive image is back . . . you will dislike me once again?"

He accepted his bowl of borscht and crusty French bread, and savored a spoonful of the fragrant soup with obvious enjoyment.

"After tonight, we will probably never see each other again . . . so,"

Her heart fluttered with sudden dread. What did he mean? Before she could think to censor the thought, it was spilling over her lips, and into sound.

"But, what about the contract?"

He finished the entire bowl before answering, leaving her to wait with both hands knotted in her lap.

"The contract has already been decided. There's no need for me to hang around any longer."

The second course of orange shrimp seasoned with bacon and herbs arrived, and the flurry of taking plates away, and putting new ones down, gave Summer a chance to think. She moved cutlery around to make room for the side dish of steaming lentils, and smiled a polite thank you when a covered basket of oven-fresh rolls and whipped sweet butter was placed directly before her.

She sampled the tangy shrimp, and let the entire tidal wave of thoughts wash over her. He fully expected her to ask whether or not they had gotten the contract. For that reason alone, she would not ask. Besides, she now knew enough about him to know that she would be unable to make him alter his decision. Whatever it was.

She looked up to find his eyes on her. There was a thoughtful, almost puzzled expression there.

"No more questions?"

She selected a hot roll from the basket, split it down the middle, spread an ample amount of sweet butter on both halves.

"No more questions. I figured you wouldn't tell me anyway."

The eyes that she had thought of as distant and cold earlier in the day, filled with sudden warmth. Crinkle lines appeared at the corner of each, and half a smile played around his lips.

He spoke, almost absently. "When you say that just so, with that tone in your voice, you remind me of Nicky."

Summer raised an eyebrow, and the wig slipped a fraction. "An old girlfriend whom you despised, no doubt?"

The expression his eyes became guarded once more. "No. My brother, actually."

Summer digested this little tidbit of information. So, there were more like him somewhere out there. It would appear that she had made quite a few incorrect assumptions about him. She had figured him for a loner. A solitary lion prowling about in his own private hell.

"Does your brother live with you in L.A.?"

"I don't live in L.A."

"But you said earlier . . ."

"I said I was from L.A., not that I lived here." His response was curt, and Summer wondered what terrible sin she had committed now. Was she not supposed to ask any questions about him at all? Would he prefer it if they sat together in total silence? She was just trying to make polite conversation for heaven's sake. Besides, he was the one who had mentioned his brother in the first place.

She speared another shrimp with a vicious jab of her fork, and took a hefty bite. What an incredibly complex man he was. She was very glad that they wouldn't be seeing each other again. She was actually beginning to look forward to the end of the evening, and to spending some quiet time with her fiancé. In the last several weeks, they had spent only a couple of hours together. It didn't seem to bother Kevin, and if the truth be known, it hadn't really bothered her much either, until now. She felt herself in serious need of some tender comforting. She wanted to be held and kissed and babied. Not ignored and snarled at for no good reason at all.

The maître d' interrupted the taut silence with a cheerful query about dessert.

"Nothing for me." They responded in unison.

"Maybe some café au lait then or a . . . liqueur perhaps?"

This time, Gavin replied, "we'll take the check, thank you."

Summer brushed a swatch of hair back from her face. During

the course of the meal, she had lost focus. For a short while there, she had actually begun to like him a little bit.

It was so easy to forget how very unpleasant he was. Sitting across the table from him, staring at his handsome face, it wasn't easy to remember that he was quite probably Satan's right-hand man. But, what he didn't know was that she was well used to handling all of Beelzebub's many helpers.

She made an attempt to brush at the hair again, and the tiniest piece of brown stocking cap peeked through. The wig was terribly hot, and she was of a mind to remove it and set her head of hair free.

Gavin watched her struggle for as long as he could. Then, sudden impatience with women and all of their many pretensions made him speak.

"Why don't you take the damn thing off? Since this is not a date by any means, it hardly matters what you look like."

A smile sloped across Summer's lips, and crazy blood rushed to her head, This was not the way she had planned it, but why the devil not?

"Thank you for being so understanding." Her voice was soft, and gave no inkling of what she was about to do. Her hand swept up, and in one smooth motion, she removed the sagging wig. From somewhere in the bowels of the restaurant, she heard a child say,

"Look mom, the lady's bald," and almost concurrently with that startled declaration, was a whispered admonition, and the sound of a sharp slap being administered.

"What do you think you're . . ."

His words were bitten off by her furious, "taking my wig off . . . and my teeth, just as you requested."

The expression on his face, was a curious mixture of disbelief, and volcanic anger. "I said nothing about your teeth . . . .Don't you dare remove those dentures . . . here. . . ."

Summer reached up for the stocking cap. In the candlelight, it probably did look as though she were bald. On account of her, some poor child had been thoroughly spanked. She would have to think of some way of making amends. But, that would come later.

Within seconds, the cap was off, and great soft waves of hair cascaded down her back.

She reached into her mouth, and peeled each denture away. The silence by then was thunderous.

"How do you like me now?" she asked, and flashed a perfect set of pearly whites.

To her complete and utter amazement, he laughed. It was the kind of uncontrolled mirth that made her think that maybe he hadn't laughed in a good long while. He leaned back in his chair with his head tilted back, and guffawed until tears trickled from the corners of each eye.

After what Summer thought must have been at least five minutes, he opened his eyes, looked at her, and broke down again. The thick husky sound of him made her feel warm inside. It was a curious feeling that began in the pit of her stomach, and worked its way down the lower half of her, all the way to the tips of each toe.

"Summer. . . ." He said her name for the first time, and it curled off his tongue like thick cream. "That name suits you. . . . I haven't laughed this hard in . . . I don't remember how long."

Summer eyed him cautiously. "It wasn't meant to be funny." She had expected anything but this. Why wasn't he angry? She had, after all, made a fool of him. Her little wig and teeth routine had been so flawlessly done, that he had actually believed that she was a bald hag with nary a tooth in her mouth.

Gavin smiled, and she saw a flash of strong, pulling personality in him. "I should have picked it up right away when you said you had no teeth."

Summer grinned, despite her efforts to remain aloof. "I still can't get over the expression on your face when you saw me for the first time back at the house. . . ."

He guffawed again. "I thought you were about to keel over . . . with those shoes . . . and your arches. That made me wonder, but I never guessed . . . never thought you had it in you."

"I'm a designer. Never forget it. And a damn good one, I might add."

They shared a smile.

"So . . ." he said after a while, "this is really you. The hair, the teeth . . . all yours. . . ."

"All mine," she nodded. "I guess you can go back to hating me, now that you know."

His eyes glinted softly at her. "No. That's one thing I'm sure I couldn't do."

CHAPTER SEVEN

The next morning, Summer was in to work early. The events of the previous day and night, had caused her to sleep soundly in her bed. It had been close to eleven last night before she made it back home. After her unveiling in the restaurant, the remainder of the evening had unraveled without a hitch. The play had been wonderful, and the company, she had to admit, not unpleasant.

In the end, when he had walked her back to her front door, she had been actually sorry that this was it. That they would never see each other again. There had been no kiss on the cheek, or anywhere else, as she had envisioned. But, both of his hands had folded around one of hers, and for some reason, unknown to her, he had thanked her. The simple feeling of pleasure that had given her had sent her right off to sleep with happy dreams, instead of the usual blank uneventful sleep.

Now, as she walked briskly toward her office, briefcase in hand, glorious raven hair swinging to and fro in one smooth pelt, she was ready to face anything, even possible failure. As she rounded the last corner, she was greeted by tooting party horns, and a shower of sparkly confetti. She came to an abrupt stop, frozen for a second, not knowing what was happening. Then, she was surrounded by the entire office. There was loud cheering, and jubilant shouts of, "Congratulations. You did it."

Her boss came forward, and the cluster of people around her parted. There was a glitter of something very like greed in his eyes.

"We've hit the mother lode," he said, his round face wreathed in smiles. He took her firmly by the arm, marched her into her office, and closed everyone else out.

He gave her a chance to deposit her things, then perched on a corner of her desk.

"You're a smart girl, Summer. You know there's gonna be a bonus in there somewhere for you . . . and maybe even a promotion. Ten million dollars. Goddamn you're good."

"Thank you, sir. But, I didn't do it alone. The other designers were as much a part of it. . . ."

He slid off her desk with a certain reptilian grace. "Modest too. I like that. I like that . . . you're gonna go far kiddo." He clapped his chubby hands together, as a sudden idea hit him. "Tell you what. Why don't you take the rest of the day off? Go out somewhere. Have some fun with that fiancé of yours . . . what's his name?"

"Kevin," she said, and wondered why she was not more excited by the news that the contract was theirs.

"Yes, Kevin. And while you're off, try to think of a way to get to Massey. I'm thinking of stealing him away from Budget."

Summer stiffened. "What? You mean to work on this project?"

Cameron's eyes became as cool as a mountain stream. "Don't get territorial on me Summer. No matter what happens, you're still gonna be heading the Aztec project. But, Massey has some good ideas. Aztec is gonna be a lot of work. And, you're gonna need all the experienced help we can muster. I see you two working together as a team. Think about it."

When he was gone, Summer sat for a moment, twiddling her pen. Cameron was a sly snake in the grass. He had probably already made an offer to Brian Massey. That was the reason behind the little meeting in his office the day before. He had intended to bring him on board all along. Maybe her job at Design International was not as secure as she had originally thought. She had been so caught up in the last several weeks with winning the contract, that the little signs that were often there, had slipped her notice. But, a sixth sense told her now, that her job probably would have been in jeopardy, had she not won the Aztec contract.

The phone on her desk rang, and the sudden noise startled her.

It was her secretary. ''I've got something out here for you. Can I bring it in?''

Summer put down the pen. She would just have to force herself to be cheerful.

''What is it?'' Her mind was already working. Maybe Brian Massey was out there. The low-down skunk had lost the fight for the contract, but, in losing, he'd also won.

The door swept open, and she realized that she was talking to a dead phone. Her secretary had not waited for a reply. She was now standing in the doorway with a huge basket of burgundy roses. She beamed at Summer.

''Aren't these wonderful? Where shall I put them? There are more outside too.''

Summer stood, gesturing toward the little window to her right. ''More? From whom?''

Jessica Andrews ran out, then in again. This time she carried a planter filled with gorgeous blue tulips. The bulbs were just coming into bloom, and the sight of them brought Summer across to the window. There was a tiny card attached to a stem and she read it without comment. Brian Massey. Her heart had beat a little faster at the thought that the tulips might be from Gavin Pagne. But, of course that was impossible. He very obviously was not the flower-giving kind of man. And, at any rate, why should he bother to give flowers to her anyway?

The roses were from Kevin. It was just the kind of thoughtful thing he would do. He had had every confidence in her. And, the flowers were his way of saying, I know you did it. I love you.

She broke a solitary head off, and twirled it beneath her nose. Of late, because of her work, she had been neglecting him. But, he was so understanding, Such a very good man. They hardly ever disagreed on anything at all. He was perfect for her, and she had the sudden urge to tell him so.

She would go home, change into that yellow linen dress he liked so well, and surprise him at his office downtown. She would take him out to lunch at the most expensive restaurant in L.A. They would have truffles and wine, and a delicious Italian dessert. Then maybe, if she could talk him into it, a movie.

The idea of it all, propelled her into motion. It was a wonderful March day. Perfect for just about anything, with its scrubbed blue skies, and breezy white clouds.

''Jess?'' she called through the open door. ''I'm going to take the rest of the day off. Remind Mr. Cameron for me?''

Her secretary's well-combed head appeared in the doorway again. She smiled. ''Have a wonderful day. You deserve it. . . .'' She lowered her voice. ''More than anyone else.''

They exchanged a knowing look, and Summer thanked her.

''Oh . . . before you leave. A letter came for you yesterday. It's from Champagne Industries. It looks important.''

Summer accepted the thick cream envelope. She turned the package over to inspect the back. The name did not ring a bell.

''You didn't open it then?''

Jess gave a little shake of her head. ''No. It's stamped confidential. I thought it best to leave it for you.''

''Hmmm,'' Summer said, and proceeded to tear open the package and pull everything out. There were a couple of newspaper clippings, and several photographs of a beach cottage in a very serious state of disrepair. She scanned it all, giving the cover letter only a very cursory inspection.

She remembered now. Several years ago, before she had begun her meteoric climb at Design International, she had applied for an international design job. She'd been younger then, and more willing to take risks with her career. The idea of living and working on the island of Jamaica, had appealed enormously at the time. But, she was older now, and everything had changed. She couldn't afford to be frivolous any longer.

It was certainly strange though, that after all this time—at least five years—they should want to interview her, very flattering too that they should remember exactly where it was that she worked.

She fitted the contents back into the envelope, and slid the entire package into her handbag. She would have a better look at it later, not that she really intended doing anything about it. It was only the cottage that had caught her eye. It was in such an utter mess. But, it had so much exciting promise too. There was a wonderful wraparound veranda, and stone stairs leading to the beach. Intricate Victorian trellis work ran up the sides. It was a bit rusted and worn, of course, but with only a spot of paint, it would be as good as new. A nice dirt patch off to one side, would be ideal for a tiny flower garden. There was even enough space under the solitary fruit tree to build a comfortable little bench.

Her eyes glazed over. It would be a prime job indeed. If she were interested in it. But, she was not. In six months, she would be married, and there was much planning still to be done on that. She couldn't afford to go gallivanting off around the Caribbean, renovating houses at the drop of a hat.

She smiled at her secretary as she walked past. "Have a nice weekend."

She took her time driving home. She rolled the top back on the tiny convertible, and let the wind wreak complete havoc with her hair. Most days, she was in a hurry. Always rushing here or there, never taking the time to just enjoy the day. Today she would enjoy. She would squeeze out every last ounce of *oomph* the day had to offer. Then, she would be ready to face the corporate world again. Ready to do battle with the Camerons and Masseys of the world.

An absent smile drifted across her face. It had been rather fun crossing swords with Gavin Pagne. She had been so certain she could never like him. He was such a complex figure. A modern-day Shakespearean, filled with ample portions of darkness and light. Maybe if things had been different. If he had come into her life before now. . . . He wouldn't have been any good to marry, of course. He had the completely wrong kind of personality. But, it would have been interesting to know him. To find out what made him so very forbidding.

Before going home, she stopped at the local grocery store. She picked up a carton of milk and two boxes of chocolate dipped golden-sponge doughnuts. It was their Saturday morning ritual to laze around the TV, watch old movies, and wolf down scads of doughnuts and milk. It was the next best thing to heaven itself. This Saturday morning, she intended to be completely lazy. She would sleep until nine, a luxury she hadn't allowed herself in weeks. Then, both she and Alyssa would vegetate in front of the set, watching old Cary Grant and Audrey Hepburn movies.

She took a happy breath. It was a wonderful thought, indeed. With brown paper bag in hand, she slammed the car door shut, then proceeded up the cobblestoned walkway. It was such a beautiful day, that her eyes were drawn by little things she would ordinarily overlook. She stopped to admire the artistry of a white-washed cupid. The intricately carved stone seemed to almost breathe, with its slightly pouted belly, chubby cheeks, and ivy-garlanded head.

At the condo door, she placed the bag at her feet, and fished around in her purse for the door keys. Alyssa would be out at work, so she would have to let herself in. It took a minute of searching, of pushing things around in the dark recesses of her purse, before she heard the tinkle of keys.

She was in the condominium and closing the door, before she realized there was someone else in there with her. For a minute she stood stock-still, listening. Then, the bag was placed on a table by the door, and her eyes hunted for the portable phone. Her fingers balled into tight fists, as it struck her. It was probably in Alyssa's room.

Her eyes lifted to the level above. God help her if the noise wasn't also coming from the upper level. And, by the sound of things, whoever was up there, was in the process of tearing the place apart.

It took a moment before she could decide exactly what to do. Her neighbors were probably also at work, so there was no point in going next door to call for help. And, if she drove back to the supermarket to use the phone there, whoever was in the condo would have thoroughly ransacked it by the time the police arrived.

Her fingers trembled a bit as she removed her heels. She'd be much better flat-footed if a chase ensued. She placed the shoes very neatly by the lip of the door, then padded softly to the curved staircase, and began to climb. Every step was taken with great trepidation, and, when a board squealed beneath her weight, she froze, heart pounding, hand pressed against her lips.

The sounds of thrashing and thudding were very loud now, and after a moment of careful listening, she realized that they were coming from her bedroom. Her breath came in short thankful gasps. At least she would be able to call for help from Alyssa's room.

She crept down the hall, her feet making not a whisper of sound. Once in her room-mate's bedroom, she closed the door behind her, and locked it. The phone was lying in the middle of the bed. She picked it up to dial, keeping one finger pressed against her ear, to keep the noises of next door out.

''It's an emergency,'' she whispered into the receiver.

A calm female voice came back. ''What is the emergency ma'am?''

Summer took a deep breath, and attempted to control her nerves. Her heart was pounding in her chest like a jackhammer, and beads of perspiration trickled unheeded down the center of her back.

''Noises,'' she stammered. ''In my condominium . . . coming from my bedroom.''

''Noises ma'am?'' the voice said. ''What kind of noises? Is there an intruder?''

Summer took her hand away from her ear. ''Yes. Of course there's an intruder . . . that's what I'm trying to tell you. I need help, someone is . . .''

The sounds of moaning coming from the next room, caused her to pause. ''It . . . it sounds like groaning. . . .'' She listened again. ''. . . you know, like someone in pain.''

There was a silence, then the voice said. ''Do you live alone, ma'am?''

Summer closed her ear with a finger again. The sounds were so loud, that she could just barely hear what the emergency operator was saying.

''No. I've got a roommate. But, what does that have to do with anything? I'm telling you there's someone in my bedroom. Someone who shouldn't be there. You've gotta help me. He's tearing the place apart.''

''What is your address?''

Summer gave it with her breath coming in short, sharp bursts. ''Please hurry,'' she said.

''Where are you now, ma'am?'' the operator asked.

''In the other bedroom . . . my roommate's.''

There was another thud from next door, and Summer shivered. ''Hurry. He's battering something against the wall now.''

''Ma'am?'' the voice said. ''Ma' am . . . can you hear me? Stay exactly where you are. Lock the door, and do not . . . under any circumstances leave the room. Help is on the way.''

But Summer was no longer listening to the phone. The hairs on the back of her neck, were standing at stiff attention. There was something about that last groan that had sounded very familiar.

With the phone still in hand, and the voice on the other end bellowing at her, ''Ma'am? . . . ma'am are you there?'' she reopened the bedroom door. Like someone in a daze, she walked the short distance to her room. Her bare feet slapped the floor like those of a sleepwalker. She tried the door, twisting the shiny gold knob with fingers that were suddenly slippery and cold. The polished oak pushed back without resistance, and for one brief moment, time stood completely still.

The phone in her hand clattered to the floor, and the voice on the other end grew even more frantic. There, in the middle of her bed, with sheets and blankets all askew, were two naked, writhing, sweating bodies.

She stood motionless, for maybe a full minute, just staring, completely incapable of doing much else. The two on the bed were so deeply engrossed in their primal dance, that they were totally unaware of her presence.

Then, like steaming lava just beginning to flow, the ice in her veins was pushed back by a flood of white-hot fury. She crossed the distance to her dresser and back to the bed in an instant. In her hands she carried a large black oriental vase of nicely arranged roses. His roses.

Maybe a board creaked, or perhaps it was just an animalistic sense of survival that made him raise his head, so reluctantly from the swollen bosom. But his reflexes were slow, and he was only able to cry out once before the entire arrangement came crashing down on his skull. The vase splintered into several pieces at the same time the front door on the first level was kicked in by heavy-tipped boots.

Alyssa sprang from the bed, taking a pink sheet with her. She knelt on the floor beside Kevin. The force of the blow had knocked him sideways, and he now lay half on and half off the bed, his eyes closed, a solitary trickle of blood running from a gash on his forehead.

"You've killed him," she shrieked. "Oh my poor sweet darling. . . ." And she erupted into wordless sobbing.

Summer whipped around as three heavily armed policemen rushed in. In the ensuing confusion, with Alyssa wailing like an abandoned dog, and the uniformed men pounding about the room in search of an armed intruder, the realization of what she had done, hit hard and Summer felt herself begin to shake. Dear God, she had just killed a man. She had killed her fiancé.

The room swung unsteadily about her, then sweet, welcoming darkness rushed in.

When she came to, she was lying on the large Roman-style divan. Her favorite chair. The policemen, surprisingly, were gone, and so was Alyssa. Her fiancé sat on the side of her bed, his head bent against a washrag he held in his hand. He was partially clad, his shirt still lying where it had been discarded earlier.

Summer sat up carefully. She still felt strangely light-headed. So, she hadn't killed him after all. . . . Her fiancé and her best friend. The two people, other than her parents, whom she had trusted most in the entire world. That they should betray her so. And all this time, pretending that they despised each other. The thought of it brought the rage back, and she had to force herself to be calm as she looked across at him and met his gaze.

They stared wordlessly at each other for several beats. Then without a word, Summer stood, and left the room. On legs that were still not completely steady, she walked the distance to her roommate's bedroom. The door was closed. She tried the knob, took a breath, and entered.

Alyssa was sprawled on the softly padded window seat, staring out at nothing in particular. Summer felt her fingers bunch into tight fists at her side. Waves of anger threatened to overcome her again.

"How long has all this been going on?"

Alyssa turned to give her a cold stare. "What difference does it make? You were never good enough for him . . . anyway."

Volcanic rage was just a hairbreadth away, but Summer made a valiant attempt to control herself.

"Why did you do this? We've been friends for years. Good friends. How could you hurt me like this? We . . . we shared everything."

Alyssa wrapped the skirt of the long terry robe around her legs. "For a cold-hearted career woman, you're very naive, my dear. I was never your friend to any degree . . . I just wanted your man. That's all. So, don't go all teary eyed and dramatic on me. You, more than anyone else should understand how these little things work. I've seen you play with men before . . . it's what you do. And don't pretend that you're so very hurt. We both know that you didn't love Kevin. He just fit in with your yuppy plans. You're a . . ."

"Enough," Summer said, her eyes sparkling with ire. "You've said your piece. You know . . ." and her eyes ran over the other woman, "you may be wasting yourself . . . working as an accountant. Your talents obviously lie elsewhere. . . ."

"How dare you?" Alyssa gasped, swinging her feet to the ground.

Summer advanced a step, her eyes blazing. "Count yourself lucky that I'm too much of a lady to consider resorting to anything physical with you." She wagged a finger. "But . . . don't push your luck with me . . . my dear."

Summer spun on her heel, not trusting herself to continue. At the door, she turned again. "You're welcome to Kevin, by the way. You both are so very well suited. I wish you two lots of luck. A word of advice though . . . you'd do well to put a padlock on his breeches unless you want this little scene repeated . . . a few months down the road."

And with that, she stormed back down the corridor, opened her room door, and closed it again with a resounding crash.

Kevin stood slowly. "Honey I . . ." he began.

"Get out," Summer enunciated crisply, and she strode to the walk-in closet and began pulling clothes off hangers. She couldn't bear the thought of spending another second under the same roof as her roommate. She pulled down a suitcase, and without any care given to folding, began tossing garments in.

Kevin was behind her almost immediately. "What are you doing? Where're you going?"

His voice brought her head up, but she continued to pack.

"We have to talk about this . . . you can't just leave . . . I won't let you."

She dragged a large duffel bag down and continued to stuff it with handfuls of silks, satins, slinky Lycra, and cotton shirts. She worked quickly, clearing the racks of belts, shoes, stockings, garters.

She felt his touch on her arm, and she spun around, her eyes spitting fire.

"Don't you ever . . . ever touch me again."

She looked down at her hand. Just for today, she had placed it on her finger, hoping somehow, that it would bring her luck. She yanked the ring off, and thrust it at him.

"Take this . . . and get out. If I ever see you again, I may be forced to commit murder."

When he remained where he stood, the gash on his head still seeping blood, she shoved him backwards with both hands.

"I said . . . go on . . . get out of here. I don't want to see you again."

He broke down then , and began to sob like a little boy. "It didn't mean anything honey. I swear it didn't mean anything. I don't even understand how it happened. She'd been after me for months, sending me gifts, writing me notes. Telling me you didn't deserve me. . . . I never would've if you hadn't made me wait to have you. All this time I've been faithful . . . years. . . . but, I couldn't wait any longer. It was . . . it was too much for me."

Summer pulled another rack of clothes down, and stuffed them into a third bag. Her heart battered against her ribs as though she had just completed a marathon. In some small part of her, she felt pity for him. Pity for the weak, lying coward that he was.

"I don't want to hear about it . . . Okay? I just don't want to hear another word." She spun around to face him again. "I trusted you. How could you . . . here? . . . in my own bed?"

He continued to sniffle, and Summer closed the bags, and went to the bathroom. Within minutes, her many bottles of creams, lotions, and perfumes, were all packed. She snatched up her toothpaste and toothbrush, and shoved those into an already bulging cosmetic bag. When she re-entered the bedroom, the crying had ceased.

"What do you want me to do?" he asked plaintively, "Tell me what you want me to say . . . tell me . . . just . . . just please don't leave me. Alyssa isn't your friend. I tried to tell you that many times before . . . but you wouldn't believe me. She envies you. She wants everything you have . . . including me. But . . . I'm yours . . . yours . . . always. . . ."

Summer stared at him, and for the first time since they'd met, she really looked at him. And what she saw left her with a sick feeling in the pit of her stomach. Was this the man she had intended to marry? This slick-tongued, soft-bellied bastard? She wondered how she had never noticed before how weak his chin was. Or how no matter what it was he said, the expression in his eyes almost never changed.

She found that she didn't really want to know how long the relationship had been going on. She didn't want to know anything at all about it. In fact, if she thought about it for too much longer, she would be violently ill.

"Aren't you going to answer me? If you wanna be mad at someone . . ." he paused, and his mouth thinned to a cruel line. ". . . be mad at your friend Alyssa." And he emphasized the word *friend.* "Ask her who started this entire thing. . . .You ask her."

Summer snapped the final suitcase closed. "There is one thing you can do for me Kevin. . . ." A measure of icy calm had come over her now

He perked up. "Anything honey . . . anything."

"Tell Alyssa that I won't be living here any longer. And . . . if she happens to ask, let her know that I'll be back sometime next week . . . in the afternoon, for the rest of my things. And . . . oh, make very sure you tell her for me, not to be in when I return."

With a suitcase in either hand, purse and duffel bag on her shoulder, she walked through the door, never turning to look back even once.

CHAPTER EIGHT

Summer drove around aimlessly for what must have been a full hour, before the full enormity of what had happened hit her. In the space of a few moments, her entire life had collapsed. All the planning, and the careful preparations, everything gone.

Angry tears trickled down the sides of her face, and she dashed them away with the ball of her palm. What an embarrassment, too, to have called the police, and to have had them burst in at almost the exact moment that she brought the vase down on Kevin's head. She could have been brought up on charges of aggravated assault, or worse. But Kevin, had obviously sent them away with one of his smooth-tongued explanations. He was good at that. He was good at a lot of things, apparently.

A Marriot sign loomed ahead, and on a sudden impulse, she turned into the drive. She would stay there over the weekend, until she decided exactly what to do about things. This was definitely not the weekend she had been looking forward to. Never in a million years, would she have thought Alyssa capable of hurting her so. For years, they had lived like sisters, sharing everything, crying on each other's shoulders. How was it possible that she could have misjudged her so very completely?

She gave the hotel valets a watery smile as they helped her from the car. ''Just these bags, thank you,'' she said, indicating the motley assortment on the passenger seat.

Once she was comfortably ensconced in the hotel room, with her bags neatly packed away, and the bellboy tipped, she picked up the phone, and like an automaton, began making calls. The couturiere, who just a day before, had nipped and tucked at the waist and sleeves of her wedding gown, happily complimenting her on her petite ribs, and long elegant back, burst into loud tears and a flood of completely unintelligible French.

Summer spent ten whole minutes calming the woman down, and assuring her that payment would be made anyway.

She canceled the booking for the reception hall, and told the very helpful clerk that talking to a premarital counselor would not help a bit. The caterers were called next, and finally her parents. In a very stilted voice, without going into much detail, she told them that the wedding was off.

There were no recriminations, or noises of disappointment, Kevin had never been well liked. In a very thin voice that indicated to her father that maybe tears were not too far off, Summer promised that she would be up for a visit, the following weekend, and that they would have a nice long talk then.

Up at Mammoth Lakes, the phone was handed over, and her mother, being the kind, understanding soul that she was, wisely decided not to ask too many questions either. She could tell by her daughter's tone that Summer needed the time to work through things. She got the phone number of the Marriot, made Summer promise to call the next day, then hung up and went immediately to see to preparations for the weekend visit.

With all of the most pressing calls made, Summer sat on the edge of the large double bed and stared blankly at her left hand. The mere sight of that lighter gold area, offended her, and she massaged the finger vigorously. She would never again trust a man. Never. They were all, as she had always thought, lying dogs. And, she wanted nothing to do with any of them ever again. Henceforth, she would dedicate herself completely to her career. She didn't need any of them. It was a very good thing indeed that she didn't believe in foolish romantic love. What an awful mess she would have been in now, if she had actually believed herself to be *in love* with Kevin.

She peeled off her snappy red suit, and went to the tiny bathroom. After a long, steamy shower, and a very thorough washing of her hair, she emerged clad in a thick cream towel, with a matching one wound tightly around her head. The hot water had not done her much good at all; she still felt icy-cold inside. Her fingers were as shriveled as prunes, and the burgundy polish on her nails was all waterlogged, and beginning to peel.

She spent half an hour tending to her thick hair, blow-drying and brushing it until it was silky smooth. Then she retired to bed, to pass the remainder of the day, rolled up in a tight ball, not moving, not sleeping, unable to shed a single tear in anger or sorrow.

CHAPTER NINE

Summer was disturbed by the ringing of the phone, at 6:00 A.M. on Monday. She had spent the entire weekend holed up in her hotel room, only leaving her bed to order room service and fresh boxes of tissue. Somehow, in the midst of everything else, she had come down with a severe bout of influenza.

When she picked the phone up, and croaked a very hoarse "Hello?," there was a small pause on the other end, then a male voice said, "Summer . . . is that you?"

She struggled into an upright position. Her eyes were severely bloodshot, and her head felt as though a steamroller had run directly over it. She fumbled for another swatch of tissue, blew her nose very heartily, then said in a voice that was hoarse and not a little grumpy: "Brian Massey. What do you want?" She had left her whereabouts on her secretary's voice mail, but how had Massey gotten a hold of it. And, why in the name of all that was holy, was he calling her at such an ungodly hour.

His cheerful laugh, and "what's the matter . . . get up on the wrong side of the bed this morning?" comment, irritated her even further. She was in no mood for levity. She had endured one of the worst weekends of her life, and saw nothing at all to be cheerful about.

"I hadn't gotten up yet. . . ." she gave a terrific sneeze, and blew her nose again. "As you can probably tell . . . I'm not at my best. Just tell me what you want and let me get back to my suffering."

His voice was immediately concerned. "You sound terrible. Now I'm sorry I woke you. I just wanted to let you know, before you got into the office, that we're going to be working together on the Aztec project, starting to . . ."

Summer sat bolt upright. "You are what?" she bellowed into the phone, cutting him off in mid-sentence.

His response was a bit startled. "I thought you knew I'd been hired on. Cameron told me you were in complete agreement with it."

Summer inhaled with great difficulty, the congestion in her chest causing her to wheeze heavily as she did. So, this was how she was repaid for winning the contract, a huge knife right dead center in the middle of her back.

She swung her legs out of bed, and winced at the feel of the soft carpeting between her toes. She did have the flu, there was no doubt about that. Every muscle in her body ached.

"I'll see you at the office in about two hours."

"You are going to come in then? . . . Even in your condition?"

A spasm of coughing took her, and she felt that maybe she was suffering now because of the trick she had played on Gavin Pagne just a few days earlier.

"Of course I'm coming in." In fact, try to keep her away. There was no way on God's green earth that she was going to let him steal that account away from her. And, she was going to let Mr. Cameron know exactly what she thought of his tactics.

"I'll see you later," she said, and hung up without waiting for a reply.

She was bathed, dressed, and well medicated in under an hour. She pinned her hair up in a soft chignon, stroked a deep kohl pencil across the very tips of her eyebrows, added mascara and eyeliner, and finished the entire picture of cool sophistication, with a hint of blush on her cheekbones, and a tinted amber gloss on her lips. She did her nails last, skillfully removing the faded burgundy, and replacing it with a translucent cream color that matched her suit almost exactly.

She soothed her raw throat with a blast of Chloroseptic, dropped a roll of lozenges into her purse, and left the room looking no worse than when she had entered it on Friday.

She was in her office, and sitting at her desk when Brian Massey came breezing through the door. He gave her the kind of smile that made Summer think of the smug Cheshire cat in the old *Alice in Wonderland* fable. Maybe it had something to do with the quantity of medication she had poured down her throat. But his lips did appear to stretch from ear to ear.

He seated himself in the chair before her desk. ''You look gorgeous. Do you ever have a bad day?''

She felt a sneeze coming on, and controlled it with great difficulty. When she looked at him again, her eyes were watery, and tinged with a blush of pink.

''So . . . we're going to be working together, then. I can't help feeling that there's something unethical about having one of the lead Budget designers, working for us . . . on a project on which we both competed.''

Massey laughed. ''You don't mince words, do you?''

Summer was prevented from answering by the ringing of her phone. She reached across to answer it, then covered the mouthpiece.

''Can you excuse me for a minute?''

She waited until the office door was firmly closed.

''There is nothing left for us to say to each other Kevin.''

She listened to the whining tone for a bit. ''Yes, I did cancel everything . . . I don't care what everybody thinks.''

She hung up when he began to moan about how everything would affect his chances to be made partner. She couldn't believe she had never seen what a very selfish bastard he was. Maybe catching him in bed with Alyssa was one of the luckiest breaks she had ever received.

She gave her watch a glance. The day was going by very slowly, and she could feel the first traces of a thumping headache beginning to beat an insistent tattoo around the area of her temples. She sneezed again, and this time, was forced to give her nose a hearty blow.

The skin around her nostrils felt dry and sore. In fact, everything about her today felt dry and sore.

The door opened and closed. And, she looked up, expecting Brian Massey.

It was her boss.

''I hear you're sick,'' he said and came to perch, as was his usual practice, on the edge of her desk.

Summer patted her nose with a tissue. ''Just a little cold. Nothing serious.''

He looked at her for a second, grunted, then came down to the meat of it.

''As I told you on Friday, Massey is gonna be working on Aztec. . . .''

Summer bit back an immediate retort. It would have pleased her heart tremendously to point out that in fact what had been said was something totally different. But, she held her tongue, albeit, with great difficulty.

''Yes, you mentioned something to that effect.''

Mr. Cameron nodded. ''I know how much you want Aztec . . . how hard you worked to get it. . . .''

Summer waited, her face serene. A slow-burning anger was beginning to unfurl itself. And, the headache that had only been threatening thus far, was now upon her.

''. . . and I would never think to pull you off it. So, I've decided to give Massey the VP spot in your department.'' He rushed on, spurred somewhat by the slow rhythmic tick that had begun to beat on Summer's left temple.

''. . . that way, you will have the benefit of his years of experience, and at the same time, have complete—or almost complete—control of the Aztec project.''

He got off the desk, drew himself up. ''Also . . . this office. It's really an executive's office. We let you have it . . .'' and he laughed, ''. . . because, quite frankly there was enough space, and it didn't matter. But, now. . . .'' he shrugged, ''space is gonna be an issue. So, we're gonna put you in one of the cubicles out front. You can have your choice of furnishings, and whatever else you'd like to include to give it a nice homey look. . . .'' He paused to give her a rather feral look. ''Well . . . what do you think? Got any ideas?''

He stood looking down at her with an air of condescension, and a hint of ''do what I say or else,'' in his voice.

Summer was on her feet before she could think to do otherwise. Unbridled anger flashed like wildfire through her blood. She had worked herself half to death, done many things, some of which she was not greatly proud, just to win that ten-million-dollar Aztec contract, and this was how she was repaid. Massey was hired into the spot she was originally promised, and, she was hustled out of her office, and into a cubicle out front.

Her voice was cold when she spoke, and only hinted at the volcanic anger that boiled just beyond the veil of her eyes.

''Will Brian Massey be given this office?''

Mr. Cameron cleared his throat, and shuffled a bit before responding. ''As a matter of fact . . . yes, he will.'' His eyes became icy. ''In this business, things can change very quickly. No one is indispensable. Not even you. Do you get my meaning ?''

''Perfectly. . . .'' And, she began to clear her desk with great sweeps of her hand.

Mr. Cameron rocked back on his heels. ''What are you doing?''

''I need a few days to think.''

Her boss rested both hands on the flat of the desk. ''You can take some time after the Aztec project is completed. We can't spare you now. You know that.''

Summer paused, her eyes glittering dangerously. ''You should have thought of that little detail before you made some of your decisions.''

Mr. Cameron's face flushed red with anger. ''The decisions I choose to make are none of your concern, miss. If you weren't such a good designer, I'd toss you out of here on your ear, right now.''

He drew breath, then charged on, his many chins beginning to wobble as he grew increasingly agitated. ''And, let's get this entirely straight. You cannot take any time. We can't spare you. Gavin Pagne needs the project done in six months.''

The throbbing in Summer's temples had spread across her forehead to settle somewhere between her eyes.

''I just got you a ten-million-dollar account for God's sake. I should at least be entitled to some time off.''

Cameron straightened, his face frigid. ''Let me make myself completely clear on this. If you walk out that door. You walk out that door. Get me?''

Pride stiffened her spine, and Summer drew herself up.

''You are . . .'' and she searched around for the appropriate words. Several occurred, but none seemed quite severe enough. To say that he was greedy, unethical, and conniving, would be a good start though.

''You are not going to make me any more upset than I already am.''

She swept the entire jumble of things on her desk into the leather bag that was already filled with bottles of cold medication and boxes of tissue. With eyes gleaming with a combination of high fever, and white-hot temper, she said, ''good-bye, Mr. Cameron. I hope you and Brian Massey get on fabulously together.''

And, with that, she stormed from the office, almost knocking over a delivery boy carrying a bunch of ''I'm sorry'' balloons, and a large vase of roses.

CHAPTER TEN

Once she got back to the hotel, she called a storage company, then began repacking her bags. When she was through, she sat on the wide double bed, and had a good cry. Her entire world was crumbling about her. First Kevin and Alyssa, now this. How was it possible that so many things could go wrong so very quickly? She had lost Kevin, and her job within days of each other. It was almost as though some force of nature had deliberately set out to do her in.

A sudden thought occurred to her, and she gave it a minute of careful consideration. What if her sudden litany of woes had not been caused by some supernatural bogeyman with a crazy vendetta against her. What if Gavin Pagne was behind the entire mess?

The more she thought about it, the more possible it became. Maybe this was his way of repaying her for humiliating him publicly. He had appeared amused then, but it could all have been an act. In fact, it was very likely that it had been an act. He was a cold, dangerous, and powerful man. One who would not take kindly to being made a fool of. It could be that he had asked Cameron to move her out of her office and into a cubicle, knowing full well, that she would be forced to quit the job in order to keep her professional respect.

It wasn't impossible either, that he might have had something to do with Kevin's betrayal. How he could have orchestrated that, she wasn't entirely sure, but she knew that he was definitely diabolical enough to have urged Kevin, who was a much weaker man, into an indiscretion.

She got off the bed and went into the bathroom for a glass of water and two aspirin. She massaged the area around her temples. The high fever was beginning to unbend her mind. Gavin Pagne could have had nothing at all to do with the string of calamities that had recently befallen her. And, it was ridiculous, not to mention quite a bit paranoid for her to even think that he might have had something, anything to do with the whole sorry mess.

For a minute, she studied her face in the mirror. She had always thought that she looked a great deal like the old fifties film star, Dorothy Dandridge. She had the same general shape of face, the same mouth and nose, the same cheekbones. The only real difference between them, was the eyes. Dorothy's had been jet-black, dancing eyes, filled with volatile quicksliver emotion. Hers were a golden fawn color that often went through subtle changes in shade, depending on her mood.

She made a face at herself. She had always been grateful for her unusual looks. As a little girl, her mother had regaled her every night with wonderful stories about her paternal grandmother. About how she had been a great beauty in her time, and had broken many a heart before she was finally tamed by her grandfather. It had been her fervent wish each night as she was tucked securely between the covers, that she would become such a beauty too. When she had turned eighteen, and was finally allowed to wear her hair loose, she had realized that her wish had been granted. From that point onward, she had carried her beauty like a badge of honor, a treasured heirloom passed down to her by her wonderfully feisty grandmother. And, everyone had paid her homage. Everyone, except Gavin Pagne, who had hated her on sight because of it.

She turned her face this way and that, inspecting the clean lines of it. Surely, as twisted as Gavin Pagne was, he could not hate her that much? That he should desire to destroy her entire life by taking away her job?

The phone on the bedside table rang just as she was giving her nose a second blow. She let it ring for a couple of seconds, undecided as to whether or not she wanted to speak to anyone. With her temples throbbing the way they were, and a band of pain beginning to tighten around her cranium, she was in a mood to do nothing but fight.

She let the phone ring for a bit more, giving the person on the other end a fair chance to escape. When the ringing persisted, she walked across to snatch the phone up.

"Yes?"

It was her secretary, Jessica Andrews, and she was, for the very first time, flustered.

"Summer . . . I . . . I heard you'd left us? Please . . . please tell me it's not true. The entire place is in an uproar." She continued without waiting for a response. "Mr. Cameron is screaming at everyone . . . he says no one knows what's going on . . . and . . . and Brian Massey practically forced your whereabouts out of me . . . I think he's on his way over. . . ."

"On his way over? Here?" Summer interrupted. "Is he completely crazy?"

"He said . . . he feels responsible for what happened."

Summer gave a short laugh. "Isn't that a scream? Is he coming here as Cameron's mouthpiece? Or on his own initiative?"

There was a slight pause, then Jessica said somewhat hesitantly, "on his own . . . I'd guess."

"Has he left the office yet?"

"No . . . I mean . . . yes . . . he's leaving right now."

Summer heard the secretary stifle a sob, and for a brief moment, she felt a rush of sympathy.

"Don't worry Jess. I'll be okay. I'm not destitute, you know. I can survive without Design International. . . ." She was about to say more, then thought better of it. ‘‘Take care of yourself. I’ll give you a call later, all right?’’

She hung up, and scooted about the room collecting her bags. When Brian Massey arrived, she would no longer be a guest at the hotel. Not that she was afraid of facing him. Nothing would give her more pleasure. But, she was sick, with what must be a very high fever, and would be in much better mettle after a good long rest in the crisp mountain air of Mammoth Lakes. It would take her only a couple hours to see to the storage of her furniture at the condo, after which she’d be able to set out for the mountains.

She checked her watch. It was almost midday. If she hurried, she would be able to make it to her parents house just before dark. She left the hotel with the cheery thought that she had made it through the worst of it. Surely, nothing else could happen to her now.

CHAPTER ELEVEN

The long road up to the resort town of Mammoth Lakes, snaked its way through some of the most beautiful country in California. The drive out of town had been taxing on her already frayed nerves, with stop-and-go traffic, and eighteen wheelers careening along at dangerously fast speeds. But, once out of the confines of Los Angeles county, with the crush of people far behind her she was able to relax and enjoy the unraveling countryside.

She took Highway 14 through the Mojave desert, then continued north on the two-lane stretch of I-395. Every so often as the road weaved its way through majestic red-brown mountains and desert flatlands, the wind would pick up, blowing balls of tumbleweed across the road. This was the part of the long five-hour drive that she enjoyed the most. The utter peace of rolling hills, the cattle grazing undisturbed in thick herds, the shimmering blue of a mountain lake. It moved her like nothing else. It was raw, eloquent, and never failed to take her back a century or two to the time when Native American tribes would have inhabited the plains.

In her mind's eye, she could see the glistening bronze bodies on horseback, hear the rumble of hooves as a stampede of buffalo came roaring down the gentle swell of a grassy hill. It was like driving through a huge movie set of the old west, complete with quaint little towns bearing names like Lone Pine and Independence.

She slid in a Barry White CD, and let the music seep into her bones. Music and this great beauty surrounding her was maybe what she needed. With the top down, sunglasses firmly in place, and the wind in her hair, she could almost believe that all that had happened to her in the last few days, had only been a horrible dream. But, it wasn't. It was real, and no amount of pretending was going to change the fact that in one clean sweep, the entire direction of her life had been forever altered. It would be years before she would let herself trust another man. Years before she would let another hold her.

The air was beginning to take on a different quality now, there was a chill to the wind that raced through her hair, and the caps on the surrounding peaks, were dusted with a recent fall of snow. At about four thousand feet, she put the hood up, and turned on the heat. It still amazed her how very suddenly the day could turn cold.

She stopped in Bishop to refuel, and decided to pick up a bucket of fried chicken and biscuits at a drive-through window. Nothing made her dad happier than scarfing down crunchy legs of golden-brown chicken, and sopping up spicy, brown gravy with soft, white biscuits.

When she was somewhere between eight and ten years old, she and her dad had had a nightly ritual. At precisely midnight, after her mother had retired to bed, they would creep down to the kitchen, turn on the stove light, and create their own extra-special midnight snack. Sometimes it was cereal and ice cream, or warm biscuits drenched in butter. But, most of the time, they both would settle on the huge container of chicken that was always in the refrigerator. It was their unspoken agreement, that dessert would be a huge chunk of nicely frosted chocolate cake, topped off with a glass of ice-cold milk.

This practice probably would have continued on into her teens, had her mother not caught them at it one night. A fond smile drifted across her face. She hadn't thought of any of this in years. Her mother had pretended great outrage of course, and had sent them both up to bed with a good scolding, but, Summer had crept back down the staircase, and surprised her at the kitchen table, quietly laughing.

She had realized then, what wonderful parents she had been blessed with, and impulsively, she had rushed over and given her mother a big sloppy kiss on the cheek. They had held each other, and a deeper understanding had been forged between them.

All the memories of childhood came rushing back to her as she urged the car into low gear, and began the final climb into town. She was up above seven thousand feet now, the air was sharp and cold, the sides of the road were lined with mounds of fresh snow. Around her, the mountains soared to amazing heights, their glistening white peaks glimmering pink and gold in the setting sun. It was so still, so perfect, that Summer pulled over for a minute to watch the changing kaleidoscope of colors. Nothing could equal this. No artist could capture such a glorious sight. She sat watching until the first blush of burnt orange slowly tinted the sky.

It was almost dark when she turned into the winding gravel-strewn driveway, and began crunching her way up. She was tired after the long drive, but seeing the house silhouetted in the darkness, warm and ablaze with light, her spirits picked up a great deal. This was home, this was where she belonged.

Her parents had moved to Mammoth when she was just a baby. She had grown up there among the fresh air, trees, and snow. But, by the time she had entered puberty, she had tired of things, and had found the pace of the quiet, sleepy little town not at all to her liking. As soon as she was out of high school, she had relocated to the city, gotten herself a job, and enrolled as a part-time student at UCLA. She had thrown herself with joyful abandon into the nightlife. The clubs, the parties, the theater. She had taken her grandmother's credo to heart, nosing out excitement and stimulation wherever it lay. She had done this for two or three years, until the sweetness of it all, gradually lost its flavor.

Now, she could think of nothing she would like better than to settle in a town very like Mammoth, where the air was soft and sweet with the scent of flowers in the mornings. Life was slower; people, kinder, genuine. She was truly tired of the corporate hurly-burly. The scheming, backstabbing, brown-nosing environment that was a normal part of the business culture in most big companies.

She honked her horn once to let them know someone was there. The front door opened, and a great big shaggy dog came tearing down the stairs. She was out of the car, and kneeling in the soft snow. The dog charged her, knocking her backwards, its tongue plastering her face with wet kisses.

"Bruno." She hugged the wiggling body tight, and felt the burn of tears behind her eye-lids. How could she have thought that she needed anymore than this? She heard her mother's voice call out from the flood of light in the doorway, "It's . . . it's Summer, Dad . . . it's Summer."

She looked up then, one arm controlling the excited dog, "Don't come down Mom . . . there's ice on the stairs."

Her father who was now forced to use a sturdy cane because of surgery on his hip, was also at the door. The happiness on their faces as Summer struggled up the stairs under the heavy weight of her bags, caused her eyes to tear up again. She hadn't visited once since Christmas. She had always put her work ahead of everything else. She hadn't fully understood, before now, the things that were of real importance. It wasn't money, or things, or even power, as she had once thought. It was this. It was home, and family. Knowing that you were loved and accepted, no matter what.

At the door, she dropped her bags and swept them both into a great hug. How lucky she was. How very lucky that she still had them.

With tears streaking down her face, she managed: "I brought some . . . some chicken for you, Dad."

Hours later, she was snuggled deep in her bed under thick, warm covers, listening to the soft fall of snow on the windows. The fireplace crackled in a corner, making the room cozier still. She closed her eyes, and contentment softened the slight wheeze in her chest. Tomorrow she would decide what to do about things. Tomorrow.

CHAPTER TWELVE

She spent all of the first morning puttering about the house, and not thinking much at all. Kevin phoned in the afternoon, and again in the evening. She refused his call on both occasions. She still had not told her parents much about the breakup, and tactfully, they had not asked. When she was comfortable enough, they knew she would tell them.

When evening fell at the end of the first day, she settled down to a spirited game of Scrabble with her parents. She was in the middle of a very thoughtful consideration of a possible word beginning with the letter *X*, when her father cleared his throat and said, "Summer . . ."

She raised her head, laughter dancing in her eyes. "Wait a minute, Dad . . . there's a word here somewhere."

His hand covered hers, and his eyes were serious. "Leave that for a moment, sweetheart."

Summer's eyes darted to her mother, then back to her dad. "Is something wrong? Are you . . . you're not sick or anything?"

Her father smiled, and the great burst of fear that had exploded in her chest, eased a bit.

"No . . . no, I'm fine. Mom's fine too. The doctor tells us

we should live to a fine old age. Must be the mountain air. . . ." And he laughed. "We've been thinking of a way to do this for the longest while though. . . ."

Summer gripped the strong brown hand that reached out to her. Her mind began to churn again. Oh God, something was wrong. They were trying to prepare her. She could feel it.

"Dad . . . you're . . . you're making me very nervous. What is it?"

He shook his head, and swallowed. "The attic. . . ."

Her mother took over when it became apparent that he could not get the words out.

"We . . . we want you to go and . . . and clean the attic dear . . . when you find the time. After you've rested a bit . . . settled in more. If you don't mind. We're getting too old to climb up that ladder. There's lots of cobwebs and boxes full of old things. Some you might like to keep. . . ."

"Maybe you could help us redesign the entire space, dear." Her father had regained his voice. He turned to his wife, and they exchanged a little look. "It's the best way."

Summer squeezed the hand still clinging to hers. "Wow . . . you had me scared for a second. Of course I'll do the attic for you. Actually, I'd been meaning to talk to you about it for a long while. . . . I never understood why you would never fix it up." She looked around at the immaculate living room, with its crystal vases, fashionable rugs, and warm colors.

"I must have gotten the design gene from you, Mom."

Her mother got suddenly teary eyed and pressed a kiss to Summer's cheek. "Yes dear . . . yes."

The word beginning with the letter *X* suddenly occurred to her and Summer grabbed the pieces and placed them triumphantly on the board. "Xylen."

Her father studied the board. "That's not a word, honey."

Summer sat up, her eyes flashing with mock outrage. "Dictionary . . . dictionary."

She groaned loudly, causing her mother to break into laughter, when it turned out that the word she'd actually been reaching for was really *xylem.*

Her father smiled. ''I've still got a few gray cells left in this brain of mine.''

The remainder of the night was passed playing more Scrabble, dominoes, then a spirited game of cards. At about ten o'clock, Summer felt the effects of the cold medication beginning to wear off. Her parents were still going strong, but she felt herself fading.

''Do you mind if I get to bed a little early tonight?''

Her mother looked at her, and the love shining in her eyes was bright.

''This is your home, Summer, dear. You can do whatever you like.'' She rested her cards on the table. To her husband she said, ''I know exactly how I put them down, so I'll know if you've had a look. Then, ''Let me fix you some of that soup Summer. A hot cup is exactly what you need for that chest of yours.''

In the warm country kitchen, she lit the stove, while Summer clattered about in the cupboard looking for bowls. The fridge, which was always packed with food, was no different tonight. Summer poked around until she found the large home baked rolls, which her mother made like clockwork every Sunday. She selected three of the largest.

''Will dad want any soup?''

Her mother was busy stirring the large pot. ''A roll will be fine for him. We have to watch his diet.''

Summer set the microwave for half a minute. ''He's okay . . . isn't he Mom? He looks . . . thinner somehow.''

The stirring stopped for a minute. ''He's on a special diet. The doctor said he needs to get his cholesterol down . . . but, other than that, he's fine.''

''And . . . you're okay too?'' It was almost inconceivable to her that her mother should not be well. She, who had never been sick a day in her life.

''I'm fine. Healthy as a horse . . . Summer, I don't want you to worry about us. What we really want is for you to be happy. . . .'' The stirring resumed. ''You know that when we're gone, this house will be yours?''

Summer started so violently, she narrowly avoided dropping a bowl. "I hate it when you talk like that, Mom."

The creamy chicken soup with large homemade noodles, and spicy chunks of sweet potato, was ladled generously into two bowls, and set on the table. Her mother eased herself slowly into one of the straight-backed chairs. "You have to face it, Summer. You are going to outlive us." She waved her hand in the familiar authoritative manner Summer remembered so very well. "Take that roll in to your dad, and tell him to stay away from my cards . . . no don't put any butter on it."

Summer returned with a smile on her face. "He was asleep. Mouth wide open."

She sat at the table, and dug in heartily. Her badly battered spirits were slowly beginning to unfurl their wings again. It didn't matter that she had lost her job. She was talented, she would get another one. A better one. And, it certainly didn't matter about Kevin. In fact, she was happy that she had found out the way she did. What a horrible mistake she would have made, if she had gone ahead with the wedding.

"Did your breakup have anything to do with Alyssa?"

Summer choked on a spoonful of soup. She sputtered for a moment, and her mother reached across to thump her on the back. "I saw how they behaved together when they were up here at Christmas. But. . . ."

"You mean . . . you knew? . . . about them?"

"I wasn't certain. But, I wondered."

"And you would've let me go ahead and marry him . . . without telling me what you thought?"

"No. We would've found some way to stop you. But, first we wanted to be absolutely sure. Your dad and I were thinking of hiring a detective. To get the proof we needed, then. . . ."

Summer had stopped eating. How had she not seen it herself? She had once prided herself on being calculating and shrewd. How was it possible that she had not seen some small sign in Alyssa's or Kevin's behavior.

"So . . . that's why you didn't sound surprised when I told you the wedding was off. I've wondered for a while why it was that you and Dad didn't like Kevin . . . but, I always thought you liked Alyssa. You seemed to."

Her mother stood and went to the sink. Even though the kitchen was well equipped with a large dishwasher, she would never use it.

"You've never had a lot of friends. So, I was happy when Alyssa came along. I wanted to like her . . . for you. But, sometimes I would see the envy in her when she looked at you. You had so much . . . and she, so much less."

Summer rose and wrapped her arms around her mother. She hadn't hugged her in this manner since she was a little girl of ten.

"I love you, Mom. I'm so lucky to have you and Dad. You've always been there for me . . . even when I went through those crazy years . . . you never stopped loving me."

Her mother returned the hug for an instant, then turned back to her dishes, her salt-and-pepper head bent. "Remember that tomorrow. Remember that . . . when you redecorate the attic." She sniffed loudly, and Summer felt a rush of tenderness.

The attic was really driving her crazy. "Mom, if . . . if you don't want it cleared out, and everything changed. I can just sweep it up a bit . . . but leave everything the same. I don't have to touch a thing."

Her mother spun around, soap suds dripping from her arms. "No . . ." She took a breath, then said more calmly. "No . . . I want everything out. Everything sorted and gone through. All the boxes and trunks . . . you understand? All of them."

Summer nodded. A slight furrow of concern had sprung up between her eyebrows. She hoped her mother wasn't on the verge of having some sort of nervous collapse. Maybe she was in need of a vacation. It didn't seem reasonable, somehow, to let one cluttered attic get you so very worked up.

"I'll start on it first thing tomorrow. Now, let me help you clear up."

"No, no . . . you go to bed child. Get some rest . . . you'll need it. . . ."

Summer left the kitchen mumbling to herself about being a

grown woman, and knowing exactly when it was that she needed to rest. She conveniently forgot that she had intended going to bed anyway.

She was up at six the next morning. She fed the dog, then took him on a long walk through the woods. With a fur-lined hood up around her ears, waist neatly cinched, and comfy old calf-high leather boots, she was warm and snug enough, even though the air was sharp with the promise of more snow.

She climbed all the way to the top of a hill, and stood looking down on the valley below. It was completely populated by houses. As a child, she had been able to see clear to the other end of it. Now, there were large custom homes puffing smoke from brick chimneys, smaller cozy-looking cottages with skis propped against the sides, and every one of them had a large 4X4 truck parked in the driveway.

Off in the distance, the sun came slowly into view, and Summer settled back against a tree.

She called halfheartedly to Bruno who had gone tearing off after something that had scuttled by in the underbrush, and was reassured by a loud volley of barks, and the sounds of more scuffling.

She pulled the hood in closer around her face This was her favorite time of day. When everything was still, and the only sounds around were the ones made by heavy boots crunching through dead leaves. It was a good time to think. To carefully sort through what it was she needed to do. Her life had come to an uncertain halt. And, for the first time, she was unsure of how to proceed. It was too soon for her to go into business for herself. She hadn't saved quite enough yet. Although, if she returned to live in Mammoth, and set up shop in her parent's attic, she would be able to cut down considerably on costs. And, she would be able to offer her custom decorating services to the wealthy residents of the ski town to start with. Then, later, she could branch out to Bridgeport, Bishop, and slowly work her way back to Los Angeles. By then, she would be a large business concern, larger maybe than Design International. She would be able to bid on and win the prime multimillion dollar contracts too.

She stood up with a flourish, sudden excitement, and renewed hope pulsing through her. With quick hands, she brushed the twigs and leaves from the seat of her pants. The idea was too good to just sit there doing nothing but thinking.

She whistled for the dog, and after a moment, he came crashing through the brush with something brown in his mouth, tail wagging furiously as he laid the prize at her feet. She jumped back automatically as the brown thing came back to life as soon as it was free, and made a wild dash across her boots.

"Bruno . . . you horrible dog, come back here."

But, he was gone again, paying little heed to the bevy of shouts that followed in his wake. It was half an hour, before Summer was able to get him properly under control. She attached the retractable leash to his collar, and scolded him all the way back to the house.

The phone was ringing when she closed the kitchen door behind her and stamped the snow from her boots. She hustled across to it, picking it up before it could ring again and disturb her sleeping parents.

"Massey," she said after a brief moment of listening. "My God. Don't you ever sleep? And how did you get this number?"

His voice came back, as cheerful as ever. "Summer . . . good morning. You sound much better."

"What do you want?" She was not inclined to be pleasant. Not to him.

There was a slight pause when Summer knew he was calculating exactly how to say what it was he intended saying to her.

"I feel really terrible about what happened. . . ."

She waited, saying nothing.

"You were sick . . . angry too . . . not thinking clearly. I wanted your permission to speak to Mr. Cameron on your behalf. He really didn't mean for you to leave . . . and I'm sure you didn't either."

A cynical little smile curved her lips. So, they had discovered that they couldn't get along without her. Now, they wanted her back. It was the kind of situation she had dreamed of for years. Being an invaluable player. But, now that she had it, she found that it meant very little indeed.

"Thanks for your concern, Massey. But, I could never return now. Not after what happened. After all the work I did . . . to be treated in such a shabby manner. . . ."

"It was unforgivable," Brian Massey interrupted. "And, . . . since I'm now the VP of the special projects division . . . it's really my call . . . and I want you here. I need you here. Aztec is your baby."

Bruno began barking again, and Summer covered the mouthpiece and hissed: "Quiet, you dog."

Massey chuckled. "Sorry . . . am I talking too much?"

Summer found herself smiling, despite every effort to remain serious. "Not you . . . it's the dog here. We just got back from a walk, and he's still very excitable."

He was pleased that her tone had changed, and decided to press home the advantage. "So . . . what do you say? Let me talk to Cameron. With a little pressure from me, he'll take you back in a second."

Summer hesitated, thinking. If it hadn't been for the wonderful idea of only an hour ago, she might have been willing to consider returning. There would have had to be a raise, of course. And a title higher than that of senior designer. But, working for herself, being her own boss, setting her own schedules, going after her own clients, was suddenly very appealing. Too appealing to just toss casually aside. "Let me think about it," she finally said.

Brian Massey released the breath he'd been holding. This was progress. He had not expected her to fold so easily. He wanted her working right beside him. He needed her talent. Together, they would make an unstoppable team.

"Take all the time you need. I'll call you again in a few days. Later, gorgeous."

With the phone back in its wall bracket, Summer spun about

the kitchen, a wave of happiness taking her. Things were turning her way again. When everything had gone wrong, and so quickly, she had thought more than once about the chain letter she had told Alyssa to throw out. She'd remembered how she'd scoffed at her predictions of bad luck. She had thought, too, that Gavin Pagne might be responsible for things. But, now that she was in a rational frame of mind, she saw very clearly that it was just plain old-fashioned Murphy's Law at work, nothing more sinister than that.

She went to the broom closet, and began taking out the things she would need for the attic. A brush and pan, a mop, a bucket. Several rags. Pine cleaners, sponges, lemon furniture polish, to give everything a nice shine when she was done. Her nails would have to be protected from the dust and harsh cleaners, so latex gloves would be needed too.

She spent a bit of time searching for these, and finally settled on a medium sized pair of pink rubber gloves. They were dingy looking, but devoid of holes. They would have to do. She placed the rags and cleaners in the bucket, set everything neatly against a wall, then sat down to a breakfast of cereal and milk.

When she was through, she poured the milk remaining in her bowl into a metal dish for the dog and watched as he lapped up every drop.

"No more for you, greedy guts," she said as the tail continued to thump hopefully. She scratched him behind an ear.

"I don't believe that love shining in your eyes for a second. You'll give your heart away to anyone who'll feed you."

The tail thumped again, and she relented, pouring more milk from the carton. She filled the bowl this time, emptying the entire carton in.

"That should hold you for a minute."

For the next half hour, she busied herself about the kitchen, tidying up the traces of her meal, taking out the garbage, lining the bin with a fresh bag and spraying it with peach-scented antiodor fragrance.

When the first flakes drifted past the window, she had already made cream of wheat, and warmed up oatmeal muffins for her parents' breakfast. She loaded everything onto an efficiency trolley, and pushed it out to sit next to the shiny lacquered table, sitting in the solarium.

"Breakfast," she called, knocking twice on the closed door. There were sounds from within, then her mother, wrapped in a terry-cloth robe, opened the door.

"You're up early," she said.

Summer pressed a kiss to her cheek, and waved at her dad who was still in bed.

"I wanted to get an early start upstairs. I made cream of wheat and muffins. There's coffee, jam, and fresh bread too. I'll be cleaning, if you need me for anything."

And, she was gone, clanking down the hall with bucket and brooms, before her mother could get a word in edgewise.

The ladder to the attic was one of those you pulled down and straightened out. So, Summer was forced to place the jumble of cleaning utensils down, jump to grab the cord, then yank it down. It took quite a bit of doing to get the brooms and bucket up the vertical ladder while maintaining her own precarious balance.

At the top, she hoisted everything above her head, laid them down on the wooden flooring above, then, hauled herself through. At the foot of the ladder, Bruno sat staring forlornly up at the empty square of space. Summer poked her head back through the opening. There were cobwebs in her hair.

"You're going to have to stay down there Brunie boy. You're a little too heavy for me to carry up here."

She pulled herself back up. It took a minute for her eyes to readjust to the darkness. There was a thin sliver of light coming through a broken window shutter, and Summer felt her way over to it. With careful feeling, she found the latch, and after a moment, pulled it back. Wintry sunlight flooded the room immediately, and for the first time in at least ten years, she was able to take a look around the attic room.

There were chests of drawers and trunks, boxes, racks of

clothing in garment bags, stacks of bound newspapers, tools, old tires, dressmaker dummies with swatches of brown paper pinned here and there, even an ancient tricycle she couldn't remember ever owning. Everything was covered by thick layers of dust, and unbelievable grime. There was a dank odor about, too, and she could see her footprints very clearly in the dust trail that weaved its way across the floor.

"Amazing." She stood with hands on hips, looking around. "Just amazing." She'd expected it to be untidy, but not like this. The air of neglect about it, was palpable. It would take her days to wade through everything. To clear everything out, as her mother wanted. Why hadn't she done anything about it before? She knew the answer to that, but didn't want to consider it too carefully. She had been busy, with her job, with other things. And, cleaning out the attic whenever she had visited, had never seemed like a priority. That was the convenient answer. The one that made her feel less guilty. But, the unvarnished truth of it was, that she had been more than a little selfish, and thoughtless. More than a little.

She rolled up her sleeves, swept her hair up and secured it with two bobby pins, and plunged in. By midday, she had pushed everything back, washed and shone the floor, cleaned the solitary storm window, and polished the wooden shutters.

From her crouched position on the floor, she looked around at her handiwork. It was beginning to look like a room again. With all the clutter up against the walls, design ideas were beginning to flood her brain. It would actually be perfect for a little utility office. She could see a warm burgundy throw rug on the floor, a shiny wooden desk in the corner by the window, a comfortable leather chair with a high back, a phone, fax machine.

She went back to her polishing. The knees of her jeans were now filthy, and the muscles in her arms ached, but she was making more progress than she had thought she would in only half a day.

"Summer. Lunch," was the call from below.

"I'll be down in a little while, Mom," she said, wiping her

brow with the back of her hand. ''Could you put it in the oven?''

Two hours later, she was still cleaning. She heard footsteps below, but was so caught up in the need to make everything sparkle, that she paid them no heed.

Outside, the snow had been falling steadily. Huge mounds of powder now wedged her car in on both sides. The sky was a dull gray, and the wind battered itself against the house, howling around the aluminum sidings like a wild thing.

Summer closed the slatted wooden shutters, turned on the roof light, and stood looking around her. The difference was remarkable. The floor was smooth and shiny. The walls, now devoid of cobwebs and dust bunnies, were actually beginning to take on some rustic character, and, the ceiling tiles that were so grimy just a few hours before, were no longer covered by spotty blotches of mildew. There was still the clutter to contend with, of course, but that could be left until after dinner. Some of the lighter things like the newspapers, and tools, she could take care of right away. It would take several trips, up and down the ladder, but it would be best to get the smaller things out of the way, before the major work of sorting, and throwing out began.

''Summer? Are you okay up there?'' It was her dad this time, and he sounded a trifle worried. Almost afraid.

Summer walked to the opening, and leaned through. ''Hi, Dad. I got caught up in everything up here. Sorry I missed lunch. Tell mom, I'll be down for dinner though.''

She heard the thump of his cane as he shifted it from hand to hand.

''What have you done up there so far?''

She grinned down at him. ''Cleaned everything up. The floors, walls, everything. You won't believe the junk up here. Old newspapers, all sorts of cardboard boxes and that sort of stuff. Should I throw them out? They're just cluttering up the place really.''

His voice sounded suddenly old and tired. ''Yes. It's been a long time. Too long. Throw them away.''

Summer lowered herself onto the ladder, and came slowly down. "Dad . . . something's been bothering you since I got here a couple of days ago. Won't you tell me what it is?"

His deep brown eyes met hers, and for a minute, she was certain there was something hidden there. He put an arm around her shoulders, gave her a little squeeze.

"Why don't you wash up before dinner?"

She smiled up at him. "What're we having?"

He stroked the back of a finger down a cheek. "Our favorite. Smothered steak with macaroni and cheese and corn bread."

"Uhmm," Summer said, "I'm hungry already."

They walked arm in arm into the living room, and before long, were settled at the dinner table, eating and chatting warmly.

The meal was over by seven, and Summer was back in the attic, stacking things, unwrapping others. She placed the huge pile of yellowed newspapers on an old blanket, and dragged the entire thing across to the ladder. With her feet resting on the first rung, she lifted the bundles one by one, first checking to see there was no one below, then tossing them down. They landed with solid thunks on the floor below, sending a cloud of dust back up, that had her coughing, and reaching for the handkerchief in the back pocket of her jeans.

As she lifted the final bundle and prepared to throw, an article on the front page caught her attention. She smoothed the surface layer of dust away, turned the faded paper to the light, and stared. Gavin Pagne. He was much younger of course, a teenager even, but it was him. The same face. The same eyes.

She plucked open the knot on the cord that held the bundle together, and removed the paper on top. She read the article slowly, struggling to decipher words that were long faded by grime and age. Every so often, she would utter a surprised, "Oh," then bend again to the paper to read some more. With dusty fingers, she turned to the center page where the story was continued, pausing for a moment to look at the face of a little girl who was listed as missing.

When she was through, she set the paper aside, retied the

cord around the rest, and dropped the bundle below. Gavin Pagne, a hero. How remarkable. She never would have thought he had enough love in him to risk his own life. But, strangely, he had done it. By fighting his way back into the blazing tenement building where he'd lived, even when several firemen had tried to restrain him, he had managed to save the life of his infant brother. He had been severely burned, the paper said, since he'd shielded the baby with his body. And, at the time of the published report, about twenty years before, he had been in hospital, in critical condition.

It was an incredible story of courage, and Summer sat, thinking on it for a while. What an interesting man he was. She had thought him cold, and uncaring, totally incapable of tender emotions. But, it would appear that beneath the surface of that icy exterior, lurked a strong and passionate man, who had loved his brother enough to risk his own life.

She stood, with the paper rolled beneath her arm. For some reason, she couldn't throw it away with the rest. There was no reason to keep it. She didn't even like Gavin Pagne, and of course, she would never be seeing him again, as he himself had pointed out. But, she still wanted to keep the article. It was the heroism of what he had done that made her feel that way. Nothing else.

She placed the paper carefully on the window ledge, and began opening the trunks. The smell of mothballs and old fabric assaulted her senses right away. She flipped the lid of the first trunk all the way back, and looked inside. Everything was stacked in neat little rows. Tiny dresses, blouses with frilly bits of fabric around the neckline and cuffs, sailor suits with big floppy collars, carefully rolled socks.

A smile flickered across her face. Her parents were so sentimental. They had carefully saved all of her baby clothes. She wiped her hands free of dust, then removed the first dress. It was a rich royal blue with soft, white hearts speckled across the front of it. In the back, there was gathered elastic, and a white bow. There were matching white socks, and tiny black patent leather shoes, that were no bigger than the palm of her hand. Everything was in pristine condition. It was like going back in time, looking into yesterday, seeing and understanding things she had been unable to understand then.

She sat on the floor, being very careful with the little dresses. She wouldn't give these away. She would save them, just as her parents had done. She dug down deep, pulling out an old skipping rope with faded red paint around the handles, a game of jacks, a Monopoly box, another of Snakes and Ladders.

She placed the games on the floor beside her. A small frown had crept in between her eyes. She had never played jacks, or Snakes and Ladders. And, she'd never been any good at skipping.

She rifled around in the bottom again. This time, she came up with a diary. A little pink and white book, with dog-eared pages, and a small golden lock. She turned it over. It was monogrammed in gold, with the initials *C.S.* She flipped through the body of it, not really seeing the collection of childish scribbles that abruptly stopped on June 18, 1968. Her mind was racing. These things, all of them, had belonged to someone else.

She dug into the trunk again, and when she found nothing more in there but clothes, she opened up the second one, and the third. Piles of storybooks, rubber balls, dolls. Her heart was beating in thick, heavy thumps. Excitement rushed through her as she pulled the contents out. It was too unbelievable to even let herself think it yet. At the very bottom of the final trunk, she felt a large flat object. She felt around the sides of it, knowing before she removed it, what it would be. An album. A picture album.

With both hands, she heaved it out. Sitting, surrounded by a pile of clothing, toys, and books, she took a deep breath, and opened the cover.

She turned the pages slowly, flipping forwards, then occasionally, back again to stare at photographs she had never seen before. Young pictures of her parents standing in a grassy yard, smiling. A little girl in pink ribbons and a white dress, smiling too. Pictures of the same little girl lying in bed, grinning at the camera. Pictures of her taking a bath. Pictures of a birthday party, a long wooden table, a cake with six candles.

Her fingers shook as she turned page after page. Each new photograph, sucking her in further. The wind hammered against the window, but she hardly noticed. She flipped all the way through, then back again. She felt happy and scared at the same time. This smiling girl in the photographs, was her sister. She recognized her somehow. The smile was so familiar. It reminded her of her dad, when he was teasing. But, where was she? Why had her parents kept her existence a secret, all these years? Was she institutionalized? Was that why? Were they ashamed of her? The questions poured into her mind, and she wanted to get up, right then and there, and ask them about her. About her sister.

But she forced herself to go on. There was more. There had to be. Maybe documents in the very bottom. Maybe somewhere in one of them, was her name. An explanation of the initials *C.S.*

She was frenzied now, pulling and pushing things aside, scrabbling around. But, that was it. There was nothing else. Just more clothes, and other knickknacks. In disappointment, she sat back on her heels. The floor around her was a complete clutter. Carefully, she refolded and repacked everything.

The sky outside was pitch-black, and with the temperature plummeting outside, the frigid air had begun to seep into the little room. She tucked the thick album beneath her arm, and stood in one smooth motion. Her parents would still be in the sitting room, playing cards, or maybe watching TV. Her mind was still churning with questions. Had they wanted her to know finally? Was that why they'd suggested cleaning up the attic? But why wait so long to tell her?

She stacked the cleaning utensils in a corner, made certain that everything was nicely tidied, turned off the light, and with album and newspaper under her arm, began climbing back down the ladder.

She was so preoccupied with her own thoughts, that when the rung beneath her gave way suddenly, she slipped and was forced to grab wildly at the rung above. The newspaper and photo album, went crashing to the ground, spilling pictures everywhere.

She dangled for a moment, looking down at the carnage below. The stack of newspapers had partially muffled the sound, so it was very likely that her parents hadn't heard a thing.

She judged the distance to the floor while still hanging on, decided to chance it, and let go. She landed on her feet and immediately flopped backwards onto her back. The ladder, relieved of its weight, recoiled neatly.

Summer wiggled her toes, then tried sitting up. Other than the slight pain in her tailbone, she appeared to be okay. The newspaper she'd rolled so carefully though, was in total disarray.

She picked up the cover page, made an effort not to dwell on Gavin Pagne's face, and began putting the paper back in order. Her eyes fell on the center page, and her heart seemed to come to a scudding stop. She picked up one of the scattered photographs, silently praying that it not be true, but knowing deep down, that it was.

With a hand across her lips, she fought back the tears.

"Oh my God . . . oh my God." She read the caption beneath the photograph in the newspaper, and a cold tear crept slowly down the length of her face. She allowed the trickle of wetness to roll its way to the round of her chin, then she raised a shoulder, and wiped the streak away with the soft fuzz of her sweater.

Her heart tightened with sorrow and compassion for what her parents must have gone through. Her sister, her beautiful sister Catherine, had been abducted. Stolen away from her family, and from her. And, she'd been just a baby. A sweet, smiling girl with chubby legs and ribbons in her hair.

How could it be though? Surely things like this didn't happen to people who were loving and careful with their children. People who watched their children all the time. Picked them up after school. Screened baby-sitters thoroughly. Always watched while they played in the yard. Never let them out of their sight.

As her parents had done with her. How could it be true? How had it happened? When? What had they done to find her? To find Catherine? And, why had they kept it to themselves for so long?

The questions raced through her. And, her cold fingers gathered the pictures up with exquisite care. From the living room, came the sound of voices, and she walked in their direction, zombie-like.

Her mother glanced up as soon as she appeared. She placed the cards in her hand on the table, reached out for her husband with one hand. Motioned with the other. ''Sit down, love.''

Summer sat, her face a mirror of confused questions. There were so many she wanted to ask. But, where to begin?

Her mother was the first to speak. ''How do you feel about it?''

Summer took a filling breath. ''What? How? Why . . . why didn't you tell me before?''

Her mother let out a sigh. ''It was a bad time for us. Very confused. Very painful. When we got you . . . you were so tiny and fragile . . . and. . . .''

Her voice broke, and Summer rushed to hold her. It was her dad who continued the story.

''. . . it was so easy then, because of all that had happened, to . . . to pretend that you were. . . . We always intended telling you. But, we put it off . . . we thought you'd understand better when you were older . . . stronger. But, time has a way of slipping by . . . getting away from you.''

Summer looked at them both, her eyes earnest. ''But, I would have understood at any age . . . it wasn't your fault, what happened. . . .''

Her mother stroked the curve of her cheek, ''so . . . you don't mind at all that you were adopted?''

Summer blinked a couple of times. She heard herself draw air into her lungs, in a distant, unconnected way. But, the single breath wasn't enough, it did not fill her, so she tried again. Suddenly, it was as though she was miles under water, struggling desperately to make it to the surface before all the air was gone. Her lungs burned with the effort, and a trickle of moisture, dribbled its way down her cheek.

From a long distance away, she heard her name. Heard them calling, and viciously, determinedly, she fought her way up. Her mouth opened with a pop, and she took in a great gulp of air.

"Quick Mavis . . . get her some water. It's her asthma. She's having an attack. You're okay, honey . . . you're okay." Her father patted her hand. "Take it easy . . . that's right . . . breathe . . . okay . . . another now." He continued to talk to her, running a slow hand down the length of her hair.

Her mother was back almost immediately. She held Summer's head, and gently forced the water down her throat. "She hasn't had an attack in years Henry . . . we shouldn't have done this. We should've waited. What good will knowing do her?"

Summer struggled to take a breath. "What? . . . do you . . . mean?" Every word cost her some air, and she panted, trying desperately to get herself back under control. She was lying flat on her back, across her father's legs. Her hair spread out around her head in an ebony cloud. She looked up and met her father's eyes directly. He'd never lied to her. Ever. He would tell her. He would tell her the truth of it. "Dad . . . what did Mom mean?" There were tears in her voice now, a hint of confused desperation.

They both held her, and she looked from one loved face to the next. Her voice was a croak of sound. "Adopted? . . . Me?"

They both nodded in unison.

"Didn't you find your birth certificate in the attic? In one of the boxes?"

The tears behind her eyes were cold, frozen. "I started with . . . the trunks. Was going to do the boxes tomorrow."

Slowly, carefully, she sat up. Her chest was tight, her neck sore from straining for breath. "But . . . I look like you do." She stretched out her soft, manicured hands. "My fingers, Mom . . . those are your fingers. . . ." She looked wildly at her father, and said with a note of pleading, "my . . . my chin. That's yours dad . . . you said so . . . so many times. I've even got the same moles you do . . . look at this one behind my ear . . . look,'' and her voice went up half an octave.

Desperately, she searched for features she held in common. Her mind racing. Blood pounding. She couldn't lose everything this way. She couldn't. This was some horrible dream. A nightmare. A joke. They were just playing a joke on her. Like they had so many times before when she was a little girl.

She found another similarity, seized on it, and pounced. ''Granny Jane . . . remember? I'm just like her. We . . . we look alike, not the eyes but . . . we're just alike. My . . . my personality . . . is just like hers?''

Her mother was crying now. Her father, twisting his hands together, incapable of speech. Uncontrollably, Summer bolted to her feet. Forced herself to sit. Then stood again.

This was crazy. Everything was crazy. Everything she knew and held sacred, was seeping away from her, like sand through her fingers.

''What about Catherine? Was she adopted too?''

With a hand pressed against her lips, and tears in her eyes, her mother wordlessly shook her head, attempted to speak, cleared her throat, then tried again. ''No. She . . . she was our biological daughter. But you Summer . . . you are no less my daughter . . . your dad's daughter . . . you couldn't be more ours than if I'd birthed you myself.''

Summer sat again, her fingers clenched. Her knees shook. Her face burned as she tried to comprehend the enormity of it all. The sadness in her was deep and cutting. She looked up, her eyes welling with fresh tears. Everything was gone now. Everything she'd had a mere week before, was gone. Forever. Her upcoming marriage. Her job. Her friendship with Alyssa. And now, even her parents. What more could she lose? What more? How much more of this could she stand?

''Couldn't . . . couldn't you be wrong about me? . . . about me being adopted, Mom? Isn't it possible that you could be?'' Silently, she prayed for a miracle. Prayed for this scene to magically disappear, and never again rise into the realm of reality. Although her question was completely without logic, she waited, hoping that they would suddenly laugh, tell her that it was not so.

Her mother left the room, and returned with a well-preserved document neatly encased in plastic. She handed it over. ''This one is the original. We kept the copy in the attic with the other things.''

Summer looked at the evidence of her birth, recorded there in black-and-white. Her eyes skittered down to the ''name of parent'' section. There was only one name there. A woman called Dorothy Moore. The truth. It was the truth. Some woman named Dorothy was her mother. And, she had no father. Oh God, she had no father.

She felt such a tearing sense of loss, that it was several minutes before she was under control again, and could raise her head to ask, ''Why? . . . why didn't you tell me before? Why did you let me think . . . let me believe all those wonderful stories? Why did you tell me this way? . . . and now?'' The questions bubbled over, and she couldn't restrain herself enough to even give them a chance to answer.

They let her speak, and when the flood was over, and she was ready to listen again, they told her about Catherine and the day she'd been taken. And, they answered all the questions, one by one. Taking care with her. Unraveling memories that had lain dormant for almost thirty years.

CHAPTER THIRTEEN

Later, Summer stood at the kitchen window looking out at the dark, the snow, the trees bending effortlessly in the gale. She was as cold inside as the iciest winter's day. She stood with her arms wrapped around herself. Alone. Hurting. Feeling everything, yet feeling nothing at all. She ached for Catherine. She ached for what her parents had gone through. The years of fruitless searching. The thousands spent on newspaper ads. Private detectives. The eventual coming to terms with the realization that they would never see their daughter again. That the smiling face was gone. Gone for good.

A shudder racked her body. She would never be warm again. Never. Everything had changed. Irrevocably. She was no one. She had no one, now.

A soft arm wrapped around her from behind, and she weathered it, as impassively as an old oak.

''Come to bed now, Summer . . . come to bed. You'll feel better in the morning.''

She turned, and let herself be led away. Was it shock? Was that the reason she felt nothing? Nothing at all? Would she ever feel again?

She lay under the covers, and let herself be tucked in like a child. She was unresponsive to the kiss on her brow, and didn't notice when the lights were turned out, and the door closed. She lay, staring at nothing. Wanting nothing. Not even rest.

It was an effort to close her eyes. But, eventually she did. And, dark, dreamless sleep came, covering her like a heavy blanket.

She awoke somewhere close to mid-morning, with heavy lids, her eyes coming sluggishly open. Bright sunlight came through the wooden shutters, casting a dappled pattern on the bed. The phone on her bedside rang, and she turned away from it, pulling the blankets up over her. Her head was throbbing, and it felt like her flu was coming back.

There was a knock at the door, and she burrowed deeper under the covers. After a moment, the door opened, and her mother came in with a tray. She placed it on the bedside table, went across to the windows, and threw the shutters open.

"It's a wonderful day, Summer. Come on, get up. I'm not going to let you lie around moping all day."

The strong words penetrated the haze, and with great reluctance, Summer opened her eyes again. She felt the corner of the bed sag as her mother sat down.

"Summer . . . sometimes life is unpredictable. But, when it knocks you down . . . you don't lie down and die. You get back up . . . you fight. You've always been a fighter. Even as a baby, when your asthma was so bad, and you were so fragile that everyone thought you might not make it. You refused to give up. . . ."

A hand stroked Summer's head, and the first suggestion of warmth crept back into her.

"Come on. . . . Nothing has changed. Nothing at all. Your dad and I didn't want to burden you with the knowledge of Catherine . . . that's the only reason we didn't tell you before. Maybe . . . maybe we were wrong to do it. Maybe, the way we let you find out was wrong too . . . but, we were having such a hard time finding the right words. . . ."

Summer pushed back the blanket, and slowly dragged herself

up. Her hair sloped silkily to her shoulders. "No . . . no, Mom. You did your best. It's . . . it's just everything, you know? Everything happening all at once. Before I even had the time to catch my breath . . . there was something else. I'm afraid . . . afraid what will happen next."

Her mother held both of her hands, gave them a little squeeze. "I'll tell you what's going to happen next. You're going to go on a vacation. A long one . . . somewhere nice and warm, with lots of sun . . . and maybe a beach. You'll feel much better after you've spent some time away. . . ."

Summer shook her head. "No, I can't go away somewhere. I have to work. I have to have something to do . . . to occupy my mind. If I don't, I think I'll . . . I'll go crazy."

"Well take a working vacation then. How about that? You could go off somewhere . . . maybe the Caribbean or Africa? Get a job there . . . stay for a couple of months? They're lots of international design jobs . . . Dad could make some calls?"

The idea appealed for a second. "But, Mom . . . you and Dad should be the ones to go. You should have a little fun. You've suffered so much, all these years."

Her mother stood and looked down at her in a very determined manner. "Don't tell me what we need young lady. Your dad and I are perfectly content. We've got all that we need right here. Besides, you know I don't like planes . . . so" and her voice held a softer note now, "eat your breakfast, have a shower, and let me know where you've decided to go."

A tiny smile twisted the corners of Summer's lips, and the smallest bit of happiness, crept back into a corner of her heart. "Yes ma'am."

After her mother left, Summer lay where she was for several minutes more, staring unseeingly at the ceiling tiles. What else could happen to her now? What else? If things continued along their present course, by month's end, she'd quite probably be bald, completely toothless, and the spitting image of the pitiable creature she had pretended to be on that evening she had had dinner with Gavin Pagne.

A trace of a smile drifted across her face at the thought of it, and she forced herself to sit up. There was a dull sensation in the pit of her stomach, and although she hadn't eaten in more than twelve hours, she still did not feel very hungry. Over the last several days, she had lost five pounds. To some, this might be reason to celebrate, but in her case, the absence of those few pounds made her face appear almost waif-like. She had to eat, whether she really wanted to or not.

Summer took a determined breath, and peeled back the white linen napkin on the tray.

Breakfast was buttered toast, scrambled eggs, orange juice, and milk. She ate the toast, drank the milk, but left the eggs and juice when her stomach began to feel queasy.

In the shower, she spent some time thinking. Maybe her mother was right. Maybe going someplace different would help her sort through things more clearly. Somewhere with miles of crystal-blue ocean and acres of sandy beach. Somewhere warm, peaceful.

She was toweling a long expanse of smooth calf, when she remembered the cottage in Jamaica. With the large terry towel still wrapped around her, she walked back into the bedroom. She remembered how wonderfully disheveled it was. If that particular job was still available, that was the one she would choose. Two or three months spent in solitary quiet, doing exactly what she loved. What could be more ideal than that?

The package from Champagne Industries was still in her handbag. She pulled it out, and had another look. The cottage was still in the same horrible shape she remembered.

Curled up on the bed, she scrutinized the cover letter. It was just a letter of inquiry, really. Not an offer of employment. A feeler, to gauge her level of interest.

She skimmed down to the bottom of it. The name signed there was Nicholas Champagne. Before she could change her mind, she picked up the phone. Within minutes she had the number of the international agency that did staffing for overseas design projects.

"This is Summer Stevens," she said when the phone was

answered. "I'd like some information on Champagne Industries."

She was placed on hold for a minute, then a recruiter came on. The voice was clipped, and a bit impatient: "I'm sorry, we're not allowed to give out any information on the phone."

Summer tapped her fingernails on the bedside table. She had expected that.

"Let me speak to Bill please. Tell him it's Summer."

She was placed on hold again. Almost immediately, Bill Sharp was on the line.

"Summer, babe, haven't heard from you in a long while. Heard you created quite a stir, walking out on a ten-million-dollar contract at Design International. . . ."

Summer grimaced. Did everybody know about that? Besides, she didn't exactly walk out, she was practically forced to resign.

"Bill," she said, cutting him off in midstream, "a while back you called me on a job in Jamaica? Remember?"

"Oh . . . yeah, . . let me see . . . ah . . ." she heard the clicking of computer keys, "Champagne Industries. Yep. What's up? Thinking of doing some overseas work? I've got a great job here for you. In Bolivia. Old Spanish Estate house. Good money."

"Sounds great, but I was more interested in the Jamaican job. About a week ago, I received a package from them. . . ."

The interest in his voice picked up a notch. "From Champagne? Strange . . . they didn't call the job in to us . . . let me check. . . ." She was on hold again.

He was back almost immediately. "We sent your portfolio over to them a while back. There was some interest then, but when you backed out . . . everything went cold."

"I didn't back out. I just decided to stay where I was. Doing work overseas can be tricky."

He seemed unconvinced. "So, what now? You want to work for them?"

Summer weighed her thoughts carefully. She didn't want to commit herself to anything just yet. "I just wanted to make sure that they were legitimate. I'm not certain that I really want to go ahead with it."

Bill sensed that she was right on the fence, and he pushed. "Oh they're legit all right. One of the larger business concerns on the island. Let me give them a call. I'll set up a phone interview for you."

"Well . . . I"

"Just a phone call, babe, nothing else. You don't have to commit to a thing. Let me see what I can do? Okay? Call you back in a couple of hours."

And he was gone before Summer could say anything more. She sat for a moment staring at the phone in her hand. Salespeople were all the same. It was always rush, rush, rush. Get the sale, close the deal. Well, she wouldn't be hurried into anything. She would take her own time. And, only if she was really satisfied with the lie of things, would she go.

She returned to her dressing, and finished up quickly. The activity had done her some definite good. She was beginning to feel like herself again, though there was a dullness inside, that she just couldn't seem to shake.

Summer carried her tray out, and set it down on the kitchen counter. Her mother was at the table, up to her elbows in dough. She shook a generous amount of flour from a little cup, onto the mound, and kneaded. Summer settled at the table to watch. Bread-making was something that had fascinated her since childhood.

After a moment of intense kneading, her mother said, "Well? . . . what have you decided."

Summer examined her nails for a minute; a ploy, to give herself more time.

"Well, I haven't really decided on anything just yet. But, there's a little cottage in Jamaica that looks interesting. It's right by the sea. You can actually walk down stone stairs, and you're right there on the beach. It's owned by a company called Champagne Industries."

"It sounds like just what you need." Her mother kneaded again, requesting that Summer sprinkle some flour on her hands.

"Kevin called earlier. I told him you were still resting. I didn't think you'd want to speak to him."

"I don't. I can't believe I was actually going to marry him."

Her mother grunted. "Not everything that has happened to you in the last few days has been bad. Getting away from Kevin was a blessing. You need a different kind of man, love."

Summer sprinkled more flour. "I don't need any kind of man, mom. They're all . . ." she struggled for the appropriate word. Thinking of several that were a little too strong to say to her mother. She finally settled on, ". . . scum."

"That's an interesting thing to say about all men. What about your dad? Do you think he's scum too?"

"Dad's different. He's one of the few good men left."

The dough was patted into a ball, carefully covered with a damp tea cloth, and left to rise. Her mother wiped her hands on her apron.

"There's one out there for you too. But, to find him, you've got to believe he's there. God will bring him to you, if you believe."

Summer sighed. Her mother would never understand that she didn't believe in or care too much about romantic love. All she wanted was a man who would be faithful to her. One whom she could trust. She didn't have to love him, and he didn't have to love her. Because, really, there was no such thing. Not the soft, selfless, romantic kind of love anyway. There was only lust, and confused feelings of dependence, which most people mislabeled as love.

"Where's Dad?" she asked, changing the subject.

"He's at the doctor this morning."

Summer felt her heart clench, then begin to beat rapidly. She had been expecting something else to happen. But, not to her father. She prayed silently. Please God.

The fear must have shown on her face, for her mother patted her arm and said, "it's a routine checkup. If things go well, he'll probably be coming home without his cane."

"Oh." Summer was so relieved that she smiled.

"Now, that's the Summer I know. Come and help me do the laundry."

She followed her mother down the stairs and into the finished basement. Over the second load of clothes, Summer finally asked the question that had been bothering her since the day before. ''Mom . . .''

''Uhmm?'' Her mother was waist-deep in the dryer, her upper torso completely out of sight as she checked the readiness of each garment.

''Do you think Catherine's still alive?''

Her mother went still for a moment, then continued pulling clothes from the dryer.

''It would be a miracle if she still is . . . after all this time. I've seen all of those terrible missing child reports on TV. Whenever a child is taken, it's usually by a man, and . . . and that's never any good.''

Summer folded and stacked, as the clothes were passed back to her. ''What if we hired a private detective? Someone really good . . . who specializes in finding missing persons?''

Her mother straightened up slowly, and there was a sadness in the depths of her eyes that Summer just could not bear. She went to her, and they held each other for wordless minutes.

Finally, Summer said in a choky voice, ''I'm sorry, Mom . . . I know it's hard to talk about it, but maybe if we tried, we might find her again?''

''Your dad and I tried everything, Summer. We printed up flyers, spoke to the FBI, hired several detectives. There were a few leads. But, eventually, they all turned out to be red herrings.''

''What about the housekeeper you and Dad had at the time. Didn't she disappear at about the same time that Catherine did?''

''Yes. She was a very pleasant woman. But, she had a lot of problems at home. Her husband was a drinker . . . and I think there was some physical abuse. She was forced to leave the state in order to get away from him. Catherine was really attached to her. Cried for days when she left.''

''Hmmm,'' Summer said. ''Was she ever checked out? I mean, does anybody know where she went?''

''She was first on the list. They found her in Arizona. She

was grilled by the FBI, and by several private detectives, but nothing ever came of it.''

They were both silent for a while, each one thinking their own thoughts on the matter.

Henry Stevens found them like this, both folding clothes in a very quiet, absorbed way. He looked at his daughter first, then his wife, wondering what other calamity had just struck.

''I've got my dancing legs back,'' he said, his voice deliberately cheerful.

They both looked up. ''Dad, they took the brace off.'' And Summer was rushing across to give him a hug. He held her close. ''No more tears Summer, honey?''

She returned his squeeze. ''No more tears.''

''She's going to Jamaica for a while,'' her mother added. ''Some sun and fun is what she needs.''

''I'll be working, Mom. . . . if I go.''

Her mother placed the neatly folded pile into a laundry basket. ''You'll still be able to enjoy yourself, even if you decide to work. I've heard there're all sorts of wonderful things to see and do down there.''

''Like the Dunns River Falls,'' her father piped in encouragingly. ''You'd love that, Summer. Huge, flat rocks . . . crystal-clear water cascading down. . . .''

Her interest was beginning to quicken, as her father continued. He described blue lagoons where the water was almost green, misty blue mountains where some of the best coffee in the world was grown, even a place called Maroon town, where runaway African bondsmen from centuries past, had established their own city. By the time he was finished, she was completely sold.

''Dad . . .'' and there was a trace of something very like wonder in her voice. ''I never knew you'd gone there. You never told me. . . .''

''There're lots of things you don't know about me, love. I'm not the old stick-in-the-mud you think I am.''

Summer laughed. Her father was many things. A stick-in-the-mud he definitely wasn't. But the idea of it appealed to her, and she teased him about it as they traipsed back up the stairs to the kitchen, heavily burdened by loads of soft, fresh laundry.

Later, when Bill Sharp called to tell her about the scheduled interview, she was ready to negotiate the best deal for herself. Already she could see the wonderful blue of the Caribbean sea, smell the tangy salt air. It would be glorious. It would be utterly peaceful. And that was what she needed most of all.

CHAPTER FOURTEEN

Summer clicked the latch closed on her suitcase, and set the combination. She stood for a moment, looking around the room, mentally checking that she had not left anything behind that she would need.

She had gotten the Jamaican job. The phone interview had gone very well. Nicholas Champagne had complimented her on her work, asked a few perfunctory questions about her background, then given her a brief history of the beach cottage. Back in the sixteenth century, it had been nothing more than a shack. A safe haven for runaway slaves on their way to sea. In the late seventeenth century, a British sea captain purchased the property, demolished the shack, and built a tiny cottage of brick and stone in its place. According to local rumor, the captain was none other than Sir Henry Morgan, the notorious pirate. Supposedly, old Henry buried several cases of Spanish gold somewhere on the property.

The bullion was never found, of course. Although subsequent owners gave the property a very thorough going over. Some, even enlisting professionals to excavate the areas surrounding the house.

Just after the second world war, the cottage passed into the hands of a Dutchman by the name of Vanderhagen. He was a cold, implacable man, well known on the island for his dark dealings in the occult. Each of the Dutchman's two wives had died violently. One flung herself from the cliffs and was dashed to pieces on the rocks below. The other set herself ablaze, walked calmly into the foaming surf, and drowned herself.

Years later, the Dutchman himself was found hanging from a large wooden beam in the basement of the cottage. Beneath him was a circle of chalk, a black candle, and a pile of kindling.

His death was ruled a suicide. But local legend had it, that during an incantation to the powers of evil, the Dutchman had become possessed by the spirits of dead slaves. And, against his will, he had placed a rope around his neck, and hanged himself. It was also believed that with his dying breath, Vanderhagen had placed a curse on the cottage.

Strangely, and certainly giving more weight to the belief that the cottage was cursed, it had never been lived in since then. It had been vacant for decades, and by the time it was acquired by the Champagne family, it had fallen into a state of terrible disrepair.

Summer had been instantly fascinated by the story. This was exactly the kind of house she liked to work on. One steeped in layers of dusty history, legend, and ghostly folklore. So, when Nicholas Champagne had offered her the job, she had very gladly accepted.

From that point on, everything had swept ahead in a whirlwind of activity. There were new passport pictures to see to, other work-related documents to secure. Tickets to purchase. Clothing to buy. Manicures. She even splurged on a new designer swimsuit made of shiny black spandex, a matching beach cape, and clog-heeled sandals.

Between shopping excursions, she managed to find the time to finish off the attic. It had been hard to climb the stairs again. And, she had had to steel herself to go up. But, the room was now thoroughly clean, with throw rugs on the floor, wonderful lacy curtains at the window, pictures on the walls, and everything stacked neatly in one corner. There was still more work to be done of course, little finishing touches that she would like to add. But, this could be done easily enough upon her return.

"Summer?"

Her mother's voice pulled her back from deep thought. "I'm in my room."

The door swung back. "Phone call for you."

Summer stifled a sigh. Who could it be this time? She had turned the ringer off on her phone just so she wouldn't have to speak to anyone else. So far, she had battled with Brian Massey, hung up on Kevin, and taken down numerous instructions from Bill Sharp.

"Can you tell whoever it is that I've already left?"

"It's Bill Sharp again, dear. He said it was important. Something to do with transportation from the airport in Jamaica."

Summer picked up the phone. "Bill," her voice was bright. "If you don't stop calling me, I'm gonna miss my plane."

He laughed. "Listen Summer, babe, we made a change in your booking. You're flying in to Norman Manley Airport in Kingston. Not Montego Bay. So, a car from Champagne Industries will pick you up right outside the terminal building, okay? And, one more thing . . . you're gonna stop over in Miami. No change of planes though. So, don't get off."

With great difficulty, she held her tongue. "You're the best, Bill."

"Don't I know it. You all packed?" Without giving her a chance to answer, he rushed on. "What's the snow like up there at Mammoth? Heard another storm's due in later today. You'll just be able to make it outta there before it hits."

Summer glanced at her watch. "Bill. I've got to go. When I get to Jamaica, I'll check in with you, okay?"

"You've got my home phone number?"

"Got it."

"There's something I've. . . ."

"Bill. I really have to go. I'll call you later."

She hung up without giving him a chance to plunge into

something else. Her two suitcases stood at the ready by the bed, and she pulled them out to stand in the hallway.

Bruno pranced happily around the bags, and she bent to scratch his head.

"You're going to be a good boy till I get back, aren't you?"

He gave her a great woof, and promptly sat up on his hind legs, front paws waving in the air. For a moment, she was flooded by a surge of emotion. She hugged the fuzzy head.

"You great-big, crazy dog. I'm going to miss you."

Two hours later, Summer was standing in line at the Mammoth Lakes Airport. Every so often, she would turn back to wave at her parents. They stood in the waiting area looking at her go with happy smiles pinned to their faces. But, behind the smiles, there was a trace of sadness. And, for the first time since she'd left home and struck out on her own, she felt a tinge of worry. They were both beginning to look so old. The strong bodies had become bowed by age. The skin, softer. They needed her now. Why was she selfishly going away? Leaving them.

"Put the bag on the conveyor, miss."

The voice of the attendant caused her to start. "I'm sorry," she said. "Daydreaming."

At the door, she turned one last time. Tears pricked the backs of her eyes. She blew them a kiss, then turned and walked briskly toward the small aircraft. She would be back in just two months. It wasn't such a very long time. And, when she did return, she'd never leave them again.

CHAPTER FIFTEEN

Thoughts of her parents still echoed in her mind, as she made her way through customs in Jamaica. It had been a long trip. First the flight back to LAX, an hour of waiting there, then a seven-hour flight to the island, with a brief stop in Miami.

She stood outside the terminal building now, on a long ribbon of winding pavement, her hand shielding her eyes against the sun. She was beginning to feel very fatigued, and not a little hungry. But, the sight of leafy coconut trees bending gently in the wind, the crush of people all around, the lilting voices belting out genuine Jamaican patois, touched something deep, almost primal, inside her.

She closed her eyes, and took it all in. It didn't matter that the car was late. Or that her bare toes had been severely trampled by dozens of feet and the odd suitcase. There was a hot scent to the air. A pulsing vibrance that swept you up as soon as your feet touched the black of the airport tarmac. So this was it. This was the land of Bob Marley. The birthplace of reggae. She could completely understand why so many fell in love with the place. There was something intoxicating about it. Something magical.

"Taxi cab, ma'am?"

Her eyes sprang open, and for a second, she felt quite foolish.

"No. No thanks. I've a car coming."

"You can sit in the shade, ma'am. If you're feeling faint."

Summer's lips widened into a smile. "That's all right. I'm fine. Really," she added when the porter continued to hover, unconvinced that she wasn't about to keel over from sunstroke.

A large Jeep pulled up to the curb, and Summer watched, hoping. It was unmarked, so there was no way of really telling if it was the car sent by Champagne Industries.

The driver sprang out, and came quickly around to her side. He was tall and trim with magnetic black eyes. "Ms. Stevens?"

"Yes. Are you from Champagne?"

"I am. Nicholas Champagne at your service. " He extended a hand, and gave hers a hearty shake.

"I'm sorry. I wasn't told . . . I didn't think that you were coming for me yourself."

"These your bags?" When she nodded, he swept them effortlessly into the back of the Jeep. There was something strangely familiar about him, and Summer tried not to stare as he handed her into the front seat. He closed the door behind her, loped around to the driver's side, and got in.

"Had a good flight?"

"Yes. Thank you. It was fine." Her eyes lingered on his face again, and he turned to meet her gaze, a wicked glint lighting somewhere in the depths of his. The Jeep started with a lurch, and Summer fumbled around for the seat belt. It was going to take a while before she got used to seeing steering wheels on the right side of the car, and traffic on the left.

"Pull up then down again. You've got to really yank it. Shall I help?"

Summer gave a mighty pull. "No . . . no I think I've got it."

When she was nicely buckled in, she swept the heavy weight of her hair back across one shoulder, and fanned vigorously.

"Is it always this hot?"

"No. Sometimes it's hotter." He swerved to avoid a chicken that suddenly ran squawking into the road.

"You're kidding, right?"

He gave her a large smile, and Summer absently reflected that he must be quite a hit with the ladies. A bit young for her tastes, but a handsome devil nevertheless, with a lot more charm than should be legal.

"You're going to enjoy being here . . . we're going to enjoy it too." The glint of mischief came and went in his eyes again. "I don't know if the agency told you, but you're going to be staying at the house with us."

"Us?" Her eyebrows rose a fraction. She had been told that accommodations would be provided. But, no one had said anything at all about sharing a house with a horde of other people.

"The Champagne men."

He had her complete attention now. "Champagne men? You mean there're more of you?"

"Just three more. You don't mind, I hope? You'll have your own room, bathroom . . . that kind of thing. Almost a private apartment for yourself. Just occasionally . . ." and he paused to shake a cigarette unto his palm. ". . . very occasionally . . . I . . . we might ask that you do some cleaning . . . cooking . . . washing. Nothing heavy-duty though.'

Washing? Cooking? Summer's mouth was agape. Was he completely crazy? She had come here to do a design job, not to work as a glorified housekeeper.

"I'm afraid there's been a misunderstanding Mr. Champagne. . . ."

He blew a puff of smoke out the window. "Nicholas. I hate formality."

"Nicholas," she began again, "I have no intention of doing any washing or cooking . . . or anything else you might have planned. The job that I accepted was that of designer, not servant."

He threw back his head and laughed, and Summer felt a

wave of déjà vu wash over her. It must be the heat, she told herself. Maybe she was coming down with sunstroke after all.

Nicholas swung the Jeep into the parking lot of a restaurant, and was out of the car before she could say anymore. He pulled open her door, extended his hand.

"I'm sure you're hungry. The food here is especially good. Come on," and he gave her hand a little tug.

Summer climbed down, and waited as he locked the door. "Look . . . I'm completely serious about what I just said. If the job has suddenly changed, I'll be on the next flight out of here."

With hands stuffed casually into his pockets, he looked down at her. And, in that moment, Summer knew that she wasn't imagining things. She did know him. But where?

Where had she met him before?

He was smiling at her again in that marvelously infectious way. "I was just kidding with you." He tucked her arm through his. "Has anyone ever told you how stunning you are?"

"Yes. Actually, I get that all the time," And she grinned at him. It was impossible not to like him.

"So . . . where are we?"

He pointed to the sign above the door. "The Hot Pot."

"Sounds sinful."

"It is. Sinfully delicious. This is the real thing though. Jamaican cuisine."

He gave the girl at the door a wink as they walked through. "Table for two."

They were seated right away, even though there was a group of women already waiting.

Summer bent to whisper. "Should we have done that?"

Nicholas bent and whispered too. "Don't worry. I've got a way with women. Never met one I couldn't charm."

Summer chuckled. "You're wicked."

He wiggled his eyebrows. "Thank you. That's the biggest compliment you could've paid me."

When the waitress came around, Summer decided to be adventurous. She ordered curry goat, peas and rice, and pink passion-fruit punch. In the background, over the soft murmur of voices, the sounds of steel band music ushered in the dusk. Tall willowy coconut trees swayed in the evening breeze, and there was a sweet scent of hibiscus on the wind.

Nicholas lit up another cigarette, and took a deep draw. Blue smoke curled around his fingers, then drifted up into the night air. "I always eat here whenever I'm in Kingston."

"Uhmm," Summer agreed. "It's a wonderful little place. You would never guess, walking through the door, that it was an open-air restaurant."

He nodded, took another draw. "So . . . do you mind about sleeping at the house? That part of what I said before is true. But, if it's going to be a problem, we can think of something else?"

Summer shrugged. "I'm a big girl. As long as there's a lock on the door. I don't see a problem with it."

"Good," he said, and leaned forward. "Is it too soon to tell you that I'm in love with you?"

She met his gaze directly, and her eyes danced. "No. Now is a good time."

He crushed the head of his cigarette into an ashtray, gathered up one of her hands. "You know. I think I'm really going to like you."

She laughed, loving the way his satin eyes filled with bright humor. "Don't be too sure about that. I make a good first impression, but . . . once you get to know me . . ."

She let the rest of her sentence trail off. He was quick to pick up her cue.

"I'll bet you've broken a heart or two in your time?"

"Never deliberately . . . but I'm sure your track record isn't spotless either."

He leaned back in his chair, his shirt pulling open naturally at the throat. "Whenever I do, I break them in the gentlest way possible. Though, of course whenever that happens, I get a lot of heat from my older brother."

"Oh? Is he one of those strict, overbearing types?"

Nicholas lit up another cigarette before he answered. "He's

a regular paragon of virtue. Doesn't smoke or drink to speak of. It's work, work, work with him. I could never measure up, so . . . I don't even try.''

The meal arrived, and Summer waited as the plates of fragrant niceties were properly laid.

She motioned to the waitress. ''Curry goat and punch for me.'' The name of the dish rolled as easily from her tongue as though she'd been ordering it all her life. She smiled at Nicholas. It was almost unbelievable to her, that she was now sitting in Jamaica, just as calmly as you please, ordering wonderfully exotic dishes, while just a day before, she had been struggling very hard to come to terms with the horrible mess her life had become.

She loaded her fork with a succulent chunk of meat, and took a measured bite.

''What do you think of it?''

Summer patted her mouth with the linen napkin. ''Wonderful. I wasn't sure I was going to like it. But it's good. Spicy, though.''

''Have a swig of punch. That'll cool it down a bit. You have to know how to eat curry, man.''

Between gulps of punch, she said, ''now you sound like a Jamaican.''

He took a bite of braised beef, and chewed with obvious enjoyment. ''I'm adopted.''

''You mean, you didn't grow up here?''

''I've lived here for a while. Years. Don't even remember how many now.''

''Must be nice. I've never lived anywhere but the States. What's it like? Living here I mean.''

''It's the best place in the world to be. I'd never live anywhere else now. Jamaica has a way of sucking you in. Making you hers.''

''It's that good?''

''It's that good.''

Summer waited, expecting him to elaborate, but he didn't. And, they fell into companionable silence for a while, with no sound between them but the clinking of cutlery.

When dessert was served, Summer chose a wonderful bowl of rocky road ice cream. With the first taste, she was completely hooked. The combination of ingredients was divine. Chunks of pure chocolate nugget, thick nuts and tropical fruits, whipped together in sweet vanilla cream. Warm fudgy syrup on the side. It was almost too perfect. And, she dived in, taking her time, savoring every mouthful until it was all gone. When she was through, she even resorted to scraping the sides of the dish with her spoon.

After a while, polite etiquette would not allow her to scrape further, so, she sat back with a satisfied sigh.

"That was the best meal I have ever had."

Nicholas smiled. "Don't pass judgment too soon. There's more. Much more." He stood, placed an enormous amount of money on the table, and gestured to her in a very continental manner.

"We've got to get going, if we're going to make it to Ochi before dark."

She followed him back to the jeep, strapped herself in, and for the next two hours, allowed herself to be drawn into easy conversation. He had an infectious manner about him, one that made her feel that maybe life in general, wasn't so very bad afterall. That maybe being adopted was not the end of the world. He made her laugh, and, she found some measure of enjoyment in bringing that wicked grin to his face.

"We're going to be friends I think," she told him as they drove through the thick greenery of Fern Gulley.

He gave her a quick sidelong glance. "You can count on it."

A short while later, Summer got her first glimpse of the beautiful resort town. In the burnished gold of sunset, Ocho Rios lay like a flawless pearl quietly nestled in a bed of gorgeous green foliage. Summer's gaze fastened on the unrolling countryside, and for the first time in her life, she felt a stab of something very like wonder. It was like driving through a living postcard. The quaint Mediterranean-style houses, the willowy palms bending gently in the evening breeze, the indescribable blue of the ocean, as it rushed up to the shoreline, curling, and slapping its foam across the powder-white sands.

She took a deep gulp of the crisp sea air. It couldn't be real. It just couldn't be.

"Like it?"

Summer turned. "I've never seen anything so . . . perfect. So completely . . . I can't even think of the right word." Her eyes had gone as golden as the sunset, and for a moment, Nicholas found it hard to drag his attention back to the road.

He nodded, because it was all he could do, articulate speech for the moment, was beyond him. It was hard to think with her sitting so close, looking at him with those eyes, and those very soft, perfectly shaped red lips. . . .

When he had devised his little plan, he had not realized that she would have been so very beautiful. He had seen her photograph in the portfolio, of course, and that was the main reason why he had chosen her. But, she was so much more sensual in the flesh. So alive and warm, full of wit and obvious passion. It would certainly complicate matters quite a bit if he himself became smitten with her.

". . . and to think I'm going to be spending the next two months surrounded by all this. It's almost . . . I can't take it all in. Finally, something good is happening. . . ."

"Yes." Nicholas said, nodding. He hadn't heard a word she said. His mind had raced ahead to the house. Robert and Mik would be finished by now. After all, he had tried to give them as much time as possible; showing up late at the airport, lingering over dinner, had all been a careful calculation designed to give them more time.

"Why're you so quiet all of a sudden?" Summer's voice splintered his thoughts, and he turned to her with a smile. "Sorry. I was thinking."

"Judging by the look on your face, I would guess it's nothing good . . . that brother of yours again?"

"No . . . well, in a way, yes." Her razor-sharp intuition caused him to shoot an assessing glance in her direction. Maybe there was more to her than just a very pretty face. If that were the case. If there was actually a brain behind all that beauty, there could be some very interesting complications.

"So . . . aren't you going to tell me about your brother . . . the older one? I am going to get a chance to meet him, right?"

"Oh yes. Without a doubt."

Summer tucked an annoying swatch of hair behind her ear. "But?"

"But . . . not right away."

"What's the matter? Don't you two get along?" She knew she was being nosy, but she felt so completely at ease in his company, that she ignored the ordinary rules of polite conversation.

"We would get along a lot better if he could only admit how very similar we both are."

"I see. I've stepped into the middle of a family feud then?"

Nicholas gave a short bark of laughter. "Don't worry. It's nothing serious. It's just a little argument we had recently about creativity."

"Uhmm-hmmm," Summer said, with great sympathy in her voice. "He wants you to show more initiative. Be more creative?"

"Right."

"I can see you've thought of something."

He smiled his devilish smile. "I have."

They turned into a neatly manicured driveway lined by coconut palms, and before long, the Jeep had come to a stop in front of a huge, rambling three-storied house. Nicholas leaned across to release her belt.

"Well . . . we're here. Hang on, let me help you down." He was out, and opening her door before she could gather enough breath to properly object. She took his arm, even though the liberated woman in her, chided her severely for doing so.

Darkness had fallen suddenly, and as soon as Summer emerged from the truck, she was treated to a cacophony of sound. Dance hall music blasted from a window on the second floor of the house, and great crashing sounds came from somewhere within. She listened closely. It sounded very much like furniture being tossed around.

"Is your . . . brother at home? The older one?" she inquired as Nicholas re-emerged from the back of the Jeep with her luggage in his hands.

"You mean the noise?"

He motioned for her to go ahead of him "No. No. That's just Rob and Mik."

"What are they doing? Tearing the house apart?"

Nicholas dropped the bags at the front door, and pounded on the polished wood. "They're just a little hyperactive. Growing boys, you know."

Summer massaged her temples. "Do they always make this much noise?"

"Always. Except on Sundays." Summer suppressed a sigh. So much for her wonderful peace and quiet.

Nicholas pounded again and attempted to bellow above the throbbing music. "Mik? . . . Rob?"

The door sprang back after another session of pounding, and a skinny teenage boy with curly black hair and strangely familiar eyes, appeared in the doorway. He winked audaciously at Summer. "What a sweet dawta."

Summer looked at Nicholas, a smile of utter incomprehension on her face. "What . . . did he say?"

"He likes you." Nicholas batted the boy's head with the back of his hand. "Take Ms. Stevens' luggage up to her room, and Rob . . ."

The boy turned.

". . . be careful with her things."

An impish grin came and went. "Yeah, man."

When he was gone, Nicholas ushered her into the large sitting room. "Have a seat. You must be tired."

Summer took a quick look about the room. There were

papers, clothes, cups, plates, CDs and other assorted paraphernalia strewn about. She took it all in, in utter silence.

"Where . . . where would you like me to sit?"

He lifted a crusted pizza box from a chair, dusted the cushion, then flung the box, crumbs and all, into a corner. "What about here?"

Summer dusted the cushion again before sitting, and even then, could only bring herself to perch on the very edge of the seat.

Nicholas rubbed his hands together. "Well . . . can I get you something to drink?"

"No." The word exploded before she could think of a more diplomatic response. If the house was in such a hideous mess, there was no telling what the inside of the refrigerator would be like.

"What about a tour of the house then?"

"Does it all look like this?"

"Yes. What do you think?" and his eyes glinted down at her, deep, dark and dancing with latent humor.

Summer wet her lips. "It needs . . ."

"Yes?"

"Well, it needs some work. A lot of work actually. When's the last time someone took a broom to the place?"

"Mik and Rob have been cleaning all afternoon."

"Oh. I see. You mean they dumped everything in this room?"

"No. Actually, they've cleared it up remarkably."

Summer looked around again. "That's hard to believe."

Nicholas considered her from behind steepled fingers, and for a minute, Summer struggled with the elusive thread of memory that had been troubling her all evening.

He smiled at her in a kind and somewhat regretful manner. "You look tired, why don't you turn in early?"

Summer stood immediately, glad for an excuse to be off the chair.

"Yes. I think I'll have an early night. I'm worn out from all the traveling. . . . If I could just use the phone for a quick call to my parents? They'll be wondering if I got here safely.''

''Certainly.'' And, he came to his feet with a fluid, panther-like grace. ''There's one in your room. Come on then. I'll take you up.''

CHAPTER SIXTEEN

Gavin Pagne pushed open the heavy wooden front door, and closed it quietly behind him. It was not yet midnight, yet strangely, the house was in complete darkness. He felt around for the hall light, flicked it on, slung his suit bag across one shoulder, and made a beeline for the stairs.

It would be good to lie in his own bed again, under his own sheets. Have a shower and shave on his own turf. As much as traveling was part and parcel of running a multimillion dollar business enterprise, he had never quite gotten used to the hectic pace of it all. The endless succession of hotel rooms, hotel food, the traffic, the jostling crowds. If it were completely up to him, he would never leave Jamaica again. Never leave the peace, the quiet. There was nothing in the world like slowly waking to the sound of waves crashing on the beach. Or like walking aimlessly along miles of powder fine sand, with nothing and no-one to disturb you but an occasional gust of wind.

There was no room for brash aggressiveness here. No room for people like Summer Stevens, who made a living by studied calculation. She was beautiful, no doubt, and over the past weeks, he had found himself thinking of her overly much. But, she was not the kind of girl he wanted for a wife. He needed someone who was soft and tender. Someone who cared more about what she was like inside than what she looked like on the outside. And, of course, the woman he married, would not be a career girl. She would be content to stay at home, bake, cook, and do all those other warm domestic things women used to enjoy doing. She would be the kind of woman who would wait up for him on nights like this. She would have a warm plate of supper waiting. Maybe she would rub his feet, cuddle with him. She would be pleasant, even tempered. Not volatile and unpredictably explosive like Summer Stevens often was.

He paused before his bedroom door, tried the knob, fiddled around in his pocket for the key, inserted, and entered the darkened room. Once inside, he narrowly avoided tripping over an object standing just in front of the door. He felt around for the light switch, and swore silently when the bulb did not light. He dropped his luggage where he stood, and felt his way to the bathroom. In a few minutes, he had stripped to nothing but his underwear. He was far too tired to bother with hunting around in the darkness for pajama bottoms. Tomorrow, he would have a look at the light. Find out why it wasn't working.

He padded over to the large bed, pulled back the sheets, and climbed beneath the covers.

It took only a moment of settling against the pillows, for him to realize there was someone else in there with him. A tired but tolerant smile twisted the corners of his mouth.

"Mik . . . ? Come on. It's too late for any of your practical jokes. Go on back to your room."

When the body lying next to him only shifted and muttered in response to his low command, he reached across and struck it firmly on the behind.

"Mik . . . did you hear me?"

Summer came abruptly awake at the sharp crack on her rump. For a brief second, cold shards of panic ricocheted through her. Someone was trying to maul her in her sleep. It took another second for her to remember where she was, and a third for her to formulate a plan of action. Another crack landed on her rump, and a male voice whispered something horrible in her ear. Something about using a stick on her.

She sprang from the bed like a sprinter coming out of the blocks. She had dropped her shoes by the side, and her hands felt around frantically for them now. The man on the bed was coming toward her, she could hear the creak of the springs as he did. She lashed out with a shoe, and heard a soft grunt in response.

"Stay away," she shrieked. Her voice was completely unrecognizable, even to her own ears.

The man launched himself at her, carrying them both, in a tangle of limbs, to the ground. She found a patch of exposed flesh, and bit down, hard. A hand was clamped across her mouth, and somehow, in the flurry of limbs, she managed to bite that too.

"Stop struggling you little wildcat."

She kneed him in the ribs, rolled sideways, and pounced again on the shoe, which had been dislodged from her grip. She swung again, landing a substantial blow against some part of him. He seemed unfazed by this, however, and flung his body across hers again, using his weight to still her struggles.

"Listen to me, I'm not going to hurt you. Do you hear me? I am not going to hurt you." It took a moment for the quiet words to sink into her terrified brain. Slowly, gradually, she stopped squirming, and lay like a slab of stone beneath him, her brain all the while, working furiously. What would he do to her if she screamed for Nicholas? How far away was her purse? And where exactly in its voluminous folds was her canister of Mace?

He eased himself off her, and she wondered at the wisdom of kneeing him heavily in the groin.

"Get up," he said. "I guess you must be one of Nicholas's girls."

Summer got unsteadily to her feet. Her knees shook, and she was forced to lean against the bedside table for support.

In a voice that was severely winded, and still ringing with

the residual traces of panic, she said, "I am most definitely not one of Nicholas's girls."

Something about the calm words struck a familiar chord, and Gavin's heart stilled, then recommenced a very furious beating. It couldn't be. Was it possible that he was losing his mind after all? Granted he had had a few steamy dreams about Summer Stevens since their dinner in Los Angeles, but to start hearing her voice too? That was not a good sign. Not a good sign at all.

Summer fumbled about for the switch at the base of the lamp. If she could see him, see his face, she would be able to adequately control the fear still running like wildfire through her veins.

Her fingers closed around the knob, turned. Her eyes met his at the exact moment golden light flooded the room. They both stared, each momentarily stupefied. Gavin was the first to recover.

"You. What the hell are you doing here? In my house?"

Summer opened her mouth to reply, and a croak of sound escaped. Her eyes scampered up the naked torso, over the thick scar tissue that covered his right breastbone, then down again to the snug fitting briefs and long sinewy legs. "Your house? . . . This is your house?" It was all too much for her, and she sank onto the side of the bed.

He made no attempt to cover himself, instead he stood before her, almost proudly, like the poster boy of some male swimsuit calendar. "Don't be coy with me Ms. Stevens . . ." his eyes swept the room, "and . . . what in God's name have you done to my bedroom?"

Summer looked around at the jumble of things on the floor. "Done to your room? I haven't done a thing. Your . . . your brothers have been cleaning, apparently."

Gavin flung a blanket at her, rapped out an autocratic, "cover yourself with this," then strode to the door and yanked it open. "Nicholas." His voice reverberated along the narrow corridor.

Within moments, there was the sound of footsteps, and Nicholas appeared in the doorway. He was still fully dressed, and he strolled into the room with a cigarette stuck in the corner of his mouth.

"You bellowed?"

Gavin turned and pointed a finger at Summer who was now thoroughly wrapped in the blanket. "What is she doing in my room? And, more importantly, what is she doing here . . . in Jamaica?"

Nicholas removed the cigarette. "I hired her."

Gavin approached his younger brother, and for a second, a flicker of uncertainty clouded the younger man's eyes. "Come with me."

With a hand pressed to the base of Nicholas' spine, Gavin maneuvered his brother outside. Summer waited for the door to close, then she went to place her ear against the wood. For the next several minutes, she could clearly hear the strident bass of Gavin's voice, and every so often, the more subdued sound of Nicholas.

When the sound of heavy footsteps echoed once again in the corridor, she rushed back to the bed to sit. The door opened, and Gavin reappeared. He was now dressed in a striped robe, and black leather slippers. A square Band-Aid sat almost directly above his right eye.

He stood there for a moment, as though unsure of exactly what to say to her, then he pushed away from the door, and approached the bed. Summer burst into immediate speech. She didn't care for the expression on his face one bit.

"Look . . . I had no idea that you . . . that this was your room. I didn't even know that you were a part of Champagne Industries. After all, the name you use is Pagne not Champagne like Nicholas."

He came to stand at the foot of the bed, his expression unreadable. "Nicholas explained. I know you probably had nothing to do with all this. He hired you as . . . a joke. He didn't have my approval."

Summer shifted her legs onto the floor, and involuntarily, Gavin found his eyes following the smooth long length of them.

"You mean there's no cottage? No job?"

Gavin met her eyes then turned and walked across to stare out the window. "There is a cottage. But . . . there is no job. Not for you anyway."

Summer looked across at his solid back, and felt the first stirrings of anger. "What do you mean 'not for me anyway'?"

He turned, and his face was cold. "Exactly that. This job is not for someone like you."

She was on her feet, blanket forgotten, breasts thrusting forward beneath the thin cotton nightgown. "Someone like me? Are we back to that again? Can't you get it through your thick head that what a person looks like on the outside is by no means an accurate gauge of what they're capable of doing? I'm very good at what I do, let me tell you . . . and, they're very few designers in the world who can do it better."

His eyes flickered over her. "I'm sure you are . . . good . . ." and he appeared to put an entirely different spin on the word *good,* ". . . but the person we hire for the job has got to be a man."

"A man?" Summer's voice was incredulous. How dared he say such a blatantly sexist thing to her. "I know you're not overly fond of women, and for that, I pity you. But I've just flown thousands of miles to be here. And, I'm not leaving until I complete the job I was hired to do. . . ."

"Ms. Stevens . . ." he interrupted gruffly. "There is no point in collapsing into hysterics. We will compensate you for the inconvenience caused, of course. And make arrangements for your flight back home."

Summer folded her arms. "I am not leaving."

"Well . . . after tonight, you certainly can't stay here."

"I'm sorry I bit you on the shoulder . . ." she waved a hand vaguely in the direction of his head, "and cracked your skull with my shoe. But, that's no reason, no reason at all to fire me. It's unfair, that's what it is. Most unfair. You after all, hit me on the behind in the dead of night, what was I to think? In my position, you would have done the same."

"It has nothing to do with the sharpness of your teeth, or the accuracy of your aim . . ." he massaged the spot covered by the Band-Aid, "which is, I have to tell you, quite potent. It's a simple matter of logistics and common sense. The designer we hire would have to live here, with us, for the entire length of time it takes to fix the cottage up."

Summer eyed him. "So?"

"So . . ." he said with exaggerated patience, "you would be forced to live here with us. Share the same facilities. A house full of men. . . ." he paused to let that sink in. "Men, Ms. Stevens."

"Uhmm-hmmm," Summer agreed. "Believe me Gavin . . ." and she called him by his first name very deliberately, " I have run into a couple of members of the opposite sex before. They don't scare me at all."

Gavin's expression grew shuttered. "I don't care how much 'running into' you've done with other men. You won't be doing any of it here."

Summer gaped at him. Did he actually think that she would be a damaging influence on his brothers? That she was some sort of morally decrepit woman who would lie in wait for the boys in the dark corners of the hallway, and maybe trick them into some sort of indiscretion? It was insulting, that's what it was. Just plain insulting.

She marched across to her handbag, zipped it open, and pulled a document from within. She waved the pages at him. "This is the contract, which I signed. All perfectly legal. If you do not agree to let me stay . . . to let me complete the job, I will sue Champagne Industries for breach of contract."

For a moment, she thought she'd gone too far. He moved so quickly, that she barely had enough time to utter a squeak of protest. He grabbed her about the waist, and brought her hard against him.

Summer squirmed vigorously. "What are you . . ." But, that was as far as she got. His lips were on hers in the next breath, warm and firm, his tongue gently stroking the soft inner curve of her lower lip. A hand came up to cup her breast, and he ran the flat of his thumb around the dusky softness of a nipple.

An uncontrollable shudder rippled through them both, and

just as suddenly as she had been grabbed, she was free. Summer's chest heaved, and suddenly, it was hard to draw breath. What had happened? What was this burning in her lower abdomen? How was it possible that a simple, not to mention, unwanted kiss had made her feel this way? She had been kissed before. Many times in fact. Why had she never felt like this?

His voice had gone husky, and several tones deeper. "Do you still want to stay?"

She forced herself to look him squarely in the face. Her heart was battering like a wild thing against her ribs. She knew the exact intent of that unexpected embrace. He was trying to scare her into leaving, but it would not work.

"I came here to do a job. I'm not leaving until it's done."

Without another word, he strode from the room, slamming the door behind him with a loud crash.

After that, sleep did not come easily. She made certain the door was securely locked, then returned to lie on the bed, her thoughts a tangle of confusion. Why had she pressed so hard to remain? To stay in a job that quite obviously would not have been hers to have, if Gavin Pagne had had anything to do with it. Was it just the island and the beauty of the surrounding country that had made her behave so? The fact that she had not yet had a chance to explore, to look at the wonderful old cottage that was just begging for the touch of an experienced hand. And why had she felt such strong, confusing emotion when he had kissed her? They didn't even like each other for goodness' sake. In Los Angeles, after her little performance, they had come to an uneasy truce, an understanding of sorts. But nothing more than that.

She lay on her back in the hard, very broad bed, and listened to the soothing crash of waves as they curled and foamed on the beach just outside. A gentle breeze stole through the open window, filling the room with the perfume of tangy salt air. And, after a while, Summer was able to close her eyes, and slowly quiet her roiling thoughts. Eventually, she slept. And, for the first time in a long while, she dreamed.

* * *

In the morning, she was awake by seven, and standing at the window staring out at the gorgeous turquoise blue of the sea. From where she stood, she could see miles of smooth ocean, white sand, sailboats with their vibrant colors blowing in the wind. There was a fragrance in the air that she didn't recognize, it was a curious blend of fruit, flowers, and warm Jamaican sunshine. It was peaceful. Exciting. And, she wanted to get out there and enjoy it all. She wanted to walk barefooted on the sand. Trail her fingers in the wonderful break of a wave. Bite into a sweet, warm, juicy fruit.

She turned away from the window, her eyes glowing. The house was still quiet. Why not go right now. Without waiting for breakfast. Without waiting for anything.

The idea of it all swept her along, and she succumbed to the pull of it. Rifling through her suitcase quickly, she found a pair of soft, faded jeans with the fashionable holes in the knees, a white tanktop, sunglasses, and black rubber thongs for her feet.

She took a quick shower, hurried into the clothes, then pulled her substantial mane of hair into a knot atop her head. With sunglasses in hand, she quietly opened the bedroom door, took a quick look up and down the hallway, then walked down the corridor, down the stairs, and out the front door.

An hour later, she was sitting on those same stairs again, dusting sand from the soles of her feet. She had wanted to walk the entire length of the property, but it had been too sprawling, and she hadn't been exactly sure that it was safe to go exploring at will. So, she had contented herself with a stroll along the beach, all the way up to where the old cottage stood. It had looked exactly like it had in the many photographs she had pored over. The wonderful brick and stone around the base of it. The wrought-iron trellis work. The wraparound veranda with the remnants of what was once a porch swing. It was every serious designer's dream house. And, when she was through with it, it would be beautiful.

She had cleaned a spot on one of the dirt-stained windows

with the edge of her top, and tried to see into the dark interior, but after several minutes of fruitless rubbing and squinting, she had given up. Instead, she had contented herself with walking around to the sea-facing side of the veranda, leaning against the rails, and staring out at the ocean.

The history of the place was so strong. The lives that had passed before, the force of them all, was still so very powerful. She could almost feel their presence. She could clearly see how it would have been centuries before: African bondsmen huddled in the cottage by day, eating what they could, saving their strength for the dangerous trek down the craggy rocks at nightfall. Maybe some of them would have slipped and fallen, screaming and clawing at the air as they plummeted to the churning ocean. But others, still, would have made it.

With thoughts of what might have gone before still milling about in her head, she had walked back along the beach toward the house, a little more solemn now that the spirit of the house had touched her.

At a few minutes before nine, Nicholas found her sitting on the stone stairs, her chin cradled in the cup of a palm, a faraway, almost otherworldly look in her eyes. He closed the front door, and came to sit beside her.

"Are you mad at me?"

Summer refocused her gaze, bringing herself abruptly back from her mental wanderings.

"I should be. God knows you would deserve it . . . but," and she turned to look at him. "You brought me here. To the cottage. I can't explain it, but I feel a strange connection with it. You know, like . . . like déjà vu or something."

Nicholas laughed. "Don't tell me you believe in that reincarnation trash."

Summer gave it a moment of thought. "No. I don't believe in revolving lives. I'm not even very superstitious. But, I went up to the cottage this morning, and I could . . . I could feel something. It was almost as if I'd been there before. I know how it sounds. Maybe I didn't get enough sleep last night."

Nicholas draped an arm about her bare shoulders. "Maybe.

Listen, I'm sorry about everything. I shouldn't have brought you here . . . the way I did . . ."

"Why did you, anyway? I mean, why me, when your brother obviously wanted a man to do the job? It would've been so much simpler to hire a Jamaican designer. Someone who lived here."

Nicholas avoided her eyes in a manner that made her immediately suspicious.

"Maybe . . . before you leave, I'll tell you why. For now, let's just say the picture of you in the portfolio, caught my eye."

"What?" Summer pushed away from him. "You mean you hired me because you thought I looked good? Not because you admired my work?"

He shrugged. "That's all you're going to get out of me now." Grabbing her hand, he pulled her up. "Let's go make breakfast, maybe the smell of frying bacon wafting through the house will help put my big brother in a better mood."

In the kitchen, Nicholas began opening doors, pulling out pans, bowls, knives. Summer stood with hands clasped behind her back, momentarily at a loss. She was no great chef. She could warm things up nicely, if they were already made, and boiled eggs and toast were not too far beyond her range of culinary skills. But, anything that involved mixing and mashing things from scratch, was completely virgin territory for her.

Nicholas turned with a thick ceramic bowl in hand. "What do you fancy? Scrambled eggs and bacon?"

"Sounds fine to me. I don't usually eat much breakfast anyway."

He gave her slim figure a cursory glance. "You could stand to gain a pound or two. Pass me that skillet. And start breaking the eggs in this bowl."

"Ah . . . look," she said, as he started passing her the milk, cheese, and eggs. "I've never made scrambled eggs before." She looked down at her beautifully manicured nails. "I'm not cut out for cooking."

Nicholas waved her protests away. "Nonsense. It's as easy

as breathing. Break the eggs first. You do know how to do that?''

''Well it can't be that difficult,'' Summer mumbled beneath her breath. ''Don't you have a housekeeper? Someone to cook and clean for you?''

Nicholas reeled off a wad of bacon, and dropped it into the frying pan. ''No, Gavin doesn't believe in them.''

Summer bashed an egg against the side of the bowl and pried the splintered shell apart.

''I should have guessed.''

''What?'' Nicholas said over the noise of the frying.

''Nothing . . . never mind.'' She dug into the bowl with the tip of a fork, and fished several pieces of eggshell out. She spent a minute trying to capture some of the smaller fragments, but gave up after a while, and bashed another egg.

''Where is he, by the way?''

''Gavin?''

''Who else?''

''Probably working. He wakes at six every morning. Even on weekends. His office is on the third floor. He'll be down by about eleven.''

''Thanks for letting me know. I'll try to stay out of his way.''

Nicholas guffawed. ''What happened between you two last night?''

''I'd rather not say.''

''C'mon. You can tell Uncle Nicky.''

Summer bashed the final egg, and let out a little exclamation of delight. She had actually managed to get a whole yolk out of this one, with only a handful of tiny eggshell bits attached.

Nicholas placed the first rasher of bacon on a wire rack, covered it with a swatch of absorbent paper, then looked at Summer expectantly. ''Well?''

She walked across with the bowl of broken yolks and swimming eggshells. ''Maybe I'll tell you before I leave.''

''Aha,'' he said with a knowing gleam in his eye.

She set the bowl down on the side. ''Don't 'aha' me. I should strangle you for what you did. Putting me in his room. In his bed.''

Nicholas removed another slice of bacon. ''Yeah, that was good. Even you have to admit that.''

Summer swatted at him with a tea cloth. ''There's not an ounce of repentance in you, is there?''

He grabbed the cloth and pulled her close. ''None whatsoever.'' He laughed down at her, and she responded with a large grin.

They both sprang apart, and Summer felt herself flushing guiltily when a voice at the door said, ''Nicholas.''

She rushed to her newly found friend's aid. ''It's not what . . . We were just making breakfast . . . kidding around.''

The black eyes were cold as they swept dismissively over her. ''Nicholas. There's a shipment of medicine coming in this morning. I want you to go down to the docks and supervise the off-loading.''

Nicholas turned back to the pan, and continued to fry. ''I'll go down after I finish up here.''

''You'll go now.''

Summer felt a surge of embarrassment creep up the length of her neck. Why did he have to be so rude and unfeeling. To speak to his brother in that manner. In front of someone else too. A total stranger. Didn't he know how that must feel?

Nicholas turned the fire down, made an elaborate play of wiping his hands. ''Summer, you finish up then, okay?'' Very deliberately, he bent and pressed a kiss to the side of her cheek. ''See you a little later.''

Gavin waited until he heard the sound of the front door closing, then he came fully into the kitchen. Summer turned toward the pan, and began aimlessly stirring the quickly blackening strips of bacon. She heard the sound of a stool being drawn out from under the table, and assumed that he was now sitting watching her.

After a long moment of silence, he said, ''If you're going to remain here for the two months, or however long it takes you to finish the cottage, you're going to have to stay away from Nicholas."

Summer spun around, a blackened strip of bacon hanging from the tip of her fork. "What do you mean 'stay away from him'?" Did he think she was poisonous to the touch?

"I mean it. If you don't, I'll put you on the first flight out of here, contract or no contract. Do you get me?"

The bacon in the pan was now on fire, but Summer paid it little heed. She wagged the dripping fork at him. "I'm getting a little sick and tired of your nasty-minded insinuations about me. I have not one iota of interest in Nicholas, you, or any other man. Do you get me?" And she made very sure she emphasized the *you.*

Without answering, he sprang from his seat and rushed toward her. Summer backed up against the stove, fork outstretched before her. "What are you. . . . ?"

He shoved her aside, and covered the frying pan with a large lid, very effectively cutting off the supply of oxygen to the leaping flames. Then, he turned on her. "What the hell are you trying to do? Burn the place down?"

Summer slammed the fork down on the counter. "I was making breakfast for you and your brothers."

Gavin picked up a blackened strip and turned it over between his fingers. "What is this supposed to be?"

"What does it look like?"

He shook his head, an expression of disbelief on his face. "You can't cook worth a damn, can you?"

Summer turned and marched from the kitchen. He was the most ungrateful, rude, and thoroughly unpleasant person she had ever had the misfortune of running into. It was hard to believe that he and Nicholas had the same blood running in their veins. As she was about to go through the front door, she heard his voice behind her. "Where are you going?"

She turned. "You may be able to order Nicholas around . . . get him to do your every bidding, but let me tell you, that's the entirely wrong approach to take with me."

He quirked an eyebrow at her. ''Is that right?'' And, there was a faintly mocking tone in his voice.

''That's right.''

''You seem to have forgotten that you're working for me now. So, I get to order you around, whether you like it or not. Don't forget, I offered you a way out last night . . . you could've been on your way back to L.A. right now . . . as we speak. . . .''

Summer cut him off. ''I seem to remember you offering me more than just a way out last night.''

Gavin's gaze skidded toward the staircase, then back to her. ''Keep your voice down. I know you . . . ''

''You don't know anything,'' she interrupted again, this time in a fierce whisper. ''That's the problem. You assume too much, and know too little. You . . .'' The rest of what she was about to say, came to a skittering halt. Her eyes darted between the man standing in the sitting room doorway, and the tall boy standing on the stairs. It was incredible. The resemblance was almost awe-inspiring in its exactness. The boy on the stairs was the spitting image of Gavin Pagne twenty years before.

Gavin straightened away from the door frame. ''Lost your tongue, Mik?''

The boy smiled, and Summer felt a flush of perspiration dampen her palms. Maybe Mik was his son. He had to be. It wasn't possible that two siblings separated by more than a decade could look so much alike.

Mik walked slowly down the stairs, his thumbs tucked into the pockets of his jeans. ''So . . . it's really true.'' His voice was not nearly as deep as Gavin's and it was laced with the lyrical cadence of the Jamaican accent.

Affection rippled across Gavin's face, and his voice lost its brusque quality. ''Summer Stevens, meet my youngest brother, Mik.''

The boy stopped directly before her, and for a moment, Summer just gaped. He extended a hand, and long fingers swallowed hers. ''Ms. Stevens. You're even more beautiful than Rob said.''

Summer nodded a smile of thanks. "I thought Rob was the youngest though?"

Her question was really directed at Gavin, but Mik answered. "Rob's a cousin. I'm the youngest Champagne man." He winked at her, and a chord of memory twanged. This must have been the baby that Gavin had risked his life saving from the fire.

"You're very like your brother," she said to Mik. He grinned at her. "Yeah man, everybody says that. But," and he pulled his collar up, struck an elaborate pose, "I'm better looking."

Summer laughed, her good humor completely restored. These Champagne men were quite a bunch.

"Mik, go up and get Rob." Gavin swept his hand in a semicircle. "I want you two to clear up the mess you made yesterday. Ms. Stevens and I are going to finish breakfast. By the time we're done, I want the living room to be clean. Get it?"

Mik saluted. "Got you."

Summer followed Gavin back into the kitchen. There seemed little else for her to do, under the circumstances.

"You run a tight ship." There was a faint note of respect in her voice.

"Yes," and he began taking glasses from the cupboard. He placed them in neat rows on the table. "Can you handle the juice and milk?"

She nodded. "Okay. I guess I deserved that, but one shot at me is all you get."

He turned, and for the first time since her arrival in Jamaica, he smiled at her.

Her lips curved in response. It was the Champagne charm, she told herself, as her heart flip-flopped heavily in her breast. All of the brothers possessed large quantities of it. Even Gavin.

Within minutes, she had everything nicely poured and arranged on the dining room table. From the kitchen, the busy sounds of frying and whisking and more frying, drifted outside.

The warm aroma of bacon and eggs settled around her, and

even though she was not much of a breakfast person, her stomach grumbled.

She stuck her head around the door. "Need help with anything else?"

"Toast? Think you can manage that?"

"Funny guy," she mumbled, just a little too low for him to hear.

They were just finishing up breakfast when Nicholas returned. He was holding a brown paper bag in his hand. To no one in particular, he announced: "Hope you left enough for me."

Summer pointed at a covered plate in the middle of the table. "It might be a little cold. I'll warm it up for you," and she made to rise.

"Sit," Gavin said, "Nicholas can warm up his own food."

"But, it's no . . ."

Nicholas dropped the paper bag beside her plate. "Brought you something."

Without really knowing why she did, Summer glanced across at Gavin, before opening the bag. He was staring firmly at Nicholas' retreating back, his jaws tightly clenched. She hesitated for a moment more before prying open the bag and looking in. She lifted out a huge golden pastry shaped very much like a half moon.

Both Mik and Rob were looking at her hopefully. "It's a Jamaican patty," Rob said in response to the unspoken question on her face.

Summer rested it on her plate. It smelled wonderful, but she was really a little too full to have any dessert.

"Do you eat it with cream?" she asked.

"Cream?" Rob's face was incredulous. "Nah man, yuh nah eat it wid cream. Yuh nyam it jus' so."

Summer blinked at him. "Ah . . . pardon me?"

Gavin bit the inner corner of his lip to prevent himself from laughing. "He said, you eat it just like that. No cream." He directed a look at his young cousin, that fell somewhere short of being actually stern. ''Rob, you know Ms. Stevens doesn't speak patois. . . .''

''Oh, that's okay,'' Summer broke in, ''maybe I can learn it.''

Rob nodded with enthusiasm. ''It's easy man. I can teach you.''

''Okay,'' Summer agreed. ''But, you have to be paid. . . .'' She opened up the brown bag again and removed more patties. ''Here's my first installment.'' She handed one each to Rob and Mik. She looked across at Gavin, and an unfamiliar emotion flickered somewhere deep within her as their eyes met.

''Would . . . would you like one too?''

He extended a hand, and she went to great pains not to touch the skin of his palm as she placed the pastry there. She watched almost hypnotically as he took a huge bite.

''Oh . . . it's filled with ground beef.'' Her surprised exclamation had them all turning toward her.

''It's only the best thing you'll ever taste,'' Mik said, and Rob nodded between large bites of the savory pastry.

''Give yours a try,'' Nicholas pulled a chair out right next to her, and sat down.

Summer picked up the pastry, gave her stomach a little pat of encouragement, and took a tiny bite of one edge. The warm, flavorful meat oozed onto her tongue, and her eyes widened.

''Uhmm, it is good.''

She finished off the rest of it in no time, and looked longingly into the bag again.

''They're finished.'' Her voice held a note of greedy disappointment.

Nicholas patted her arm. ''I'll get you some more this afternoon when I take you exploring.''

Summer perked up immediately. ''Exploring? You mean it?''

Before he could answer, Gavin said, ''No. He doesn't mean it.''

"What? . . why? . . . oh." She had forgotten what he had said earlier about staying away from Nicholas. What did he think she would do for goodness' sake?

Mik and Rob exchanged a speaking look, and immediately excused themselves from the table, taking their plates out to the kitchen.

"Wash them," Gavin said to their retreating backs.

Nicholas continued to eat as though nothing had happened. And, as soon as the two boys re-emerged from the kitchen, Gavin scraped his chair back and stood, his thumbs tucked through the unbelted loops of his jeans; Every inch of him the dominant male.

Summer stood, too, before he could tell her to get up and wash her plate. She knew very well that he was quite capable of issuing such an order without a flicker of misgiving. He was a very hard man to get along with, as poor Nicholas probably knew very well. But, she was no Nicholas, as she had told him earlier: She would not be ordered about by him or anyone else.

With her chin tilted defiantly outward, she walked toward the kitchen.

Gavin followed.

"We'll go have a look at the cottage as soon as you're through."

Summer put her plate in the sink, and turned the water on, making very certain that the steam did not come into contact with the varnish on her nails. Gavin settled his plate on top of hers, and stood a little too close for Summer's liking. She took a step away.

He looked down at her. "What's the problem?"

"Where're your gloves?"

Gavin raised an eyebrow. "Why would we need those?"

"You wash with them," she said with exaggerated patience. "Everyone does. They protect your nails."

He took a step toward her, and Summer fought back the urge to put more distance between them.

"Your nails? Don't be ridiculous. You're just going to have to wash the plates without them."

Summer turned the water off. ''I will not.'' And, what did he mean by 'plates'? Surely he wasn't expecting her to wash his too?

He turned the tap back on. ''If you're going to remain here. They're a couple of things you're going to have to get straight. One. Everyone here looks after themselves. There are no housekeepers or cooks to fetch and carry for you. Two. I don't have any tolerance at all for any of the frivolous nonsense that you seem to be accustomed to. If you eat, you wash. Clear?'' He paused, folding his arms across his chest. ''If you find this situation not to your liking, I'd be very happy to book you a flight back to the United States?''

Summer took a calming breath. So that was it. He was trying to make things as difficult as possible for her, so that she would eventually get fed up and leave. Well, he quite obviously didn't know her very well. She was always at her best in difficult situations. In fact she thrived on them.

Before she could rethink the wisdom of her actions, her hands were on his arms, sliding silkily up to his shoulders. She saw the surprise in his eyes, felt the muscles tighten beneath her touch. Then, as quickly as he had grabbed her the night before, her lips were on his. With soft, skillful pressure, she pulled his bottom lip between hers, stroking it gently with her tongue. For a moment, he was passive, and she sensed the deep struggle in him. Then, he moved, his hands coming up to touch her. She felt that he would surely resist then, maybe even push her off.

But the long fingers stroked across her back, dipping down to rest lightly at her waist. Then, they tightened and he dragged her close, bending her to fit his body until she was crushed against the hard warmth of him. Somehow, somewhere in that moment, the balance of power shifted. She was no longer kissing him, he was kissing her. He pulled her up, propped a knee between her legs so that she was now straddling him. And, very effectively, he deepened the kiss, pushing past the tender barrier of her tongue, growling with satisfaction when she matched him, caress for caress.

She was the one to break away this time, and when she did, he pulled her back, his eyes hot, fierce with dark need. She tried to move her head, to put a stop to what she had so foolishly started. But, his lips were on hers again, pulling sweetly, depriving her of every drop of breath, taunting her with maddening half kisses, until they were both clinging feverishly to each other, each giving as much as taking.

What would have happened next, Summer wasn't exactly certain, but the clink of cutlery, and a voice saying, "Oh, excuse me," brought them both back from the haze.

Nicholas stood in the kitchen doorway, looking inordinately pleased with himself, and not at all surprised to see them standing as they were. "I'll come back," and before either could mutter a protest, he was gone.

Summer stood stock-still, not knowing what to say. How to explain what had just happened. She had only kissed him to show him who was in control. She had used this very device on many men before. Invariably, they had all become as malleable as jelly as soon as her lips touched theirs. But, this time, things had gone very wrong. She had lost control. She had actually wanted him to continue, and she had felt strangely cheated when he had pulled away.

"Go get your purse."

She blinked at him for a moment. "What?"

"Your purse, go and get it."

"I mean what . . . what for?" Was he going to march her to the airport and forcibly put her on the next plane?

"I'll get you the damn gloves."

For a moment, she gaped at him. So it had worked after all? Was that the way to get him to do what she wanted? A kiss? Granted, it had been a lot more than just a simple kiss. Something strong and wild had sprung up between them when their lips had touched. It was like the front of a storm, raw and undeniably powerful.

"Be back in a second," and she very nearly sauntered to the door, a tiny smile curving the corners of her lips. Now that she knew how to handle him, everything would be just fine.

But, he took the smile right off her face, with his next words: ‘‘Be very careful you never do that again Ms. Stevens. I'm not the kind of man any woman can toy with.’’

CHAPTER SEVENTEEN

Shopping for dish-washing gloves, turned into several hours of happy browsing in the main open-air market in Ocho Rios. Gavin was surprisingly tolerant of her wide-eyed fascination. He made no complaint when she repeatedly stopped to pore over wonderful wood carvings, intricately woven baskets, pottery, hand-fashioned jewelry.

And, when she stopped to have a long and very wordy philosophical chat about Jah, and the state of the world, with a Rasta wearing long flowing dreadlocks, and a huge kangol, he even joined in, translating here and there when the patois got a little too thick for her untrained ears.

She bought more Jamaican patties, some delicious-looking cookies called coconut biscuits, and a hand of huge green bananas everyone seemed to call plantains. She would have also bought several bags of juicy black mangoes, so called because of their characteristic spotty appearance. But, Gavin forestalled her by pointing out that the mango trees on the Champagne property, were heavily laden with fruit.

Somewhere near mid-afternoon, wearing a jaunty straw hat,

her purchases tightly cradled between her legs, she agreed to head back to the property.

"Everyone's so friendly," she said, turning to give Gavin a bright look. "It's like a whole different world here."

Gavin turned his attention from the road for a brief moment. "You'll find good and bad here, just like anywhere else. Don't make the mistake most tourists seem to make . . . assuming that reality is somehow suspended, and that Jamaica's some wonderful trip through the land of Oz. You have to be just as careful here as you would be in any city in the United States."

"I know that," Summer said. "I just meant that . . . oh I don't know what I meant really. It's just that I've never left the States before, and seeing a different country is . . ."

"I know what you mean. It was like that for me, too, when I first came here."

"Why did you leave L.A.?" The question was out before she could stop herself.

He was silent for a long while, and Summer, thinking that maybe he wasn't going to answer, hid her embarrassment by rooting around aimlessly in one of her bags.

"Nicholas. . . ."

"What?" her head shot up from her busy activities.

"I left mostly because of him."

She could see very clearly by the expression on his face, that it was a subject better left unprobed, but the headiness of the day had thoroughly unhinged her tongue, and she couldn't prevent herself from asking, "Why Nicholas especially? What about Mik and Rob?"

"It's not something I talk about." He swung the Jeep into the gateway of the Champagne property, and Summer cast a quick sidelong glance at his impassive face. What would it be like to share his confidences? To be the one he came to when he needed a shoulder to lean on? Had he ever let himself be that weak? Or, depending on how you looked at it, that strong?

"I'm sorry I asked . . . I didn't mean to pry."

The big shoulders shrugged, and she felt the sudden need to massage away the tension she saw there. Would he let her if she tried? Or would he think that she had some dangerous ulterior motive in mind? Never before had she ever had to pursue a man. They had always been more than willing to chase her. Just days before in fact, she herself had sworn off the male gender entirely. But sitting beside Gavin Pagne now, sensing the loneliness in him, something came back to life in her. Something that maybe had never been fully alive until now. She could finally admit it to herself. She wanted him. At least for as long as she stayed in Jamaica. And, she would have him too. She knew all the many tricks on how to get a man.

Gavin Pagne would be no different. But first, she would have to find out what the problem was between himself and Nicholas. Then she would know what she was up against.

"Are we still going to take a look at the cottage?"

"I've got some work to do. Nicholas will take you."

"I thought you wanted me to stay away from him?"

"Forget what I said before . . . just be very careful. Don't try any of your flirtatious stunts with him. You don't know him as I do."

Summer gave him a calm stare. "I wouldn't with him."

"You did with me . . . and almost got yourself into some trouble."

"It's different with you." She wanted him to turn and look at her, so that he would see her eyes, and the soft promise flickering there. But he continued to stare straight ahead, focusing intently on the gravel drive, almost as though she had not spoken.

When he pulled the car to a stop, he said: "I'll bring in your bags."

He waited until the front door had closed behind her before he let himself relax. It would be difficult, very difficult living under the same roof. His reaction to her earlier in the day, was proof enough of that. Never before had the simple taste and touch of a woman so completely inflamed him. He had known the reason behind her actions of course. The reason why she had kissed him. Clearly she had thought to bend him to her will by using her physical attractiveness on him. He had known that, and yet, he had not possessed enough of a will to push her away. To tell her that her infantile little tricks would not work on him. Because, he had wanted her to touch him. Had dreamed of it just the night before, and awoken covered in a fine sheen of perspiration, wanting her. It was crazy the way she had taken a hold of his senses. It didn't make any sense at all that he should experience such a confusing weakness whenever she walked into the same room. He wanted to take a hold of her, shake her, tell her to set him free from this madness.

There was only one thing to do if she were to remain in the same house with him for the next two months. He would have to get himself a woman. Maybe he had been too long without one. Maybe that was the real reason his feelings for her were out of all realistic proportion. He just needed a warm body. Someone to slake his desire with, who could also cook a decent meal for him. Someone who wouldn't be so very anxious to jump down his throat at the slightest provocation.

His mind was thoroughly made up as he lifted her bags from the truck. Until he could find someone suitable, he would do his utmost to stay clear of her.

Later that night, Summer lay in bed making detailed sketches of the interior, then the exterior of the cottage. Quite a lot of work would be required on the infrastructure of the house. Many beams had been spoiled by the salty, wet sea air. Floor boards in all three bedrooms, had become soft and bowed with age and neglect. Mildew and mold stained most of the walls. The entire kitchen would have to be torn out and redone. There was much to do. And, two months might not be nearly enough time. It might actually take at least that long, working with an architect and a team of builders, to get the house itself back into livable shape.

She stopped to consider this, then began sketching again, a thoughtful furrow creasing her brow. If she stayed for four months instead of two, she would have that much more time to work on Gavin Pagne. And, work on him she would. There were many things about him that puzzled her. Like why he had changed his name from Champagne to Pagne, for one. She would have to remember to ask Nicholas. He would tell her, she was certain.

She fell off to sleep with her sketch pad on her chest, her mind drifting smoothly from conscious thought, into soft dreams.

Shortly before midnight, Gavin walked quietly by her door. He had done so exactly three times in the last two hours. As he passed, he slowed to listen. Was she asleep? What if she had taken ill suddenly? After all, she had barely touched her dinner. She might be sick. Might be lying in there, waiting for someone to come to her aid.

He turned, walked quickly back to her door, and pounded. Summer sat bolt upright, spilling the pad on her stomach onto the floor. For a minute, she couldn't tell where the sound had come from. When it came again, she slid off the bed, and padded to the door.

"Who is it?"

"Gavin. Are you okay?"

She scraped her hair back from her face, ran a hand down her jeans, then opened the door.

"I'm fine . . . why?"

He was dressed for bed in his striped pajamas, a black robe, and leather slippers.

"I thought I heard you call out."

She smiled sheepishly. "I must've been having a bad dream. I was asleep."

"Oh."

And, he still continued to stand there, just looking at her. Summer widened the space between where she stood, and the door frame. Blood sang madly in her ears. She'd know that look anywhere. He wanted her. He actually did. But, he was still fighting it. Still fighting her.

"Would you like to come in for a minute? It is your room. . . ."

He stepped back, almost as though she had struck him. "No.

I just wanted to make certain you were alright. Living under my roof, if anything happened to you, it would be my responsibility entirely.''

She met his dark gaze, took a calculated gamble. ''Okay then. I'll see you in the morning. There're a few things about the cottage I'd like to discuss,'' and she began closing the door.

He cleared his throat, and she stopped, leaving the door open no more than a crack.

''Yes?''

''If it's really important, maybe we should discuss it now.''

She smiled. ''Come in then.''

For the next two hours, sitting on the floor in front of the large four-poster bed, she went over every detail of the cottage, pointing out what would need to be done. How long it would probably take. The possible cost of it all. He listened well, only stopping her when a point needed clarification. Finally, she was all talked out, and too exhausted to do any more of anything. She sagged back against the bed. From between half-closed eyes, she saw his hand reach for her, and her heartbeat quickened. She was too afraid to even breathe, lest the slight movement sway him from his purpose.

His fingers hovered, then dipped down to pull a bit of fuzz from a strand of her hair. She sat up again, trying hard to hide her disappointment. Had she misread him? Was it possible that he had really only wanted to discuss the cottage?

''I guess I'd better let you get off to bed now.'' He pulled himself effortlessly to his feet, then extended a hand to help her up.

Summer wanted to ask him to stay. But she knew that with a man like him, she couldn't. He would have to be the one to suggest it. Even if she prodded him into doing so, the words would still have to come from him.

She smiled her sexiest smile. ''Thanks for listening to me ramble.''

He looked at her for a long moment, and Summer tried to guess what he might be thinking. Did he know what she was up to?

"I'll get an architect out here tomorrow . . . so we can get this thing rolling."

"Yes. Tomorrow," was all she could manage.

"Good night then."

She watched him walk through the door, waited until it was firmly closed, then heaved one of the bed pillows at the plain wooden face of the door. She would never figure him out. Never. Not even if she lived to be a hundred years old, would he be less of an enigma to her.

She walked into the bathroom, stripped off her clothes, took a cold shower, then tumbled into bed still muttering vile things about Gavin Pagne beneath her breath.

The next week passed quickly. First she met with the architect and went over plans with him. Then the builders and contractors. She spent most of her time up at the cottage, measuring windows, rooms, kitchen space, bedroom space. At the end of each day, she would return to the main house, hoping to see Gavin, but he would never be there. Her dinner would always be waiting for her on the stove, and sometimes, she shared it with Nicholas, Rob, and Mik. She had grown quite close to them all. They were like the brothers she had never had. And, during these moments, she discovered that the matter of her adoption, did not hurt quite so much anymore.

With some skillful prodding, she learned that Mik was a premedical student at the University of the West Indies, and that Rob was still in high school, which she had assumed anyway. But when she had tried to unearth anything more personal than that, they had all clammed up, and in very short order, excused themselves from the table, leaving her even more curious than before.

On Friday evening, she decided to take the bull by the horns. She cornered Nicholas in the kitchen, and went to work on him.

"Where's Gavin tonight?"

He flung a dish towel over his right shoulder. "Out somewhere I guess."

She removed the towel, and began drying the dishes. ''Does he always work this late?''

Nicholas paused in the scrubbing of a pot to give her a speculative glance.

''No. Usually he's home by now. Maybe he's out on a date.''

Summer dried some more, and tried not to reveal how much the idea of that disturbed her. ''Is he seeing someone, do you think?''

Nicholas shrugged. ''Maybe. There's a girl up Exchange way.''

''Serious?''

Nicholas turned the water on full blast, letting it fill the huge pot almost to the brim, before inquiring, ''Why are you suddenly so interested?''

''No reason. I was just curious, since he never talks about himself at all.'' She rested the plate she had been drying for the last several minutes on the kitchen table, and turned to pick up another.

His next question had her so completely flustered, that she almost dropped the plate in her hand.

''What?'' she asked.

''You heard me. I asked you whether or not you want him?'' and he continued to wash as though they were having a simple conversation about the weather.

''By 'want him' I assume you mean in a romantic way.''

His eyes gleamed at her. ''If you like.''

''Well . . . I haven't really given it much thought . . . I'm . . .''

''The hell you haven't,'' he cut her off. ''You've been mooning about the place all week, picking at your food, asking a million and one questions about him and where he might be. Don't tell me you haven't given it much thought.''

Summer put the plate down since she had now dried the same spot at least a dozen times. She was unsure whether to be upset or not.

''Are you always so blunt?''

"Yes. If you want to know something, why not just come out and ask it?"

A reluctant smile twisted her lips. He was right. Why not just ask it?

"Well, do you?" he said with a trace of impatience in his voice.

"What are you going to do if I say yes? Tell him all about it?"

"I could maybe . . . help you. Since you don't appear to have come up with any original ideas yourself."

"Hah," Summer snorted. "No original ideas? I've come up with a few beauties in my time. In L.A. I . . ."

"I know, he told me all about the dinner . . . the teeth and everything."

Summer was momentarily taken aback. "He did?"

Nicholas chuckled. "He did."

"Why do you want to help me?" Summer asked, a twinge of suspicion creeping into her voice.

"Why not? I like you. He's my brother. He works too hard. Maybe you'd be good for him. Help soften some of his edges."

After a moment of careful consideration, Summer said, "Okay. What do I do?"

Nicholas finished up the final pot, turned the water off. "It's simple. You've got to become the kind of woman he wants."

"The kind of woman he wants?" Summer repeated. "And what kind is that? Some poor barefoot and pregnant creature who rushes about boiling and mashing things, while somehow managing to bow and scrape whenever he enters the room? Well no thank you. I don't want him that much."

Nicholas looked at her for a long moment, the corners of his lips twitching. "Alright. Do it your way then. Believe me, you'll get absolutely nowhere with him."

Summer flung the dishcloth onto the counter. "Well that suits me just fine."

She walked out of the kitchen, almost barreling into Gavin's broad chest. He steadied her with a hand, and she dropped into an immediate curtsey, "Your highness."

Gavin's puzzled gaze followed her across the floor and up the stairs. When she had disappeared from sight, he stepped into the kitchen. The sound of Nicholas quietly laughing, made him inquire, ''What have you said to her now?''

Nicholas nodded approvingly. ''That girl is perfect for you, Gav. Why don't you do something about it?''

Gavin came to perch on a stool, his expression unreadable. ''That's why you brought her here, isn't it?''

''I had to see what she was really like. All that beauty often means no brains. But, this one's got it all . . . and a temper to boot.''

Gavin chuckled. ''I know.''

''So?'' Nicholas prompted. ''What are you going to do about it?''

Gavin stood, arching himself into a long stretch. ''Nothing. Absolutely nothing. I'm not into girls like her anymore. I've been there . . . done that. I need someone different. Someone special. Not a . . . a good-time girl. Maybe if she wasn't living here with us . . . with the two boys, I might have had a toss with her. She's good-looking enough to stir any healthy man's blood. But . . . since she is here with us . . . I can't take the chance. . . . Trust me, when I marry, it will be to a girl who at the very least knows how to cook.''

''Well . . .'' Nicholas unfolded his arms, and went to clap Gavin on the back, ''you can't say I didn't try.''

''Nicky?'' Gavin said as his brother prepared to leave the kitchen, ''when is Sheila due?''

Nicholas glanced at the stairs before answering: ''About a week.''

''And she still hasn't changed her mind about not wanting to keep the baby?''

''No. Her agent thinks it would be bad for her career. An infant would get in the way. . . .''

A pair of shapely jeans'-clad legs appeared at the top of the stairs, and both men stopped talking almost in unison. Summer came slowly down. She had reconsidered her hasty exit from the kitchen, and come to the decision that she had been terribly rude to Nicholas, when all he'd been doing was attempting to help her.

Both pairs of black eyes were upon her as her foot settled on the last stair. She cleared her throat before speaking, trying all the while to avoid looking at Gavin. Seeing him standing there in the doorway so tall and unconsciously sexy, did queer things to her stomach.

"Ah . . ." and she gestured a bit with her hands. "I'm sorry . . . am I interrupting something?"

Nicholas shrugged. "Nothing important."

"Would you . . . would you like to go for a walk on the beach?"

Nicholas shot a quick look at Gavin before saying, "Sure."

Summer smiled. "I'll meet you outside then."

She made a beeline for the front door, and was through it and outside before it struck her that she had not said a single word to Gavin. Not even "good evening."

As soon as the door closed, Gavin said: "What was that about?" All thought of anything else, had been driven from him by the simple sight of her.

Nicholas chuckled. "Maybe she's got a thing for me."

Gavin's brows drew together, and a slight ridge appeared between his eyebrows. "Don't. Not with her."

Similar black eyes clashed for a moment. "You don't want her. So why should it matter what I do?"

"I mean it Nicholas. Don't touch her . . . not even a hair on her head. She's . . ." his voice tailed off.

"You more or less said that she's free and easy, and isn't worth. . . ."

"I know what I said," Gavin interrupted, impatience making his voice rough. "Let's not get into it now . . . okay?"

Nicholas stuffed both hands into his pockets "Fine. I won't touch her."

Gavin was unconvinced. "I mean it." His brother's easy acquiescence worried him.

Outside, Summer paced impatiently. What was taking him

so long? It had been more than five minutes. In a second, she would go back in.

Just as she was making up her mind to do just that, the door opened.

She turned. "What were you doing in there?"

Nicholas draped a lazy arm across her shoulders. "You are an impatient one, aren't you?"

Summer smiled up at him. "No . . . well, okay, maybe a little. But I wanted to apologize before I lost my nerve."

Nicholas let that little comment slide off him without bothering to make a response.

When they were halfway down the cobblestoned path, which led to the beach, he said, "I've got to hand it to you. You're making more progress than I thought."

"Progress?" Summer was immediately alert. "With Gavin you mean?"

Nicholas pulled her in closer. "No, with me . . . of course with Gavin."

Her heart thumped a little harder. "Did he . . . did he say something?"

"Yes and no."

Summer's brows wrinkled. "I hate it when you try to be mysterious. What did he say?"

"It's more . . . what he didn't say. Get me?"

They walked down the thick stone stairs to the sand, and silence settled over them for several paces.

"Why didn't you ask him to go for a walk on the beach . . . instead of me?"

Summer dug her heels into the sand, and looked behind her at the trail of deep footprints.

"Because he would have refused. He's been avoiding me all week. Besides, I'm way more comfortable with you."

Nicholas made a noncommittal sound. "If you want him, you have to go after him, you know? Don't leave him guessing. Tell him. Better yet, show him."

"I dunno . . . he's hard to figure out. One minute he's

friendly. Next, he looks at me like I've committed murder or something.''

''He doesn't trust women.''

''I know that . . . believe me. I don't know why I even want to bother.''

''You two would be great together if you'd only give yourselves the chance to find that out . . . and he likes you. Trust me on that one. Half the battle's already won. Now all you've gotta do is pull out the big guns.''

''You mean cook?''

Nicholas nodded. ''Among other things.''

They had walked a great distance down the soft sand. Summer bent to roll up her pants' legs. She looked at Nicholas, her eyes sparking with sudden mischief. ''Let's go in.''

Nicholas hesitated. ''Ah . . . no. Not a good idea.''

''Come on,'' Summer teased. ''We can take our pants off and wade in up to our waists.''

''You go in . . . I'll watch from here.''

Summer laughed. ''I can't believe you're a prude.''

''Believe me,'' Nicholas said, ''that's not the reason.''

''Then what?'' She began unbuttoning her jeans, and Nicholas turned his back to her, digging his hands into his pockets.

''The last time I received a lashing from Gavin, I think I was about sixteen years old. Twenty-eight is a little too old to have that particular experience repeated.''

Summer flung her jeans onto the sand. ''Oh ye of faint heart,'' she said, and within seconds, she was in the water.

''Careful,'' Nicholas bellowed at her as she continued to walk out. When she was at waist level, she turned and beckoned. ''Come on in, Nicky. The water's beautiful. It's nice and warm.''

Nicholas tapped his watch. ''Five minutes. That's all I'm gonna give you. Then you're coming out of there.''

Summer picked up a handful of water and tossed it at him. ''You're no fun.''

He sidestepped the tiny sprinkle, ''I'm counting.''

She began wading toward the shoreline again. When she was

close enough, she said, "Why are you so afraid of your brother? If he says jump, you break your neck trying to do it."

Nicholas handed her the sandy jeans, and turned again. Summer was into them in two wiggles of her hips.

"So . . . ? Don't I get an answer Mr. Champagne?"

"Do you really want one?"

She squeezed water from one end of her T-shirt, then tied it in a knot at her waist. "Of course."

"You're going to catch cold."

Summer waved a hand airily. "Don't try to distract me. Let's have it."

"Never let Gavin know I told you this. . . ."

She was serious now. "I won't say a word. You can trust me."

He took her arm, hooked it through his, and as they walked back up the beach, he told her bits and pieces of it. How Gavin had raised them all. Had quit school to do it. Had built Champagne Industries single-handedly into a multimillion dollar enterprise.

"So . . . I have a huge amount of respect for him. Even though many times . . . many, many times, we don't see eye to eye on things. But still," and he shrugged, "I love him. He's my father . . . my brother. . . . and the best friend anyone could ever want to have."

Summer blinked, a thin film of moisture had come suddenly across her eyes. "Were . . . were you the one he pulled from the fire . . . I saw the scar on his chest."

"No . . . that was Mik."

"Oh." She fell into thoughtful silence for a brief moment. "What happened to your . . . parents," she asked after a while.

"Never really knew my dad. He left us after Mik was born. My mom died of ovarian cancer when I was about eight. So I don't really remember her much either. Gavin does though. He was eighteen when. . . ." His voice faltered.

Summer gave his arm a squeeze. "I'm sorry Nicky. . . . You don't have to talk about it. Sometimes I'm just too darn nosy."

They walked back up the stone stairs, and across the lawns

to the house. From a window on the third floor, a dark silhouette watched their progress. In the moonlight, with arms linked, they appeared like lovers out for an evening stroll.

For no clearly discernible reason, a long shudder suddenly rippled through Summer. Nicholas rubbed the flat of his palm up and down Summer's arm, massaging away the goose bumps.

"I told you not to go in . . . if you get sick, you know I'm gonna get blamed for it."

"Don't worry. If I get sick—which I won't—I'll tell Gavin it was entirely my doing. When does Mik come up from college?" she asked, switching subjects neatly.

"He's up every two weeks . . . why?"

"Nothing. Just wondered."

"So . . . what about the cooking? Are you gonna try it?"

Summer laughed. "I think this is all part of a bigger plan. You just want me to be the one to cook dinner for a while. Right?"

Nicholas gave her arm a pinch. "You'll thank me for this later."

They were still laughing as they walked through the front door. Gavin was standing in the living room as they entered. His eyes swept over her, then Nicholas.

"You're wet," he said to her.

Both she and Nicholas erupted into an immediate bout of explaining. Gavin stood stone-faced, arms folded across a white T-shirt with the words *Jamaica,* emblazoned across the front.

"I want to talk to you," he said after a long silence, and a finger came out to jab in her general direction.

"Good luck," Nicholas whispered in her ear, and he was gone from the room before she could even think of a reply.

Summer squared her shoulders and prepared to do battle. After all, they had done nothing at all to be ashamed of. Except for the part when she had gotten a little crazy and waded into the ocean, everything had been conducted completely within the boundaries of polite behavior. She and Nicholas were just friends for heaven's sake. Like brother and sister almost.

"Look," she began, attempting to forestall whatever tirade

was in the offing. ''Nothing happened just now between Nicky and I . . . and nothing will ever happen. . . .''

''You expect me to believe that the two of you just spent more than an hour on the beach . . . talking?''

Summer nodded, all the while telling herself that she would not lose her temper. No matter what he said, what he implied, she would remain calm. ''That's right. Just talking.''

He sat in a chair, and motioned to her to do the same.

''I'm sorry. . . . I'm wet.''

He looked at her, and his eyes were cold. ''I suppose you got that way . . . just talking too.''

''Look,'' she almost bellowed, ''I'm not one of your brothers. You're not my parent. You're not my anything. So don't treat me like a half-witted child.''

He stood in a single movement. ''You're my employee . . . or have you forgotten that? And, I don't want you treating my brother like one of your playthings. Got it?''

Summer forced herself to count very slowly to ten. This was what he wanted. For some reason, he needed her to get upset. Maybe this was his way of getting his kicks. Well, she just would not oblige him. Not this time.

''I'm going up to my room.''

''We're not finished yet.''

She gave him a cool stare. ''Yes we are . . . and don't even think of kissing me,'' she said, as he made a move toward her.

He rocked back on his heels. ''Kiss you? You are a conceited miss, aren't you?''

She undid the knot in her T-shirt, and gave him a slow, considering look. ''You want me,'' she said, ''why pretend you don't, when we both know you do.''

A muscle in his jaw bulged and relaxed, but he made no denial of what she had just said.

She continued, driven by some crazy need. ''If I walked across to you now, and kissed you softly on the mouth . . . are you saying you would push me away?''

His voice was silky soft when he replied, ''Why don't you try me?''

She walked slowly toward him, and for the few seconds it took to close the distance between them, uncertainty flickered within her. She knew that this was not the way to get to him. He was angry now, it was there in his stance, in his eyes, in the stiff way he held his mouth.

When she hesitated, he said, ''Changed your mind? Don't you think your charms are potent enough?''

She ignored his taunt. ''I won't now, because I can see how much you really want me to.''

He grabbed her arms. ''You will. You started this. Now, finish it. Let's see how you work.''

Summer pulled away from him, her eyes filling with sudden hot tears. So that was what he thought of her. How could she have been so foolish as to encourage his belief in her promiscuity. What would he do if he knew the truth of it?

A tear streaked down the flat of her face, and she tried to catch it with a finger. Large hands turned her slowly.

''I'm . . . sorry,'' he said, and he cuddled her in close, wrapping both arms around her. She buried her head in his chest, making sniffling sounds. After a moment, she lifted her face, ''I'm sorry too. I didn't mean . . . mean all that . . . I was just . . .''

''I know.'' He bent his head, and touched his lips gently to hers. The light touch of his skin against hers sent another shudder through her. He pulled her in closer, and his lips were on hers again, stroking back and forth gently. She kissed him back, winding her arms about his neck to force his head down to her. He gave, she took. He took, she gave. The total and absolute synchronicity of it all was like nothing she'd ever experienced. She felt the warm heat of his skin, and the strong press of his fingers as they wandered at will, across her back, then dipped beneath her T-shirt to stroke smooth, bare skin.

He tried to pull back for a moment, but she wouldn't let him. It was too good. Too sweet. Too absolutely right to end so very quickly.

''No,'' she muttered.

He groaned a sigh into her mouth. ''God. . . .''

When she opened her eyes, his were filled with bright heat. They stood together, chests heaving, eyes locked. Something was happening between them, Summer realized. Something cosmic. Something beyond their control.

He bent his head to take her lips again, and she met him halfway, greedy for the feel and taste of him. Of all the men she had shared this with, none had possessed such a tongue. So rough, so very soft. She groaned her satisfaction, and a deep tremble raced through him.

From somewhere, he dredged up the strength, and he wrenched himself away. Summer clutched unashamedly at him.

"No." His voice was several shades deeper.

She looked at him, eyes golden-brown and fawn-soft. "Why?"

He ran a rough hand across his face. "We can't do this."

"Why not?" Desire was still written plainly on her face. "You want it . . . I want it . . . we're both adults. . . ."

"We're not going to do this, and I don't expect you to understand why," he snapped, and his eyes were black chips of ice again. She made as if to touch him, and he warded her off with a hand.

"This will never happen again between us . . . agreed? Never."

On legs that were not completely steady, she turned and walked away from him without uttering another word. Her mind churned with a curious mixture of confusion and budding anger. Had he expected her to argue? To beg and plead with him like many women before her must have done? Well, he was in for a surprise; a big one. Within the month, he would be the one doing all the pleading. She would make him want her until it was all he could do not to get down on his knees and beg her to do a lot more than just kiss him.

Her spine was ramrod straight, and she refused to look back at him. She knew he was watching her. She could feel those hot eyes on her back. But, she wouldn't give him the satisfaction of that. He obviously thought that he was the one in control here. That he could kiss her one minute, and send her packing, the next. Well, it wouldn't be like that. Not anymore.

From below, Gavin watched as she walked up the stairs. His heart was still pounding in his chest, and the sweet taste of her was still warm on his lips. He wanted to call out. Ask her to come back down. Apologize for his harsh words. Explain why they couldn't go any further. Why it could never be between them.

But reason stilled his tongue, and logic slowly took the place of passion. It was only wild lust that he felt for her anyway. Nothing more lasting than that. And it was certainly nothing that a good toss with a woman wouldn't cure him of. Granted, he had never experienced anything quite this strong before, but lust was lust, all the same.

What he really needed was a good night's rest. A soft and peaceful night, where sleep would come easily without hours spent lying flat on his back, counting the number of nails in the boards of the ceiling. It would be good to have a dry and exhausting sleep with dreams filled with anything but her.

How did she know exactly how to touch him, where to touch, and when? And why did the mere scent of her make his blood sing? He had tried to stay away all week, working extra long hours, coming home late just so he wouldn't see her or catch a hint of the fragrance she wore, in the hallway. But the need to see her had been strong. So very strong. Why, of all the women in the world, did she have to be the one to have that strange and powerful effect on him?

''She's having it.'' Nicholas came tearing down the staircase, his shirttails flapping, water still in his hair.

Gavin brought his attention forcibly back to his brother. ''What? . . . Now? Are you sure it's not a false alarm?''

Nicholas cleared the last step, his fingers already buttoning up the front of his shirt. ''No . . . it's the real thing. Her doctor called. He's on the way to the hospital . . . said to meet him there.''

Gavin took a hold of his brother's shoulders and shook him.

''Nick. You have no shoes on. Go up, get your shoes, and meet me outside in the car, okay?''

Nicholas grinned sheepishly. ''Shoes . . . right. I'll need those. It's not every day you become a father you know?''

Gavin gave him a little push. ''Hurry then.''

Summer was just emerging from the shower when she heard the screech of tires, and the rapid acceleration of a car up the long drive. She went to the window and looked out just in time to see the red taillights of the Jeep disappear into the darkness. She sat on the bed to dry her hair, and spent quite a while running the soft terry towel up and down the thick fall of hair that hung in one wet swatch somewhere just below her shoulder blades.

She was so very involved in the process of getting her hair dry, that it was a few seconds before she heard the knock on the door. She lifted her head from its bent position.

''Did someone knock?''

''It's Rob.''

Summer gave her hair another rub. ''Just a minute.'' From the closet she selected a pair of soft corduroy pants, and an oversized T-shirt. She pulled those on quickly, swept her still-damp hair into a tight bun, and went to pull open the door.

She smiled at the lanky teenage boy. ''Rob. Thought you'd be in bed by now.''

The boy gave her an incredulous look. ''Not on a Friday night, man.''

She held the door open. ''Would you like to come in?''

He blinked at her, shuffled his feet shyly. ''Yuh sure, it's alright?''

Summer nodded. ''Sure.''

''I'll bring my cards then . . . and some music?'' he said hopefully.

''What will Gavin have to say about that? Music at this time of night.''

It was Rob's turn to give her a smile. ''That's what I came down to tell you. Gavin said . . .''

"Yes?" Summer took a breath and waited. What new edict had her wonderful employer now issued?

". . . to make sure I told you that he's gone to the hospital. . . ."

"What?" A rush of sudden panic clamored at her. Was he ill? Was that the reason why the Jeep had torn out of the yard at such a terrific speed. Maybe he'd had a heart attack or something. If that was it, it would surely be her fault. She'd gone and gotten him all worked up.

"What's . . . I mean . . . is it serious? Where's Nicky? Has he gone with him too? I should dress . . . go down . Which hospital is it?" The questions poured out of her, almost without pause.

Rob looked crestfallen. "But, I thought we were going to play some cards."

"Rob," Summer managed with great patience, "your . . . cousin is sick. You should be more concerned about him, than with whether or not we're going to play cards."

"Sick? Who's sick?"

Summer gave the boy a stern look. Teenagers these days were impossible. "Gavin is sick. You just told me that Nicky rushed him to the hospital."

Rob made an attempt to restrain himself, but failed. Between great chuckles of amusement, he managed, "Gavin's gone to the hospital because of the baby."

"Baby?" It was her turn to look bewildered. "What baby?"

Rob shrugged. "Gavin's bringing home Sheila's baby."

Summer felt the blood drain slowly from her head. Could this be happening to her again? Another man whom she had decided that she wanted, was also deeply involved with another woman?

"Who is Sheila?" she asked, and waited fearfully for the answer.

"Oh . . . just a dancer . . . she came here about two years ago. She's from the States too. She dances at the resorts around here. . . . I'll go get the cards."

He was gone before she could ask anything more. Summer

closed the door, and went to sit on the bed. Her hands were trembling, and a strange numbness had begun to creep across the width of her chest. How could he kiss her the way he had, when he knew that he was committed to another woman? Had gotten this Sheila person pregnant, no less? She hadn't felt very much more than initial shock, and the fleeting pain of abandonment when Kevin had betrayed her, but this, she felt. This cut her to the very quick. All men were pigs. Kevin. Gavin. They were all the same. Jamaica had seduced her into forgetting this. But she wouldn't again.

Her brow furrowed. Maybe he planned to bring mother and baby back to the house. Maybe he would give them both her room, or better still, have them share his. She stood suddenly, spurred by the thought of it. If that happened, she would leave. She would not live under the same roof as he and his . . . his concubine. A solitary tear trickled from the corner of one eye, and she wiped it away with an impatient hand. Where the numbness in her chest had been, there was now a very palpable pain. It could be that she was the one now having a heart attack. Suddenly, she didn't feel well at all. It hurt to breathe, and there was a strange buzzing noise in her head.

She walked into the bathroom to splash some water on her face. What in the name of heaven was the matter with her. Finding Kevin in bed with Alyssa had never affected her this much. There had actually been a part of her that had been relieved.

''I'm back.'' Rob's head appeared around the door. He carried a portable cassette player in one hand, and a deck of cards in the other.

Summer dashed another tear away. ''I'll be right out.'' Why was she crying? So what if Gavin Pagne was having a baby. So what if he actually loved this other woman. So what if she'd never have him now. There was sure to be plenty of other men if she got too lonely while she was here in Jamaica. She'd seen enough of them when she'd gone shopping for supplies for the cottage. And, they hadn't been shy about letting her know how they felt about her.

She wiped the corners of both eyes, and dabbed a bit at her nose. She didn't need Gavin Pagne at all. One man was just as good as any other, anyway. They all had the same parts. The touch of any particular one should not be in any way special to her.

By the time she had emerged from the bathroom, there was only the faintest tinge of red in her eyes. Rob was seated on the floor in front of her bed.

"So . . ." she said, a little croakily, "are you going to teach me patois too?"

For the next several hours, they played gin, old maid, several hands of poker, and a varied assortment of other card games. Between hands, Rob also explained some of the rudiments of Jamaican patois to his pupil. At one point, following several unsuccessful attempts at mimicry, he said, "put your tongue between your teeth like this."

Summer followed his suggestion for a minute, then gave up when she caught sight of her face in the mirror. "I can't do it."

Rob put his cards facedown. "Look. It's easy. Say . . . okay, say you wanted to tell someone: 'I spent all of my holiday on the beach.' "

"Uhmm-hmmm," Summer said. "How would I say that?"

"You'd say: 'Mi spen all a mi haladay pon di beach.' Get it?"

Summer repeated it, getting the intonation completely wrong.

Rob shook his head. "No. No. Lawd yuh head tough. You have to go up and down when you say it."

By 3:00 A.M., Summer was completely worn out, and couldn't muster the strength to play any longer. The arduous twisting and turning of her tongue in her failed attempt at mastering patois, had taken its toll too.

She put her cards down. "Gin . . . and that's it for me. I've got to get some sleep. You too."

"One more hand, man. Just one more." The black eyes looked pleadingly at her, but this time she resisted.

"You've been saying 'one more' for the last two hours.

We'll play again tomorrow night if you like. But, I've really got to get some sleep."

He perked up immediately. "Tomorrow? You, me, Nicky, and Gavin?"

"You , me, and Nicky maybe. I'm sure Gavin will have his hands full with the baby and all. He won't want to play."

Rob gave her a sly little look. "He likes you, you know?"

Summer nodded. "Yes. I guess he likes girls in general." Not what she had thought originally, but who could tell with Gavin Pagne?

Those words were still echoing in her head as she turned for the thousandth time on her pillow. She knew why it was she couldn't sleep. Why every fifteen minutes, she felt compelled to look at her watch. Gavin still hadn't returned from the hospital, and she wasn't sure whether to be glad about that, or not. She wanted to see his face when he walked into the house carrying another woman's child. His child. He would probably be as brazen about it as he was about everything else. There would not be an ounce of shame in him, she was certain.

She pounded her pillow with a balled fist. Why did men have to be such evil, deceitful creatures? Why? Was it some defect in their genes that made them so? Or was it that somehow, they just didn't care what they did, or who they hurt?

At some time just before dawn, she fell into a fitful sleep. She awoke at eight, with faint shadows beneath both eyes. The Jeep was parked again beneath the window. She lay in bed a few minutes more, wondering what she would say to him when their paths crossed again. The thought of him lying with another woman made her see red. Not that she had any proprietorial claim on him. But why had he felt the need to go to this Sheila, whoever the devil she was, when he could have had her just as easily.

She hated him for it, and didn't want to see him again. She couldn't bear it. She would move out. Into the cottage. It didn't matter that everywhere was still in a mess. That there were ripped up floorboards, cans of paint, nails, and metal bars all over the place.

So what if she broke her neck or something. He wouldn't care. Not with his precious Sheila around.

An hour later, she was in the kitchen pouring herself a glass of passion-fruit juice. The house was completely silent, and she was glad that she hadn't run into him in the hallway or on the stairs. She made herself a sandwich for lunch, slid the keys to the cottage into her right pocket, and let herself quietly out of the house.

Hours later, she was down on her hands and knees in a small cobwebbed-filled alcove attached to the master bedroom of the cottage, when the sounds of footsteps pulled her from her busy work.

"Summer?"

She put the ancient-looking jar she had been inspecting onto the floor, wiped a hand across her brow. The voice called again, and for a moment, she considered not answering. Why had he come in search of her? Why couldn't he leave well enough alone? She didn't want to speak to him. She didn't even want to see him.

"I'm in the back room," she called out when it was clear that he was determined to find her.

She heard the sounds of heavy footsteps, then suddenly, he was there in the doorway. A shiver ran through her as their eyes met for a moment. She turned abruptly away, plunging her upper body back into the alcove. She was so acutely aware of him, that she knew exactly when he left the door and moved in closer.

"What are you doing?"

"Working." She lifted a couple of dusty books out, and placed them with great care on the floor beside her.

"On Saturday?"

"Why not? That's what I'm here to do, isn't it?"

She felt him sit on the floor beside the growing pile of odds and ends. He picked one of the books up, turning it over to look at the faded lettering on the cover. "This looks old," he said.

"It's a ledger of some kind."

Gavin flipped open the book, and began reading the long list of names on the first page. "What do you think it is?" he asked after a moment.

Summer gritted her teeth. Why didn't he just go away and leave her in peace? The warm smell of him filled the entire room to such a great extent, that she could just barely concentrate on what she was doing.

He was obviously waiting for her reply, so she said, "I'm not sure. But given the history of this cottage it could be anything at all."

Gavin laughed, and the husky sound of him made a feeling of heat rush through her. "You don't believe those stories Nicky told you about pirates and runaway slaves do you?"

She forgot to be angry with him for a moment, and turned to him with earnest eyes. "Why is all that so impossible? Pirates did frequent these oceans, and African slaves did run away from the plantation houses to the sea. So why couldn't this cottage have been used for that purpose. It's close enough to the ocean to be ideal for just about anything . . . anyway," she said turning away from him, "I'm sure you didn't come down here to talk to me about dusty old books."

"I wanted to ask you a favor."

Summer swallowed. A favor. He had never asked her one of those before. "What is it?" she asked cautiously.

"I'd like you to come with me to the hospital this. . . ."

"No," Summer interrupted.

"No?" and there was a note of disbelief in his voice.

Summer bit the soft inner flesh of her bottom lip. Go to the hospital indeed. Of all the nerve. To actually come out and ask her to do that. Undoubtedly he was under the impression that all he had to do was snap his fingers, and she would be more than willing to do his bidding, whatever that happened to be. But, she wouldn't do it. Not for him or his precious Sheila.

"You see . . . it's for. . . ."

"I know what it's for," she said snappily. "I know all about it. The baby. Sheila. The whole thing." She stood, dusting her hands against the seat of her jeans. "And let me tell you, I think you're a . . . a . . . just a sick . . . sick man.'' She shook a finger at him. ''You, with your self-righteous attitude . . . and all along you're one of the worst. The absolute worst. How can you stand to look at yourself in the mirror?''

The expression of blank surprise on his face irritated her even further. ''Don't look at me with those big innocent eyes. What kind of an example are you setting for your younger brothers, I ask you? What?'' Her eyes flashed up at him, glowing almost yellow with suppressed rage.

He came slowly to his feet. ''What in the name of heaven are you raving about?''

''Oh, I know you don't think it's anything so very much, with the baby and all. But, let me tell you, there're codes . . . codes of ethics still, . . . even in this day and age.''

His jaw tightened. ''I gather, that in addition to all your other petty likes and dislikes, babies don't rank too high up on your list either.''

''Don't you dare lecture me about my likes and dislikes. At least I have some morals to speak of.''

His lips twisted. ''Just to speak of . . . but none at all when we really get down to the practical application of them.''

Her nails bit into the soft flesh of her palms. Why was she even doing this? Whenever they tried to converse on anything, it always ended this way, with them bellowing at each other.

''I don't want to talk to you anymore,'' she said, and with that, she was back down on her knees, plunging wild hands into the darkened alcove. He was silent for so long, that she found herself praying that he had gone. But when she turned to take a quick look, she found that he was still there. Just standing, looking down at her.

Finally he said in a voice that was more than a little tired, ''Why do we always fight like this?''

Summer shrugged. ''I guess we're just not compatible personalities.''

He leaned on the wall right next to her. ''I think we are.''

She looked up at him with serious eyes. ''I am not going to the hospital to help you pick up your girlfriend and . . . and new baby . . . so you can just turn the sweet stuff off. Cause it's not gonna work on me.''

There was a moment of silence, then he gave a bark of laughter. ''My baby? . . . Where did you get that idea?''

She blinked up at him, almost too afraid to hope. ''Well . . . Rob said last night that . . .'' She couldn't stand it, she had to know. ''Whose baby is it?''

''Nicky's.''

Her jaw dropped. ''Nicholas? Nicholas has a baby?''

''He does now.''

''But . . . but how?''

''The usual way . . . I'm sure I don't need to explain how all that works to you.''

Summer was so bowled over by the news that the baby was not his, that she completely ignored the taunt in his voice.

''Is that what you meant when you told me . . . told me to be careful with him?''

Gavin gave a noncommittal grunt. ''Nicholas is still very young . . . and still very wild. This baby is an offshoot of some of that. But he's going to take care of the infant, I'll make sure of that. This, if nothing else, will help make a man out of him.''

''But . . . oh, you mean they're getting married?''

''No. Nicky will have full custody of the baby since the mother doesn't want it.''

''Doesn't want it?''

''Well don't look so surprised. You just told me minutes ago that you don't care for babies either.''

''I said nothing of the sort.''

''You refused to go with me to the hospital. . . .''

''That was . . . that was only when . . . when, I thought you were . . .''

''Forget it,'' he said, and he turned to go. ''I'll select the baby clothes myself.''

''What is it? I mean what did . . . did Sheila have?''

''A little girl,'' he said, and there was a new tenderness in his voice now. ''A tiny baby girl with round pumpkin cheeks, huge black eyes, and dark curly hair. A Champagne through and through."

"Oh," Summer said, and her heart turned over at his description of the baby. "She sounds beautiful."

"She is."

"I'll . . . I'll come with you . . . but I'll have to go back to the house first . . . take a shower."

For a moment he stood looking at her with those intensely black eyes, a faintly puzzled expression creeping in between his brows.

"You don't have to do this . . . if you really would rather not, you know . . . it's not part of your. . . ."

"I want to help," she said. And, she really meant it. She was ashamed and embarrassed by her behavior of just minutes before, and, as they walked back up the beach together, she wondered about some of the things he had said. Was she really selfish and petty? Because she painted her nails, and wore impeccable makeup all the time, did that make her superficial?

"Do you like boiled bananas and mackerel?" she asked after a long and very thoughtful silence.

The black eyes turned in her direction. "Boiled bananas. . . ?"

"Rob told me about it . . . it's a Jamaican dish. I just wondered whether you liked it or not."

He gave her another glance. "How much paint have they put on the walls of that cottage?"

"What?" Summer said, "what does that have to do with . . ."

"Well . . . just out of the clear blue sky you ask me do I like boiled bananas and mackerel. I figured that the fumes from the paint . . . you know?"

Summer smiled at him. "I feel fine . . . I've just been thinking about cooking. Something Nicky said a little while ago."

He surprised her by reaching for her hand and holding it. "Thank you for coming with me," he said. And, Summer felt her heart pause in her chest, then resume a furious beating.

"It's . . . it's," she stumbled, "no problem at all . . . really. Thank you for asking me."

They stood at the lip of the stone stairs looking at each other, and never before in all of her twenty-eight years, had Summer ever felt so much like being held by a man.

But, after a long moment, he dropped her hand, and ushered her before him with the words, "Let's go up."

CHAPTER EIGHTEEN

Summer held up a little flower print dress with a narrow ribbon of lace around the throat.

"What do you think?"

Gavin came across to stand beside her. Under his arm he held several bundles of disposable diapers.

"Do babies sleep in dresses like these?" he asked.

Summer laughed. "No. This is something she might wear if you took her out for some air in her stroller. . . ."

He appeared doubtful. "Well . . . if you're sure. What about those?" And he pointed to a thick pair of blue denims, better suited for a three-year-old.

"Definitely not," Summer said decisively. "They're not for an infant, and besides she's a little girl, not a boy."

She wandered away again to look through another rack of baby things. When she wasn't looking, Gavin picked up the denims, and slipped them into the already overflowing basket hanging from his arm.

Half an hour later, they were walking back to the Jeep pushing two shopping carts laden with things.

"Where's Nicholas, by the way," Summer inquired, when they were once again seated in the truck.

"Waiting at the hospital. He . . . ah . . . insisted on being present during the delivery. But I think the entire process was a little too much for him."

"You mean he fainted in the delivery room?"

"No. But, he was sick all over one of the doctor's shoes."

"Poor Nicky," Summer said, and she tried very hard not to chuckle at the image in her mind.

"I think it's more like poor doctor. He had to leave the room . . . change everything he had on."

This time Summer laughed, and the throaty sound of her caused Gavin to cast a quick glance in her direction. With the wind whipping through the truck, and wisps of ebony hair blowing madly in the breeze, bare shoulders a smooth golden-brown, she looked exactly like what she was: a vibrantly beautiful woman. One whom he would very much like to take to bed, and might yet, if he continued to feel the way he did.

Summer turned toward him with a comment about the narrowness of the streets, and for a quick moment, their eyes met and held. Then the black eyes shifted away from her, and back to the road.

Hot blood pounded in her veins, as her eyes ran over the strong capable fingers that handled the wheel of the Jeep with such exquisite skill. What would it be like to be held and caressed by those wonderful hands? To feel his lips on her neck, her shoulders, her breasts. . . . Her throat clenched in a sudden involuntary movement. She had to have him. She just had to. Even if it meant cooking and baking and mashing things. She would have him before she left Jamaica.

"We're here." Gavin's voice brought her back from the smoky heat of her thoughts. "St. Andrews Hospital."

A short while later, Summer was standing in a private hospital room staring in disbelief at the woman lying in the narrow bed. In her arms, Summer held a warm, squirming bundle of arms and legs. "Won't you even have a look at her?" she asked again. "She's such a sweet little thing."

The woman in the bed rolled over onto her side, presenting Summer with the long and still very shapely lines of her back.

"Take her away," she said. "I told them I didn't want to see her. I don't want to be a mother . . . do you understand me?"

She turned again, and Summer was taken aback by the blazing anger in her eyes. "Just get out," she snapped, ". . . take her away, please. . . ." Then, she flopped back down on to the pillows, and began a terrible sobbing.

Summer held the warm bundle protectively against her bosom, hesitated for a moment more, then turned and left the room. In a way, she felt pity for the woman. She seemed so young, almost a child herself. She looked barely twenty. What could have been going through Nicholas' mind? How could he have been so horribly irresponsible? Because of their nights of thoughtless passion, a baby had been brought into the world. A beautiful, soft little thing, who would probably grow up with the knowledge that her mother had not wanted her.

She cuddled the gurgling bundle closer, as if to shield her from this, and the tiny head moved against her chest, searching instinctively. She peeled back the pink blanket, and pressed a soft kiss upon one cheek. The huge black eyes opened to stare unblinkingly at her, and Summer felt compelled to touch one of the rounded cheeks with a finger.

"I'm going to have to cut my nails short for you little girl," she whispered to her. "Don't want to poke you with them . . ."

"Has she seen her?"

The question brought Summer's head back up. Gavin was halfway down the hall, a tray of some sort in his hands.

Summer shook her head. "She's probably suffering from postpartum depression. Some women do, you know. She'll want to see her later, I'm sure."

Gavin rested the tray on the table. "I've brought you some sandwiches, and something to drink. "Here . . ." he said stretching both hands toward her, ''I'll hold the baby for a while.''

Summer gave the little thing up with marked reluctance. It was the most curious feeling, but she could almost imagine that the child was hers. Hers and Gavin's.

The sudden clarity of that thought brought her eyes up to his face. He held the baby with great care, making sure he cradled the neck in one large palm. She never would have thought it possible that he could be so gentle, so very tender.

He looked up and caught her watching him. ''What's the matter? Don't you like the stuff I got?''

''Oh . . . no. That's not it. I've just never . . . never seen you like this before.''

He rocked the baby gently when she began to make little cranky sounds. ''There's a lot you don't know about me.''

Summer took a bite of sandwich. ''I know.'' Without thinking, she offered him the un-bitten half of the bread. After a momentary hesitation, he opened his mouth and said, ''put it in.''

She let her index finger stroke deliberately down his top and bottom lips, and the black eyes settled on her mouth, then flicked away again. She felt the warmth of his breath against her skin, and the hairs on her arm stood at rigid attention. What was happening to her? Wasn't she the same person who just weeks before had discounted the existence of such powerful emotion?

''What's. . . ?'' she croaked, then tried again. ''What's . . . Nicky doing?''

''Paperwork. He'll be here in a minute.''

''Oh . . . I . . . there's no hurry.'' She really didn't want Nicholas here just now. She had only asked for him because she'd been unable to think of anything else to say.

She went back to chomping on her sandwiches. When the silence became too long, she asked ''What's her name going to be?''

''Amber,'' and he bent his head to kiss the baby's cheek in

exactly the same manner she had. "Amber Allison Champagne."

"A pretty name. Did you choose it?"

"Uhmm," he agreed.

"Gavin. . . ." she began, "if the mother doesn't snap out of it. . . . you won't tell the baby that she wasn't wanted . . . will you?" Suddenly it was terribly important for her to know this. She wanted to spare the little girl the pain of rejection that her own parents had lovingly kept from her. And, for the first time in weeks, she realized that she could actually think of her own adoption without experiencing any of the gaping hollowness.

Gavin shifted the baby into the crook of his arm. "We may never tell her the whole truth . . . that sort of knowledge can destroy a child. . . ."

Summer nodded. She understood now that her parents had done the right thing. Not telling her, letting her grow up young, happy, carefree, had been the right thing to do.

"You're a . . ." she began, but the words halted in her throat at the sound of approaching footsteps.

"Well . . . everything's set." Nicholas said as soon as he was close enough. "I've never had to fill out so many forms. . . ."

Gavin stood with the sleeping infant. "Go in and talk to her before we leave. She still refuses to see the child."

Nicholas gave Summer a quick look. "Come with me?" he asked.

Summer dusted the crumbs from her pants. "It might be better if you spoke to her alone, Nicky. I don't think she took very well to me . . . somehow."

"We'll wait for you in the truck," Gavin intervened before Nicholas could think of some other bit of persuasion.

"Let me carry the baby," Summer said, stretching for the tiny bundle. The round little face was so sweet and peaceful, that her breath caught in her throat for a moment. There was the tiniest hint of rose on the cheeks, and the soft pink mouth, which was slightly pursed in sleep, was perfection itself.

Summer stroked one cheek with a finger as they walked out

to the truck. "If she grows with the same features . . . she's going to be a beauty."

"Like you, I guess?"

He opened the front door for her, and Summer got in. Her heart was suddenly racing in her chest. So, he thought her beautiful then? This was news indeed. She now held a chip of his armor in her hand, and the knowledge of that made her almost giddy with delight.

Gavin closed the door behind himself, and in the stillness of the evening, she could hear herself breathe. He glanced at the baby.

"Is she okay? She seems to be sleeping a lot."

Summer stroked a hand across the mop of curly black hair. "Don't worry, this won't last for long. Just be thankful that she's asleep now."

He made a noncommittal sound in response, and rested a long arm on the wheel.

"You seem to be good with babies . . . why aren't you married yet?"

The suddenness of the question had Summer scrambling for an appropriate response. She hadn't thought of Kevin or Alyssa in weeks. Had made a conscious decision not to. And, she didn't want to have a discussion about that part of her life now. It was dead and better off buried. But, this was also the first time he had ever asked her anything that was even remotely personal in nature.

"I . . . was. . . ." her voice tapered off.

The black eyes glided over her, finally settling on the burnished gold of her eyes. "You were married?"

"Not married. Engaged." She prayed that he would not ask her anything further. The anger she had thought dead, swelled in her breast, making it difficult for her to think clearly.

"A long while ago?"

"No. Recently." Why didn't he leave it alone? She had tried so hard to wipe away the image of Kevin and Alyssa together. But, it was still there. She could still see them. Still hear them.

"What happened?"

''I'd prefer not to talk about it.'' Her voice was brittle.

She saw his jaw clench, and something wild flared for a brief instant in his eyes. ''Where is this man?''

''I don't want to talk about it . . . him,'' she repeated, her voice rising ever so slightly.

Nicholas knocked on a side window, and they both turned to glare at him.

''What did I do?'' he asked, as soon as he was in the truck.

Gavin flicked on the headlights, and slid the car into gear. ''Did you let her know you'd be back tomorrow to pick her up?''

''Yeah, she knows.'' Nicholas pulled a cigarette from a packet in one of his shirt pockets. He twirled it between his fingers, then slid it with practiced ease, between his lips, and hunted around for a match.

Before Summer could formulate the words, Gavin voiced them. ''Don't even think of smoking that in here,'' he said. ''The baby. . . .''

Nicholas swore softly. ''I'd forgotten for a minute there.'' He wound down the back window and tossed the entire pack out. ''That's it for me.''

The two-hour drive back to Ocho Rios was passed largely in silence. Summer stole a glance or two at Gavin's profile, but his face was, as always, completely unreadable.

Tomorrow, she decided, she would try cooking a meal. Dinner. Everything from scratch. She'd even bake some bread. After all, she'd watched her mother do it any number of times. It wasn't difficult at all. And, he'd be forced to think of her differently then.

Half an hour outside of Ocho Rios, just for the sake of saying something, she asked: ''Nicky . . . you asleep back there?''

Gavin glanced in the rearview mirror. ''He's asleep,'' he said.

''Oh . . .'' then encouraged by the fact that he seemed to have gotten over his earlier disgruntlement, she said, ''have you got a room and a crib all prepared for the baby?''

‘‘There’s no crib. But, we’ve set up a small bed in the room that I’m in, she should be. . . .’’

‘‘A small bed?’’ Summer’s voice was incredulous. ‘‘Does the bed have protective bars around it?’’

‘‘Bars? What for?’’

‘‘She’s a baby Gavin, she might fall off. She can’t sleep in a regular bed.’’

‘‘She can’t do that much moving around. She can barely keep her neck steady.’’

‘‘She should have a crib,’’ Summer insisted.

‘‘Tomorrow then.’’

Summer waited until they had pulled to a halt in front of the house before she said, ‘‘and a nanny too.’’

Gavin shifted in his seat, in the darkness he appeared coldly unapproachable. ‘‘She won’t need a nanny. We’ll all be here to look after her.’’

‘‘Three men who have never looked after a child before?’’

He turned fully in his seat. ‘‘For the record, I have had some practice in this area.’’

‘‘You mean Nicholas and Mik?’’

‘‘And Rob.’’

Summer’s eyebrows lifted a fraction. ‘‘You raised them all from birth?’’

‘‘Rob came to us when he was ten. Mik was two when our mother . . . went away. . . .’’

‘‘Oh,’’ Summer said, and she was immediately sorry for questioning him. ‘‘I . . . just thought it wise. . . .’’

‘‘I know what you thought,’’ Gavin said, turning in his seat to shake his sleeping brother’s knee. ‘‘In your own way, you’re quite sexist.’’

Summer’s mouth worked for a moment. ‘‘Sexist? Me? Don’t be ridiculous.’’

He gave her a neutral glance then turned to shake his brother again. ‘‘Nicholas.’’

The sleeping infant stirred, opened a coal-black eye, peered at Summer for a moment, then released a volley of bellows worthy of an opera singer. The wailing jerked Nicholas abruptly out of sleep.

"What the. . . . ?" he began.

"Your daughter," Gavin said. "Come on help unload some of the stuff we bought."

Summer shifted the baby to her shoulder and rocked and cooed to her to no avail. Finally she was forced to say "She must be hungry."

Several hours and two bottles later, Summer sank wearily into a soft overstuffed chair. The baby had fallen into a fitful sleep, from which she would immediately awaken, whenever Summer attempted to place her on the tiny bed in Gavin's room.

She had tried handing the child to Nicholas, too, but this had caused the wailing to ascend to another octave entirely.

The room door opened and closed and Gavin came to stand beside her. He was dressed in pajamas and the now-familiar robe.

"Good . . ." he said, "you've gotten her to sleep. I can't thank you enough for this."

Summer looked up at him, and her eyes darkened to liquid amber. "You can . . . thank me I mean."

He shoved his hands deep into the large pockets of the robe. For a long minute, his chest just rose and fell, and there was no other sound in the room but the ticking of a clock on some distant wall.

"Put her on the bed," he said, after what seemed like an eternity.

Summer got slowly to her feet, making very sure not to wake the baby. "Don't you ever ask nicely?"

It took a moment for her to place the baby on the bed, and another for her to stack pillows in a box-like pattern around the sleeping infant. When she was finally satisfied, she carefully lifted off the bed and said, "there . . . that should make her safe enough tonight."

She turned to look at Gavin. He hadn't moved from where he stood. She took in the tenseness of his body, and cheered internally. The telltale signs of strong attraction were all there. She could also see the struggle in him too. Whatever his reason, it was clear that he did not want to feel whatever it was he felt for her.

The blood drummed in her ears, and in that moment, she threw caution to the wind. "Aren't you going to thank me, then?"

The hands in the pockets became fists. "Not in the way you would like me to," he said.

Some part of her felt vague embarrassment at being turned down so bluntly, but the need in her was so great, that she pressed harder still. "What can it hurt? There's no one here but you . . . and me."

He shifted. ". . . and the baby."

Summer gave the bed a quick look. "She's fast asleep."

"No," he said. "I meant what I said last time. That. . . . will never happen between us again."

Summer felt the blood begin to creep slowly up toward her face. How could he treat her in this way? Forcing her to humiliate herself by literally throwing herself at him. She had never had to beg a man before. Never. Who did he think he was? Did he really think that she couldn't turn around right now and walk out of his room?

"If you don't . . . kiss me now, I will never let you again . . . never," she said, placing great emphasis on the word *never.*

He gave her a smile that didn't quite reach his eyes. "I think I'll live."

Their eyes battled for a minute. Finally she said, "Why do you dislike me?"

He turned toward the window, presenting her with his back. "I don't dislike you. . . ."

"Well you do a good job at pretending you do," she said, and there was more than a little trace of hurt in her voice.

He was silent for several beats. "It's a long story . . . nothing to do with you really. . . ."

Summer walked across to the window. She felt more than saw him shift away.

He turned to her, and in the half light, his eyes glowed like warm embers.

"Go to bed, Summer."

"Not until you do what we both want."

He made no attempt to deny her assertion. "We can't always have something just because we want it."

She placed a hand on his and stroked. "We can have this."

He hesitated for a moment more, and the faintest whisper of a smile crept into his eyes. "I've never been seduced by a woman before."

She slid a soft hand inside his robe and in slow circles, caressed the hard strength of his chest, gently fingering the raised area of scar tissue. "You'll never be able to say that again."

His hands reached for her then, and she went willingly into his arms, pressing eagerly against the hard length of him. In an instant, the calm was gone. Dark heat flared in his eyes. His head lowered to her, and she was there to meet him half-way. His sigh mingled with hers, and the warmth of his breath intoxicated her. He kissed her roughly, but she clung unashamedly to him, giving herself up to the raw elemental feel of him. His heart thundered against her breast, and the fingers of both her hands clawed at his back, pressing him closer still. When his mouth left hers to wander across the side of her face, she could only manage a bemused, "Gavin. . . ."

Strange and powerful sensations swept through her when his lips finally came to rest on hers again. It was all she could do, not to tell him all she was feeling. A warm tear trickled from the corner of one eye, and he kissed it away, gentling her with his hands. Everywhere he touched felt good and right. With her body trembling the way it was, and her breath coming in uncontrollable gasps, she felt as though she might do anything at all for him. Anything he asked her to, even cook and bake and mash things in bowls . . . every day.

He raised her chin with the blunt of his thumb, and she turned her lips against the hard calluses on his palm. A tight shudder ran through him, and her lips stretched into a pleased smile. He did like the feel of her against him.

When she parted his robe to press a line of warm kisses across the ridge of his collarbone, his hands tangled in her hair, and he drew her up again to meet his lips. This time his kisses were soft and deep, and mingled with throaty, unintelligible sounds.

When they were finally spent, she stood in the circle of his arms, her head resting against the flat of his chest. One hand ran slowly up and down the length of her back, and she closed her eyes and fought for control. What was happening to her? Had she gone crazy? Why did it feel so right when he held her? She was almost afraid to stir, afraid to put an end to this tender sharing. She had never felt this way for Kevin. In fact, not for any other man on the face of the earth. What would he say if she told him that? What would he do?

She felt his hand thread its way through her hair, and shivered with pure enjoyment when his long fingers gently massaged the round of her scalp.

"Summer. . . ." his voice rumbled at her, as deep and soft as black satin.

"Uhmm?"

"Lift your head for me."

Her head came away from his chest. There was a smile in her voice. "Yes, Gavin?"

"Kiss me," he said.

"I thought you said . . ." she began playfully.

"Forget what I said," he growled, and his lips were upon hers again.

CHAPTER NINETEEN

The following morning, Summer awoke with a general sense of well-being. For a while, she lay unmoving beneath the covers, savoring the sounds of the ocean, and the melodic cooing of the tiny brown doves nestled in the wooden window boxes just beneath the ledge. There was a sweet scent in the air that was uniquely Jamaican. It was robust and warm, salty and fresh.

She released a breath of pure contentment when a soft gust of wind entered the room, stirring the leaves of a gnarled mango tree just outside. For the first time in a long while, she felt completely at peace with herself. It was strange, the effect he had on her. It was almost as though whenever he touched her, her troubles just melted away into total insignificance.

Last night had been magical though. So much so, that she was almost afraid to face him now. Afraid to discover that maybe she had dreamed it all. She had wanted to stay with him all night, but he had been such a gentleman about everything, content to just kiss and hold her, without pushing things to the natural next level. In a way, it had shamed her to know that she had wanted it more than he. Strange, too, that she had wanted to at all. When she had been engaged to Kevin, she had insisted on remaining celibate until after they were married. Sex had never really interested her that much. For the most part, she had found it largely overrated. A lot of heaving and panting, without much else to recommend it. But, with Gavin, it would be different. Every instinct in her told her that she was right about this. And, she would have him before she returned to the States. But, how? It was important that he respect her too. She wanted that from him. Needed that, somehow.

But, surely everything would be easier now. After what they had shared last night, they just had to be.

She would have a nice leisurely bath first, bake some bread, cook lunch, do the housekeeping and then invite him on a nice little walk with her. Maybe a lovely Sunday picnic somewhere on the property. They could both sit under a tree, feast on crackers, cheese, and wine. Then, in the pink glow of evening, with the salty breeze rushing in from the ocean, she would position his head in her lap, and feed him sea grapes dipped in thick milk chocolate. It would be wonderful.

She turned onto her side, and allowed herself a long and very lazy stretch. Her mother had been absolutely right about her spending time in Jamaica. It had been the best decision she had made in years. Somehow, she was slowly beginning to regain little pieces of herself, and discovering facets to her, too, that she had never even known existed.

The sound of a car pulling to a stop just outside, had her sitting up and shaking back the sleek hair from around her face. The doorbell rang a moment later, and curiosity pulled her out of bed and to the window. A tiny, rather weather-beaten beetle of some indeterminate color sat just below. From where she stood, she could just see a pair of shapely, nicely hosed legs, standing on one of the stone stairs. She watched as the legs walked back down the stairs and became part of a smartly dressed woman. A frown sprang up between her brows as a pair of long jeans-clad legs also appeared on the stairs. She watched the legs come slowly down the stairs, and knew even before he came fully into view, that they belonged to Gavin. The woman thrust her upper body into the interior of the car, and wrestled for a moment with a huge oddly shaped package. Gavin came around to help her lift it out. Then, she was back in again, and lifting something out that looked very much like a cake of some kind.

Summer expelled the tight breath she had been holding. Her contentment was all gone. She turned from the window and went straight to the closet. Without spending the usual time in careful selection and coordination of colors and fabrics, she grabbed the first things her hands fell on. In five minutes flat, she was dressed and shoving her feet into black leather sandals. She left her hair loose, only pausing to run a quick comb through it to remove some of the tangles. In just minutes more, she was on the curving staircase, and walking quickly down.

On the last rung, she deliberately slowed her pace. Voices. She recognized Gavin's husky rumble immediately, and cringed at the soft and obviously flirtatious sound of the other woman's voice.

She took a breath to calm herself. At least they were talking, and not doing something else entirely. She smoothed her palms down the length of her thighs, flicked a swatch of hair back from her face, and walked determinedly in the direction of the sounds.

Gavin was standing with his back to the sink, both arms folded across his chest, and an unexpected thrill rippled through Summer at the sight of him. How was it possible that a man could look so handsome and sexy in just a white T-shirt and a pair of blue jeans?

He looked directly at her as soon as she appeared in the doorway. Their eyes locked for a brief instant, and some of the irrational panic that had pelted through her at the sight of the other woman, receded. He still wanted her. It was there in the darkness of his eyes.

"Janet, this is Summer. Our genius designer."

The woman turned, and they both exchanged a look tinged with mutual dislike. Summer's chin lifted a fraction. So she had been right after all. This woman was a rival.

"Nice to meet you," she said, without a trace of conviction in her voice.

The woman gave her a brittle smile. "I've heard a lot about you. Gavin says you're among the best at what you do."

"Well, I've been at it for a good, long while." Summer came fully into the kitchen. Her glance swept over the other woman in a quick and very analytical way. She was attractive, and had a good shape, but would be no match for her if she really put her mind to it.

"Do you work for Champagne Industries?"

The woman's laugh tinkled, and a surge of annoyance raced through Summer.

"No, thank goodness. I couldn't handle one of those boring nine-to-five jobs. I model for some of the local magazines and newspapers." She walked around the table and threaded an arm possessively through the nook of Gavin's arm. "Walk me out, Gavin?"

Flecks of bright amber stood out in Summer's eyes, and she fought hard for control. After all, she told herself sternly when they had left the kitchen, she had no proprietary claim on him. They had just exchanged a couple of very heated kisses. It wasn't as though they were in love with each other, or had promised to spend the remainder of their lives together.

She looked at her watch, and counted the minutes that he spent out in the courtyard with her. Pride more than anything else, kept her rooted to where she stood in the kitchen. She couldn't bear the thought of peeping at them from behind a living room blind, and maybe seeing him take the simpering Janet into his arms in the same way he had done with her just the night before.

She hadn't long to wait though, and when he again appeared in the kitchen, the first words out of her mouth, even though she had firmly decided not to ask him about it at all, were, "Who is that woman?"

"A friend," and he gave her a completely neutral glance, walked across to the fridge, opened the door.

For several moments, Summer just let herself breathe. When she was finally calm enough, she said, "What kind of friend?"

He re-emerged from the open fridge with a carton of milk. "Let's not play these games with each other Summer. Nothing has changed between us."

Her mouth opened and closed wordlessly. What a cold bastard he was. After all that had happened, that he could still treat her this way. Why did she not turn away from him, as she would surely have done with any other man? Tell him to go to the devil, or some such thing. What was it about him? Why was the need to have him so very, very strong?

"What is it about me?" she said. "I don't understand. Why do you treat me this way? When I was in L.A., I made a joke of it. But this is serious now. I want to know what it is."

He set the milk on the table, selected a glass, poured. "There's no polite way to explain Summer, so . . . I'd rather not get into it."

Summer stepped forward, already she was beginning to bristle. "No. Let's get into it. If you're going to treat me like a leper, I think I deserve to know the reason why."

He looked up, and his eyes were as smooth and emotionless as black marble. "Okay. I generally don't have anything to do with women like you."

She sputtered. "Women . . . women like me? What do you mean, women like me?"

He took a swig of milk. "Women who are vain, selfish, immoral, money-hungry gold-diggers. Women who go after anything with a pulse, as long as there's a thick wallet dangling somewhere at the end of the chase. I can't stand women who wear makeup as thick as mud . . . who have long curving painted nails . . . need I go on?"

Her jaws were clenched tightly shut, but she yanked them open to say, "and . . . that's, that's how you see me?"

He downed the remaining milk, wiped his mouth with the back of his hand. "Yes."

"That's your reason for treating me the way you do? Because

you think I'm immoral, and after your money?'' Her voice was dangerously calm.

''That's it in a nutshell.''

She took a breath, released it. ''Are you completely stupid?''

''And . . . that's another thing about you I don't like,'' he said, jabbing a finger at her, ''that temper of yours. You can never control yourself. The very first thing you did in L.A. when we ran into each other in that parking lot, was belt out of your car like a bat out of hell . . . and holler your lungs out at me.''

Summer propped her hands on her hips. ''I do not holler. And anyway, even if I did, you were extremely rude to me. So, you got exactly what you deserved.''

''Well,'' he said, ''that about sums the situation up. So why don't we leave well enough alone, and not mess things up further by trying to have some sort of romance. We're obviously completely incompatible. We can't even have a normal conversation without it turning into a massive argument.''

Her eyes narrowed to tiny slits. ''Okay Mr. Pagne. But, I promise you . . . you're going to want me so badly that . . . that you won't be able to sleep nights. . . .''

He folded his arms across his chest, and gave her a bland look. ''I don't want you now . . . and I certainly won't want you then . . . whenever that is. And, as to my sleeping habits, they're many ways to lull a man to sleep . . . Janet knows them all.''

Jealousy, raw, powerful, and completely alien seized her violently. She couldn't bear the thought of them together. Of Janet touching his arms, his chest, kissing him. He was hers, and no one else would have him. At least, not until she no longer wanted him. Not until then.

''If . . . if you go to that woman . . . I'll . . . I'll . . .'' she searched desperately for something to say. Some terrible thing. ''I'll leave here without finishing the cottage,'' she finished lamely.

''You'll stay and complete your contract,'' he said. ''You

wanted this. I won't let you leave now . . . and don't turn the tears on, they won't work this time."

She blinked nobly. "I would never shed a tear over you. Never."

"Funny," he said, "last night . . ."

"Oh, shut up," she said. "I don't care what you say to me now. I know I'm the one you dream of at night. Not Janet. I'm the one you want. I'm the one you need."

There was a moment of silence as they both absorbed her words. Finally he said: "and, am I the one you dream of at night? Or is it that man you were going to marry?"

"I don't dream at all. I never have . . . very much. At least, I don't remember when I wake up, if I do."

He unfolded his arms. "Everyone dreams. But . . . my dreams are not of you. I'm sorry to disappoint you."

She met his eyes. "You say my name in your sleep. I've heard you."

He blinked, and she knew then, that she had him with that, even though, she hadn't really known it to be true when she'd uttered the words.

"Come here," he said.

She approached and stood directly before him, arms at her side.

"So . . ." he drawled, and his eyes slid over her, " you want me . . . do you?"

She met his eyes without a flicker. "You want me just as much . . . and, I won't let another woman have you."

He actually smiled at her audacity. "Is that right?"

"That's right."

"And even though my opinion of you is so low, you still want me? Still want my kisses?"

"Your opinion of me is much higher than you think. You don't really believe any of those terrible things you said to me."

He shrugged. "Maybe. But . . . this thing between us, it's just . . . We're just attracted to each other. It doesn't mean anything. It's happened for both of us before."

"Not like this. It was never this strong before."

"Not even for that man you were going to marry?"

Summer suppressed an internal sigh. She might as well tell him and be done with it. "That man that you keep harping about . . . he . . . he . . ."

"Yes?"

"I caught him in bed with my roommate. . . ." her voice faded, and it was impossible to conceal the traces of hurt still lingering in her eyes. He reached out to touch her hand.

"I'm sorry."

She nodded, and turned away, but his hands slid over hers from behind, and he turned her back. His fingers stroked the fine golden-brown hairs on her arms. "Why do you want me?" he asked softly.

She hesitated a moment, not sure how honest she wanted to be with him. "I . . . you're . . . different from most other men I've met," she finally managed.

"Different?" he said, pulling her to him. "How so?"

"Tall . . . and sexy. . . ." There was a hint of breathlessness in her voice, "And there's a quality of . . . of goodness about you, that I've not seen before. . . ."

"Hmmm," he said, and bent to pull the fat of her lobe into the warmth of his mouth. Summer stood perfectly still as his tongue caressed it. Without actually willing it so, her eyes closed, and a sigh drifted across her lips. A thick haze settled somewhere in the core of her, and she found herself thinking mistily, that this must be what heaven was like. Surely, nothing could be any better than this.

He turned her, and her lips were ready for him. Before his settled, she said, "I don't want to see that woman here again. Ever."

He paused. "Jealous are you?"

"You're mine," she said.

He laughed, and it was a husky, pleased sound. "You're an amazing woman. Completely unstoppable."

She nodded. "I always get what I want."

He pulled her in closer. "I'm not so sure that's good for you . . . to get everything you want. . . . Maybe I should . . ."

She pulled his head down. "No. We won't start with my not having you. I won't let you."

Later that afternoon, with her arms coated with ample quantities of white flour, she finally admitted to herself that the bread baking was not going well. The dough, which should have been nice and firm owing to the large quantities of flour she had poured into the mixing bowl, was instead quite sticky and seemingly more intent on clinging to the bowl and her hands than anything else.

She looked up with a furrowed brow as Nicholas strolled into the kitchen. The baby was cradled snugly in his arms. He observed her efforts for a moment, then hooked a foot about the leg of a chair, and sat.

"What are you doing?"

She waved him into silence. "Don't talk to me now, I'm trying to think."

"More flour," she said, and poured a heaping quantity from yet another bag. She plunged both hands into the bowl, and kneaded with determination.

Nicholas hid a grin behind his hand. "What are you making? Jamaican buns?"

"No . . . no, just regular bread. Nothing fancy."

"You seem to have a bit too much flour in the bowl . . . and not enough moisture. Maybe if you put some more water in?" he suggested helpfully.

Summer looked up at him. There was a large patch of flour on one cheek. "Do you think that might work?"

Nicholas shrugged. "It couldn't hurt."

"Is Gavin back yet with the cradle? I want to be finished by the time . . ."

Nicholas smiled. "So, you've finally decided to take my advice about the cooking."

Summer kneaded the dough again. ''No. I just felt like baking some bread. . . .''

''And frying mackerel? Just out of the blue?''

She shot a thoughtful glance in his direction. ''You're not going to say anything to Gavin . . . I mean, tell him that . . . that I'm doing this for him?''

Nicholas gave her a familiar wink. ''Not a word.''

He shifted the baby as she began to stir. ''How're things going with him?''

Her brow furrowed. ''I'm not sure most of the time.''

''Well,'' he nodded, '' this cooking should do it like nothing else can.''

''Uhmmm-hmmm,'' she agreed, then changed the subject just as neatly as he often did. ''Where's Rob?'' she asked.

''Out with his friends. They went up to Thatch Hill to have a cookout. You know, curried goat and mannish water, that kind of thing.''

Summer stopped her kneading for a moment. ''Mannish what?''

''It's a kind of soup made from goat head.''

''Soup . . . out of a goat's head?'' Her nose wrinkled. ''It doesn't sound very appetizing.''

Nicholas bit the corner of one cheek. ''I dunno . . . it's Gavin's favorite thing. Maybe you should try making that too.''

Summer rolled the solid ball of dough from the bowl onto the flat of the tabletop. ''I'm not cooking anything that involves boiling and mashing some poor creature's head.''

Nicholas gave the ball of dough a little prod with a finger. ''It looks a bit hard.''

''It's supposed to be hard,'' Summer said. ''It'll be nice and soft in an hour or two . . . after it's risen.''

''Ah . . .'' Nicholas nodded. ''So, what's next? The fish?''

''I thought I'd do the green bananas first. Then the fish. Then the sauce.''

His brows lifted. ''Sauce?''

''Sauce. I found a recipe for a savory coconut gravy in a

recipe book in one of the drawers. Should go nicely with everything else.''

''Well,'' Nicholas said, coming to his feet, ''I'll leave you to it. I guess . . . you and Gavin will be wanting to eat alone tonight . . . so, I'll be dining out. . . .''

Summer flashed him a grateful smile. ''I owe you one.''

Gavin returned an hour later and was immediately greeted by the pungent smell of burning fish and something else he couldn't quite make out. He heaved the crib through the open door, and bellowed: ''Nicholas.''

It was several moments before his brother's head appeared at the top of the staircase.

''What the hell is that odor?''

Nicholas came down slowly. ''Summer's cooking.''

Gavin pushed the door open wider and took a great gulp of fresh sea air. ''She's what?''

''Cooking.''

Gavin shoved the ornately carved wooden crib toward his brother. ''Why in the name of God didn't you try to stop her?''

Nicholas gave his brother a completely innocent stare. ''She was quite determined. You know what she's like.''

''Take the crib up,'' Gavin said. ''I'll have a talk with her.''

Nicholas hoisted the baby bed with little effort. ''Gavin. . . .''

''Yeah?''

''She's been cooking all afternoon. Be gentle with her.''

Gavin exchanged a look with his younger sibling. ''You put her up to this didn't you?''

Nicholas threw back his head and laughed. ''Come on. Would I do that?''

A smile played around Gavin's mouth. ''Okay,'' he said nodding, ''but don't be too surprised if I jump into the game too.''

A look of mutual affection passed between the two men. Nicholas propped the crib on his knee. ''She's a nice girl you know . . . not at all what you might expect.''

Gavin nodded. ''I know.''

In the kitchen, Summer was hard at work over the sink, scraping valiantly at a pile of severely scorched hunks of flesh, barely recognizable as fish. Everything had gone wrong. First the pan of oil had caught fire, then an entire loaf of bread had fallen from her hands and broken into pieces on the floor. She had spent a good long while down on her knees cleaning up the crumbs. Then, to top it all, every last piece of fish had stuck and burned in the pan. She had been very careful with the quantity of oil she poured into the frying pan the second time around. But, by the looks of it, it had not been at all sufficient. The only thing that had come out even halfway decent, was the coconut gravy, which had somehow developed a nice and creamy consistency. Everything else, was in total shambles.

Gavin came to a halt in the doorway, and grappled for a bit, with a strong urge to break into gales of uncontrollable laughter. She was, very earnestly, removing huge chunks of charred flesh from each fish, and attempting to conceal their battered appearance with pieces of lettuce.

When he was finally in control of his mirth, he said, ''Can I help . . . with anything?''

Summer spun around, and dismay flashed across her face. ''Oh . . . I didn't hear you come in. I . . . I'm not finished yet.''

Gavin rubbed a hand down the length of his jaw, and carefully considered his next words. ''Would you like to take a break from it?''

Summer blinked at him. ''A break? No . . . no, I'm almost finished. It's dinner you know. If you go up and change, I'll be done by the time you come back down.''

''Don't need any help setting the table?''

She smiled, and Gavin's heart turned over. ''No. I can manage . . . really,'' she said when he still hesitated. ''I cooked your favorite meal. . . .''

Gavin bent his head to hide a chuckle. ''Really? . . . and what's that?''

''Boiled green bananas and mackerel. Freshly baked

bread. . . . and a coconut surprise sauce. 'Rundown,' I think it's called.''

''Ah,'' Gavin said since it was the only thing he could manage without giving vent to the mirth bubbling within him. ''Well, I guess I'd better go up and change. Is this a formal dinner? I mean, do I need a tuxedo or anything like that?''

''Silly,'' Summer grinned, ''no, you don't need a tux. Just clean hands. . . .''

Gavin gave his hands a glance. ''Right. I'll be back.''

By the time he was back down, Summer had managed to arrange most of the food on the table. She had been forced to use the largest bowls she could find, since there were no serving platters to be found. The fish, which was the dish in need of the most assistance, had been placed on a bed of dark green lettuce, and the scorched parts hidden by carefully cut circles of onion and bright red tomato. The boiled green bananas were put into another dish, and draped attractively around the circumference of the bowl. The bread, which had been a bit difficult to cut, had been sawed into two hunks, nicely buttered, and garnished with a handful of sea grapes. She brought in the gravy boat filled with the coconut sauce known as rundown, last.

She was in the process of carefully positioning a colorful spray of bougainvillea in the middle of the table, when Gavin reappeared at the top of the stairs. He had changed into a black silk shirt and tapered white pants. His brow furrowed for a moment at the sound of clinking that was coming from the little dining room. The entire house was just filled with the tangy aroma of burned fish, and he was momentarily glad that the rest of the Champagne clan would not be at the table. The dinner would require the utmost tact and skill on his part, if Summer was to survive it without her feelings being put through the wringer. He was just beginning to realize how very easy it was to hurt her, and, that was the last thing in the world that he wanted to do now.

Summer turned at the soft sound of footsteps. The table was all ready, and if she did say so herself, looked quite presentable.

Gavin took a steadying breath, and entered. Maybe it wouldn't be so very terrible. After all, how bad could it really be? The important thing was that she had tried, and very hard, too, by the looks of it. The very least he could do was pretend to enjoy the meal.

Summer waved a hand. "Well . . . what do you think?" She was almost light-headed with the strong sense of accomplishment that swept over her.

"It's . . ." and Gavin struggled for the appropriate word, "very . . . colorful." And it was, with a variety of vegetables and flowers arranged on plates and in vases. What she lacked in culinary skill, he noted with reluctance, she certainly made up for in artistic flair.

"You can sit there," Summer said, pointing to the chair at the head of the table.

Gavin sat, then remembered his manners and stood again until she was seated. He unfolded the linen napkin that had been rolled and fitted into a fluted glass.

"You spent a lot of time working on this . . . are you sure I deserve such a spread?"

Summer smiled. "I just wanted to show you that I'm a woman of many talents."

"Uhmm," Gavin said, and placed the napkin in his lap.

"Where's Nicky?" she asked after a moment of shifting cutlery about.

"Upstairs with the baby."

"Oh," she paused, then after a bit of thinking, said, "he was supposed to be eating out . . . should I invite him down?"

The suggestion, galvanized Gavin into speech. "No. . . ." he said, before he could control his response. Then more calmly, "No. He's . . . he's definitely going out. Friends . . . an invitation. . . ."

"Is he taking the baby too?"

"No, he'll leave her with us . . . me."

"I'll be happy to look after her," Summer said, and she spooned an alarming quantity of soggy bananas onto his plate.

Gavin touched the back of her hand when it appeared that

she was going to give him the entire lot in the bowl. ''That's . . . that's more than enough bananas, how about some fish?''

Summer set the bowl back on the table. ''How many pieces do you want? I made plenty. Enough for tomorrow too.''

''One . . . one is good.''

She picked up the gravy boat. ''And some sauce?''

Gavin gave the creamy concoction a doubtful look. ''What kind of sauce is it?''

''It's called rundown. Don't you know it?''

Gavin nodded. ''Yes, but not as a sauce. It's a whole separate dish . . . you know?''

''Oh . . . it is?'' and an expression of disappointment crept across her face. ''So, you don't want any of it then?''

''Yes. Yes . . . I do. It looks creamy. Good and creamy.''

Summer poured a generous amount onto the bananas and fish, then proffered another dish. ''Bread?''

Gavin accepted one of the hunks and placed it on his plate. ''Well . . .'' he said, after waiting for her to dish her own food. ''Let's eat.''

He speared a piece of banana and a chunk of fish with his fork, placed both into his mouth, and chewed. Summer watched, an expression of happy anticipation on her face.

''How is it?'' she asked after a couple chews.

''Water . . .'' Gavin said hoarsely, ''where's the water?''

He grabbed wildly at a glass and chugged the entire thing in a single shot.

''I put some scotch bonnet peppers in the fish. Nicky said you like it spicy.''

''Remind me to have a talk with Nicky later.''

Summer took a bite of the fish on her plate. After a bit, she said, ''mine's not so bad.''

Gavin picked up a hunk of bread, and struggled to break it in two. ''I think I bit into an entire pepper . . . that's probably what did it.''

They ate in silence for the next several minutes. There was a brief moment of grave concern when Gavin wondered whether he'd broken a tooth on a piece of bread. Never before in his very varied experience with breads and the like, had he ever come across anything that was quite as hard. But, he struggled on valiantly, deliberately soaking everything on his plate in the coconut sauce, the only thing on the menu that was anywhere close to being halfway decent. In just ten minutes, he had managed to swallow several chunks of banana and fish whole, finding it entirely more practical to do it that way. By the time his plate was almost empty, he found himself praying that there not be any dessert to follow.

Finally, he placed the knife and fork on his plate, and Summer shot a quick glance in his direction. Strangely enough, he appeared to be enjoying the meal a lot more than she was. "More?" she asked, her hands poised to serve additional quantities of bananas and fish.

Gavin patted his stomach, which felt more than a little bit unsteady. "That's it for me, I think." He sat back in his chair, and ran a hand across his forehead. It was over, thank God. Never, never again, would he allow her to cook for him. He'd be willing to do just about anything at all to prevent it. Even hire a housekeeper, or a cordon bleu chef. Anything.

"Sure you don't want some more? There's plenty."

"No, no. I can't take a morsel more."

Summer grinned. "Well, it's a good thing I threw your . . . friend Janet's cake out then."

"You threw the cake out?"

"I did."

Gavin shook his head. "You are probably the single worst employee I have ever had."

Summer sat back, crossed her legs, and pointed a mild look in his direction. "Is that all I am? An employee?"

"I don't think I'd better answer that before I get myself into some trouble."

"Coward," Summer said, then, "so . . . did you like the dinner?"

"I've never had another like it."

At almost that exact moment, Nicholas poked a head through

the doorway. ''Ah . . . dinner's over.'' He walked across to slap his brother on the back. ''Had a good meal?''

Twin pairs of black eyes met for a moment, and Gavin smiled. ''Summer's prepared some for you too. I told her that you were going out .. but since you're still here, with all this food . . . it seems such a shame to waste it. Doesn't it? Summer . . . would you mind dishing him a plate? Growing young man that he is. He needs to keep his strength up.''

''Sure,'' Summer agreed before Nicholas could utter a word of protest.

Gavin pulled out a chair, and motioned to it. ''Sit.'' He unfolded the extra napkin that had been used as additional decoration on the tabletop, and threw it onto his brother's lap.

With a very characteristic Champagne wink, he reached across, patted Nicholas on the back, and said: ''Enjoy.''

CHAPTER TWENTY

Later that evening, Summer was in bed nicely propped against the pillows. A large floor plan of the cottage was unfurled across her chest, and her hair hung in thick ebony waves about her shoulders. One hand zipped across the paper, making changes here and there, adding cryptic notes, and occasionally pausing to score a line through a diagram. She was so engrossed in her work, that it was several moments before the soft knocking on her bedroom door caught her attention. She paused for a moment and listened. At night, there were always noises about the house. Sometimes it was a can rattling about, caught by a sudden gust of sea air. Other times, it was the sound of floorboards creaking.

When the noise came again, she asked, "Is someone there?"

She put the paper aside, slid into the soft bedroom slippers at the side of the bed, and padded to the door.

Gavin? Her heartbeat picked up a pace. Maybe he had come to ask her to his bed. She ran quick fingers through her hair, adjusted the shoulders of her silky white pajamas, and pulled open the door.

She peered into the darkened corridor, and a wave of disappointment swept through her. ''Rob?''

The boy was leaning against the far wall, apparently in some manner of distress. ''Can you .. tell me where my . . . room is?'' A shard of fear shot through her. ''Oh . . . oh my God . . . Rob, what's happened?'' The boy attempted to push himself off the wall, but gave up after a few ineffectual tries. Summer felt about for the light switch. ''I'll go get Gavin . . . you're hurt.''

''No . . . no Gavin,'' the boy slurred, and a strong wave of alcohol drove Summer backwards.

''You're drunk,'' she whispered fiercely. ''Gavin's going to kill you.''

The boy put a finger up to his lips, and a slack grin twisted his lips. ''Sshh . . . don't tell . . . I . . . feel . . .'' and with mercurial suddenness, he bent over and was sick all over the floor.

Summer took a breath. She could already see the backlash from all of this. And, she would be blamed for it of course. Gavin would find some way of making all of this her fault. There was little else to do though. The boy was in no condition to face his older cousin, who would, quite likely, give him the hiding he deserved.

''Come over here,'' she said, glancing up and down the hallway. ''You can sleep it off in my room.''

Rob weaved for a moment, then somehow propelled himself into motion. ''I . . . I just had a little . . . Jamaican rum. . . .'' He raised a hand to show Summer how much he'd had.

''Are you sure that's all you had. . . ?'' she whispered.

''Maybe . . . maybe a bit more. . . .'' and, he threw back his head and cackled loudly.

''Hush,'' Summer said, and she hurried him into her room and closed the door. ''Go and stand under the shower,'' she said, ''while I clean up outside.''

Rob blinked at her like a forlorn puppy. ''In my clothes? . . . I'll . . . I'll get all wet.''

Summer gave him a little shove toward the bathroom door.

"Take the clothes off first. I'll bring some of Gavin's things in . . . he's got a closet full of stuff in here. Go on."

She waited until she heard the sound of the shower, before going to the large dark wood wardrobe. She was in the middle of hunting through stacks of pants and shirts, when there was another knock on the door. Her hands stilled, and for a minute she considered not answering. After all, the shower was going. Maybe, whoever it was would just go away.

"Summer?"

Her heartbeat slowed a bit. Nicholas. She went to the door, pulled it open, and dragged him inside.

Before he could say a word, she said, "don't mention a word of this to Gavin . . . okay?"

"About you being sick in the hall? I don't think he'd be upset about that . . . he's not himself either."

Summer's ears perked up. "Not himself? What do you mean?"

"That's why I came down . . . do you have any stomach medicine?"

"Stomach medicine?" Summer repeated stupidly.

"You know . . . kaopectate . . . that sort of thing."

"Oh . . . yes . . . yes, I think I brought some with me. It's in . . . in the bathroom."

Nicholas nodded. "I'll get it."

Summer grabbed his arm. "Rob . . . Rob's in there. He's drunk."

Nicholas whipped around, and his eyes took on a gleam very much like the one that was sure to appear in his older brother's eyes, once he found out about this little episode.

"What do you mean drunk?"

"Don't ask me what I mean. He's in there taking a shower, and he's stinking drunk I tell you. He's the one who was sick on the floor. Not me."

"Gavin's going to blister that little idiot's tail. . . ."

"Not if he doesn't find out . . . he doesn't have to Nicholas. I won't tell him. You . . . you don't have to either."

"If we let him get away with this, he'll probably try some of this tomfoolery again."

"Come on, are you going to tell me that you never did something stupid when you were his age?"

"I did, and I paid for it dearly."

"I think he's suffered enough. Gavin's not feeling well anyway, let's not bother him with this." She touched his arm. "Nicky? Give him a chance this time? If he ever does this again, I'll not interfere."

"You know if Gavin ever finds out that we did this. . . ."

"I know . . . it'll be hell to pay for everyone concerned."

"And . . . this doesn't bother you?"

Summer blinked. "Not very much. The poor kid, I think he's had enough for one evening."

"Well . . . you take the medicine up to Gavin then. I'll stay here with my idiot cousin."

Summer raised up unto tiptoe, and pressed a kiss against his cheek. "Sounds like a plan . . ." then, as an afterthought, she said, "get him into bed . . . and don't damage the plans, put them on the bedside table . . . and, . . ."

"I know," Nicholas said with a long-suffering sigh, "clean up the floor outside."

Summer grinned. " And get me the bottle from the medicine cabinet in the bathroom."

Minutes later, she was standing outside Gavin's room on the third floor of the house, bottle and spoon clutched tightly in hand. She raised a hand, and knocked. A voice that was barely recognizable as Gavin's, bade her enter. She pushed the door open, and padded softly to the bed. He lay on his side, back toward the door.

"Gavin?"

He turned over, and glared at her with shiny eyes. "Where's Nicky?"

"He . . . he's down on the second floor. . . ." That was true enough.

"He went to get me something."

"I've got it."

Gavin turned onto the flat of his back. "God. What did you put in that coconut stuff you made today?"

Summer sat on the edge of the bed, unscrewed the bottle cap and prepared to pour a spoonful. "Are you saying that you're sick because of me?"

"Damn right that's what I'm saying."

She shoved the spoon at him. "Don't swear at me. Drink."

He propped himself up on his elbows, and gently, she placed the spoon in his mouth.

"You're not finished yet . . . open," she said when he prepared to ease himself down again.

His brow furrowed, and his eyes took on a petulant boyish look. "I hate that stuff. I don't want anymore of it."

"Come on," Summer insisted, "just one more. You'll feel so much better in an hour or two."

"I don't want it."

She stroked the side of his face. "Come on . . . just one more."

After a moment, he opened, and she placed the spoon in his mouth again. He swallowed with a grimace, and sank back onto the pillows.

"Were you sent here by one of our competitors to finish me off? Was that the plan?"

Summer replaced the cap on the bottle, and rested it on the bedside table. "Let me rub your stomach for you."

"After all you've done . . . you want to rub my stomach?"

"I haven't done anything . . . I ate the same things you did this afternoon. Nicky did too. Why aren't we sick?"

"I dunno. Maybe you took an antidote or something."

Summer reached forward to feel his brow. "Well. You're not feverish . . . so I guess you can't be delirious."

He gave her a very intent look, then allowed his eyelids to close. "Has Rob gotten back in yet?"

Summer swallowed. "Yes. He's in."

"The baby?"

"Fast asleep in Nicky's room I think."

His eyes came open again. ‘‘I’m never sick. Do you know that?’’

Summer nodded. ‘‘I know,’’ then when she sensed that he was calmer, said, ‘‘let me rub your stomach for you.’’

He made no attempt to move away from her as she slowly rolled up the large T-shirt. The black eyes watched as she came fully onto the bed, and prepared to lean across him.

‘‘Be careful what you rub,’’ he said, ‘‘I’m not that sick.’’

Summer smiled, and the warmth of it was clearly reflected in her eyes. ‘‘Don’t worry babe . . . when I decide to rub you there, you’ll be fully able to appreciate it.’’

He laughed then grimaced when a spasm gripped at his innards. ‘‘Rub away . . . babe.’’

The pet name rolled easily from his tongue, and for one delirious moment, Summer was able to convince herself that he really meant it.

Her hands circled his abdomen in slow, easy strokes. The hard, washboard muscles rippled beneath her fingers, and his eyelids lowered to hide the smoky beginnings of passion. She massaged until her fingers were tired.

‘‘Feel any better now?’’

His hands came up to still hers. ‘‘Much.’’

Summer leaned lower to press a kiss against the hard flatness of his stomach. ‘‘I’d better go back down.’’

His fingers tangled in her hair. ‘‘So soon?’’

A ripple of surprise, which she hurried to conceal, flickered for a brief instant in her eyes. ‘‘You mean you want me to stay?’’

‘‘Do you have something else to do?’’

She thought of Rob lying in her bed just below, and slowly shook her head. ‘‘No. Nothing. But, even if I did, I’d put that all aside for you.’’

He smiled, and the inky blackness of his eyes sucked her in. ‘‘You would? Just for me?’’

‘‘Just for you.’’

He peeled back the corner of the blanket, and patted a spot just beside him.

"Come under."

Summer kicked off her bedroom slippers, and slid her long limbs beneath the covers. He turned onto his side, a hand propped against one temple.

"So? . . . Ms. Stevens, here you are in my bed . . . and here I am as sick as a dog."

She ran a finger down the side of his face. "A very cute dog."

He stilled the finger, and brought it to his mouth. "You know . . . that in order to put this thing between us to rest . . . we're gonna have to . . ."

She leaned forward to kiss his chin. "Uhmm . . . I agree."

He turned his head to gently sample her lips. His mouth wandered across the side of her face, leaving a line of little kisses. "But . . ."

"Uhmm?" She was almost breathless with anticipation.

". . . not here."

Her head jerked back. "Not here? What do you mean?"

"I mean. We can't here."

"Here . . . in this bed. . . ?" She moved her head and took one of his earlobes into her mouth. A thrill of raw sensation raced through her at the sound of his harsh intake of breath.

"No . . . in this house . . ."

"Gavin . . ." and, she bit the lobe gently.

A sound of pure pleasure purred from the back of his throat. "We have to wait . . . until the cottage is fixed up. Then . . . we can. . . ."

She drew back, and her eyes were as pulling as liquid honey. "I don't want to wait any longer . . . don't ask me to. . . ."

His fingers threaded their way through her hair, and her neck arched involuntarily.

He placed a warm kiss against her throat. "I have a feeling that . . . we're gonna need a lot of privacy . . . lots of space . . . soundproof walls . . . or at least, a great distance between wherever we are and wherever everyone else is."

Summer lay back against the pillows. Her eyes were the

color of dark brandy now. "You mean . . . it's going to be that good?"

His tongue snaked into the depth of one ear, and a tiny squeal of sound bubbled from between her lips before she could prevent it.

"Need I say more?"

"No . . ." she said breathlessly, "but I'll say it . . . more, please."

He rolled her completely into his arms. "I'm a sick man. Have some mercy."

Summer forced herself to take a calming breath. After all, this was exactly where she had wanted to be for the longest time. "Okay. But, we'll have to talk about something sterile." She reached out to massage his temples. "Think."

"Ahh . . . okay. Let's talk about you. Did you have a good childhood?"

"Yes." Summer snuggled into the groove of his neck. It felt so good to be held by him. So very, very good. His hand came up to massage her neck. "Tell me about it. Everything about it. I want to know."

"Everything?" Summer looked up at him, and a sunburst of enlightenment broke slowly somewhere deep inside her. And, this was accompanied by a rush of thick confusion. It couldn't be love that she felt for him. She didn't even believe in it. It was all a ridiculous lie made up by the Hollywood hit machine. It didn't exist. And, even if there was some remote chance that it did, it couldn't be happening to her. Not now, not with a man who didn't believe in it either.

And, the man in question lay on his side, looking down at her, completely oblivious to the earth-shattering revelation that had just occurred deep inside her. "Summer?"

She blinked a couple of times. "Hmmm?"

"Why did your parents give you that name?"

She relaxed into his arms again. "My . . . my sister was abducted in the summer of '68. So they decided to name me Summer . . . so that . . . well, as a sort of memorial to her."

"Abducted?"

"Yes."

"How?"

"Walking . . . walking home from school one day. She . . . just never showed up. . . ." This was the first time in weeks that she had thought about it, so it was a while before she could get the words out with any semblance of coherency. But, he let her talk at her own pace, and when she struggled, he just held her, and waited. She found herself telling him everything that had happened. She started at the very beginning, and worked her way up. She told him about the chain letter, about catching her fiancé in bed with Alyssa, about losing her job, about finding out that she was adopted. When she was through, it was as though a huge weight had been lifted from her. She felt strangely reborn.

He stroked her neck. "And then I showed up to give you more hell." He lifted one of her hands, and very subtly changed the subject. "You haven't had a professional manicure since you got here to Jamaica."

Summer gave her nails a totally unconcerned inspection. A month ago, this would have worried her greatly, but now, she found that she couldn't have cared less. There were more important things.

"They're shorter . . . you don't like them?"

He kissed each pink shell-like nail. "I like you."

"You . . . do?" The disclosure rattled around in her head like a loose ball in a pinball machine.

"I do."

She beamed. "How much?"

He traced the outline of her lips. "I guess . . . about as much as you like me . . . maybe even a bit more."

"Oh." And hot blood rushed to her face, but she didn't care even if he could see how happy he had just made her. Of course, he wasn't to know that she had just discovered that she might be in love with him. But it didn't matter, he had admitted to liking her, and that was a massive step in the right direction.

She wrapped both arms around him, and the huge empty space that had always been there inside her, filled a bit.

"Are you going to go back to treating me as though you . . . hate me? Tomorrow I mean?"

"No. Not tomorrow." He pulled her in to rest against the warmth of his chest. "Just . . . promise me something. . . ."

"Anything."

"Don't ever cook for me again?"

"What?" She attempted to rise, but he held her still until her struggles quieted. "Promise me."

"You mean . . . I'm no good?"

He shook his head. "You're no good. Not at cooking anyway."

Summer laughed despite herself. "And you ate all that food this evening."

He nodded. "Just goes to show you how much I . . . like you then."

"Uhmm." That response satisfied her, and she settled in closer, sighing in pure contentment as every breath of his stirred the soft fragrance of her hair.

"Gavin?"

"Yes?" And a hand came to rest softly against the skin of her back.

"Who is Janet?" There, she had said it. He had avoided answering her earlier, and it made her suspicious. Very suspicious. The thought that there might be some other woman out there whom he was secretly seeing, made her crazy.

She tilted her head to look at him. "Are you seeing her?"

He smiled. "Are you always this possessive?"

"You're not taking me seriously," she said, and there was a trace of hurt in her voice.

He stroked a gritty thumb over her top, then bottom lips. "Janet . . . is no one for you to worry about. We agreed years ago that a romantic relationship between us would be a bad idea."

"You mean . . . you agreed. She didn't seem convinced on that."

"Trust me on this one," he said, "she is not my type, at all. Not like you . . . however."

"Didn't you tell me that I wasn't your type either a while ago?"

A husky laugh rumbled from somewhere deep in his chest. "Surely, I didn't say that . . . exactly?"

"I dunno . . . if it wasn't that exactly, it was something pretty darn close."

"Ah," he said.

"Is that all I'm going to get? Just an 'ah?' "

He tilted her chin up to press a quick kiss on her lips. "For now."

CHAPTER TWENTY-ONE

Over the next several weeks, Summer worked like a demon on the cottage. She was up sometimes even before the first streaks of dawn tinted the morning skies. Breakfast would be a hurried affair of orange juice and toast, then she would let herself quietly out the front door, and walk the distance up the beach to the cottage. She would spend her entire day there, keeping a close eye on the builders as they ripped out walls, replaced floorboards, and enlarged certain spaces. When they got around to working on the bedrooms, she was there, too, helping with the removal of the ancient and very mildewed wallpapering, making sure that the form and substance of each room remained essentially unchanged.

It was during one of these very extended sessions of stripping away layers of papering from the bedroom walls, that her tool fell against a rectangular metal plaque that had been inset somehow into the very fabric of the foundation. It took a bit of doing to get all of the paper out of the way but when it was all gone, the dim yellow of the bronze plate winked back at her.

She ran a finger along the flat of it, feeling out the blackened rows of lettering. Her heart pounded with excitement. The plaque was rough and appeared to be very old. And, the language scratched upon the face of it, was definitely not English, or even one based on a standard Latin alphabet.

With careful hands, she cleaned the face of it with a tiny toothbrush, scrubbing gently until she could clearly read the words carved into the metal face. She worked with a quiet intensity, head bent forward, eyes slightly squinted because of the detail work. She was so absorbed, that when two long arms folded around her waist from behind, she actually started.

"Nicholas. Why do you always creep up on me like that? You almost scared the life out of me."

He laughed, and spun her around. "Did you think it was one of your builder friends getting a little too fresh with the boss?"

She shoved the blackened toothbrush into a small can of soapy water, then rested both hands on her hips. "Where's the baby?"

"At home. . . ."

"All alone? Have you lost your mind?"

He leaned forward to give her a quick peck on the cheek. "I love the way you talk to me. No, she's not alone. Mik's here."

"Oh, that's right. He's up from college this week."

"Yeah. Poor kid. Needs a break from all that studying. He's doing a research paper on Jamaican traditions and how they're tied to Africa. I promised to help him."

Summer's eyebrows rose. "You?"

He gave the tip of her nose a little tap. "Me. I know I don't look it, but I was quite a good student in my time."

"Oh . . . I didn't mean . . ."

He wrapped an arm about her waist. "I'm just kidding with you. Don't get all serious on me now." His eyes swept the room. "The place is just tore up isn't it?"

"It'll look a lot better in a couple of weeks." She tugged at his hand. "Come have a look at this. Do you know what language that is?" and she pointed to the metal on the wall.

Nicholas squinted at the small letters. After a brief look, he said, "Haven't a clue. But," and he looked at her with a smile, " I know someone who might. Why don't you take down the inscription, and you can come with Mik and me when we go see the Obeah woman in Thatch Hill."

He rubbed the metal with the flat of his thumb. "It looks very old. Chances are it was written by a runaway African bondsman. Madame Kofo might know what it means though. . . ." He gave her a squeeze. "That's if you can tear yourself away from my big brother for one evening."

Summer gave him a friendly little shove. "Shaddup. Who's this Obeah woman anyway? And why are you going to see her?"

Nicholas took up a comfortable position on the floor, leaned back on his elbows, and stretched his long legs before him. "You know what Obeah is don't you?"

Summer turned back to the wall, and resumed scrubbing the metal. "Nope. I don't. What is it? A secret society or something?"

Nicholas clucked his tongue in mock disgust. "Haitians call it *juju.* The rest of the world knows it as voodoo. In the Caribbean, it's called obeah. It's essentially the same thing though. There's been a bit of divergence in practice between the islands over the years. But, the core of it is the same."

Summer had paused in her vigorous brushing of the metal, and her mouth had fallen slack with disbelief. "And . . . you . . . you want me to go with you there . . . to this . . . this juju woman?"

"Obeah," Nicholas corrected obligingly.

"Whatever," Summer said, and waved the toothbrush absently, splashing the ground liberally with soapsuds. "I . . . why would I want to go to a woman like that? I'm a Christian, don't you know that? I don't believe in any of this . . . this hoodoo, Obeah, or whatever you want to call it."

Nicholas sat up. "I can see you've been thoroughly brainwashed by western thinking. Obeah is a legitimate African religion. As legitimate as Christianity."

"Well that's not what . . ."

"I know," he interrupted. "That's not what you've seen on TV. But, that's just Hollywood. Why don't you come and find out for yourself firsthand?"

Summer rested the toothbrush in the rusty can, wiped the face of the metal with a soft cloth. "Will there be any slaughtering of animals?"

Nicholas grinned. "Nope."

"Any drinking of blood?"

"No drinking of blood."

"What about incantations to the forces of darkness?"

"There may be incantations, but not to. . . ."

"That's it," Summer cut him off. "I'm not going."

Nicholas came to his feet in one easy movement. "This is a once in a lifetime opportunity. Something that you'll remember when you're back in the States. . . ."

Summer shook her head. "No. As long as there's any incanting going on, I'm not going."

"I'll be there . . . Mik will be there," he added persuasively. "You'll be perfectly safe. There's nothing to worry about at all. She may even give you a little something to help you snare Gavin."

Summer slanted a sideways glance at him. "Gavin?"

Nicholas nodded. "Many women who want to trap . . . ah . . . coax their men into matrimony or whatever, go to visit Madame Kofo. Her success rate, I've heard, is legendary. She's been known to save marriages on the brink of divorce, to bring the most unlikely of lovers together. . . ." He let the remainder of his sentence trail off. It was clear that he had her full attention now.

"And . . . how does she do all this?"

Nicholas winked. "The only way you'll know is if you come with us this evening."

"But, Gavin . . ."

"He can spare you for one evening."

"He won't like it though. I'm sure."

"Since when have you cared about whether he likes something or not?"

Summer blinked. "I care. Nicky, I don't see why you want me to come so very much."

He shrugged, then turned away to stare out a bald window. "I like doing things with you . . . that's all. Of late, you've been spending a lot of time with Gavin in the evenings. Playing cards, talking. . . . Hardly any time with me. We used to talk . . . remember?"

"I remember. And we still talk. . . ." She went across to give him a hug.

He held her for a minute, and Summer wondered why it was that she felt absolutely no attraction at all for him and every possible ounce of feeling for his older brother.

"I'll go with you then," she said after a bit. "Even though I'll probably be scared out of my wits the whole time."

He held her at arm's length. "You'll go?"

She smiled. "Yes."

"We can't tell Gavin though. . . ."

Before Summer could think of a suitable reply, a voice from somewhere in the doorway said, "Can't tell Gavin what?"

Summer spun around, a smile on her face. "You're home early."

Gavin came fully into the room. He was dressed in tapered black slacks and a white shirt, slightly open at the neck. And the simple sight of him, with hands in pockets, so relaxed, so terribly sexy, caused a flush of excitement to stain Summer's face.

Nicholas pressed Summer's hand. "I'll see you back at the house." He exchanged a knowing glance with his brother, then hustled through the doorway.

Gavin turned to watch him walk through the tiny sitting room. "I have a feeling my brother's got a crush on you," he said after a minute.

Summer wiped her hands on a cloth rag. The situation would certainly be ironic, if that were the case. "Nicky's just affectionate. His feelings for me are strictly brotherly. Nothing more."

Gavin closed the distance between them, removed the cloth from her hands. "How long before the cottage is done?"

Summer did her best to adequately control the tremble in her knees. "Another month . . . maybe two."

He bent his head to take her lips in a soft kiss. Against her mouth, he murmured. "I can't wait that long."

Summer ran her tongue along the inner curve of his bottom lip, pausing to sample each dip and curve, probing and tasting the entire length of it, like a bee foraging for honey. His hands came up to cup her shoulder blades, and he deepened the kiss, curving her to fit his body.

From somewhere on the perimeter of the house, the sounds of hammering came, but neither heard nor cared.

"We can go to a hotel," Summer murmured against the side of his face.

Gavin turned her lips back. Between sweet little kisses, he said, "Tonight?"

"Uhmm," Summer agreed. Then, she remembered Nicholas. She pulled her mouth away. "No. Not tonight. It can't be tonight, I promised Nicky. . . ."

Gavin ran his hand up the flat of her back, sticking a finger under the lace bra, tugging impatiently. "Promised Nicky what?"

She was almost delirious with need. The words stumbled from her lips. "That . . . I'd go with him . . . and Mik . . . research."

He pulled back for a moment. "Research?"

She nodded, and tried not to look too guilty. "Afro Jamaican customs . . . that sort of thing."

"Ah," he said, "Mik's paper. But what do you have to do with it?"

Summer massaged the small of his back. "Nothing really. Nicky just invited me along."

Gavin brushed a swatch of hair back from her face. "Have you noticed that whenever we're in the same room . . . we can't keep our hands off each other?"

Summer nodded. "I'd noticed."

"And you're willing to turn all that down for an outing with Nicky?"

"I promised I'd go."

He smiled, and a faint glimmer of some emotion shone for a brief instant in his eyes.

"Ok. But, Friday . . . Saturday . . . Sunday. Those days are all mine."

It was early evening when they all piled into the Jeep. Gavin leaned into the driver's side window, the baby safely cradled in his arms.

"Nicholas . . ."

"You worry too much Gavin," Nicholas interrupted. "Trust me, everything will be fine."

Gavin nodded. "That's what worries me. Your fine and my fine are often two different things entirely." He looked across at Summer, and a little crease broke the smoothness of his forehead. "Sure you still want to go?"

Three pairs of black eyes were leveled on her for a moment.

She swallowed, and boned up her flagging courage. "Yes. It'll be fun. Something I'll never forget I'm sure."

Gavin straightened away from the window, tapped the side of the Jeep. In a low tone that only Nicholas was able to adequately decipher, he said, "bring her back in one piece."

Nicholas threw the truck into gear. "We'll be back in a couple of hours."

Gavin stood watching until the Jeep was out of view, and all that remained, was a cloud of brown dust circling in the air. Then, he turned and walked back into the house, and up the stairs to the third floor. He put the baby down in the crib, and played with her for a while. He kissed the tiny feet, and tickled her stomach.

"You look a lot like me don't you?" he whispered to her. The baby stared back at him with what he was certain was great understanding.

He covered her carefully with a light blanket, "time for bed

. . . go to sleep.'' The huge black eyes blinked at him for a moment, then she released a volley of strenuous bellows. Gavin reached into the crib, lifted her out again, and bounced her on his shoulder.

''Rob?''

When there was no reply, he walked down the hallway. Throbbing music reverberated from just beyond the closed door. He pounded on the wood. ''Rob.''

The door swung back almost immediately. The boy was dressed in an oversized T-shirt, droopy jeans, and tennis shoes.

Gavin gave him a tolerant look. ''Go down and warm up a bottle for the baby,'' he said. ''. . . and turn that music down.''

The baby had quieted almost as soon as he lifted her out of the crib. She lay on Gavin's shoulder now, making contented little burbling sounds. Gavin patted the little back with one of his large hands.

''You like being held by me, hmmm? You're like someone else I know.''

He went to sit in a comfortable chair facing one of the windows. The sky had turned a delicate pink in the approaching dusk, and a comfortable ocean breeze drifted through the wooden slatted window. It was the kind of evening that a mere month or two ago, would have brought him some measure of contentment. But, it brought him none whatsoever tonight. He found himself glancing at his watch, and wondering repeatedly why he had allowed Nicholas to take Summer out into a rugged country area like Thatch Hill, and at night too. Mik would be okay, of course. He was a young man much accustomed to the antics of his brother, but Summer. . . . If anything at all happened to her, he would thrash Nicholas himself, he decided.

The baby made a few cranky sounds, and Gavin rocked her gently back and forth.

He turned in his seat to bellow at the open door: ''Rob? Where's that bottle?''

''Be right there, '' was the response from somewhere in the lower half of the house.

There was the sound of running feet, a loud crash, then a flood of Jamaican swear words.

Gavin stood. "Rob? What in the name of . . ." He broke off as the teenager appeared in the doorway. "What was that crash?"

Rob extended the bottle. "The large vase in the hallway."

Gavin tested the milk on the underside of his wrist before putting the nipple into the baby's mouth. When she was suckling contentedly, he said, "broken?"

Rob nodded. "In just three pieces though. But, I think I can glue it back together."

Gavin went to sit at the window again. "Don't bother. Just throw it out . . . and Rob . . ."

The boy came into the room, and perched on the side of the large double bed. "Yeah?"

"I don't want to hear about you drinking . . . ever again. Understand me?"

"Drink . . . drinking?" the boy stuttered. "How? . . . oh . . ."

"Summer didn't reveal your little secret . . . and don't bother to ask me how I know. I was your age once."

The boy propped his head against the ball of his palm. In the half light, with his face in partial silhouette, the beginnings of the Champagne beauty was already clearly evident.

"Why don't you marry her?"

"What?" Gavin swiveled in his seat to stare at the boy on the bed.

"I mean . . . you're not getting any younger . . . and at your age, you should be married."

Gavin frowned. "And what do you know about marriage?"

"Not much. I just think that Summer . . . she'd be a good choice for you. You suit each other somehow."

"She can't cook to save her life. What kind of wife would she make?"

Rob shrugged. "She can play cards . . . and . . ." his eyes burned with a strangely adult light for a second, "she's irie all over, man."

Gavin removed the half-full bottle from the baby's mouth,

and gestured to Rob. "Hold this a minute." He positioned the baby on one of his broad shoulders. "Are you watching how I do this? You'll be in charge of feeding and burping her tomorrow."

Rob straightened from his slouch. "It's not my turn. Mik. . . ."

"Mik had her for most of today," Gavin interrupted. "You'll take care of her tomorrow evening . . . after school."

Rob muttered something low and heated. Gavin turned to observe him with steady black eyes. "Did you have something to say?"

"Tomorrow's Friday . . . I don't want to take care of a baby on Friday night . . . I've got things planned."

"What things?"

"A group of us are going up Fern Gully way . . . a nature hike."

"Would you rather give up Saturday night then?"

Rob sighed in a long and very mournful manner. "No."

Gavin nodded. "We all take care of baby Amber. Even if it's inconvenient. Understand? We're Champagnes, and that means we go out of our way for one another. And nothing is ever too much. Get me?"

"Yeah. Okay." The boy stood, long and lanky, his eyes still holding the telltale signs of recalcitrance. "Did you need me for anything else?"

Gavin waved a hand in the air. "Go."

When he was alone again, Gavin allowed his thoughts free rein. Marry Summer Stevens indeed. His entire family was conspiring against him. First Nicholas, now Rob. And before long, it was very certain that Mik would be added to her long line of admirers.

Somehow, within the last two months, she had managed to bewitch them all. Sometimes it was hard to think of the house without her being there. When she was around, things were vibrant, alive, exciting. Even the air seemed to be charged with a certain energy. With those little shorts she wore sometimes, her long, golden-brown legs seeming to go on forever. Perfect little breasts thrusting proudly beneath some gauzy, cottony thing. Many days, it was all he could do, not to throw her down in the sand and take her right then and there. Physically, she was all any healthy red-blooded man could ever want. But, she was not the one for him. When he did marry, the girl would be a lot like her, but different too. She would be a cordon bleu chef. She would be a quiet, reserved type. She would not be volatile and argumentative. She'd be innocent, untouched. Something that Summer Stevens was definitely not.

He got carefully to his feet, the sleeping baby cradled in his arms. Marriage was completely out of the question. She was entirely unsuitable. She had managed to hold his interest, admittedly. But it was purely a physical attraction, surely? Albeit, a very strong one, but physical nonetheless. It had to be. He had never loved a woman before. His brothers. Rob. Them, he loved. But, no one else.

He rested the infant in the crib, and stood for a while looking down at her as she slept. He resisted the urge to look at the shiny face of his watch. It was only a mere half hour since they had left. There was no need to panic yet. On occasion, Nicholas could be trusted to be responsible.

''Let's stop there for a minute, Nicky,'' Summer said leaning out the window and pointing at a rather ramshackle-looking little building with the slogan D&G soft drinks emblazoned across the front of it. ''Maybe we can pick up something nice and cool to drink.''

Nicholas slowed the Jeep to a crawl, the steep incline of the hill making it possible for him to do so without stepping on the brake. There was a long rickety wooden table standing near the open door of the establishment. Four men were hunkered down at it, and every so often, a sharp clacking sound would rend the air as a hand shot up then slapped back down against the flat wooden surface.

In the rearview mirror, Nicholas exchanged a brief glance with his younger brother.

''It's one of the local rum shops . . . you know. . . .'' he said after a moment. ''Women don't . . . ah . . . that is, only certain women . . . hang out in there.''

Summer waved an elegant hand. ''Oh come on . . . you're beginning to sound like Gavin now. What could it hurt? This place just oozes with local color.''

''It oozes with a lot more than just that . . .'' Mik muttered from the backseat.

''What do you mean?'' Summer turned in her seat to direct a golden glance at the young man sprawled in the back. It continued to amaze her how very like Gavin he was.

''Is there an undercurrent of . . . of crime here?''

Mik shrugged. ''Maybe. You'll find all sorts of people in a place like this.''

Nicholas pulled the Jeep off the road, and parked on a little patch of loose gravel. ''We'll take you in . . . you pick out a drink, then we leave. . . . Deal?''

Summer smiled. ''All right. But, I'm not sure I like you all serious and . . . responsible like this.''

Nicholas released his belt. ''Don't smile at me like that. I can see you're trying to get me into some sort of trouble tonight. . . . If Gavin . . .''

''Come on . . . forget Gavin for a while. Let's have some fun.'' She was out of the car before Nicholas could say a word more. She stood for a moment, and took in her surroundings. The hillside was peppered with huge leafy trees and quaint-looking little houses.

''Everything is so fresh . . . and raw around here,'' she said as Nicholas came around to join her. ''And the air smells different too . . . sort of like burning wood.''

''There're some Rastas living up the hill on that ridge over there.'' Mik said, pointing to a high point that jutted out from the smooth symmetry of the surrounding landscape. ''Maybe one of them's lighting up a spliff.''

''Spliff? You mean . . . joint?''

''That's exactly what he means.'' Nicholas folded her arm through the crook of his, and led her past the table of men.

As they passed, the domino game paused, then resumed with vociferous abandon.

The interior of the shop was dark, and it took a minute for Summer to accustom her eyes to the smooth dankness of it. There were ragged little tables scattered about, an ancient jukebox jutting out from a wall, and from what she could see of it, a body of indeterminate sex, slumped across the flat of one of the tables in the far corner of the room.

Summer stared. "My God . . . you don't think he's . . ." she paused, "well it looks like a man . . . I think. . . . You don't think he's dead do you?"

Nicholas gave a short bark of laughter. "No, that wouldn't be my first guess."

"Passed out," Mik said helpfully.

Nicholas gave a little tug on the arm that was still looped through his. "Come on. Let's get you your drink. You're beginning to attract too much attention. I don't want to have to fight off a whole pack of men."

Summer grinned. "There's no one in here. Besides, I think you can handle a couple of drunks."

"Don't be too sure about that," he said, urging her along to the back of the shop. "These hands weren't made for fighting."

She gave him a sidelong glance. "You mean you let Gavin do all your fighting for you?"

Nicholas shrugged. "He's good at it. Trust me."

Mik nodded in agreement. "Gavin's the kind of guy you want to have on your side in a brawl."

Summer blinked at him. "Brawl? Gavin? Seems totally out of character for him."

"He's mellowed with age. You should've met him about fifteen years ago."

Summer rested both elegantly shaped hands on the long glass case. "There's more than just liquor in here. Why's it called a rum shop?"

"Men come to these places to drink, and socialize . . . three kola champagnes," Nicholas said, motioning to the clerk standing behind the counter. The man came forward. He was thin, dark, and very neatly groomed. His gaze ran over Summer in a bold but friendly manner. "Just kola champagne ma'am? How about some coconut biscuits or some bulla?"

"Bulla?" Summer whispered questioningly to Mik.

"It's a firm round cake," Mik whispered back.

Summer nodded at the man. "Okay. I'll try the bulla."

"A bag of Jamaican patties too," Nicholas added, "and give me half really hot . . . and the other half mild."

"We made some with Scotch Bonnet peppers. You want those?" the man asked.

"Yeah . . . I'll try the Scotch Bonnet," Nicholas nodded.

"It really hot though, so make sure you eat it with plenty wata' around," the man cautioned while placing the warm flaky pastries into a brown paper bag.

Nicholas accepted the bag with a smile. "Don't worry about me, I've got a heavy leather lining my stomach."

"Awright bwoy," the man said, "stay irie."

Outside, the men at the table were still hard at their game of dominoes. Summer took a swig of the crystal-cold drink, a small bite of the bulla cake, and sighed with pure enjoyment.

"People back in the States really don't know what they're missing . . . that crazy hurly-burly, nine-to-fiving, rat racing, corporate jungle backstabbing environment. And the traffic. The traffic on those L.A. freeways is just unbelievable."

"Don't forget the smog," Nicholas added.

Summer grimaced. "Don't remind me. I've probably lost at least ten years off my life because of just that alone."

"Why don't you stay then."

Summer crammed some more bulla into her mouth. Between chews she said, "Stay? What do you mean?"

"He means stay here with us," Mik said. "We think you're good for Gavin. He hasn't been . . ."

"Let's get back to the truck," Nicholas interrupted.

Summer found herself being dragged along by the arm, and she looked up at Nicholas, a frown of puzzlement beginning to crease her forehead.

The front door of the truck was yanked open, and she was

handed in. When Nicholas was once again sitting in the driver's seat, she said, "What was that all about, Nicky?"

He started the engine, then turned to look at her with veiled eyes. "What was what?"

"You practically dragged me back to the truck just as Mik was about to tell me something about Gavin."

Nicholas turned in his seat. "Mik, were you about to say something about your brother?"

"No . . . nothing," the younger man said, and he turned to stare in a very fixed manner, out the window.

"Okay. But, I'll figure whatever it is out. You should never have said what you almost did, Mik. I'm like a pit bull when it comes to getting to the bottom of things."

"Oh God," Nicholas said, and turned the key in the ignition.

The road to Thatch Hill was rugged and quite steep. Mango and avocado trees pressed heavily against the road in places, almost seeming to resent the intrusion of the noisy vehicle. Summer rolled down her window, and let the soft evening breeze whip through her hair.

"This is wonderful," she said, after a moment of enjoying the wind. Her eyes had gone a deep honey-brown. "Everything's so . . . so completely natural. Nothing man-made here at all."

Nicholas nodded. "This is the Jamaica that few tourists will ever see. No resorts, none of the people who usually hang around the tourist area. . . . just good, clean, wholesome living."

Summer turned from the wind. "What people?"

Nicholas eased the Jeep in and out of a huge pothole, before answering. "There're lots of people who hang around the hotels and the cruise ship docks . . . shady characters who help reinforce the idea in the minds of tourists that Jamaica is some sort of narcotics den."

Summer swept an errant swatch of hair behind a perfectly formed ear. "Yes, I'd heard that . . . one of the people at my last job took a Caribbean cruise once. She told me that when the ship docked in Ocho Rios, she was literally rushed by people trying to sell her all sorts of things. . . ."

"Ganja mostly," Mik added from the backseat.

''Uhmm-hmmm.'' Nicholas shifted into a lower gear as the hill got a bit steeper. ''American and Canadian tourists get the worst of it, I think.''

''Because of the money thing?'' Summer asked.

''Yep.'' Mik leaned forward, propping an arm on the smooth leather back of the driver's seat. ''Lots of Jamaicans are very poor . . . there is that small percentage that's wealthy, of course. But, because of the economic downturn the country suffered in the eighties, the average Jamaican has to struggle to make a living. So . . .''

''So . . .'' Summer interrupted, ''shady characters tend to descend on American tourists who're seen as wealthy by comparison.''

Nicholas turned to beam at her. ''You're not just a pretty face, are you?''

Summer gave him an audacious wink. ''I have my moments.''

Mik leaned back against the soft leather, resting his head against the flat of both palms. ''When you finish working on that cottage, I think we should call it Summer Champagne.''

Summer whipped around in her seat. ''Summer Champagne? I'm not certain that Gavin would be too thrilled with that idea.''

''How about Champagne Summer, then?'' Nicholas suggested. ''That kinda has a certain ring to it.''

''How about just Champagne?'' Summer said, getting into the spirit of things.

Mik made a sound of disgust. ''Champagne? That's a little too ordinary don't you think? Where's your creativity Summer Champagne?''

''Why is he calling me that?'' Summer asked, turning to Nicholas with humor brimming in her eyes.

Nicholas grinned. ''Why're you calling her that young'un?''

Mik leaned forward again. ''Ever heard of the power of suggestion?''

''You guys are beginning to scare me,'' Summer said with mock sternness, ''It's starting to look as though you're trying to marry your brother off to the first available woman.''

''Not the first,'' Mik said.

''Shaddup Mik.''

Summer glowered at Nicholas. ''Don't let your brother intimidate you, Mik. Go on . . . you were saying?''

Mik shot a glance at his brother in the rearview mirror, then appeared to come to some sort of decision. ''You're not the first girl we've tried this with.''

Summer felt her heart beat increase by several measures. ''Tried what?''

''Setting Gavin up with.''

''Setting him up?'' Summer repeated stupidly.

''Sheila was. . . .''

''Enough Mik.'' This time there was a trace of steel in Nicholas' voice.

The younger man sighed, and retired to the confines of the backseat again.

Panic swelled in Summer's throat. ''Wait a minute, Nicky, you can't stop him now. What was he going to say about Sheila? Did she and Gavin. . . .? . . . .I mean, is . . . is Gavin the baby's father? Has all this been a lie?''

She waited, terrified to hear the truth of it. Terrified to know that maybe Gavin really was baby Amber's father. ''Well?'' she prompted when the silence stretched.

''No. Gavin isn't her father. He wouldn't have anything at all to do with her.'' Nicholas shrugged. ''She was too young for him, I guess, and maybe not his type.''

''So . . . there was nothing between them . . . ever?''

Nicholas gripped the wheel. ''Nothing.''

''So . . . how did you end up with her?''

''It just kinda happened I guess. We drifted into it. Gavin was . . . distant at best. Completely unresponsive to her flirtations . . . I found myself consoling her many a time. . . .''

''Oh . . . Gavin was like that with me too . . . the same exact way. . . .'' Summer muttered, more to herself than to anyone else.

Nicholas laughed. ''Who're you kidding? He can't keep his

hands off you. All you have to do is crook your little finger, and he comes running.''

''Are we talking about the same guy?''

Nicholas gave her arm a friendly tap. ''You still don't understand him, do you?''

''No, I don't.''

He paused to think for a bit. ''Gavin is a pretty complex guy. . . .''

Summer nodded. ''I'd already figured that out.''

Nicholas turned to flash a grin at her. ''. . . there's more. He doesn't trust women . . . mostly because of our mother.''

''. . . but she died of ovarian cancer, you told me. He can't blame her for that.''

Nicholas cleared his throat. ''She's not dead.''

''She's not dead? You mean she survived the cancer?''

''She never had it. I just told you that.''

Summer pushed the heavy weight of hair off her shoulders and knotted the entire length of it at the nape of her neck. ''My God . . . you Champagnes are a lying bunch of men aren't, you? I don't know what's real and what isn't anymore. Where is your mother then, if she isn't dead?''

''Somewhere in Arizona I think. Gavin knows for sure. He sends her money each month. Me . . . I don't want anything to do with her. She's probably one of the most shallow, and self-centered people to ever walk the earth.''

''Uhmm-hmmm,'' Summer agreed in a noncommittal manner. ''Did Gavin really raise you all . . . or was that part of the lie too?''

''No,'' Nicholas sighed, ''that's true. He had to. Our dear mother walked off and left us in foster care when the man she had her sights set on announced that he didn't want a ready-made family.''

Summer stared. ''Oh, how terrible.'' She gave Nicholas' arm a quick squeeze. ''I'm sorry.''

Nicholas swerved to avoid something in the road. His voice was a bit gruff when he said, ''yeah . . . well. It doesn't matter now. Anyway . . . that's at the root of the problem he has with women. Maybe it's part of the problem I have with them too. Thank God, Mik wasn't affected by all this too much. He was a baby when she left. . . .''

Summer was silent. It all made sense to her now. Why it was that Gavin was fighting her every inch of the way. He was afraid to trust. Afraid to give his heart. Afraid that if he did, she would treat it with as much regard as his own mother had done. But, couldn't he tell that she was different? That she would never hurt him? All she wanted to do was love him, after all.

The thought of that, rattled around in her head, and she savored it for a while, getting used to the strong and varied texture of it. She had scoffed at the emotion once. Had held it up to scrutiny, and trashed it with ridicule and disbelief. But, it was real. It wasn't the myth she had once thought it. It was embodied by a living, breathing human being, with black eyes and curly, black hair. A man who had spent a good portion of his life taking care of his younger siblings. Who needed her, perhaps more than she needed him.

''Are we really going to see this Obeah woman?'' she asked after a good, long while had passed.

''Of course we are . . . why else would we be up in these hills at this time of night.''

Summer chuckled. ''Well . . . after all the lies and schemes, I don't know what to believe anymore.''

Nicholas turned, and in the half light, his resemblance to his older brother suddenly struck her. His features were sharper, perhaps, his forehead more narrow, his lips not as generous. But the likeness was there.

''Believe this . . . I brought you here to Jamaica for Gavin . . . maybe that wasn't the right thing to do . . . but . . . I . . . we did it for him. It's been a long time since he's been really happy . . . you know? For the last several years . . . he's just kinda existed. Living only to work. I would do anything for him . . . we all would. . . . Now that we're all grown, the best thing we can do for him, is to give him back his life . . . understand?''

Summer blinked away a film of moisture. She never would have thought it possible. What a strange and powerful thing love was. Nicholas loved his brother. Really loved him. Almost to the point of irrationality. She had never noticed that before.

She wiped the corner of an eye, and attempted to hide a little sniffle.

"Do you . . . do you believe in God, Nicky?"

"God? What brought that on?"

"I just wondered if you did or not. It's strange that you should have chosen me out of all the hundreds . . . thousands of women. . . ."

The shoulders shrugged. "It was just luck . . . that's all."

"No . . . not luck," Summer disagreed. "Something more . . . something more than just random chance was involved here. . . . My life was in such a mess a couple of months ago. I'd given up on so many things . . . and what was the likelihood that Gavin and I would've hit it off? No . . . something more than luck was at work here. . . ."

"If it makes you happy to think so." Nicholas pulled the Jeep off the road, and parked it almost directly before a tiny concrete house. There was one solitary light shining in the front window.

"Is this it?" Summer released the catch on her seat belt. A coldness had settled somewhere in the pit of her stomach. Outside, night had fallen, dark and silky. The trees whispered in the light wind, and from somewhere far off, came the sound of a yapping dog.

"Aren't you going to get out?" Nicholas urged when she made no attempt to remove herself from the seat.

"Don't hurry me . . . don't hurry me."

Summer gave the house another uncertain look before fumbling around with the handle on the door. Mik came around to help her down, and she clung unashamedly to his hand.

On the short walk to the door, she found herself wondering repeatedly why it was she had allowed Nicholas to talk her into coming to this place. She waited with great anxiety as Nicholas pounded on the wooden door.

After what seemed like a very long while, but what in reality must have been only a half a minute, she said hopefully, "maybe she's not home?"

"She's home. She's expecting us." Nicholas pounded again.

There was the sound of footsteps, and a latch being pulled back. Summer staggered backwards as a blur of fur launched itself through the open door, and landed somewhere on her chest.

"Lawd Jesus have mercy. That dog. Percy . . ." Madame Kofo bellowed at someone lurking in the bowels of the house. "Cum and get ounu dog."

For one terrified moment, Summer thought she was being attacked by the fur ball. But, after the initial panic had faded, she realized that the exuberant little thing was attempting to plaster her face with its tongue.

It took the efforts of both Mik and Nicholas, to remove the excited animal from Summer's chest.

Somehow, in the ensuing confusion, one of the animal's claws had become firmly wedged in the fabric of her shirt, and it was only with a lot of pulling, tearing of the garment, and attendant yelping by the now subdued dog, that the whole tangle was properly sorted out.

When it was all over, Madame Kofo came forward.

"You alright dear?"

Summer nodded. She wasn't at all certain that she was all right. Her shirt certainly wasn't. There was a huge tear sitting somewhere high up on her shoulder, and her heart was racing like she had just completed a hundred-meter dash. The woman took her hand. "Come inside, little bit. I got some nice broth fuh steady yuh nerves."

Summer took a gulp of air, and tried to explain that she didn't need any broth at all, and that her nerves were quite steady under the circumstances. Madame Kofo would hear none of it. She handed Summer into a tattered chair, motioned for Nicholas and Mik to sit, then took herself off to the kitchen for the broth.

She returned within minutes, holding a steaming cup, which

she pressed into one of Summer's hands. "Mannish wata'," she said. "Good for whatever ails you."

She took herself off again, and Summer seized the opportunity to whisper fiercely to Nicholas who was laughing at her from behind his hands.

"Is this the goat brains soup you were telling me about?"

"Try it," Nicholas said. "It's good."

"I don't want to try it," Summer said. "You have it since you like it so much."

Mik stretched a hand. "Give it here," he whispered. "I'll drink it."

Summer handed over the cup. "Careful, it's hot."

Mik blew on the surface of the broth, then proceeded to gulp the whole thing down. When he was through, he handed back the cup. "That was good," he said. "The best I've ever had."

Summer peered at the bottom of the cup, then up at Mik. Gratitude was written all over her face. But, before she could adequately express her thanks, the woman was back.

She took a quick look at the cup in Summer's hand.

"You're hungry," she said sympathetically.

Summer's "no . . ." was drowned out by Mik and Nicholas' enthusiastic response.

Madame Kofo beamed. "I made some nice ackee and salt fish with roast bread fruit."

Summer's stomach churned. It was altogether likely that this ackee and salt fish was nothing more than a skillful attempt to conceal another healthy serving of goat brains, this time without the broth.

"Well . . . I'm not very . . ." she began, but thought better of it once she got a good look at the expression of enthusiasm on the old woman's face.

"I'll have some of yours Nicky," Summer said, sending a look of great pleading in his direction.

Nicholas grinned, and Summer knew by the expression of devilish enjoyment on his face, that he wasn't going to help at all.

"She's just a little shy, Madame Kofo," he said. "Give her a huge helping of the ackee."

"You just wait 'til I get you outside," Summer mouthed as soon as Madame Kofo was out of earshot.

Nicholas gave her a broad smile. "Gavin isn't here to help you now."

Summer shook a finger at him. "I don't need Gavin to help me with this, believe me bwoy," and she stretched the syllables of the word *boy,* getting the Jamaican intonation just right.

Mik guffawed. "Where did you learn to talk like that?"

"Rob," Nicholas said without hesitation.

Within minutes, steaming plates of ackee and salt fish were set before them. Madame Kofo had taken Nicholas at his word, and filled Summer's plate to capacity. Long, cool glasses of fruit punch were brought in on a highly polished silver tray. And, only when Madame Kofo was satisfied that everything was nicely situated, did she leave them to the business of eating.

Mik and Nicholas were almost halfway through their meal before Summer gathered enough nerve to place a tiny forkful of the ackee, which, to be completely fair, did smell quite appetizing, into her mouth. She sampled another larger amount, before declaring, "it doesn't taste like brains at all."

"That's because it's not," Nicholas said between hefty mouthfuls. "Ackee is a fruit. It grows on some of those trees we passed on the way up here."

Summer sampled again. "A fruit . . . how strange. It looks kinda like scrambled eggs . . . same yellow color . . . same texture"

"Uhmm" was the only response Nicholas gave for the next several minutes. In the period of silence, Summer polished off her entire plate, and then sipped happily on the chilled glass of fruit punch.

Madame Kofo returned to remove the plates. By then, Summer was feeling quite comfortable with where she was and why she was there.

"I'm glad you forced me to come," she whispered to Nicholas. "What's going to happen now?"

Nicholas squeezed her hand. ''Wait and see.''

For the next hour, Summer was treated to a lesson in African history and religion. Madame Kofo spoke with an eloquence and erudition worthy of any university professor. She told them of the powerful Dahomey kingdom, and of a fiercely proud people called the Koramante. She spoke of herbs and potions that had been used by her ancestors for centuries past, some of which were only now being discovered and bottled by big pharmaceutical companies in the United States.

Summer listened with rapt attention, soaking up every word. And, when it was all over, she continued to sit there, hoping that maybe there might be more.

Nicholas gave her a little nudge. ''Ask her about the inscription you found on the cottage wall.''

Summer reached into her breast pocket. She had nearly forgotten about it.

She handed over the slip of paper, with a brief explanation. Madame Kofo's gnarled fingers smoothed the paper. For a long while, she was silent. Then, she looked directly at Summer, and her eyes were filled with the wisdom of her ancestors.

''It's written in one of the old tongues of Africa. It says 'the biggest trunk cannot hold, all the treasure of which I'm told. You will know it, when you find it. A king's ransom in gold.' ''

''Oh my God,'' Summer said excitedly, ''it's the treasure . . . it's talking about the treasure.''

''You mean old Henry's gold?'' Nicholas laughed, ''that's just a myth. There's no gold on the property.''

Summer turned to him. ''No one ever found it . . . right?''

Nicholas nodded. ''Right.''

''That's why it must still be there.'' There was a note of triumph in her voice.

Mik, who until now had remained quiet, said, ''why not Nicky? There might be something to it. Maybe Henry Morgan buried the bullion somewhere beneath the old cottage. Maybe down in the basement.''

''Maybe,'' Nicholas said, coming smoothly to his feet.

He thanked the old woman warmly for the dinner and the

wonderful information that came afterward. Then, he took Summer by the arm, and led her outside. When the door was neatly closed behind them, he said, "before morning, that information is gonna be all over."

"Oh," Summer said, "I didn't think . . . I mean I thought that whatever was said here, was said in confidence?"

"Only up to a certain point," Nicholas replied, handing her into the front seat of the Jeep.

Summer groaned. "Oh no. But, there may not even be anything to it at all."

"Well," Nicholas said, "let's hope I was able to sidetrack Madame Kofo. We don't want to have people crawling all over the property. And you, Mik," he said turning around to look at his brother, "should have known better."

"Yeah," Mik said, a little shamefacedly. "I forgot for a minute where we were."

On the journey back down the long, dark hill, Summer sat immersed in thought. "It was written in an African language," she finally said. "So that probably means that whoever wrote it must have been a runaway from one of the plantation houses."

Nicholas shrugged. "Could be."

Summer gave him a pensive little look. "Why aren't you more excited?"

"I've heard all the stories. People have been searching for that gold for centuries. It's just not there."

"You know," Summer said, "you're beginning to sound more and more like Gavin every day."

Nicholas gave her a quick grin. "That must be a good thing then . . . hmmm?"

"Hmmm indeed," she nodded. "Just don't change yourself too much. How's Sheila doing, by the way? You and Gavin are so tight-lipped about everything."

The hands on the steering wheel tightened for a moment. "She's okay . . . I guess. She's gonna be leaving for the States next week. She got a job in L.A."

"Is she going to see the baby before she goes?"

''Doesn't seem so. She wants to pretend Amber doesn't exist.''

Summer shook her head. ''Strange . . . I want to thank you, Nicky. . . .''

''For what?'' Nicholas raised his voice so that he might be heard above the deafening snores coming from the back seat.

''For opening my eyes . . . on this . . . on everything. What a very learned woman that Madame Kofo is. She's deep. Very, very deep.''

''Yeah . . . she's famous on the island. I've heard that even politicians come up here to see her sometimes . . . usually at election time.''

''She gave me something as I was leaving. Something she said I would need soon.'' Summer pulled out the tiny bottle of lavender liquid, and held it up to the light. ''Looks pretty ordinary to me. Kinda like purple Kool-aid or something.''

Nicholas took the tiny bottle out of her hand, and turned it over in his hand. ''What did she say to do with it?''

''Well . . . not much really. She was kind of insistent that I attach it to a piece of string, and hang it from my neck. . . .''

''I would do it,'' Nicholas said, handing back the bottle. ''She might know what she's talking about.''

Summer slipped the tiny bottle back into her top pocket. ''I guess it can't hurt . . . I mean . . . to wear it for a while.''

Nicholas nodded, and shifted to make her more comfortable when she snuggled against his shoulder, and promptly fell off to sleep.

CHAPTER TWENTY-TWO

Gavin was standing at the front window when the headlights of the Jeep came slowly down the long driveway. It was all he could do not to open the door and rush down the stairs to meet them. Over the past hour, he had been tormented by the mental image of her lying broken and twisted in a ditch somewhere. Somehow, it had made perfect sense that Nicholas would have either run them off the road, or crashed headlong into an oncoming bus or some such thing. He had paced the front hall when they had not returned by ten, and considered calling the police quite a few times between the hours of eleven and midnight.

Now that they were back, he didn't know whether to be angry with Nicholas, or grateful that they had all returned safely. What he did know though, was that he wanted to hold Summer. In the few hours that she had been away from the house, he had missed her, missed her in a terribly lonely, aching kind of way.

He stood by the window now, watching as they walked slowly toward the house. Her laughter carried on the wind for a moment, and the sound of it made his heart beat just a little faster. He was there to open the door, even before Nicholas could insert his key.

A lightning glance at his older brother's expression, told Nicholas all that he needed to know. He hustled Mik ahead of him. To Summer he said: "See you in the morning."

Within moments, she and Gavin were alone in the foyer.

"I guess . . . everyone's kinda tired," Summer began, not knowing exactly how to read the silent expression on his face. He just stood there watching her, almost like some sort of giant sheepdog.

"Your shirt is torn," he said gruffly, after a long moment of staring.

Summer looked down at the oddly shaped rip in the fabric. "It's . . . a long story. I'll tell you all about it tomorrow . . . I'm gonna go off to bed now . . . I'm tired."

She made as if to walk around him, and he stepped aside to let her pass.

"Do you want something to eat?" he asked when she was almost to the stairs.

She turned to answer him, and noticed for the first time, that his hands were balled into fists by his sides. He held himself proudly, rigidly. And, a lightning thought shot through her head. Could it be that he wanted her to stay with him, and didn't know how to ask? She retraced her steps slowly, until she was again standing directly before him.

"Did you eat?" she asked gently.

"No. I couldn't . . . didn't feel hungry."

"I'll fix you something . . . don't worry . . . I do sandwiches well."

He followed, protesting the entire way. "I don't want anything to eat . . . anyway you said you were tired. . . ."

She paid absolutely no attention to him, and proceeded to fix him a large ham and cheese sandwich, with the edges neatly cut off, just the way he liked it. She set this, as well as a large glass of fruit juice before him. A wave of tenderness swept through her when he intercepted one of her hands, and pulled her to sit on his lap.

"Do you want me to feed you too? Is that it?" she joked.

A hint of a smile played around the corners of his mouth. "If you like."

She lowered her head to press a light kiss on his lips, and he wrapped his arms around her.

"You weren't hurt, were you?"

His fingers played with the tear in her shirt, and his mouth wandered across the area to press warm kisses against the exposed patch of skin on her shoulder.

"No . . . just a little accident . . . funny really. I'll tell you about it later." She pressed her mouth to the strong column of his neck, and bit. His heated groan sent a shock wave of electricity through her. Blindly, instinctively, she found his mouth again. And they clung together for mindless moments, each glorying in the taste and feel of the other.

When she lifted away so that she might breathe, he pulled her back down. She feathered light kisses across the skin of his face, and he turned obligingly, giving her access to both cheekbones, his throat, and again, his lips. She stroked the curly folds of his ear with the flat of her tongue, and listened in satisfaction to the harsh thickening of his breath.

"Do you suppose," she whispered between nibbles on his ear, ". . . that other people kiss as much as we do?"

A hand came up to play with the long, silky strands of her hair. And, when he shifted her down to lie in the cradle of his arms, there was a certain fondness in his eyes. "No one can kiss as much as we do . . . babe, . . . it's just not possible."

A huge smile stretched her lips. "You called me babe. . . ."

"Well . . . you are a babe . . . aren't you?"

She blinked dusky-gold eyes at him. "I wanna be your babe—nobody else's."

He stroked her cheek with the back of a finger. "I must've done something really good . . . sometime in my life . . . hmmm?"

Summer looked up and met his eyes, and in that moment, she felt such a tremendous closeness with him, that it was an effort to tear her eyes away.

''Are we spending the weekend somewhere. . . . ?''

He nodded. ''I got a villa just outside Port Antonio close to a spot called the Blue Hole.''

''Far away from other people?'' Summer asked with a wicked glint in her eyes.

Gavin laughed. ''It's very exclusive, so . . . we'll be the only people around for miles.''

''Sure you don't want to start tonight?''

He shifted her onto her feet, and gave her a playful smack on the rump. ''No. Not tonight. Tomorrow.''

It was difficult getting to sleep after that, but somehow, maybe out of pure exhaustion and not much else, Summer drifted into a soft slumber. Gavin said good night at her room door, and she had known then that, had she pressed, he would have remained with her, high ideals or not. For a long minute, while their lips clung, the temptation to do so had been strong. Passionate thoughts had flashed through her. How wonderful to spend the night wrapped in his arms, lulled into gentle sleep by the warm scent of him. To awaken to the dawn with the ocean breeze rolling through the window. To have him wake her in that special way known only to lovers. Surely that would be heaven itself.

But it was important to him that they behave in a completely circumspect manner around his brothers, and, she respected him for wanting that. The average man would not have turned away from the unequivocal invitation in her eyes. But Gavin was not average in any sense of the word. This was something she had come to terms with for quite some time now. He functioned on a completely different level, and demanded that people around him do the same.

It would seem that Nicholas had been right about his brother. He did seem to want her, even though it was a struggle for him to show it. And, God knows, she wanted him. Thinking back on her life just a few short months before, on her relationship with Kevin, it made her angry, angry that she had been so shallow, and so very willing to settle for something so much less than what she should have known was hers. But she hadn't had the belief in her then. Hadn't had the faith. But now she did. This thing with Gavin had opened up a new spiritual capacity in her. And even though he didn't love her yet, he would.

She drifted into sleep with that thought beating an insistent tattoo in her head. And when she awoke early the next morning there was a new determination in her. She was going to marry Gavin Pagne. But he would be the one to do the asking.

Since it was Saturday, she allowed herself the luxury of a long, refreshing soak in the tub. She lathered her long legs with foam, and gave them a good shave. Then, she washed her hair with a silky shampoo that smelled like wildflowers. After a while, she emerged from the bathroom with head and body wrapped in thick white towels. She spent long minutes massaging fragrant cream into every inch of skin, then stood at the window with blow-dryer in hand, gazing out on the sparkling azure blue of the ocean.

It was a golden day, peaceful, quiet, the long coconut palms bending gracefully in the wind, the occasional sound of a dog barking, the only thing to disturb the utter quiet of the early morning. The house was still asleep, so she went about the business of drying her hair, then packing a small leather valise, with the minimum of noise. She was just snapping the locks closed on her little case, when there was a knock on the bedroom door.

She gave her reflection a quick glance before crossing to pull the door open.

"Gavin." Her heart gave a tiny lurch at the sight of him standing there. He was dressed in a navy shirt, which hung outside the waistband of his pants, and a pair of well-worn blue jeans.

"You're awake," he said, and there was a smile lurking somewhere in the depths of his eyes.

She gave him a cheeky grin. "I'm an early riser. Besides,"

and she stepped back a bit to invite him in, "I had some packing to do."

He walked in and went straight to the window. Summer closed the door, and stood there for a moment. There was something bothering him, but she would give him the time to work around to whatever it was.

"There's a dog wandering around out there," he said after a good stretch of silence.

She came to stand beside him. "Looks half-starved . . . must be a stray . . . poor thing."

He half-turned to her, and the expression in his eyes was completely unreadable. "You like dogs?"

She nodded. "I've got one at home . . . Bruno. A great big shaggy thing. We've had him for years. . . ."

"Years? You and your roommate . . . I forget her name."

Summer felt her throat clench. "No . . . not in L.A. . . . not with Alyssa. Up at Mammoth."

He turned back to the window, and she knew that the subject of the dog and Mammoth was already gone from him. A furrow had sprung up between his brows. "What are we going to tell them?"

"Nicholas and the boys?" She knew very well what he meant, but chose to stall for a bit in order to give herself some time to think. How could she tell him that his brothers already knew about their planned weekend away together. That they in fact had probably been instrumental in arranging the entire thing.

"They'll wonder . . . where I am . . . where you are. It might affect the way they . . . look at you afterwards." He gave the ocean a rather fierce glare. "They all . . . like you, you know?"

"And you think they might not after we get back?"

"Nicholas is free and easy with everything . . . so, he won't lose any respect for you. But . . . Mik and Rob . . . especially Rob . . ."

She bit back the immediate retort that rushed to her lips, and gave herself pause to think.

"Would you rather we not go then?" It was a gamble asking

that question, but she took it anyway, waiting anxiously, praying that he would not call the whole thing off.

"I haven't wanted anything this much in a long time. . . ." he broke off to fiddle with the latch on the window. ". . . maybe ever."

She laid a gentle hand on his back. "The boys are grown now, Gavin . . . almost grown in the case of Rob. They don't need you to soften the blows for them anymore. . . . they'll understand. They want you to have a life too."

"I was thinking of you . . . not me so much."

She slid an arm around him, and skittered into the space between where he stood, and the windowsill. "Don't worry about me . . . I can handle myself with those three."

He smiled. "I've noticed. But . . ."

She covered his lips with a finger. "We're gonna go. We're gonna have fun. What is it they say again? 'You get out of life what you put into it'?"

He bent toward her. "That's what they say . . . I'm not sure if they're right though."

She stood on tiptoe to place feather-soft lips on his. "They're right. Trust me on this one."

His hand came up to cup the back of her head, and he deepened the kiss with a slight tilt of his head. A rush of sensation coursed its way through her at the velvety soft stroke of his tongue. He kissed her slowly, thoroughly, and with a new quality of tenderness that hadn't been there before. She was breathless, and her heart was pounding heavily in her chest when he raised his head to say, "God . . . you're so soft."

He buried his nose in the fragrant strands of her hair, and right then and there, she was of a mind to maneuver him onto the large double bed just behind them, and rip the shirt from his back. Never before had such dark and powerful emotions held her. Never before had she felt such a tearing, utterly animalistic need. If he didn't stop all this kissing and hugging right this very minute, she would be forced to break her not-so-firm resolve of circumspect behavior.

"Let's go. . . ." she muttered heatedly. "Now. . . ."

He eased her back, and she wondered if he could see how much she wanted him. Wondered if he would respect her less if he knew.

The black eyes were turbid. "No breakfast? No good-bye to the boys?"

"No breakfast . . . and we can leave a note for Nicky and the boys."

She was sorely tempted to let him have the truth of it. To let him know that she could not wait a moment longer. That there was a very good chance that as soon as they got up to the Port Antonio Blue Hole, or whatever it was called, she would very likely ruin the set of clothing he was now wearing.

He held her for a moment longer, as though unwilling as she was to let go.

"Is that your bag on the bed?"

She could do scarcely more than nod, and croak a very shaky, "Yes."

He ran slow hands down the length of her arms. "I'll write a note for Nicky. . . ."

"I'll get my bag and . . . meet you downstairs."

"Leave the bag," he said, "I'll take care of that for you."

She nodded. "See you down at the Jeep then?"

She scurried about the room after that, collecting a few last-minute things, which she dropped into her huge leather handbag. She was standing by the passenger door of the Jeep when he came walking down the front stairs, a case in each hand. He unlocked the truck door for her, handed her in, then went around behind to heave the two bags into the huge area in the back. The space in the truck suddenly seemed to get much smaller once he climbed into the driver's seat, and closed the door.

"I gave the dog some milk . . . but I think he needs real food."

Gavin gave the big-boned mongrel a glance. "Rob will take care of it once he's up. He has a thing for dogs."

"Are you sure?"

"Positive. Are you ready?" He held her gaze for a long,

searching moment, and she reached out a hand to softly touch his cheek.

''Ready.'' The simple truth of it was, if she were any more ready, she would quite probably burst a blood vessel or some such thing.

He started the engine smoothly, shifted into gear, and from the corner of an eye, she spied the front door open up a crack, and a familiar form come to stand in the doorway. She wasn't certain whether or not Gavin had seen him, so she did not return his cheeky salute. It wasn't until a full fifteen minutes later, that Gavin said, ''Nicholas seemed happy enough to see us go . . . that worries me. Makes me wonder what new scheme he's come up with.''

Summer let herself take full advantage of a very luxurious stretch. ''You worry too much babe . . . Nicky loves you . . . maybe more than you know.''

He gave her a speculative little look. ''Have you and Nicky been having long talks about me?''

''Not particularly. Nicky would never discuss anything private . . . I mean something I shouldn't know about you, with me. He's completely loyal you know . . . to you anyway.''

He considered this for a moment. ''Nicky likes you well enough though. . . .''

She gave him a great big smile. ''And why shouldn't he? I'm a very likable person. . . . as you're soon to find out.''

''Oh really?'' and humor sparkled in his eyes. ''Modesty is not one of your strong points is it?''

She nodded sagely. ''It's a problem I've had since I was about eleven years old.''

She had his attention again. ''Eleven? What was so earth-shattering about that age?''

''I started growing in certain areas.''

His eyes flickered to her chest, then ran smoothly up to rest on her face again. ''And grow very nicely . . . you did.''

She gave him a warm look. ''You didn't do too badly yourself.''

The next several hours were passed in friendly banter. She

told him all about Madame Kofo, the riddle on the metal plaque, and the possiblity that Henry Morgan's gold might really be buried somewhere on the property. He teased her playfully, when she suggested that maybe she might be the one to find it.

Summer found herself relaxing, and becoming really comfortable. And, the further away they got from the house, the more relaxed Gavin seemed to become.

The road weaved along the coast between Ocho Rios and Port Maria, then went inland for a bit until they arrived in a quaint little town called Annotto Bay. Along the way, Gavin stopped to buy hearty quantities of jerk chicken, rice and peas, and nicely chilled coconut water. He parked in a windy spot while they had their meal, then continued on through Buff Bay, and finally into the town of Port Antonio.

It was just before noon when they arrived at the turnoff that would take them to the Blue Hole. All around, the coastline was dotted by small mysterious coves into which huge foamy breakers crashed, tossing up ample amounts of spray, and every so often, setting a wild flock of gulls to flight. The country was raw and breathtakingly beautiful. With the towering majesty of the mist veiled Blue Mountains off in the distance, and the pounding surf just minutes away. It was almost too perfect, and Summer found herself looking from one to the other with something very like awe on her face.

''My God,'' she said, ''do people actually get to live here year-round?''

Gavin nodded. ''You haven't seen anything yet.'' He pulled off the main road, and began heading down a neat cobblestoned drive. Thick greenery overhung the road, creating a cool, cozy feeling. In the distance, as the road bent and curved its way along, an ultramodern two-story wood cabin with nicely polished convex windows, came suddenly into view.

''Is that it?'' Summer asked, and a tinge of great excitement crept into her voice.

''Uhmm,'' Gavin said, ''we're the only cabin around in a two-mile radius.''

She looked at him. "You were really serious about that then?"

His lips twitched. "You thought I wasn't?"

She placed a hand along the back of his seat, and ran a slow finger down the length of his neck. "Who would have thought it? You and me in a place like this . . . especially after what I did to you in L.A."

He cut the engine. "I know. I should've known you were trouble then . . . you with your shedding wig and buffed teeth."

Summer chortled. "You have to admit, that was good. I had you going for a while there."

He shook his head, and there was a trace of reluctant admiration in his eyes. "You and Nicky are so much alike. It's no wonder you get along so well. Are you sure it's me you want and not him?"

She leaned across, stopping just short of his lips, letting him feel the warmth of her breath on his mouth. "Come inside with me and I'll show you whether or not I really want you."

He leaned in, bridging the distance between them in half a beat. "You are a wicked woman Summer Stevens. . . ."

Summer pulled gently at his bottom lip. "Uhmm. . . ." she purred throatily, "but only with you, babe. Only with you."

He scooped her into his arms as though she weighed nothing at all, and somehow managed to lift her from the truck. He kicked the door shut with one leg, and headed straight for the front door of the pinewood villa. Summer uttered a token protest, "I'm too heavy Gavin . . . let me walk. . . . You'll hurt yourself."

"I've carried grown men twice your size young lady," he said.

He sprang easily up the short flight of wooden stairs, and placed her on her feet, only when it was necessary that he remove the key from his pocket. With this done, she was in his arms again being carried effortlessly across the threshold and into a sunken living room of unbelievable luxury.

White, thick pile carpeting stretched for as far as the eye

could see, and a huge saltwater aquarium took the place, from floor to ceiling, left to right, of an entire living room wall.

"My God. . . ." Summer gaped as Gavin set her gently on her feet. It was gorgeous, absolutely gorgeous. And, the choice of color for the decor was wonderful too. It gave everything a light and refreshingly airy appearance. "It's . . . it's," but, the right words escaped her for the minute. Her eyes darted over the huge plush chairs, intricately carved pieces of wooden sculpture, finely wrought inset lights, and she felt hot and cold all at once.

She wandered around the room, touching things, running the flat of her palm along the surface of a fat, marble, green Buddha, pausing to stroke the proud bust of a piece of Jamaican sculpture. Then finally, stopping to stare in fascination at the huge multicolored tropical fish, which swam unperturbed behind the thick wall of glass.

Gavin came to stand beside her. "Well . . . what do you think?"

She spun around to give him a completely unrestrained hug. "You're . . . just amazing. This must be costing you a fortune." She swept her hands in an expansive circle. "Who in their right mind wouldn't absolutely love this place. God, it's beautiful."

He nuzzled her ear. "There's a Jacuzzi right out there," he pointed to a pair of sliding glass doors. "A steam room through there," he turned her gently in the opposite direction. "Kitchen . . . through those double doors . . . and upstairs . . . a huge bedroom with a balcony overlooking the sea. . . ." He tasted the fleshy lobe of her ear, ". . . also upstairs . . . a fully stocked library . . . a small gym. . . ."

"No bathroom?" she said somewhat breathlessly.

He bit down on the lobe, and a bolt of heat fired her blood. "They're two bathrooms. One up and another down."

A sudden thought occurred, and a shard of jealousy lanced painfully through her. "How is it you know this place so very well? . . . Where everything is I mean. Have you brought other women here before?"

He turned her to face him. "I own this property . . . and no,

I've never brought anyone here before . . . not even Nicky . . . or Mik . . . or Rob.''

''Oh.'' She went silent for a bit, savoring the enormity of that and what it could possibly mean, if anything at all.

He dragged her in closer, so that she might feel the full length of him. ''Is that all you're going to say? Oh?''

She smiled, and there was a soft seductive glint in her eyes. ''I never know what to expect with you. You never do what I expect . . . say what I expect. You're a very confusing man.''

''And you,'' he growled softly, ''I have waited for . . . for long enough. Let's go upstairs.''

CHAPTER TWENTY-THREE

Gavin watched with mixed emotions as she slowly undressed for him. The long, elegant fingers on the buttons of her cotton blouse, were completely without tremor. Much too steady for a woman unaccustomed to undressing before a man. Just how many men had she had before him? And, why couldn't he have been the first? Although all he felt for her was strong lust, and a certain amount of irrational affection, he couldn't bear the thought of another man's hands touching the smooth golden skin, the beautiful curve of her neck, the dusky gold nipples beneath the lacy white bra.

She looked up at him as her shirt fell away to land in a crumpled pile at her feet.

"Your turn. You take something off."

His heart beat in heavy thumps against his breastbone as his hands lowered to unfasten the thick black leather belt about his waist. He pulled the entire length of it all the way out, then let it fall softly to the floor. Uncharacteristically, he struggled with the button at the waist of his pants, and she watched his efforts, motionless, like a particularly sleek jungle cat sizing up its prey.

When the jeans were off and on the floor, he said, ''You.''

The long well-shaped fingers again mesmerized him. She would go for the jeans she was wearing next, he knew that without question.

But, she surprised him by reaching around and carefully, hook by hook, releasing the fastenings on her bra. His fingers folded into fists at his sides, and involuntarily, he took a step toward her.

''No. Stay where you are,'' and she backed up until her legs touched the side of the huge four-poster bed.

He stopped himself with great effort, his breathing harsh and thick in the quiet of the room. She slid one cotton strap over her shoulder, then the other. And, like some exotic dancer, she slowly removed the lace, letting it fall to the ground.

The reaction of his body was immediate. He removed his shirt in a single tug, not caring that several buttons went when he did. She presented him with the smooth unblemished length of her back, and his blood pressure went through the roof. With a little wiggle of her hips, she was out of the jeans, and standing before him in the briefest of black string bikinis he had ever set eyes on.

That was it. He would play this game no longer. Before she could properly turn to face him again, he was there behind her. He slid the fingers of both hands beneath the tiny strappy elastic that ran over each hip, and removed the scrap of satin in a single tug. She made no protest at his discontinuance of the game, but instead, wound silky-soft arms about his neck, and allowed him to gently lower her to the bed.

She lay passively on the flat of her back, watching him with eyes that had turned an indescribable shade of brown. He dispensed with the single barrier of clothing between them, and came to lie beside her.

''What's the matter?'' he asked softly when she continued to lie unmoving. This behavior, was definitely not what he would have expected of her.

''Nothing,'' and she blinked at him, endeavoring to look not unlike a frightened doe trapped in the headlights of a rapidly oncoming vehicle.

He stroked the flat of a palm down the length of her arm. There was no denying it. As crazy, as utterly impossible as it would seem, she was scared. It didn't make any sense at all. Why would she be, after all the talk? After this tantalizing little striptease?

"Come here," he said. And, she came to lie with him, willingly enough. He wrapped his arms about her, and pulled the blanket up around them both. His body was crying out for satisfaction, but, it would have to wait. Making her comfortable was of far more importance than fulfilling the throbbing need within him.

He tilted her chin up so that he could see her eyes. "You're not afraid of me are you?"

She wrapped soft fingers about the hand holding her chin, and pressed a kiss to the flat of his palm.

"No . . . that's not it."

He waited. "Then what?"

"Sex . . . I don't like it. I thought it would be different with you. But, it's happening again. I freeze up when it really comes down to it . . . I'm frigid, I think."

Gavin propped an arm beneath her shoulders to draw her up. "Frigid? You can think that even after the way you've kissed me these last months . . . after the way you undressed for me just now?"

She bowed her head. "It's all just an act. . . ."

"You've never had a good experience . . . not even once . . . with all those men?"

A flicker of a frown rippled across her brow for a moment. "All which men?"

"I thought. . . ."

"Well . . ." she said in a very pensive manner, "I . . . there's not been . . . I mean .. it's just a defense mechanism . . . you know, to prevent people from guessing. . . ."

"There have been no men then?"

"One . . . or two."

Gavin felt the hope in his heart shrivel and die. ''Your ex-fiancé was one of them . . . I suppose?''

''No . . . not him. I . . . we . . .''

Gavin stopped her. ''Don't . . .'' and, he let his voice taper off, lest she get the wrong impression of what he meant. He really didn't want to know anything at all about the men she might have lain with. The thought of someone else touching her, made him almost crazy.

He leaned down to gently take her lips, thinking that he might distract her in this way. She responded to him immediately, much like a flower opening its soft petals to the glow of the sun. He caressed her with his free hand, dipping down to stroke the silky triangular patch at the soft point between her legs, then drifting up again to gentle the quivering in her limbs.

''Gavin?''

''Uhmm?'' He raised his head to look down at her.

''Do you just want me . . . for sex, I mean?''

The question took him by surprise, and the gentle stroking of his hand paused.

''What do you mean?''

''I mean . . . could you ever love me? Or do you want me just for sex?''

The frown was back between his brows. ''This is a strange time to ask me that.''

''Strange or not . . . do you think you could?'' She persisted even though he no longer appeared receptive to questioning.

''I haven't given it any thought . . .'' He was immediately regretful of answering so very bluntly, at the expression of hurt that flickered in her eyes.

''I . . . care about you. . . .'' he struggled, and was rewarded by a burst of happiness in her eyes.

A tenderness for her touched him. ''Babe,'' he said, and wrestled with the right words to say. ''There's . . . you're my . . .''

She reached up and kissed him into silence. His lips left her mouth to press a line of kisses across her shoulder blade, then wandered purposely down to the dusky gold of a wide nipple.

A feeling of satisfaction went through him at the soft gasp she made as he drew the fullness of it into the warmth of his mouth, and suckled. He pulled on it as fiercely as a hungry infant would, and her fingers came up to hold his head and press him closer. He bit gently down on the tiny nub, glorying in the soft sounds of encouragement she made. When his mouth drifted across to the other, she attempted to pull him back. He gentled her with a soft admonition, and drew the dewy softness of the rosy mound into his mouth.

She called out his name then, and he raised his head to observe her, an expression of supreme satisfaction on his face. She writhed beneath him, and he held her legs steady so that he might go lower to taste. With the first flicker of his tongue, she arched upward with the power and ferocity of a wildcat, fingers clawing the air, limbs thrashing. He stroked her until he himself was shaking, and could wait no more.

In one smooth movement, he parted her legs, and eased into her. She stiffened for a second, her hands bunching on his shoulders as if to shove him off. But the hands slowly relaxed when he began to move. His thrusts were deliberately slow, deliberately long. The fingers on his shoulders curled against his skin, and involuntarily, her long legs came up to wrap tightly around the small of his back, holding him to her for a half second longer. She moaned softly, and began to arch against him in response to his rhythm. Soft purring sounds bubbled from her lips, and he kissed her fiercely, devouring the softness of her lips, groaning in response, when she turned her face into his neck and bit the skin there.

She called his name again, and from somewhere in the thickness of pleasure, he roused himself enough to rasp a response. Summer's neck arched involuntarily. It was so good, so very good, that it was almost an agony. Her lips rounded in a surprised *O,* at the good, solid feel of him. And, without conscious thought, her nails curled into the skin of his back, urging him on. Gavin growled with the pain and soul felt pleasure of it. And, he quickened his pace.

Crystal teardrops thickened the spiky length of her eyelashes, and a solitary tear rolled free down the flat of her face. He caught the raw, sweet feel of it with his tongue, and she cried out, not caring who heard her, not caring if a nuclear device went off next door. Her voice arched its way through the afternoon quiet like the call of some exotic island bird, and his rhythmic groans satisfied her like nothing else ever had. Was it possible that anything, anything at all, could be this good?

Incoherent words of love trembled on her lips, but with superhuman effort, she held them back. He held her steady, drawing her up, tilting her back so that she was perfectly poised to receive him. Each thrust brought her closer to the edge of sanity. Her breath sobbed slowly from her throat, and from some very distant point, she realized that she was crying, moaning, begging. His face was contorted with the power, the beauty, the absolute eloquence of it all. And all she could do was hold on.

There came a point of such absolute synchronicity between them, when they were so much in rhythm, so much in synch, that they were almost like one single undulating body. Each groan that was torn from his throat, took her to a higher degree of sensation, each muttered entreaty from her, was more than sufficient to drive him into a crazy, pounding rhythm. He held her hair, wrapping the thickness of it around one wrist, pulling so that her neck was stretched as taut as the string of a bow. He rode her hard, responding to her soft cries of encouragement like a man possessed. When the first wave of spasms washed over her, he held her close, catching her shrill cries in his mouth. And when it was his turn to succumb to the rollicking crescendo of pleasure, he called out her name in wild satisfaction.

It was several minutes before either could formulate an articulate sentence. Gavin was still lying within the cradle of her thighs, her long legs tightly wrapped around the small of his back. He raised his head slowly, and their eyes met.

''That was . . .'' he began slowly.

''Incredible . . .'' she finished for him.

He pressed a kiss to the smooth skin of her forehead, and

prepared to shift. But, she tightened her legs around him, and whispered a very persuasive, "Stay."

He lowered himself to her again, and there was a smile in his eyes. "And you think you're frigid?"

She wrapped long arms about his neck. "It's never been like this before . . . not for me."

He spun her expertly, so that she was now lying atop him. "Not for me either."

She gave him a long, considering look. "You mean I'm the only one who's ever made you feel this way?"

He stroked a finger down the deep well-defined ridge running the center of her back, and, the black eyes became suddenly shuttered. "Why do you always ask so many questions?"

She rolled away from him, and he reached out immediately to bring her back.

"I'm not good at . . . at sharing my feelings . . . there're certain things I just can't do."

She sat up, giving him an ample view of her golden bosom. "You can do anything you think you can. You just don't want to . . . . that's all. Not with me anyway."

He sat up too. "What do you want from me?"

She gave him a look that was almost tearful. "If I've got to tell you that, it's hopeless."

"You are the most impossible woman I have ever known, do you know that? I never know where I am with you."

She swung a heavy curtain of black hair back across one shoulder. "Me? Impossible? You really need help."

He reached across to hold the hand that was intent on fidgeting with the bedclothes. "Well, help me then."

"What?" He'd taken her by surprise again.

"You heard me. Come over here and show me how. . . ."

She came slowly, and he sat where he was, unmoving, eyes never wavering once from her face.

"Give me your hand," he said. And she reached out to lay it against the flat of his chest. She felt the thunder of his heart beneath her fingertips, and his hand came up to hold hers there.

"Kiss me. . . ." he said leaning toward her.

Her eyes darkened a shade. ''Where?''

''Anywhere,'' he muttered huskily.

She leaned closer and pressed a deliberately soft kiss to the side of his neck. At the gentle touch of her lips, his heart thudded beneath her hand like a wild thing trapped in a cage.

''Words can be manufactured,'' he said, ''but this . . . this can't be. Do you understand?''

''I turn you on . . . that I understand. But, I've known that for a while . . . even back in L.A.''

He gave a crack of laughter. ''In L.A.? I didn't even notice you then.''

She smiled. ''You've always wanted me . . . from the very first time you saw me . . . even when I had on the wig and false teeth . . . there was something . . . something you couldn't explain.''

He pulled her closer. ''What are you, a psychic or something?''

''Look at me and tell me truthfully that you didn't always want me . . . always . . . since the very first time.''

He gave her a direct look, his eyes smoky, ''I didn't want you . . . always.''

She shoved at him with the flat of her palm, ''You're a liar Gavin Pagne.''

He caught her and flipped her neatly onto her back. His eyes were brimming with laughter. ''You're a little too self-confident for a frigid woman.''

She kissed the side of his mouth, and he shifted slowly, to give her access to the entire length of it.

''Do you like it when I do that?'' she asked.

He gave her a smile, ''Uhmm . . . yes.''

''Would you feel the same,'' she continued, pressing wandering kisses across the width of his face, ''if . . . say . . . another woman was doing this . . . instead of me.''

He took a minute to consider this, then he said, ''Lips are lips . . . right? It should be the same feeling, regardless.''

She bit the lobe of his ear, and he gave a little yelp of pain. ''Is that right?''

He turned her to face him, tracing the curve of her lips with a finger. "What do you think?"

Her golden eyes turned genuinely pensive, "I don't know."

He kissed the side of her face, then her neck, then the round of her shoulder, then the dusky tip of a breast. "What do you think now?"

She wet her lips with the tip of a very pink tongue. "I still don't know."

His eyes glowed inky black, "you want me to say it . . . is that it? You want me to say that . . . that my life was empty before you came . . . that you make me happy . . . and crazy . . . and that I want you, only you?"

She nodded, a huge smile stretching across her lips. "That would be a good start," then, more seriously, "Do I really make you happy?"

He lowered his head to take her lips in a very prolonged kiss. "Sometimes. . . ."

She wrapped her arms about him. "How come you've never told me before?"

"You're already too conceited . . . as it is." He parted her legs, and drew her up to him again. "But . . . I aim to get that out of you . . . one way or . . ." and he gave a soft growl, ". . . another."

CHAPTER TWENTY-FOUR

Afternoon became dusk, and dusk meandered gently into evening. And, still, he had not had his fill of her. This was not the way he had envisioned it happening. His need for her was not supposed to grow stronger every time he held her. Was not supposed to make him crazy at the simple thought of maybe never having her again; never kissing, touching loving her again? What was this thing that had him in its grip? Why did the thought of empty years spent without her fill him with such crushing emptiness? He had been alone before. He had had women before. Many women. But, none had held him so. Why did she, of all the possible women in the world, have to be the one to have this strange, and totally unexpected effect on him?

"Gavin?"

She had been asleep for a while now, resting against him, her hair spread out across the broad expanse of his chest like a silky ebony cloud. But he had been unable to sleep, his mind filled with things he still had no acceptable answer for.

He ran the back of his finger down the smooth bridge of her nose. "What is it, babe?"

She shifted a long swatch of hair behind her ear, and propped herself up on one elbow to look down at him.

In the darkened room, her eyes glowed like those of a much-satisfied feline. ''Don't you think . . . we should get something to eat? We'll need our strength . . . you will especially.''

He chuckled. ''Tonight, you'll be the one doing all the work, my girl.''

She sighed. ''You're such a difficult employer . . .'' and she moved a long, soft leg across the flat of his waist. His body reacted immediately, forcing him to still the wanderings of the leg with a gentle hand.

''If you keep that up . . . we won't be getting anything at all to eat for . . . at least, another two hours, or so. . . .''

She rolled away from him to sit on the edge of the bed. ''I have never come across a more insatiable man.''

He moved behind her to press a kiss to the round of her right shoulder. He nibbled at the smooth skin, ''I wish you had never come across any men at all.''

She turned to look down into the beautiful black eyes. ''I would've waited . . . if I'd known you were there. . . .''

He pulled her back down to lie in his arms. ''You always know the right thing to say to me.'' He stroked the hair back from her face, ran a finger along the smooth length of each eyebrow. ''Am I just another one of your conquests? . . . or is it more with me?''

She caressed the scar tissue on his chest, looking up at him with steady eyes. ''Oh . . . you're just another notch in my belt. . . .''

He threw back his head, and laughed. ''Funny girl. . . .''

Summer gave him a look of mock sternness. ''What? You don't believe me?''

He bent to rest his forehead against hers. ''No.''

She kissed the corner of his lips. ''You're even more conceited than I am then.''

He smiled. ''It would seem like we're made for each other . . . doesn't it?

Summer shook her head. "Oh . . . I don't know about that . . . I'll be moving on pretty soon."

He stroked the curly folds of her ear. "I'll find you. Wherever you go."

"I'll go to Alaska. . . ."

"I'll find you there."

"Chile?"

He kissed her slowly. "You can't escape me, my love . . . I'll find you, believe me."

She wound her arms around his neck, her head ringing with the sound of the casually given endearment, "We'll see."

It was another hour before they were able to tear themselves away to explore the contents of the refrigerator. There were neatly made Jamaican cheese sandwiches nicely covered beneath a silver dome. Another plastic-wrapped platter bearing pungent *eschovietched* fish, garnished with rings of onion and hot peppers. There were huge soft slices of roast bread fruit, rice and peas, succulent pieces of roast beef, and a generous amount of thick brown gravy in an expensive looking gravy boat.

"There's lots to eat here . . ." Gavin said, and he began taking things out and handing them back over his shoulder to Summer. "We can warm up whatever we need."

Summer rested each dish on the center island. "Where did all this food come from?"

Gavin closed the fridge door and turned to her. "There's a woman who lives in the area . . . she gets the place ready for me, whenever I'm coming up."

Summer nodded. "Young woman?"

He pinched the tip of her nose. "No, miss possessive . . . an old woman. A very, very old woman."

"Good." She ripped back the plastic to take a bite of roast beef. "I love it when it's cold . . . piece?" she offered him half the slice. He opened his mouth, and she put the entire thing inside.

He chewed with obvious enjoyment. "Why does everything taste so much better when you're around?"

She walked into his arms. "I'm your little piece of magic. . . ."

He bent his head to whisper. "Do you know that song?"

She looked up. "Song? Which one?"

"I'm your magic man . . ." he crooned softly, "won't you let my little magic hands touch your heart. . . ."

"Oh," she said, "that's an old one. It goes . . . it goes . . . I will hmmm, hmmm, hmmm, da, da, da, magic hands something, something."

He kissed her. "You can't sing, . . but I like you anyway."

She laughed. "I know, I'm tone deaf. But you, you've got a great voice. Kinda like Larry Graham . . . Remember him?"

Over plates stacked with food, they lapsed into a heated discussion of music, which then drifted into things of a more general nature.

"How's that design project going with the company I used to work for?" She had wanted to ask him about that for weeks, but the right time had never really presented itself.

He gave her a suddenly pensive look. "Slowly. The new guy in charge at Design International . . . name's Massey or something like that . . . ran into a few hitches. . . ."

"Hitches?"

"Come here," he said, grabbing a hold of one of her hands, "I want to talk about you . . ." he kissed a finger, "and . . . me. . . ."

"You . . . and me?" She pressed her mouth to the side of his neck to make little blowing sounds.

He knitted his brows at her, and his eyes were filled with laughter. "What are you doing?"

"Nothing much. What were you saying about you and me?"

He traced her nose, then her beautifully defined mouth.

"What are we going to do . . . about us?"

She gave this some thought. "Why do we have to do anything at all?"

"Because . . . when we go back to the house . . . I'm gonna need you with me every night . . . every night. I want to wake up each morning with you in my bed."

"Well . . ." and she paused. "How're we gonna work that out? You don't want Nicky and the boys to know that there's anything between us. I'm a wicked woman remember? The kind you bed but don't marry. . . ."

A flash of something darted across his face. "Where did you hear that said?"

"You've told me that in many different ways over the last several months."

He was silent for a long while. When he finally spoke, his voice was somber, "You're right. I never meant to hurt you though . . . I would never do that."

She sat up, "Well . . . it doesn't matter. I'll be finished the cottage in another six weeks. The builders will be through with the structural stuff next week. Then I can start the redecoration. With a little luck, I'll be out of your hair in under two months."

He held her still. "You want to go? You want to leave me?"

She weighed her response to that carefully. "I came here to do a job. . . . I never meant for any of this to happen. I didn't want to get involved with a man again. . . . Ever. But, I guess, you can't always predict these things. . . ."

"No," he said, "you can't. But, that still leaves the question of what to do. Maybe . . . if you wanted to, you could stay here in Jamaica . . . for a while. I could get you a house . . . car . . . whatever you liked. . . ."

She turned to glare at him. "You mean . . . become your mistress? Someone to pass your nights with. Your little secret rendezvous? Hidden from Nicholas, Mik, and Rob?"

He tried to persuade her with a kiss, but she remained unresponsive. "It wouldn't be as bad as you think. You would have everything you needed to be happy . . . money, clothes . . . a housekeeper . . . me?"

"No." And she turned her head away as he tried to kiss her again. "Is that all the respect you have for me? Is that all you think it would take to make me happy? Things?"

His jaws clenched. "What do you want then?"

She turned flashing eyes to him. "You. I want you," she

almost shrieked, " Why is that so very hard for you to figure out?"

"But you have me."

"Not the right way. Not the way I want."

He stood to walk across to a window. He stared out at the dark body of the ocean for long silent minutes. "I can't give you that . . . it's the only thing I can't give you."

"It's the only thing you won't give me . . . is what you really mean. You won't give your heart to me. I can have your body . . . your possessions . . . but not the one thing that really matters. . . ."

He half turned to look at her. "I can't handle this . . . this giving your heart . . . love . . . what the hell is all that?" He paused, took a deep breath. "I'm just not the right man for it. I don't even know what it is . . . most people don't even know what it is."

Her voice was soft, persuasive. "We can find out together. I don't know too much about it either."

He turned back, his hands bunched into fists in his pockets. "No. I can't give you that."

She stared for long moments at the hard, immobile back. So she had tried. So she had failed. Well, she wouldn't stay with him after the cottage was finished. She wouldn't stay. Not even if he begged her to, would she stay with him as his mistress. Eventually, the time would come when he would tire of her. When he would find someone else. Someone suitable. Someone untouched. Someone he wanted to marry. Then, he would let her go. Gently, of course, maybe even with some remorse. And when he did, it would destroy her as nothing else ever could. No. She would take all that he offered of himself, now. But she wouldn't stay once the cottage was finished.

She walked across to him, placed a hand on the small of his back. "Let's go back up."

He turned, and his eyes were filled with raw, turbid emotion. "I don't expect you to understand."

She rested a hand on his arm. "I do understand. You don't love me . . . you've made that clear."

He stared down at her without reply, his chest rising and falling. Then, he said, "I'll go out to the truck to get our bags."

She nodded, and watched him walk away toward the front door. There were tears pricking at the backs of her eyes. She turned to stare at the dark body of water, struggling with her thoughts. God, how very terrible it was to love someone who didn't love you back. It was probably one of the worst things in the entire world.

They returned to Ocho Rios early Monday morning. They had passed the entire weekend in bed. Only rising to shower and eat. Nothing more was said on the matter of her remaining in Jamaica. He had held her tightly during the night, almost as though he were afraid that if he didn't she might not be there when he awoke in the morning.

She had gentled him during the course of the night, when he had awoken from the depths of turbulent sleep calling for her. Her soft kisses had brought a sigh of contentment to him, and in some strange cosmic way, a certain peace had settled over her.

Now, as he pulled to a slow stop in the circular courtyard outside the house, he turned to her to say, "Stay with me tonight?"

She took a breath. "And what about what Nicky, Mik, and Rob will think?"

A muscle clenched in his jaw. "To hell with it. I don't care what they think."

She raised an eyebrow. "To hell with it? You don't care what they think of me either is that it?"

He gave her a frustrated glance. "Of course I care what they think about you." He sighed and ran a hand through his hair. "God, you're making me crazy."

"I'll try to finish up the cottage as soon as I can . . . so I can get out of your hair."

The black eyes were almost fierce. "You're not going anywhere when you finish that cottage."

She opened the front door, and slammed it behind her with considerable force. "We'll see about that."

She was up the front stairs, and bashing on the door, before he could even cut the engine. Within minutes, Nicholas was pulling the door back, a huge grin on his face.

"How'd it go?"

She brushed by him with an "Ask your brother that."

Gavin climbed from the car, retrieved the cases in the back. There was a thunderous expression on his face, and Nicholas found himself muttering: "Oh God, what now?"

He came slowly up the stairs. At the door he asked, "The baby alright?"

Nicholas nodded. "She's fine." After the door was closed behind them both, he said, "How'd things go with Ms. Stevens?"

Gavin set the cases at his feet. "That woman is impossible. She doesn't know what she wants if you ask me."

Nicholas gave his older brother a speculative look. He was right on the threshold. Right there waiting for someone to give him a helpful little push over the edge. Summer had him wrapped around her little finger, and he didn't even know it yet. It would be interesting to see what would happen if the ex-fiancé were to put in a passionate call.

Nicholas picked up Summer's case. "I'll take this up to her."

Gavin gave him a look of immense gratitude. "Yeah . . . I don't think she wants to see me right now."

As his brother turned to go, he remembered. "Nicky . . . a new shipment of medicine's coming in today. . . ."

Nicholas nodded. "I'll take care of it." He would take care of a few other things too.

CHAPTER TWENTY-FIVE

Over the next two weeks, Summer devoted all of her time to the cottage. She watched the builders with a hawk's eye, making absolutely certain that they did everything to her exact specifications. She walked around the outside of the building, inspecting beams, and piping, pulling and tugging at things. She even got down on her hands and knees in the semicircular flower bed, and helped to transplant specially grown white and yellow roses into neatly arranged rows. Everything would be done just so. She would do the best job she had ever done. Maybe, in the years to come, he might remember her. Remember that she was the one who had restored his cottage to the beauty it had once been. Maybe he would regret turning away the love she had so freely offered him. Maybe by then he would have figured out what he had lost . . . what they had lost.

At night she lay in her bed, unable to sleep, listening to him as he paced outside her door. She was so very acutely in tune with him now, that she even knew the cadence of his foot falls. He had asked her only once more to share his bed, and he had done this with a hint of frost in his eyes, and an unmistakable coldness in his voice. She had refused him, and he had walked from the house without another word, slamming the door behind. That night, he had stayed out until three in the morning. She was still awake when he returned to make his silent way up the stairs to his room on the third floor. His footsteps had paused for a moment outside her room door, then slowly continued on.

Things had progressed in exactly this manner for the entire two weeks since returning from Port Antonio. She went to great pains to avoid being in the same room as he, and he apparently, took equal care.

One evening, while walking down the stairs to the dining room, she had passed him on the stairs. Their eyes met for a brief electric instant, then she shifted hers away with a polite little smile curling the corners of her lips. His eyes had followed her back down the stairs, blazing with a hunger that would have surprised and enlightened her had she turned right then.

Nicholas observed the situation between the two for several days, before he started making a few phone calls. Late one evening in the third week, he came to her room. He gave the flat of the door a sharp knock, and when her voice bade him come in, he entered and went to perch on the side of the bed. She was lying, fully clothed, dressed in cut-off white shorts and a sleeveless vest, her hair cascading to her shoulders in smooth soft waves.

She looked up from the book she was reading, and said, "Don't start telling me about what Gavin needs . . . all over again Nicky. You Champagne men are all seriously mental."

He raised both hands in mock protest. "I'm not here to talk about that . . . I have a message for you. . . ."

She put her book aside, folded her arms, and prepared herself for the blow. "Okay . . . Gavin wants me to move out. . . . is that it? Wants me to go stay in a hotel for the remaining time?"

Nicholas shook his head. "Gavin would sooner have me move out than you, my pretty. How blind can you be?"

Summer blinked gorgeous golden eyes at him. "I think you're the one who's blind Nicky. You just see only what you want to see. Not what's actually there."

Nicholas stroked a thoughtful finger across his lips. ''Right. Anyway, the message isn't from Gavin . . .'' he pulled a slip of paper from one of his pockets. ''It's from somebody called . . . Kevin?''

Summer resumed reading. ''I don't know anyone by that name. Must be a mistake.''

''Kevin Jones. Said he was calling from L.A.''

Summer snapped the book closed. ''Kevin Jones? Are you sure?''

Nicholas nodded. ''That's what he said. Is something wrong? He seemed like a nice guy.''

Summer snorted. ''Nice guy? My ex-fiancé? Don't make me laugh.''

''He said he'd be calling again tomorrow.''

Summer made a noise of disgust. ''How in God's name did he track me down here? My parents wouldn't have given out any information. I'm sure of it.''

''Well . . .'' and Nicholas spread his fingers, ''it might help things with Gavin . . . if you took the call when your ex phones tomorrow. . . . and, you acted really friendly. Get me? It would . . .''

''I'm through playing games, Nicky,'' she said, cutting him off, ''that . . . that Kevin person is scum . . . lower than scum. I've got nothing to say to him. And there's no way on earth I'm going to play up to him with the hopes of maybe making Gavin jealous.''

Nicholas was silent for a bit. ''Okay. Why don't you tell Kevin that there's no reason to hope anymore. He should leave you alone after that. . . .''

''I've told him, believe me.'' She turned over to lie on her stomach, presenting him with long expanses of smooth golden-brown legs. Nicholas stood slowly, hands in pockets, eyes pensive. ''You know, if you weren't Gavin's girl . . . I'd make a play for you myself, Summer Stevens.''

She turned back over to give him a very baleful look. '' No you wouldn't . . . and I am not Gavin's girl. And from now on

I'm going to try my best to stay away from all you Champagne men . . . as I said, you're all mental.''

Nicholas chuckled. ''We'll see.''

He turned, and was gone from the room before Summer could question him on that last little comment. She pounded her pillow in frustration. That Nicholas, he was always up to something. What in the name of heaven was he planning now? Whatever it was, it wouldn't work though. She was through pandering to Gavin's ego. Through with the whole miserable situation.

Minutes later, Nicholas was relaying the same piece of information to his older brother.

Gavin was standing at the window in his room, glaring out at nothing in particular. He rapped out an irritable come in, when his brother pounded on the room door.

Nicholas experienced a surge of pity. Only he knew how very much his older brother was suffering, and how hard it would be for him to back down from whatever stand it was he had taken.

''Don't you think this situation with Summer has gone on for long enough?''

Gavin turned. ''Has she said something to you?''

Nicholas came in to sprawl on the bed. ''Yes and no.''

He had Gavin's full attention now. ''What does that mean . . . yes and no? Did she or not?''

''Well . . .'' and Nicholas paused deliberately. ''Her ex-fiancé called today. . . .'' It pained him to do this, but he knew that it had to be done. ''. . . she seemed happy to hear from him . . . thought you'd want to know. . . .''

There was a long period of silence, during which time it would have been possible to hear a pin fall. Nicholas shot a surreptitious little look at his brother's face, and was struck by the agony there. God, it was so obvious that he loved her. Why couldn't Summer see it, too, and relent a bit? They were so much alike, that sometimes it was frightening. If she came to him now, he would only struggle a very little. He did have his pride.

''When. . . ?'' Gavin stopped to clear his throat. ''When did this . . . man call? What time?''

Nicholas shrugged. ''Oh, I dunno. Two o'clock . . . maybe three.''

Gavin digested this piece of information. ''So . . . has she invited him down . . . from the States, is that it? Or . . . is she planning on going back to L.A. a little early?''

Nicholas gave his chin a thoughtful little scratch. ''Why don't you ask her?'' He waited for a slightly anxious moment. If Gavin did, that would be the end of the entire plan. And he just might be thrown from the house after all.

But, he had little to fear, Gavin reacted in the very manner that he would've predicted.

''No . . . she has to make up her mind. If she wants me . . . she has to come to me. She knows where I sleep.''

Nicholas stood. ''Well. . . . I've done my duty. Keep an eye on the baby will you? I'm going out.''

Gavin's voice stopped him half way out the door. ''Nicky . . . you understand women better than I do . . . how do you get them to do what you want them to?''

''You don't,'' Nicholas said, leaning on the doorjamb. This was definitely a first, Gavin asking for advice. If only Summer Stevens knew the changes she had brought about. ''You give a little . . . and if you've got the right woman . . . she'll give a little too. Compromise is the thing.''

Gavin savored the word, ''compromise . . . I always thought that was a word for the weak.''

Nicholas chuckled. ''Not the weak, big brother . . . the strong.''

At precisely 2:00 P.M. the following day, Kevin Jones called. Gavin, who had found a reason to work at home, answered the phone with a very abrupt, ''Yes?''

He listened for a moment to the voice on the other end. ''Summer is not available,'' he barked into the receiver. ''No,

I wouldn't advise coming down to Jamaica,'' he said after a moment of listening. ''Summer and I are engaged.''

He slammed the receiver into the cradle, and sat back in the huge leather chair, a pensive frown beginning to ripple the smooth lines of his forehead. God. He was going out of his mind. Why in the name of heaven had he just said that?

He got up to pace the room. Summer Stevens was like a fever in his blood. He was in such a state now, that he couldn't focus on his work. And, this was something that had never happened before. Strangely enough, he seemed to need her with him. Even though they constantly butted heads on almost everything, he still needed her. Wanted her. God . . . he loved her.

There was a sudden knock on the door, and he stopped his pacing for a minute to call an abrupt: ''Come.''

The door pushed back, and Summer poked her head in. This was the first time in days she had spoken to him directly.

''Nicholas said you wanted me?''

Gavin drew a tight breath. Nicholas again. His brother was as relentless as a pit bull. ''Come in,'' he beckoned, when she stood uncertainly on the threshold. ''There is something I want to say to you.''

Summer entered, and closed the door behind her. ''There's something I want to say to you too.''

''Yes?'' he said softly, his eyes devouring her.

She nodded, then blurted it out without further thought. ''I can't stay here anymore.''

''You can't what?'' He was before her in an instant, hands in pockets, eyes fierce.

Summer took a breath, and steeled herself. ''The two of us living together in the same house . . . with things being as they are . . . is just too stressful for me. And I can't do it anymore.''

The hands came out of his pockets, to rest on either side of her head. ''Why're you doing this? Haven't you made me suffer enough?''

She blinked at him for a moment, bemused by the unexpected

disclosure. "You suffer? I didn't think you cared, one way or another."

He leaned in closer. "I care."

"Enough to tell Nicky, Mik, and Rob about us?"

"Enough to tell the whole damn world about us." He pressed his lips to one corner of her mouth. "Enough to tell my mother . . . even."

Summer was startled. "Your mother? . . . Why would you want to do that?"

Gavin chuckled. "I'll send her a telegram. I'll say: Found perfect girl. We're made for each other. Love, Gavin."

Summer laughed, her eyes sparkling. "You're just as silly as Nicky."

"What?" he teased, "You don't think we're made for each other?"

Summer wound her arms about him. "I've known that we were . . . almost from the start."

"So . . . are you gonna stay with me then?"

Summer nodded. "I'll stay."

Gavin sampled her lips again. "And what about this Kevin person?"

"Who?" she murmered hazily.

"Never mind . . . we'll talk about him later," and he bent his head to pull her fully into his arms.

"Uhmm," Summer agreed. "Later."

On the other side of the door, Nicholas stood listening. When there was nothing more to be heard but soft silence, he made his way back down the corridor. There was a tiny smile playing around the corners of his mouth. Step one was accomplished. Now, all he had to do, was get them both to the altar.

A June wedding would be ideal.

ABOUT THE AUTHOR

Niqui Stanhope was born in Jamaica, West Indies, but grew up in a small bauxite mining town in Guyana, South America. Because her parents traveled quite a bit, and always took the entire family along, the summers of her childhood, were spent exploring the rich culture of the Caribbean and South America. In 1984 she emigrated to the United States with her family. She admits that novel writing never occurred to her until after she had graduated from the University of Southern California with a bachelor of Science degree in chemistry.

Niqui Stanhope now lives in Los Angeles. *Made for Each Other* is her second book.

e-mail: NiquiJ@aol.com
PO Box 6852
Burbank, CA 91510

COMING IN JUNE 1999 . . .

PIECES OF DREAMS (1-58314-020-4, $4.99/$6.50)
by Donna Hill
Tragedy brought Maxine Sherman and Quinten Parker together years ago, until another woman stole Quinn away from her. Since then, her nights were filled with dreams of his return. When Quinn returns to rekindle their love, Maxine has a new life. But a secret binds them forever.

SUDDEN LOVE (1-58314-023-9, $4.99/$6.50)
by Angela Winters
Author Renee Shepherd decides to visit her sister in Chicago and is drawn into an investigation surrounding the suspicious death of her sister's colleague. The executive director of the company, Evan Brooks, is somehow involved in all this, and it'll take much trust and faith for Renee to risk everything for sudden love.

A MAGICAL MOMENT (1-58314-021-2, $4.99/$6.50)
by Monica Jackson
Atlanta lawyer Taylor Cates is dedicated to helping battered women at a non-profit shelter. When the shelter's reputation is threatened by a series of mysterious deaths, private detective Stone Emerson must uncover the truth while pursuing an unexpected love.

LOVE BY DESIGN (1-58314-022-0, $4.99/$6.50)
by Marcella Sanders
Interior designer Daniella Taylor returns to New Jersey to bury herself in work and avoid romantic relationships. But working at Parker's Art she'll have to face the owner, Brant Parker, who will not let her forget the passion and the love they once shared.

Available wherever paperbacks are sold, or order direct from the Publisher. Send cover price plus 50¢ per copy for mailing and handling to BET Books, c/o Kensington Publishing Corp., Consumer Orders, or call (toll free) 888-345-BOOK, to place your order using Mastercard or Visa. Residents of New York, Washington D.C., and Tennessee must include sales tax. DO NOT SEND CASH.

ALSO IN JUNE . . .
LOOK FOR OUR NEW BRIDES MONTH SERIES

WEDDING BELLS (1-58314-016-6, $4.99/$6.50)
by Qwynne Forster, Francine Craft, Niqui Stanhope
Every girl dreams of walking down the aisle with her prince charming. Qwynne Forster's "Love for a Lifetime," Francine Craft's "A Love Made in Heaven," and Niqui Stanhope's "Champagne Wishes" will restore faith in marriage, when three couples discover that the true test of love is the joining of hearts and souls against all odds.

GIVE AND TAKE (1-58314-017-4, $4.99/$6.50)
by Anna Larence
Yvette Williams had it all—a career, a house, a husband and a son. The only thing missing was a second child. And although she and her husband Derrick had decided to wait, she intentionally got pregnant. Derrick, feeling betrayed, almost gives into temptation, but searches his soul for answers to staying true to the love of his life.

SOMETHING OLD, SOMETHING NEW (1-58314-018-2, $4.99/$6.50)
by Roberta Gayle
Attending her twin sister's wedding reception alone, Dorinda Fay finds that four of the guests are ex-boyfriends. When she sees her first true love, Matt Cooper, she's not willing to risk more disappointment. Matt has no intention of letting her go this time and is intent on getting her to walk with him down the aisle.

I PROMISE (1-58314-019-0, $4.99/$6.50)
by Adrianne Byrd
Christian McKinley is taken by surprise when Malcolm Williams publicly proposes. He's sure she cannot turn him down. Only, she mistakenly shares a kiss with his twin brother, Jordan, and the sparks fly. As a family feud threatens to explode, neither Christian, nor Jordan, can deny their desire for one another.

Available wherever paperbacks are sold, or order direct from the Publisher. Send cover price plus 50¢ per copy for mailing and handling to BET Books, c/o Kensington Publishing Corp., Consumer Orders, or call (toll free) 888-345-BOOK, to place your order using Mastercard or Visa. Residents of New York, Washington D.C., and Tennessee must include sales tax. DO NOT SEND CASH.